Force 12 in German Bight

To Mary & Wayne
with all best
James Boschert

Force 12
In German Bight

By

James Boschert

www.PenmorePress.com

Force 12 in German Bight -By James Boschert
Copyright © 2014 by James Boschert

ISBN: 978-1-942756-00-2 Paperback
ISBN: 978-1-942756-01-9 Ebook

BISAC Subject Headings:
FIC002000 FICTION / Action & Adventure
FIC022080FICTION / Mystery & Detective /
    International Mystery & Crime
FIC047000FICTION / Sea Stories

Address all correspondence to:
M James
920 N Javalina PL
Tucson
AZ 85748. USA
Or visit our website at:
www.PenmorePress.com

Table of Contents

Dedication

To Danielle
Markus and Simone
Sophia and Eva
All Precious to mine eyes

To all who go to sea in boats
Or anything at all that floats.

Acknowledgements

I want to thank:

Danielle for her unflagging efforts to help get this book off the desk and onto the printing press;

Roger Paine and Tim Millhouse for their suggestions and kind words of praise;

and the dedication of Chris Paige, editor extraordinaire, and Christine Horner for their work in bringing the book to its conclusion.

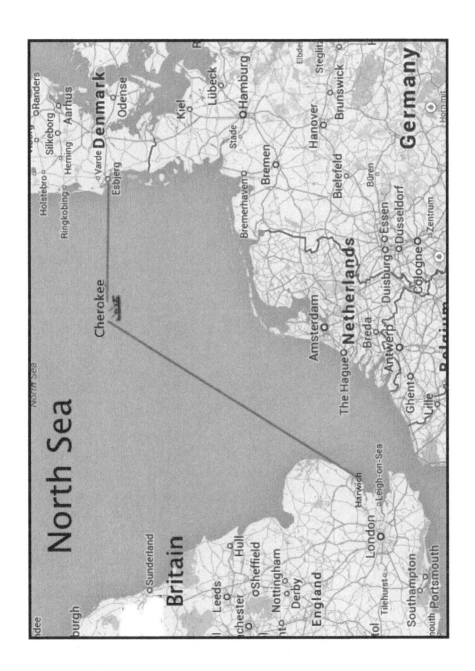

Barge Location North Sea

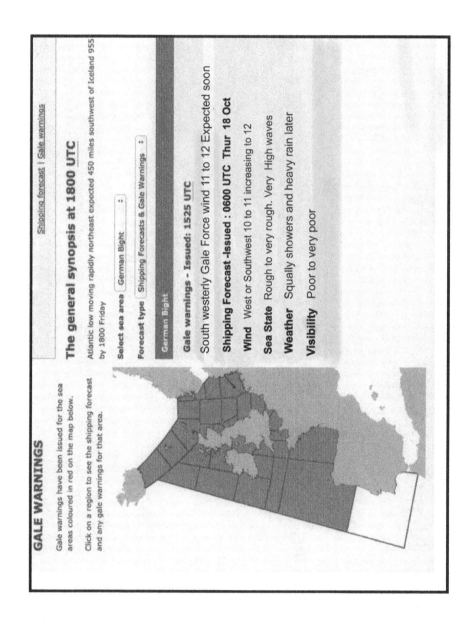

British Met Report for German Bight

X

Cherokee

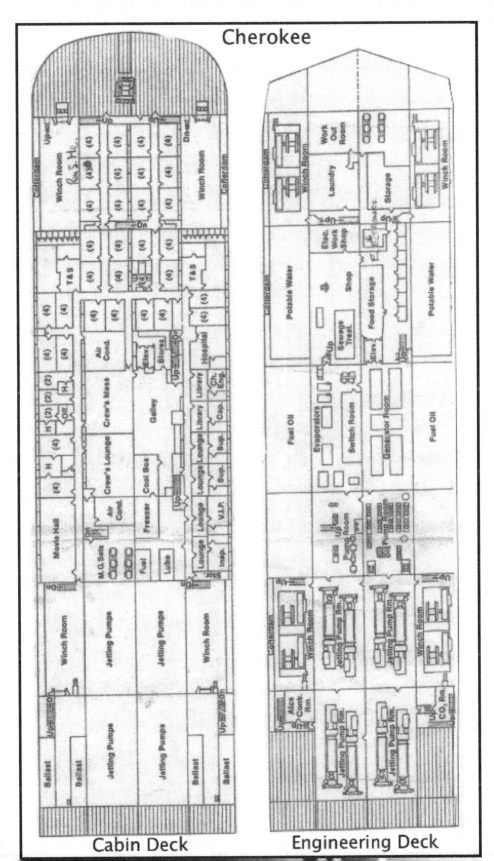

Cabin Deck

Engineering Deck

Cherokee

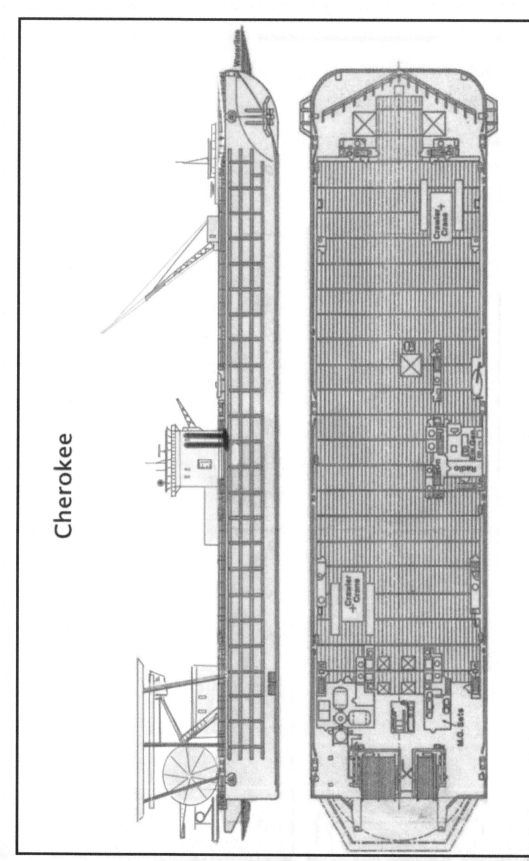

Review

by Tim Millhouse

FORCE 12 IN GERMAN BIGHT

James Boschert, in a departure from his 12th century landscape and the adventures of Talon, has masterfully crafted a modern day action thriller of murder, intrigue and a fight for life on the high seas.

Set in the backdrop of Mother Nature's most dangerous and unpredictable body of water, the North Sea, Boschert brings to life the offbeat and isolated world of ocean barge dredging operations. The crew, a rugged group of salty, hard-drinking characters from all walks of life, make these floating giants of steel their home and risk their lives daily to, as they say "stay on the pipe."

When a bizarre turn of events makes the barge the target of high seas piracy, the crew must fight for their lives, not only against one of the worst storms in the history of the North Sea, but the drug dealers who have taken control of the barge and a conspiracy that makes all hands suspect. Not until a female police officer and an engineer band together is there hope. As the storm reaches force 12, the barge is adrift and the 65 foot waves crashing down on the deck began to take their toll. The barge is breaking up, and Mother Nature is determined to send them all to the bottom. Story telling at its best.

T.J Millhouse Major USMC

Introduction

by James Boschert

Life at sea has always been hard; even today it is fraught with unpredictable situations and dangers. In the North Sea it can be very hard on vessels and men alike. This story is set in the eighties, when computers were in their infancy and communications at sea relied upon high powered radios that didn't always work. The vessels that were used in the oil industry construction business were definitely a forgotten corner of the Oil industry as a whole, most of them being rusty old ships and barges that were constantly having to be maintained by men who knew how to improvise. These old work horses of the nineteen eighties would never be permitted to float nor work in today's world of safety conscious technocrats. Some have gone to the breakup yards, while others have been given a new lease of life by other companies who reconditioned them.

For the disparate group of men who worked them, this was a living that brought good wages but often at a price. The unforgiving sea and the work itself were not for the faint of heart.

Chapter 1

Paddington

The electric train rattled and weaved its way along darkened tracks toward Paddington Station, still several miles away. A light rain reduced visibility to about thirty yards, even though the train's headlights were full on. The well-lit carriages were sparsely populated by passengers, most of whom were tired businessmen on their way back to London from visits to Bristol or Reading.

Without warning, a man leapt in front of the train, only ten yards in front of the engine. The driver swore and reached for the brakes. The lancing lights illuminated the face of a desperate looking man, who turned as he landed in the middle of the tracks, avoiding the electric rail; but as he spun around he jerked, his hands flew wide and his mouth opened as though to scream something before he pitched over backwards to fall on the rails in the path of the train.

The driver slammed on the brakes, but he knew with dreadful certainty there was no way on earth he could avoid running over the man now lying across one of the tracks. He sat, frozen with horror, his hands hauling on the lever while the train jerked and shook as the brakes took hold, and the three-carriage train screeched its way for another fifty yards before coming to a shuddering halt. The driver felt only the slightest of bumps as the front wheels went over the body. He remained where he was for a long moment, sick to his stomach, then he began to move.

Ignoring the shouts of surprise and pain from the

1

compartments behind, where passengers had been thrown about, he checked the instruments, made sure the train was fully stopped, and stood up to get out of the front compartment. He grabbed his torch and opened the door, letting in the rain, which had begun to come down with more force. He was uneasily certain it had not been the train which killed the man and wondered fearfully who else might be out in the inhospitable darkness. He just remembered to pick up the phone on the dash panel and report the incident before he left the warmth of the cabin to make his way back along the track, dreading what he was going to see.

*****

Detective Inspector Steven Greenfield received the call after he'd just gone to bed. He picked up the receiver and put it to his ear as he groggily tried to see what time it was. The electric clock with the digital numbers silently informed him it was 11.30 pm.

Grumbling to himself he clambered out of bed and dressed in the bathroom so he would not wake his wife, Jenny, who was a teacher and needed her sleep.

A half an hour later he walked in the rain along the dark pathway that followed the rails leading out of Paddington Station, with Detective Sergeant Toby Wilson for company. He regarded the dark gleam of the tracks, lit only by infrequent lights, with apprehension. One wrong step and a person would be fried by that third rail. Through the drizzle he could see bright yellow flashing lights in the distance, which marked the location of the incident. A large engine stood parked on the rails, its lights flashing as a warning to other trains. Its spot lights shone onto the space between the rails and illuminated the scene of the incident.

They were greeted by one of the constables, who respectfully touched his helmet and guided them towards a huddle of people clustered around something on the rails half way along the train, almost at the junction of two carriages. He found himself standing alongside a silent but well-lit electric train with several constables and railway officials, who were trying to keep dry on the lee side of the carriages.

"Who found him?" Steven asked the men nearby.

One of the constables motioned to a short person in British

Rail uniform among the men huddled against the side of the train. "The driver, sir. He ran over the...er, body. But he says there was something else."

By this time Steven could make out the bundle on the ground that had been covered with a white sheet. But then he noticed there were two bundles.

"Shine your light here," he indicated the one at his feet. He lifted the sodden bloody sheet; the body had been cut in half, the torso and the head were here, minus a hand. He noted the mess on either side of the track, intestines and feces with blood splattered everywhere. The stink was enough to make Steven pull out his handkerchief and hold it over his nose and mouth. The face of the corpse was gray and bloodless, the eyes wide open, the teeth bared and bloody with a look of horror frozen onto the features.

Although Steven had seen this kind of thing before, he still had to wipe his shaking hand across his mouth to hide the involuntary grimace. The corpse looked like one of Dracula's victims in one of the 'B' movies he'd once seen. He was shocked at his thoughts and glanced up, hoping no one had witnessed his behavior, but his sergeant was retching a couple of yards away and no one else seemed to have noticed.

The dead man, whomsoever he might have been, wore a cheap poplin blue-striped shirt and short wind jacket. Once cream colored, it had been splattered with blood and dirt, which obscured the chest region. But Steven noticed something. He bent to examine the corpse more closely, ignoring his sergeant, who looked on in shock at the gruesome remains of what had once been a man.

Just as he began to speak, a huge engine materialized out of the darkness in the distance, coming towards them. Its horn blared, filling the night with noise, and its huge front light blinded the group of men on the rails. To Steven, when he glanced up, it seemed as though the train came straight towards them. He stepped closer to the stopped train in an involuntary reaction to the massive form behind the light, as it loomed black and menacing in the darkness. It drove slowly towards them, causing the rails and the ground to shake before it had even passed by. It thundered past, two rails away, with its diesel engines rumbling in a metallic roar and its laden trucks rattling and squealing.

Steven sighed. This was going to be a long night.

Early the next morning a tired Inspector Steven Greenfield walked into his office and reached for the coffee his sergeant had thoughtfully placed on his cluttered, paper strewn desk. He had barely taken a sip when the phone rang and his commander asked him to come to his office and report.

Steven gave the glass door of the office a light tap, and on the command, "Come," opened it and let himself in.

His portly senior officer stood in his favorite position of 'At Ease', with his hands clasped behind his back and his feet the regulation distance apart, gazing out of the window over the jumble of factory roofs and low rent houses that stretched into the still darkened distance. Winter was around the corner and the weather did nothing to alleviate the gloom and grime of west London's Paddington area.

Commander Reginald Pollock turned toward Steven, who observed a florid, mustachioed face that had long ago gone to seed from too much alcohol; the small broken veins on his nose attested to that. The man was, however, dressed immaculately in the blue uniform of the Metropolitan police and had the single laurel wreath with crossed batons in gold on his shoulder tabs. His 'stay bright' brass-colored buttons had definitely been rubbed today, and his shoes looked as though a guardsman had worked them with spit and polish to a mirror finish.

He in turn regarded Steven with mild distaste as he came into the room and faced him, still holding a polystyrene cup of coffee in his hand. The commander seemed about to say something about the coffee cup but decided not to and instead sent a fierce look at his subordinate. Steven's returning gaze was bland. His boss didn't like him much, that was obvious, but from Steven's point of view it was something of an advantage. The commander had a military background and let everyone know it with his pompous ways.

Steven had decided long ago the man was lucky to have a job at all, even in this dark corner of the London Metropolitan Police force. For the most part he left Steven alone, as he knew little about the nuts and bolts of police work. That suited Steven just fine, and apart from discussions of this kind, he had little contact with the man. His business was catching villains, not dressing up for parties.

Steven was a tall man, about four inches taller than his boss, who was forced to look up at him when he stood too close. Steven also wore clothes badly, to the despair of his wife, who insisted he was a fairly handsome man and could do better. His tie was askew, his two day old shirt had a grimy collar, and he still wore his gray raincoat to keep out the chill of the day. Police stations were poorly heated places at best. This lack of attention to attire did little to please his boss on a cold and wet morning when strange things were happening in his bailiwick.

"I got your note about the incident, Detective Inspector Greenfield. Has the doctor confirmed your findings?" His boss had a bark of a voice, which Steven attributed to his having to shout orders at artillerymen while they fired their guns.

"Yes, sir, he did. Two bullets, one in the chest and one in the right thigh. He seemed to think they were nine millimeter, but the autopsy will confirm it."

"By Jove! Murder and a train accident." The senior rubbed his hands together in an agitated manner. "You said the body was cut in half by the train? Nothing missing? Any ID?"

Steven resisted the urge to say "No, sir, by Jove" but held himself back. This was no time for disrespect. Instead he said, "No, sir. That's what I find odd. He had no wallet, nor any other papers on him. White male, about thirty. Cheap clothes. We will have some fingerprints and dental photos sent to the labs for checking."

"Go on," his senior officer said.

"He looked as though he'd been beaten up before he arrived on the rails. The injuries to his face did not seem to me to have been part of the accident with the train, but the doc has to confirm this at the autopsy. He agreed, in principle, that the dead man might have suffered fatal injuries before he was run over. You know, the usual complicated terms, but I got the gist."

"You know what this means, Inspector, don't you?"

"Yes, I do, sir. Scotland Yard will have to be told."

His senior nodded his head unhappily and his jowls wobbled.

Force 12 in German Bight

The prospect of Scotland Yard moving in, even temporarily, did not appeal.

"Not just an accident, nor suicide, so we have to stand aside and let them take hold of it, I suppose."

Steven nodded reluctantly. The incident intrigued him and he wanted to stay with it.

"By the sound of it, the man might have been running away from his killers when the train happened along. The driver was pretty shaken up about it."

"I can imagine. Puzzling about the lack of ID. Very well, I will notify the Yard today. Let me know when the autopsy report comes in. Sergeant Wilson is new here, isn't he?" The commander seated himself at his desk.

"Yes, sir. Just down from Yorkshire. He tossed his breakfast, or supper, not sure which. Not surprising under the circumstances. It was messy, but he will be OK, sir."

"Well, that's life at the sharp end." Commander Pollock smirked as though he knew about the nasty accidents that occurred on railway lines first hand. Steven doubted he did.

"Some people prefer a train to a bridge, I suppose. M'self, I would rather take a bullet, ahem, don't you know?"

"The old boy means it too," Steven thought to himself as he turned away.

His senior officer continued.

"If he stays with us in this area he is going to see the same sort of thing often enough. Very well, dismissed, Detective Inspector." The commander spoke in an offhand manner while he sifted through the papers on his desk as though they were important. He ignored Steven as he left.

The nickname of 'Pillock' the commander had acquired while in the station was well deserved, Steven thought as he exited the office, careful not to slam the door.

Steven decided he wanted to do some checking before he dealt with the men from Scotland Yard. They were bound to want to talk to him and his sergeant, but there was as yet, little he could tell them other than what they would find out quickly enough from the body.

6

He had a suspicion he knew where the man might have come from, but wanted to confirm it, if possible.

He made his way to a small cafe not far from the main railway station on a corner of Westbourne Street. Before he left he had made a call and expected someone to be there.

Steven was not disappointed. The man he wanted to talk to was waiting for him. He lived a couple of houses down, above a paper shop cum Post Office run by a Pakistani couple.

"Hello, Bertie," he said as he sat down with his cup of tea in hand. "Good of you to come. I brought some cakes." He placed cupcakes on the table, knowing Bertie had a sweet tooth.

"How you doin', guv?" Bertie asked. He was unshaven and wore a cap, which to Steven's mind likened him to the famous Andy Capp of the cartoon series. Steven thought ruefully that Bertie was probably better dressed than he was today, or at least no worse.

"I'm fine, Bertie. How's the Social Security thing going?"

Bertie had the grace to grin. A lot of his teeth were missing and his light brown eyes were watery. "Can't complain, guv. You know how it is. Work ain't everywhere no more."

"I dare say, Bertie," Steven said.

He figured Bertie, who was an out of work housebreaker and owed his minimum sentence to Steven, couldn't be trying very hard to find real work. He nodded and sipped his tea. "Have a cake," he said.

"Don't mind if I do," Bertie said.

"So, what's the street saying these days, Bertie?"

"Not sure what you mean, guv," Bertie said, feigning innocence while he chewed on the cake with his mouth open. Steven glanced down so he wouldn't have to watch.

He repeated his question. This time he put on his policeman's expression of authority, and his blue eyes bored into Bertie's.

Bertie appeared thoughtful and continued munching, trying not to appear to be intimidated.

"Somethin' happened last night, I believe."

"Like what?"

"I 'erd a guy got clobbered by a train."

Force 12 in German Bight

"What else did you hear?" Steven asked him, and moved the cakes out of reach for the moment. Bertie acted coy, so Steven pushed a ten pound note over the table. It disappeared like magic and Bertie eyed the cakes wistfully.

"Like what, Bertie? Christ! This is like pulling teeth, and you don't have that many left!"

"OK, OK. Word is the guy was from Germany, one of those workers there."

"A *gast arbeiter*?" Steven asked.

"Dunno wot that means, but he was one of those furriners. Hung around the Three Crowns for several days."

What was he doing there?"

"I dunno, but he had a lot of cash and didn't mind spendin' it."

"Was he Turkish?"

"Na, but he had an accent. Think he came from one of those other places. Yugoslavia, maybe?"

Steven sighed. Yugoslavia was a long way from Germany. "Were you in the Three Crowns last night?"

Bertie looked shifty.

"Well, were you?"

"Yeah, I was hopin' he'd be buying, you know; Beer is expensive these days. I remember when it was only a couple of bob, now it's more'n a pound a pint!"

"That's tough, but you know how bad drinking is for you. Was anyone there with him?"

"Yeah, he had some company. They wasn't buying neither."

"Did you know them?"

"I recognized one." Bertie glanced around the grimy coffee shop as though he was checking on who else might be in this shabby place. This was no Ritz café.

"Well? Who was it?"

"I didn't stay, but I could bet it was Nigel Spencer."

"Spencer? You sure of that, Bertie? I thought he was inside."

"Think he's out now."

"So was there another man there? Who was the other man?"

"Yep, there was, but I've never met 'im, guv."

8

"Would you recognize him if you saw him again?"

Bertie began to appear agitated, which meant he felt he had spent too much time with the inspector. He didn't want to be seen is such company.

Steven understood, but he wanted to ask one more question.

"Who do you think Nigel would have gone to work for, Bertie?"

"Well, no names and no pack drill, as they say," Bertie said.

Another tenner crossed the table.

"That fella who was in the Royal Marines might be able to tell yer, guv. Don Saunders, he's all over the place these days. Big shot, I hear."

"Where would I find him?"

"Same place probably, guv," Bertie said in a low tone, glancing about him.

He got up and shambled out of the coffee shop, peering right and left before walking out in the rain to disappear into the crowd.

Steven took a deep breath. It was time to go home and get a few hours' rest.

Chapter 2

Edinburgh

The pubs were open and the inhabitants of the city of Edinburgh were either having supper or heading for the nearest 'local'. It was a damp evening with darkness shrouding the great castle that glowered down from its perch on the hill, dominating the lamplit city.

A crowd of people made their way along Forest Street up the hill past the National Museum. Among them strode a large man in a leather bomber jacket and well fitting jeans. He would slow down occasionally and check the signs of the pubs ahead of him. He was in search of a specific pub.

He crossed Cowgate and continued on up the slope towards The Royal Mile. Across the street was the pub that he wanted. He sauntered towards it and cast a quick glance behind him as he entered. Donald Saunders stood back against the wall just inside the entrance as a small group of students, already tipsy, filed out of the smoke-filled main room through the narrow doorway. Two of the girls glanced approvingly at him when they passed, and one even managed to rub her backside against his jeans as she walked out. He gave her a brief grin, but he had other things on his mind.

He walked into the room slowly, his eyes going everywhere as he searched the crowd. The bar was already half full, even on a Wednesday. The booths were filling up fast with an assortment of elderly people in a variety of drab grey woolen coats and scarves, the odd tourists who appeared as though they had forgotten to go

Force 12 in German Bight

back home from their summer holidays, and more students in their usual rag tag clothing, most of which looked as though it had been bought or even stolen from Oxfam.

His eyes settled on a man seated alone in a booth at the far end of the room. The man stood out due to his manner of dress. He was clearly not a local; his clothes were of a very different cut, albeit casual. The red check flannel shirt was uncommon, as was the white wind jacket lying on the bench nearby, and it was hard to miss the expensive watch on the hairy left wrist. He was balding, his face clean shaven, but the jowls and sagging fat around his collar told Donald he had neglected to keep fit for a long time.

Donald went to the bar, ordered a pint of Guinness, and again looked around the room to make sure no one met his watchful eyes or appeared to be taking an interest in him. With his pint in hand he walked casually over to the man in the booth and nodded to him. The heavy set man looked up from his Jack Daniels, which he had been morosely contemplating, and asked, "You the man from London?" His voice betrayed a distinct accent from the Deep South of the USA.

"Yeah," said Donald, observing the man he knew as Daryl Galay with care. He took a seat without being asked and managed to get his back more or less to the wall so he could watch for anything untoward going on in the pub. He didn't take off his jacket, even though the room was stuffy and humid.

"Been expecting you. You're late. A'hm Daryl."

"Well I'm here, and we've got things to talk about. I'm Donald." They didn't shake hands.

The American nodded and sipped his whiskey thoughtfully, as though waiting for Donald to make the first move.

Donald leaned over the table so there was only a foot between his face and that of his companion. He spoke softly, but there was no mistaking the quiet threat in his tone.

"We know all about your... problems, Mr. Galay. But I'm here to help." He smiled.

Daryl looked into pale blue eyes that regarded him as impersonally as a predator. The short blond crewcut and the grin did nothing to reassure him. He looked away, unsettled. Not for the first time, he wondered what he might have gotten into.

"All right, Ah'm listening."

"When do you go back to that ship of yours?"

"It's a barge. Couple of days. Ah've been on vacation for a while. Ah flew in yesterday from Atlanta."

"How was she? Your wife I mean." Donald grinned nastily. "Yeah, I know your wife is spending you out of pocket. Rumors are easy to pick up in small town, aren't they? We can help. And as for your little habit, well, that'll be easy to take care of, too, but..." Donald paused.

Daryl looked up at Donald with a startled expression on his face.

"Yeah," Donald said, and smiled. "We've been doin' our homework, see? That's why it took so long. Got to be careful these days. I'm sure you can understand."

Daryl nodded. He had seemed depressed when Donald arrived, but now he looked as though he saw a glimmer of hope in his future. He took another swig of the Jack.

"OK, Ah'm listening," he said with more enthusiasm.

"Well, y'see, it goes like this." Donald lowered his voice even more, although the noise level all around had increased as the crowd at the bar began to get into their drinks and talk louder. He reached into his bomber jacket and pulled out a thick brown envelope and slid it across the table. Daryl didn't even look at it, he slid it onto his lap and out of sight, then looked back at Donald with a question in his eyes. He had to strain his ears to hear what the man across from him said.

"This is an advance. You owe ten grand. Yeah, we know all about it. Your wife is one of the last of the great spenders, and then... there's your own little habit. In there is enough to pay it all off, with some left to pay for... *assistance* on the ship, and for your little... needs. We can always provide for that, of course. Cheaper than out on the street and a lot less risky, if you get my point, but there are conditions."

Daryl nodded and wondered what Donald meant. He longed for a snort of coke. It was hard to find here in the UK unless you knew people, and even then it was dangerous. He had a stash on the barge, but it was a good couple of days away. Conditions always came with a loan, but the man in front of him was from an organization large enough to have investigated him thoroughly. He felt a tingle of fear but also anticipation.

"We... my boss and his 'company', might have a need for your services out on that thing you call a barge one day, in fact it won't be too much longer, I'd say. If a package can disappear out to sea with no trace, it's easier to bring it in some time later somewhere else, ain't it?"

Daryl's expression of surprise seemed to amuse Donald, who smirked as he observed the fat man opposite him and took a swig of his pint. "Yeah, I mean it, and all you've got to do is be there and in charge when the call comes, alright?"

"But... but what do you want?"

"You're the captain of the ship, ain't you?"

"I'm a Super, if that's what you mean. There are two of us in charge of the vessel, one for each shift."

"Right, that's what I mean. When and if... might not happen, never know, but *if* the call comes, you have to be there, ready to take it and to tell us when would be a good time to come by."

"You have to tell me more than this. Will a boat come out? Or what?" Daryl was intimidated by this large, tough looking man staring at him with cold eyes, but the vagueness of the instructions irritated him. He fingered the package in his lap and wondered if it was in dollars or those Brit Pounds, which could be difficult to change in high quantities. He shifted his heavy shoulders uncomfortably and glowered at Donald.

"I need more details of what you're planning. I can't just sit out there and wait for something to come along."

Donald put his face closer to Daryl's.

"It's a large package we want to bring over here. The cops watch the roads and the highways through France, Belgium and Holland, but not so much the ports off the beaten path, if you see what I mean. You'll get a call over the radio. I want all the details of how we can reach you, and on a given day, or night, a boat will call by with a load, a container probably. I'll need accurate information as to where your barge is, too, so you have to call in from the barge on a daily basis. We'll want you to look after it for us, for a while. Just provide the coordinates." Donald had been in the Royal Marines for a few years and knew all about radio procedures; he spoke with the cool authority of a man who is sure of his ground.

"What's in it?" Daryl blurted out.

Donald grinned at him. "You don't need to know, mate. But remember: two hundred thou is a lot of cash, so don't fuck it up, or your pretty little blonde wifey will have a visitor, if you get what I mean."

Donald caught the flicker of fear in Daryl's eyes before his eyes shifted away. He grunted with satisfaction; the man would do as he was told.

"Just be there, and all will be well, and there'll be more of that stuff. Much, much more. Here's a phone number in Denmark. Use it if you need it in an emergency." He gestured towards Daryl's lap. "Now I need some information from you." He showed a smile that reminded Daryl of an alligator about to strike. Donald had very pointed teeth.

*****

Donald returned to London on the night train from Edinburgh. As the train hurtled though the night he slept comfortably in one of the first class sleeper cabins. On arrival at King's Cross station, he went straight to the block of offices overlooking the Thames where, despite the early hour, his boss would be working.

Charlie Pettigrew was a dapper little man, whose increasing weight was disguised by a carefully tailored pinstripe suit. He liked to dress in hand tailored suits and was well groomed right down to his shiny toe nails, now comfortably enclosed by black handmade Italian loafers.

When Donald knocked on the door and gently opened it, he found his boss standing behind his desk, staring down at the line of cars moving from traffic light to traffic light on the street below. It was a dark, gray morning with splatters of rain on the glass plated walls outside. Charlie tapped the back of his comfortable leather desk chair with the fingers of one manicured hand.

Donald, who knew the signs, tensed. This tiny outward display of agitation was a strong indicator of trouble, either recent or to come.

Force 12 in German Bight

He walked across the thick pile of the expensive carpet to stand loosely at attention in front of the desk and coughed low to ensure Charlie knew he was there.

Charlie turned and looked at him for a moment from under thick, gray brows with his slightly protuberant black eyes, then motioned to a leather chair near Donald.

"Sit," he growled.

"Everything OK, Charlie?" Donald knew something was up but didn't want to press his boss, as he would be told in good time. He respected Charlie, who behaved much as one of the officers might in the Marines. It fit his idea of structure.

"Yes, but tell me how it went in Edinburgh first," Charlie said, as he seated himself in the deep leather chair. This gave him an advantage over anyone sitting opposite, as the two chairs on the door side of his desk had shorter legs, so any person seated there had to look up at him.

Donald gave his report of the meeting and what had been said. When he finished, Charlie leaned back in his chair, crossed his legs and asked, "D'you think he got the message?"

"Oh, yeah. I watched his face when I told him what would happen to his wife if he screwed up. He knew I meant what I said. That fella will do as he's told, don't worry, Boss."

Charlie nodded, and Donald waited. After a deliberate pause Charlie uncrossed his legs and leaned over the table, staring at Donald.

"D'you know what those goons of yours have done?"

Donald gulped. "No, Boss, what've they done?"

"Didn't I give orders for them to take care of that guy Mirko, that Yugoslavian guy?"

"Yeah, what happened? I haven't heard from them yet." Donald felt his neck grow hot but restrained himself from reaching for his collar.

"They fucked up is what. They were told to make him disappear and leave no trace back to us." Charlie's tone was soft, but Donald could sense the anger beneath the apparent calm. He nodded, his mouth dry.

"They haven't reported back yet, but... coincidentally, last night the police at Paddington were very interested in a body

16

minced by one of their trains. Have you read the papers today?"

"No, Boss, I came straight here. Didn't think to buy one."

Charlie tossed a newspaper on the table. The *London Evening Standard* headlines blared: "Man found cut in two on railway lines outside Paddington."

Further down, Donald read the police were investigating the incident as a crime rather than a suicide.

"If that has anything to do with those two goons and comes back to my bailiwick, someone will pay for it. You get my meaning, eh, Don?"

Donald sat up even straighter than before. "I'll look into it, Boss. What do you want me to do about them? Pete and Nigel?" he asked, referring to the men who had been ordered to do the job.

Charlie stared back at him with hooded eyes. "If this has anything to do with them, they're incompetent. Find a way to get rid of them, and make sure the next ones can be trusted to do a job properly. I don't like to hear of buggered up jobs showing up in a police back yard. OK if they're not involved with this mess, but if they are, you need to do something about them."

"Gotcha, Boss." Donald made to rise, but Charlie motioned him back down.

"Let's talk about the trailer and when it gets to the Danish border," he said.

Donald relaxed. His boss didn't dwell too long on a subject once he'd delivered the message. He assumed it had been heard; if not, the consequences were usually dire. Donald had risen in the ranks because he paid attention to what Charlie told him.

"Now, I want you to go to Harwich and call on these people. They have a boat, ship, whatever, that can stay afloat in the North Sea. They're waiting for their marching orders and you have to make sure they understand them.

"You can pick up Mark and Jonah there, they're going with you to Denmark. They'll be waiting for you near the ferry. Sammy is here in the office, don't forget to take him with you. You're not taking those two morons of yours on a job this important."

Donald nodded emphatically.

"When you get to Denmark you will call these guys." Charlie

pushed a slip of paper across the desk with some names on it and a phone number. "I've worked with Hans before; he's a tough Danish guy, former navy. Knows his stuff. They know the area and are in this with us. Good so far?"

"Yes, Boss. No problem. Who's the leader on this gig?" Donald asked, feeling the first twinges of excitement at the commencement of an operation.

"You are, and Hans has been so informed. No need to lay it on too thickly with him; he'll do as asked, and he has backup and shooters if needed."

Donald asked a couple more questions, Charlie set him right on time tables and actual destinations, then said, "OK, Don. A lot depends on you and this Yank on the barge. The boys in Harwich will be waiting to hear from you as soon as you get to the American ship. Make sure to leave no trails, and make sure those idiot goons are dealt with before you leave, understood?"

"Sure, Boss, I'll... I'll deal with it, don't worry. Sammy and I can deal with it."

"Good man. And Don..."

"Yes, Boss?"

"This is very big. Could be one for the books. We're looking at well over sixty big ones here. Don't let anyone fuck this up, you hear me?"

Chapter 3

A Welcoming Party

Patrick jerked awake to a hand shaking his shoulder. He rolled over into a seated position and opened his eyes.

"We're there!" called a crewman as he left the cabin lounge.

The deep throb of the ocean-going tug's engines vibrated up through the metal deck below his feet and into the lounge where Patrick and two other men struggled awake in the darkness. The dimmed lights of the cabin were turned up to full on by a crewman, bringing a harsh, artificial brightness to the cabin that made him squint. The lounge was cluttered with all the usual things: weather jackets of bright yellow, and rubber sea boots, among which their own cases and bags were scattered. The lighter items slid about on the slick linoleum and fell into corners. The roll indicated to Patrick the sea was agitated. He hoped it wasn't too rough outside, or they'd be unable to get off the tug.

He pushed himself up off the couch, rubbed the sleep from his eyes, and glanced around for his cases and bags. Patrick was fully clothed except for his boots, which he hastened to put on and lace up. He was tired and wanted a shower. The tug had carried them nearly one hundred miles due west of Denmark's coast, taking almost all night to get here. They would be called out on deck any minute.

In a thick Danish accent the crewman told the milling passengers to load their bags onto the net for lifting onto the barge. Patrick could feel the tug boat dipping and corkscrewing in the choppy seas, and told himself he would welcome the steady decks of the barge.

He desperately wanted a cup of tea, but that was not forthcoming. The tone of the tug's engines changed and he sensed they had slowed even more. The sea-going tug began to roll and the pitch became more pronounced as its forward impetus died. Patrick found himself hanging onto the fixed tables and rails in order to stay on his feet.

There was some loud radio chatter from the bridge above his head as the captain talked to someone on the other vessel. The tug shuddered as its engines went into reverse. The deep rumble of the motors below as they revved up and the screws bit into the water focused Patrick's attention. It was time to go out onto the rear deck. Matt, one of the other men accompanying him, looked pale in the harsh light. He was seasick; Patrick had heard him vomiting in the head earlier in the evening. He gave Patrick a sickly grin.

"Ah never could abide the sea. Goddammed stupid living! Dunno why Ah keep comin' back."

Patrick understood; it was the money. These men earned a lot living on the sea, but she was not a kind mistress to work for.

He led the way with a bag over his shoulder and his case in hand. He forced open the steel door and had to hang onto the handle of the door as the wind grabbed at it and tried to slam it back on its stops. Night noises rushed in and surrounded them. Over the keening of the wind and the hissing of waves passing the hull, he could hear the whine and clank of winches and cranes, operating high above them, hidden behind the blinding light of the arc lamps from the huge ship towering over them. Deep inside its massive hull he could hear the howl and scream of large engines rise to a deafening level.

Those would be the pumps, he surmised. He was surprised that the barge was still working the pipe despite the rough weather and the late time of year. Patrick squinted upwards but could see little due to the glare from lights shining down on the tug.

Small figures leaned over the side of the ship above, dark shapes wearing safety hats. It started to rain, which created streaks of light within the beams of the lamps. He peered off to the seaward side of the tug but could see nothing other than the ominous dark mass of the seas and the occasional whitecap that drifted by.

He was forced to pay attention and to hang onto a rail as the tug lifted and twisted on the black, ten foot waves that smashed against its hull. The captain skillfully played a game of positioning to keep his boat from being hammered against the walls of the ship and remain long enough for his cargo of passengers to be lifted off his heaving deck. He yelled down at them from the open doorway of the bridge to hurry up.

Patrick and his two companions huddled in the shelter of the walkway and waited to be called by the very busy crew members, who were clearing a space in the middle of the cluttered afterdeck.

Someone shouted in warning and a dark object blotted out the lights briefly before it swung down to land with a loud thump onto the cleared space. It was a flat, round platform encased in red painted canvas about four feet across with a rope net tied all round. This net connected to a huge metal hook and a cable that disappeared into the darkness.

One of the tug crew members shouted at the huddled figures and beckoned them. Patrick joined the other two as they grabbed their bags and tossed them into the middle of the platform. The three men then staggered forward to stand on the edge of the platform, holding onto the net.

Patrick grabbed at the net just in time as the impatient crewman bawled into a portable radio and the whole thing took off. They were hauled into the air at such a rate that, as often before, he had to hang on for dear life and. Within seconds the tug had become very small beneath them, but he only got a glimpse before they were swept over the deck of the ship. Within moments they were descending with dizzying speed through the darkness into the glare of the lights to land on the deck of the larger vessel with a jarring thump that almost threw Patrick off.

A large man with a safety helmet on his head and a small portable radio in his hand approached them, shouting.

"Get off and git below! Ah need the net. Hi yer, Pat!" He gave a friendly wave.

It was Steve, a deck rigger who had the night shift. Patrick waved a brief acknowledgement but hurried to get his bags off the net and made haste to follow the others toward the steel island that loomed on the starboard side.

They needed no persuasion to leave the area; it began to rain harder, which created inches of spray when the droplets bounced off the wooden decking. They retrieved their bags and hurried in the direction of the tall metal structure and a large steel door. On their way across the bustling deck they passed the welding shop with its hellish blue glare of welding arcs flashing on and off, throwing out streams of sparks as the night welders worked their shift.

Patrick wanted to get off the deck quickly; he didn't want to get in the way of one of the fifty ton cranes, which rumbled about on the wide, wooden-clad steel deck like huge dinosaurs, lifting cargo off the back deck of the tug, and swinging it up onto the larger vessel. Unless one knew what was going on, the upper deck of the barge was a dangerous place to loiter.

He caught a glimpse of another oceangoing tug on the other side of the ship, backing up to the barge, and men working furiously to bring in one of the massive buoys. There must be a storm coming, Patrick decided. The sea was too rough for the kind of work they were doing.

The leading man undid the metal door clasps and heaved, the steel door opened against the wind and they went through into a short corridor. The door clanged shut behind them, muting the noises of the outer deck, which were replaced by a relative quiet and the distant hum of engines far below. There was a pervasive, familiar smell of oil and paint, but Patrick paid it little attention.

He wanted to get to his cabin and catch some more shut eye. His watch told him his shift would begin in four hours. He joined his companions as they trotted down the first set of steel stairs and strode along the quiet corridor with sleeping cabins on the right hand side. These belonged to the senior supers and visiting inspectors. At the far end, near the corner where it took a left, was the hospital cabin.

They hurried along this corridor, turned left again, and reached Patrick's cabin. The other two men waved to him and went on to their own cabins while he opened the door. He didn't know if his opposite number, Joel, would be hiding in the cabin, or asleep, or if there might be someone else sharing the space by now.

He'd been away for three weeks.

The cabin was lit, which meant Joel was out and about somewhere. He dumped his bags and sat on the large easy chair for a few minutes to get his bearings. He hated coming back to this rust bucket. The three weeks he'd been away were like a dream. Not that it had been great; in-law fights were never much fun. Now he had a minimum of three months to work on the barge. He wondered how things were going, rubbed the middle of his forehead with the tips of his fingers, and yawned.

His thoughts were interrupted as the door opened and Joel slipped in. Joel was a slight, almost skinny man with a wisp of a mustache. His light brown hair was, as usual, long and in disarray. His pale blue eyes were tired but lit up when he saw Patrick. He was clearly glad to see him. Three weeks of one engineer being away meant the other carried the whole system on his back for the duration and rarely slept more than a few hours each night.

"Hi, Pat! Boy, am I glad you're back!" Joel had the soft blurred accent of a man from Tennessee. When he sat down on the edge of one of the spare bunks and turned his head in an arc to relieve some of the tension in his neck, he looked older than his twenty-eight years.

"Hi, Joel. How's it goin'?" They shook hands.

"Ya really wanna know?" Joel grinned.

"No, but I guess I need to; I'm on in about four." Patrick sighed.

"OK, I spent most of last night fixing the radio... again. The tuning servo is on its last legs. Got it going, but it needs parts. I made a list. Number two generator is down. We have to strip the main brushes out and replace them. I'd started working on that when I heard you were back. The super is yelling for the power and we need to get it up and running."

Patrick groaned. "I hate those fucking generators!"

"Yeah, I know. But the work you did before you left helped keep them going for a long time without tripping off, so we are doing *somethin'* right."

"How many times did they trip off while I was away?" Patrick asked.

"About ten or twenty times I'd say, but that's a hell of a lot

Force 12 in German Bight

better than last month!"

"OK, then. Come on, lets get some tea and talk some more," Patrick said. He resigned himself to little sleep this night. He pushed himself off the chair and led the way along the corridor to the main galley where they would get their tea and coffee.

The well-lit galley was almost deserted at this time of night, as it was far too early for anyone on the next shift to be up and the current shift were all working hard to bring in the anchors.

"Seems like they are getting off the pipe," Patrick said.

"Yeah. Another blow from the north. Wonder how long we'll be off this time. At least you and I can work the generators at half power and deal with some of the problems," Joel said.

They talked for a while longer, seated at one of the tables in the galley, until Joel got a call and left. Patrick made his way to the cabin, and after a halfhearted attempt at unpacking he crawled into bed to catch up on some sleep before midnight.

*****

He woke in the dark of his bed with the curtains drawn and Joel calling him awake from the other side. Sliding out, he found the cabin brightly lit and Joel sitting in the only real chair in the cabin, smoking.

"Bit of a storm out there, mate!" he told Patrick, imitating his Brit accent.

"I can feel it!" The barge creaked and moved in slow, up and down motion. Although it was slight when a ship the size of the *Cherokee* moved in this way it had to be a rough sea outside.

Patrick accompanied Joel to the galley once more; which was now full of people in a variety of colored dungarees and overalls. The ones going off duty were for the most part filthy and stained. The men coming on duty, especially the riggers, were in an assortment of clothing from bright clean orange overalls to heavy waterproof yellow jackets and trousers.

Everyone either stood in line waiting for the food to be served or were already seated, eating. Almost to a man they were chewing on a steak or beef stew with potatoes and salad. The smell of frying bacon was pervasive.

The riggers ate in a hurry, as they had to relieve the others on deck, and those men were not inclined to do more than their allotted twelve hours. They would bitch loudly at slow replacements.

Patrick went for the eggs and bacon with hash browns, and filled up a coffee mug. Being from the engineering and tech group, neither Joel nor Patrick needed to hurry. They took their food to a space between some of the winch men, who greeted Patrick as though he'd been away for a year rather than a couple of weeks.

"Where ya been, Limey?" Virgil asked in a loud voice, with a grin.

"'E's been home to mammy! That's what," said Steve, one of the control riggers. He was a large man from Mississippi with big black eyes and sallow skin, He had a good nature however.

"How was it, Pat?" Someone asked.

"Man, it was good. I just don't know why I keep coming back to this shit hole and you bunch of wankers!" Patrick said with a grin of his own.

"What's a wanker?" one of the crewmen asked. Ryan was from Alabama, and the rest of them found him a little vacant on occasion. His question was greeted with snickers of derision.

"He means a jerk-off like you, Ryan," Joel said, and made some vulgar movements with his hand over his groin.

Ryan scowled at Joel but dipped his head and concentrated on his stew without responding. There was bad blood between Joel and some of the riggers. They didn't like his cocky ways much.

"Did ya spend all yor loot?" One of them asked him. It was Matt who had come on board with him.

"No but I bet you did." Patrick answered.

"Sure did, even bought a car, Corvette!" Matt bragged.

"Bloody Hell bet that cost a packet." Joel exclaimed.

"Did too. Got it on the jacks until Ah git back." Matt informed them placing a fresh chaw of tobacco in his mouth the moment he had finished his meal.

"Bet your wife sold it raht off the jacks the moment yew left the house, Matt," Steve told him with a grin.

The others hooted at that but Patrick knew it might well be

true. The wife wouldn't have had money by the time Matt left to come back out to sea. He listened with half an ear while the others bantering with one another. Even though they made fun of Matt, they were all the same he thought to himself.

Joel headed to the cabin to clean up and get some sleep, while Patrick finished his meal and greeted several of the men coming off duty. After a few minutes he got up and headed down to the lower deck to check on the generators. These were the lifeline of the ship, and he knew the super would ask about them as soon as he came onto the bridge at 6 am. He wondered which one it would be. He'd heard Daryl Galay had been off the barge for some reason.

The generators were on the machine deck below the cabins in a long, wide area with a low ceiling. There was only seven feet between the floor gratings that held the pipes and cables and the roof, where even more cables and pipes ran in every direction like some orderly layout of thick and thin spaghetti. The entire floor was made up of gratings that rattled whenever a man walked across them. There were five huge diesel Caterpillar generators in the room; three of them were running.

Each one could produce eight hundred kilowatts, enough to run a small town in Scotland, Patrick figured. But they were old and in dire need of a factory overhaul; often enough they could not even manage to carry their designed capacity, and they required constant maintenance. This time the problem was the worn brushes that carried the current to the power boxes, where it was converted for use on the massive drag anchors. Two of the midnight shift techies were already there, crouched over one of the dismantled machines.

Patrick walked across the grating, which rattled and clanked as he trod on them, to crouch next to Johnny, the lead technician, and another techie called Dan; both were Scotsmen from the UK. The noise in the generator room prevented any normal conversation so he had to shout.

"Hi, guys, how's it going?"

"Hey, Pat, how was it?" Johnny called up with a friendly grin.

"Fine, Johnny. Hi, Dan," Patrick shouted.

Dan lifted his hand and nodded a greeting. He pointed to the blackened stumps of the brushes they had taken out of the generator. Generator covers and tools lay strewn about on some canvas to prevent them falling into the wells below the gratings.

"The efffing brushes have worn out well before their time, Boss," he called up.

"Clean the commutators then, that might help, then replace the brushes. We do have some, right?" Patrick asked.

"Yep, Joel got hold of them yesterday."

"OK, see you later. I'm going to see Jock in the pump room. Let me know when you're done, as we'll have to re-adjust the regulators and balance the generators—I'll do that."

Patrick got a nod of acknowledgement from the men and stood up. He headed toward the rear of the ship, staying on the same deck.

His tour of the ship took him all around the engine rooms where the huge seawater pumps were located. They were silent, as the barge was 'off the pipe' due to the bad weather. Patrick continued through all the chambers and along the passages that led from one to the other in a bewildering maze of tunnels and pipe laden passages, but he knew his way about the barge blindfolded. He took his time and checked on every thing he could.

The loneliness of the first day back always weighed on him, and he was in a morose mood as he went. His last trip back to Scotland had not been as good as he would have liked. Family matters and quarrels were not something he needed when all he wanted to do back home was to relax, drink a good Oban malt whiskey or two, and sleep normal hours. This tub was like a prison to him, even if it did pay him a huge amount of money compared to his former eight to five job in the UK. It brought him back again and again, like everyone else, but he hated it all the same.

He reached the rear of the barge and climbed the steps that led all the way up to the heli pad at the aft end, hoping the kestrel that lived up in the pipes high above deck was still there. It represented the only natural creature on this floating prison other than the men, and they didn't count to Patrick. It meant a great deal to him. He fed it food when he could.

He couldn't see very much in the gray of the dawn, with a cold wind coming in from the North. He tucked his head deeper into the thick padded coveralls collar and pulled his wool cap down hard over his ears.

The barge shouldn't even be out here, he reflected, but the powers that be had sent instructions to get the barge out onto this particular pipe and dredge it before the year ended. Given the extensive repairs needed, the barge should be in port for a modest refit, but no, here they were, hoping to get off the pipe before November, when the real storms came. Being off it would not please the supers, he surmised. Time off the pipe was money lost.

He stood on the second gangway looking up at the base of the helipad, with its own dense array of pipes and beams, and had the satisfaction of seeing the flutter of wings. The kestrel was still there. His life on the barge was self-imposed, but as he looked around the cheerless seascape, he wished he'd been able to stay out in the deserts where he'd once been posted. At least creatures were visible and to hand, not like this desert of water, where living on a barge more and more resembled a steel jail.

He reflected morosely that most of the men from the USA and Britain, other than the Filipinos, were lifers who had been divorced at least twice. He didn't care to think how the Filipinos managed a whole year on the ship, but they went home rich men in their own country for their trouble. He sighed. Not much longer and he could afford a house without a mortgage in among his beloved mountains north of Stirling. He got up, sent one last glance toward the kestrel and trotted back down to the main deck, and then to the machinery decks to see how the techies were faring with the generators. That is, if they hadn't skived off to smoke a joint in the meantime.

*****

Patrick opened the door of his cabin at the end of his shift to find it was full of people and smoke. He'd just come back from the primitive gym and wanted a shower, but it looked like there was a party in progress.

"Hi there, Patrick!" Johnny the electrician techie shouted from the large black office chair, the only chair in the room. He was waving a polystyrene cup in the air. The rest of the visitors were seated on either a bunk or a suitcase.

'We're havin' a party, laddie. All for you! Welcome back!"

"So I can see," Patrick said dryly. "You found the whiskey, eh?"

"Nope. Where the hell do you hide it man? We all know how much you like the malt! But we brought some Wild Turkey and some grand old Jack with us. Jimmy here has some, and there is more to come I'm told, on one of the tugs due in next week."

Combined with the acrid tobacco smoke were the unmistakable smells of whiskey and marijuana. Both booze and drugs were banned on the North Sea, but as far as Patrick could tell the barge was awash in liquor of one kind or another, and he knew full well drugs were smoked or snorted by a lot of the men, even by some of the more whacky riggers.

He noted with wry amusement that several of the techies wore the pipes he had designed. The slim toke pipes were about four and a half inches long and were clipped to their overall breast pockets, just like a pen with a gold top.

"I see you still have your pipe, Johnny," he remarked as he took a cup.

"Ah love my wee pipe, Pat. It's so... elegant!" Johnny beamed. He took it out and lifted it up for a look in the light. "Ah would have paid ye a hundred dollars and no problem, Pat. It's well worth the fifty!"

Patrick had made it out of fine, stainless steel tubing, with black shrink tubing, normally used to insulate fine electrical connections, as a cover. The actual burn section for the weed was a gold-plated electrical signal connector, soldered onto the steel pipe. It even had a formed mouthpiece, a stopper and a clip, so the idiot riggers and techies could smoke pot right out there on deck. It always amazed him no one fell overboard from too many tokes, but so far no one had.

"Ah walked through the customs in Copenhagen, this time wi' it and no one noticed a thing!" Johnny bragged. Patrick didn't mind his bragging. Neither did he mind smoking the odd joint of Danish Gold, but drew the line at the harder stuff some of the riggers took.

He took the proffered cup from Johnny and sipped the bourbon.

"You're no a snob then, Pat? I'd have thought wi' all the malt you always talk about, bourbon might not be the thing."

"I've got no pride," he told Johnny. "Least of all when I'm with a gang of ruffians like you bunch of mindless misfits."

Johnny laughed and tipped his cup to him. "You're no so bad, Pat. Bit dour, but then Ah don't know a fuckin' highlander that isn't."

There were at least five other people in the small cabin and he knew all of them by name. One, a diver called Leonard, was a strong, lean, bearded man who seemed to be well on his way towards inebriation. Patrick nudged one of the people and sat next to him on the edge of the bunk.

"What's Johnny up to, Danny? I can smell something in the air."

Danny, who was another electrical techie, giggled. "That's the pot, Pat! I dunno, but I think he's got it in for Lenny. Don't know why Lenny's even here. Real bigmouth, and Johnny hates him."

"I can tell him to leave... it's my cabin," Patrick said. He knew and liked Leonard well enough.

"Nah, leave 'im. So what if Johnny's up to something. Lenny can look after himself."

The noise level rose and the smoke grew more dense. No one bothered to keep an eye out for the supervisor or the crew leaders. They knew this kind of party was common and helped keep the lid on the pot. Although he was one of the ship's engineers and nominally the man in charge, Patrick rarely used his authority, and then only when a situation called for it.

The men seemed to appreciate that. The supers and senior riggers would stay away unless there was an emergency. He kept half an ear open for the tannoy, which could summon him at any moment to deal with some irksome problem, but it was silent.

A joint was passed to Patrick. Why not? he thought, it's been a long day. He took a drag and passed it on to Danny.

The jokes got under way and the group giggled its way through several, then settled in for a long session. Danny drew the short stick from the matches and had to go off and get a mountain of sandwiches for the guys who were now getting the 'munchies'.

He shambled off to the mess hall in his bright orange overalls and a pair of dark sunglasses on his nose to grab as many Snickers bars and peanut butter sandwiches as he could pillage from the galley.

Patrick felt good and the bourbon tasted reasonable, although to his mind it couldn't come close to a good malt. While he didn't want a hangover in the morning, he knew he'd end up with one. A twelve hour shift was interminably long when one's head was aching. The music was good tonight. Someone had brought a guitar, and Bane, one of the few American techies, sat on one of the top bunks and played.

Bane could only play when high, so Patrick made sure he got lots of smoking done; whereupon he complained about the light, which had already been turned down low to the point where the people were indistinct shapes. He retreated to the deeper darkness of the upper bunk, drew the curtains, and played music as good as any Patrick had ever heard. The notes rippled and soared, lending a surreal atmosphere to roomful of dazed and half drunk men.

Peering around him with blurry vision, Patrick saw men, young and old, shaven or not, in dirty or clean orange overalls— the standard uniform on the barge. All were clutching polystyrene cups of bourbon, their heads wreathed in smoke, talking loudly in a variety of accents as the atmosphere grew denser. The poorest joke was now being greeted with howls of laughter and "Yee Haws" from the Southern boys, and Patrick's sides were beginning to ache.

Danny sidled back into the room accompanied by Joel, who smelled a party and wanted some of it. Although he was on duty no one would really mind unless the barge came to a stop.

The cheese, peanut butter, jelly and salami sandwiches were quickly devoured by hungry men, and the drinking and smoking resumed to the accompaniment of Bane's guitar.

"Sing us a song, Patrick. Y'know the one aboot that camel. You ex squaddies know bunches of em," Bane said.

"Yeah, come on, we need some singing!" The men nudged him.

"It's not a song, it's a ditty," he informed them.

"C'mon, Pat."

"OK, OK!"

He took a swig of his Jack and started.

Force 12 in German Bight

The sexual life of the camel
Is a truly peculiar thing!
One day in a fit of passion,
He tried to bugger the Sphinx.

Now the Sphinx's anal canal
Was blocked by the sands of the Nile,
And that accounts for the camel's hump
And the Sphinx's inscrutable smile!

They roared out the second verse, followed by yells and applause, and at one point Johnny said loudly in his thick Scots accent, "Away, Pat, me old pal. Yu've got some fine whusky here!"

Patrick, who was smashed by this time, peered back at him with a stupid look on his face. "It's not whisky, it's bourbon, and it isn't mine. Anyway, who cares?"

"But it's not the best thing ye have in here, is it, me old bugger?" Johnny said.

"Wot yer talking about, Johnny?" he slurred, but he knew perfectly well that the bastard was after his malt.

Johnny pointed. "Ah'm talkin' about that stuff!"

Patrick followed the line of his finger. All there was on the shelf over the mirror was a toothbrush and a large jar of Vicks cream for colds and flu. He'd often wondered what it was doing there, and figured it must be a leftover from the previous occupant.

"I don't know what you're talking about," he said. Things were moving more slowly now.

Everyone peered at the Vicks jar as Johnny waved his finger at it. "Do ye no understand me, man? That's the best stuff since sliced bread, and away better than the shit we've bin smokin' tonight!"

Danny started to giggle and Patrick laughed. "OK, Johnny, you first!"

Leonard asked, with a glance at Patrick, "You mean that stuff, Jock? It's for colds, you rub it on your... your chest. What the hell are you going to do with it?'

"Ar'l show yer. This stuff will send ye tay the other side o' the moon, me good man. There's nothin' like it!"

Leonard appeared to be interested. "You're joking?" He sounded uncertain.

Danny chimed in. "No, he's not, man. That stuff is the way out when you've had a few drags of shit, then you take this stuff and it sends you the rest of the way. Ah think it's better than coke, and it's not even addictive! Ha Ha!"

The hysterical giggling began again, Leonard laughing with the others.

"Go on, Johnny. Take some of it and show us how," Patrick said. His eyes were watering and he laughed. Joel on the bunk next to him was spluttering with suppressed laughter.

Patrick took the jar down and handed it to Johnny, who made a great ceremony of taking the lid off and making sure Leonard could see he took a huge dollop of Vick's cream out with his index finger. It sat there, a pale glob of goo, and then he pretended to push it up his nostril. In fact he didn't, he left it hanging off the left side of his nose like a massive greasy booger. Leonard could not see that, though, and before anyone could react Johnny pretended to go off into a new world. Strange things appeared to be happening to him.

Patrick laughed so hard he nearly fell off the bed. The mere sight of Johnny, pretending to be in ecstasy, rolling his eyes and waving his hands in the air with the dollop of slimy sludge on the side of his nose was too much for the three men on the bunk.

Patrick, Joel and Johnny started crying with laughter, and this was infectious, so the whole room started to howl, most not even knowing why. Even Bane stopped playing to peer out between the curtains, his dark glasses slipping down his nose as he did so.

Still shaking with laughter and with tears running down his cheeks, Patrick made a great show of digging his finger into the muck in the jar and pretended to ram it up his own nostril. He shoved the goop behind his ear, where it began to burn.

Johnny and Joel did the same, and all three started to act as though they were losing it. Joel laughed so hard he farted, and the room dissolved into hysterics.

Force 12 in German Bight

"Ah'm off to another planet! See y'all there!" Joel yelled with a great 'Yee Haw!' He fell back, his eyes streaming, while Danny hung off Patrick's shoulder howling like a sick dog. Patrick shook so hard he thought he was going to pee his pants. Johnny, meanwhile, cooly continued to deliver his best performance to the enraptured audience.

"Ye are no a man until ye've gone the whole whack, me boy!" he shouted.

Leonard was still a bit uncertain, but the combination of the booze, the marijuana and the idiotic performances of the others convinced him something must be working for them.

"How do I do this?" he asked.

"Well, ye take yer finger, dip it into the sludge in the jar, and take a large scoop. Ye ram it right oop yer nostril like we all did, and then ye snort it right up yer nose," Johnny said, looking owlish.

"Like this?" Leonard asked, and did as he'd been told: he rammed a huge plug of Vicks right up his nostril and snorted.

It took a few seconds and there was a pregnant pause in the whole cabin as everyone registered what had just occurred. Then Leonard went nuts. He coughed and blew and waved his head about, clawing at his face and yelling like a madman.

He pulled out a dirty handkerchief and blew as though he wanted to blow his brains out through his nose. All around him the others dissolved once more into hysterical, screaming laughter. Men were crying on each other and weeping with mirth. The poor man left the cabin in great haste, with the jeers and laughter following him down the corridor.

The drunken crew began to chant the rags of Eskimo Nell.

"Ooohooo we're up in the North! The cold, cold North.
Where a fuck is a fight and they fight all night,
And the nights are six months long!
Where even the dead lie two in a bed
And the skeletons rattle,
In amorous battle
And the babies masturbate!"

James Boschert

Patrick woke up for his shift the next day with a blinding hangover, fuzzy vision and aching ribs. The cabin was a shambles; it stank of old whiskey and reeked of stale marijuana smoke. He hoped to God the barge would behave itself during his shift.

Chapter 4

The Finding

He reflexively rolled out of bed to put his bare feet on the linoleum of the cabin floor, then leaned down with his head in his hands.

"I feel like I got bashed on the head last night, and my mouth tastes like a gorilla's armpit!" he groaned.

"It's all right for you, mate. I had to go to work!" Joel liked using the Brit terms of familiarity, although he came from Tennessee. "I don't know how I got through the shift myself. We're back on the pipe and the generators went off twice while you were taking your ease. Weather isn't too bad out there today."

"Bet it's that umbilical cable that's acting up. We need to go after it when the next bad weather comes in and we're off the pipe."

Joel nodded, but he was too tired to say more than "Go up to the bridge and check the radio, would ya? I can't figure out the problem this time, and Stan is mad as hell because he can't pick up the weather report from the UK Met office."

Patrick nodded and went to get a shower and wake himself up with some strong coffee in the galley. A tousled group of men about to begin their shift were there already. Some greeted him with waves, but for the most part people said little and ate large meals. They would be busy with their duties for many hours to come, with few breaks in between.

Force 12 in German Bight

He did the same, then he took his coffee and climbed the stairs all the way up to the bridge. As it was now 6:30 am, the sky was light in the east behind them, although the sun had not yet disbursed the darkness to the west.

"Good morning all, and good morning, Rock!" he called out. This last address was to a small, round stone that had come up from the bottom of the sea, on which he'd painted a couple of eyes and sexy red lips. It lay on a shelf nearby. Some of the console drivers were chary with their good mornings, so he would call out to it and ignore those he knew to be surly. No one dared remove the rock after a certain incident on the bridge, which Skillet had instigated. No one messed with Patrick after that.

He found his friend Skillet watching the activity down on the deck. He stood next to the NAVAID equipment, the gyro and the radar console. Four large consoles were in the room, placed in pairs back to back. Another stood at the front of the bridge, which was full of dials belonging to the sledge sensors. Men sat at the four back-to-back consoles for the anchor control systems and murmured into microphones to the two tug boats doing their bidding out at sea. The tugs lifted and placed anchors at their command.

They nodded to one another and Skillet murmured, "Good mornin' to you, Pat. Heard there was a good party at your place last night. I'm just real hurt I wasn't invited. Heard the only thing missing was the whores." He pronounced the word as whooores, which made Patrick grin despite his headache.

"Neither was I, and it was in my own cabin," he replied. "And before you ask, I don't remember much about it. Didn't see any whooores, neither."

Skillet grinned and pressed the microphone on his hand-held radio. "Pay more attention to the buoy when the tug comes in, Stanley. That cable gets broken I'll skin you!"

He turned to Patrick, who watched the goings on below with bloodshot eyes. "Incompetent bastard, that Stan guy. I'd like to run him off," he said in a low voice. No sooner had he said this than there was a yell behind them and Dana, one of the console operators, started to work his console frantically. He turned switches and looked up at the dials, which seemed to have gone wild.

"You stupid bastard!" he yelled at no one in particular. They heard a great snapping noise outside and one of the cables coming out of the starboard area sped back toward the barge, far too fast, almost as though it were a gigantic rubber band.

"It's broken, Skillet!" Dana shouted in despair. "Stupid Italian skipper over there went too fast for the winches to pay out!"

"Shut the fucking thing down! Turn off that winch altogether!" Skillet called sharply over to Dana, who was near to panic.

Dana did as he was told and the cable vanished into the sea, except for where it exited the cable hole in the barge.

"Now start the winch up again and bring it in slow and easy," Skillet ordered, and Dana calmed down.

"Rest of you clowns keep your eyes on your cables! I don't want a repeat of this," Skillet called to the other three console men, and his tone brooked no backchat.

He changed frequency, thumbed his mic and spoke softly into it to the Skipper of the tug boat that had helped break the cable.

"Giovani, how many times have I asked you to pay attention to the console, man? You were going too fast out there and now we have another broken cable. Gonna take several hours to fix and it's *your fault*! Now PAY attention or we might have to hire another tug! Git that buoy back here, and make sure you do NOT lose the anchor as well." He snapped off the key. "Bastard. Where did we find that clown?"

Skillet was angry. "That's the second cable he's helped break in two weeks! I'm going to run him off as soon as we can find a replacement tuggie."

Patrick didn't hear the rest. He hurried to check the console that belonged to him. This console measured all the sensors on the 'sled' as it was known, that rested astride the 48 inch pipe at the bottom of the sea, one hundred and fifty feet beneath the barge. He was just thankful the whole accident hadn't tripped off the generators again.

Apart from a few nervous flickers, the needles on the dials didn't give him anything to worry about. He mentioned this to Skillet, who merely nodded and went back to dealing with the cable repairs under way on the main deck.

"We can keep moving while we repair that cable," he said.

Force 12 in German Bight

Patrick went down one level to the radio room, where Stanley, the radio man, sat with Hamesh, the admin worker on the barge.

"Ah, there you are, Pat. Been waiting for you," Stanley said by way of greeting. "Joel is pretty useless when it comes to fixing this piece of shit." He referred to the 1500 watt radio, their main source of communication with the outside world, and an important piece of equipment. However, it had malfunctioned so often Patrick wondered which was worse: the generators or the radio. The barge had a dozen other malfunctioning pieces of equipment, including the radar and the gyroscope, but these two items were by far the worst to deal with.

"What's happening this time?" he said.

"Can't get it to tune accurately, and when it finally gets tuned it won't stay in place," Stan said. He was a good radio operator who knew what he was doing, but the nuts and bolts of the machine were Patrick and Joel's province.

"Is the 'Sailor' working?" he asked. This was their back up radio, but it had no long range and couldn't reach land. They sometimes used it to talk to the tug boat captains.

"Yeah, that seems to be OK, but I need to get a weather report in ASAP, Pat. The Sailor can't get it for me. Can you see what you can do?"

"OK, I'll go up and check it out. Stay off the thing until I come back. I don't want to get a nasty shock just because you're impatient, you old bugger."

Stanley was a balding, slightly overweight Englishman, who wore glasses and was into his mid fifties. He grinned and gave Patrick the finger as he left.

"I saw that, you old fart. Just you wait!" Patrick said amiably as he went up into the radio cabin located behind the main bridge structure.

He worked the system for a long hour or so, knowing all he achieved was a temporary fix till the next time it broke. Several of the tuning capacitor dials were so old they didn't function properly, and the antenna servo mechanism had so much drift, it was no wonder it couldn't hold its position.

Eventually he climbed down and asked Stan to try again. The tuning took place and they could hear the shipping news. Stanley smiled. "I'll buy you a coffee for that, Pat," he said.

"Gone off coffee, especially the Irrawaddy river mud *you* call coffee. This one's worth at least a bottle of Tobermory," Pat said as he left.

"Fucking extortionist!" Stanley called after him. Patrick laughed.

*****

Patrick made his way through the first bulkhead of the generator room and into an area just as full of machinery. The eight massive Wesley high pressure pumps sat in place, four pairs in a long, poorly lit chamber that stank of oil and diesel. He was well used to the thunder of the pumps under normal conditions, and they were hard at it today. He adjusted his ear pieces to keep the din out.

Their job was to supply the water pressure to the sled which was astride the pipe and blow the trench out beneath the pipe. He made his way along the gratings to the port side and headed for the next major compartment door. This led into the fore port side anchor winch room, where he wanted to make sure the winches hadn't suffered anything bad because of the breakage. If they had, the smell of burned wiring from an overdose of amps would let him know.

He heaved at the levers of the clamps on the door, hauled it open and stepped over the combing into another large chamber. This was again busy, but a good deal less noisy, since the winches were moving at a slow pace as they hauled the barge forward along the pipe. The huge servo motors in the shallow well near him were humming, and one of the winches at the far end turned slowly. The other was still while the repairs to the cable continued on the main deck. The sound of dripping water came to his ears, but otherwise the room hummed and vibrated, smelling of winch motor brakes and oil. There was no visible damage. His eyes roamed over the room to assess the machines.

The room had been painted in a neutral faded yellow that badly needed attention. Rust patches and moisture trails coated the walls and struts, while the grating was polished bare of the green paint that once covered it. The railing Patrick leaned against was in a similar state. He set off for the next middle chamber, which housed even more machinery, when his eye caught something on the catwalk grating near the second anchor winch.

In the dim light of the room it looked like a bundle of rags, but something about it made him want to investigate further. He walked towards it and discovered it wasn't a pile of rags at all. His eyes rested on a booted foot, and he realized it belonged to a body.

Patrick was instantly alert. He moved toward the body, which was still. He looked about him first to make sure he was alone, then he crouched over the body. The man lay sprawled face down on the grating, his head near the winch barrel, with one arm reached over his head and the other by his side. Patrick knew it was Charlie, one of the riggers.

Charlie was from Louisiana, one of the American crew whose job it was to control the gangs of Filipino workers on deck. Patrick noticed the back of Charlie's head seemed to have been smashed in. There was a lot of blood, and Patrick saw what he thought might be brain matter. The back of Charlie's coveralls was stained black with blood. Patrick reached forward and touched the man on the back of his neck. The body was still warm. He touched the blood on the coveralls; it was still wet.

Whatever had killed Charlie had only just occurred. He glanced behind him again. The atmosphere in the dimly lit chamber felt suddenly menacing. Patrick was no stranger to dead people; he had served in the British army in several of its less pleasant postings, but this was the first time he'd encountered a dead man on the barge. Accidents happened all the time, but none that he could remember down in a winch room. Most took place on the work deck where the cranes lumbered about, swinging large buoys and anchors, and high pressure valves sometimes exploded, injuring people in the process.

He knelt over Charlie's body and felt for the pulse along his neck. He didn't expecting anything, but wanted to be sure. It was still, the man was dead. Patrick peered closely at the wound, then at the metal frames and even the winch itself, but he saw no sign of blood on anything in the immediate vicinity.

He stood up, walked back the way he had come, and exited the chamber. Without acknowledging any greetings from people he passed along the corridors, he made his way to the bridge. He hoped to find Skillet still up there and was not disappointed.

He was greeted by one of the console men, who had missed him earlier.

"Hi there, Mr. Patrick. How the fuck are you today?

"Fuck you, Bobby, and good morning. Hey, Skillet," Patrick said. His eyes went automatically to the main sled console. The needles twitched gently but nothing was out of place. Patrick spoke in low tones so Bobby couldn't hear.

"Got a problem below, Skillet. Need you to come. Right away." His eyes locked with Skillet's. "It's serious, mate. Need to hurry. Get hold of a couple of the riggers from the deck."

Skillet hesitated only a moment before he hurried after Patrick's retreating back down the stairs. When they came to the main level Skillet opened the door onto the deck and shouted for two of the men nearby to join them. They walked down the stairs to the machine deck where they followed Patrick, who was already halfway along the corridor and headed for the Fore Port winch room.

"What's goin' on, Skillet?" one of the riggers asked as he jogged after his boss.

"Dunno, but Patrick said it was serious. He might be a Limey but he knows what's what. Hey ,Patrick, ease up man, what's the hurry?"

"Got your flashlights with you? You know these lights are unreliable," Patrick called. Moments later the lights in the corridor indeed went out, almost as though he had predicted it, and left them in total darkness for a few seconds before the red, emergency lights came on.

"God damned generators have gone off again!" Skillet said without much feeling. The problem was endemic, and Patrick had fought with it for almost six months now. Skillet knew how mad it made the Brit, because he couldn't figure out what was causing all the problems.

"Goddam is right. Watch your step," Patrick said, and produced his small but intense flashlight. The other three men did the same.

"Come on, it's in here." He heaved the locks on the bulkhead door, allowed it to crash open against its stops, and stepped

Force 12 in German Bight

through into the darkness beyond.

His ears picked up the sound of another door on the other side of the room shutting. He paused and listened, but other than the growl of the winches and the steady drip of water into the main well there was nothing else to concern him. He was sure of one thing however; someone had just left the main winch room and didn't want to be seen. He resisted the urge to chase after who ever it might have been, as there were a thousand places to hide and even turn on a pursuer. His main concern right now was to make sure Skillet saw the body.

"Right, now what the hell is all this about, Pat?" Skillet said when they'd followed him into the large winch chamber, and Patrick shut the door with another clang.

"Over there." Patrick pointed with his torch beam to the bundle huddled against the winch on the other side of the room. "You'll find Charlie there. He's been killed."

In the stunned silence that greeted his statement he moved along the grating to stand over the body once more. The emergency lighting did very little to illuminate details around the room, but his flashlight was sufficient to show Skillet and the other two men Charlie's corpse. It looked as though someone had tried to lift it, but had given up and let it drop.

"It's been moved since I was here, Skillet. I could swear someone was here just now and left through the door to the engine compartments."

Skillet drew a sharp breath at the sight of the body. "What the hell happened here?" But Skillet, too, had seen his share of dead men, and his background came to his aid. He glanced behind him at the two riggers and then at the doors.

"You two stay by the doors and let no one in till I tell you," he growled at the two riggers, who, even in the dim light, looked shaken.

"Is it Charlie?" one of them asked.

"Looks like it." Skillet's response was terse. He knelt by the body, which now lay on its back, and placed his fingers against the neck. "He's dead all right, but got to make sure," he said for Patrick's benefit.

"He was warm when I found him, Skillet. Someone had only

44

just clobbered him."

"Yeah, he's not cold yet so it wasn't long ago," Skillet looked at his watch. "Near 10 am I'd guess, if you came to find me right after?"

"I came right away. You're the duty officer."

Skillet turned the head over to have a look, keeping the beam of the flash light on the head. "You were right, Pat. Someone meant to kill him. Anything else, any other wounds you saw before he was moved? How was he lying when you found him?"

Patrick showed him the position Charlie had been in and pointed out he hadn't seen any kind of blood on the steel bulkhead, the winch nor the railings, which made him think it hadn't been an accident. Skillet verified the claim by roving over the area with his own flashlight.

"Nothing looking like an accident," he said and shook his head. "Wonder what's going on? Charlie, eh," he said aloud. Then he called over to the riggers. "Hey, Matt, go and find Guillaume the Medic and bring Roger down here. He's the super on duty."

"Might still be in his cabin, watchin' one of those scary movies he likes, Skillet. Don't like to be disturbed," the rigger said.

Skillet's voice went up half an octave. "So get him out of his fucking cabin and bring him here. We've got a problem to deal with!"

The rigger opened the door and ran off down the corridor. At the same moment the deck began to vibrate and the lights came back on.

"God damned generators," Skillet said. "Well, now we can see what's what. This is a police matter, Pat, big time. OK, thanks for your help, you probably want to go and find out what's going on with your toys, so that's OK. We'll call you when we need you."

"Been a busy day for you, Skillet."

"Tell me about it," Skillet responded without looking up.

Patrick nodded and left.

Chapter 5

The Danish Police

Erland leaned against the straps of his harness to allow himself a better view of the ship the helicopter headed for. The pilot in the left front seat jerked his head and spoke on the intercom.

"That's the boat," he said, and began the descent toward the strange looking craft below.

To Erland the vessel resembled a small aircraft carrier in that it had a large, wide flat deck and a bridge located on its right-hand side, but after that, the whole picture changed. There was a massive structure on the rear of the craft, a platform colored green with a huge 'H' painted on its wide surface. The helicopter turned toward it.

He stared at the rest of the ship. He noticed two heavy cranes on the top deck, placed at either end, but more interestingly the whole vessel looked somewhat like a massive water bug, as no fewer than eight steel cables came out of the front and rear of the ship. They led to large orange buoys, each about a quarter of a mile from the vessel. Two seagoing tugs were in the water nearby and seemed to be busy; one of them had a buoy attached to its rear as it ploughed away from the mother ship.

The deck bustled with activity, and he saw the blue glare of welding going on off to the right. He glanced at the other passenger. Hedi also stared down at the ship with interest as they approached. Not for the first time, Erland caught himself admiring the good looks of the red-headed assistant detective, who had insisted on accompanying him on this unusual trip. His superior had pointed out to her this was an oil vessel and a rough place. He'd tactfully refrained from saying what both he and Erland were thinking: this might not be good place for a woman to visit. But Hedi had had that stubborn look on her face, so no one said anything else and along she came. Six months before she'd been posted to Esbjerg from Copenhagen, and she appeared to have settled in reasonably well with her colleagues. She was intelligent, and seemed to know her job well enough, with several arrests under her belt already. And so far she'd not been involved in any of the standard dating games that went on in provincial police centers.

The call had come in to Esbjerg's police offices during the day. There had been an accident on the pipe dredging ship the *Cherokee,* some 100 miles out at sea. The radio operator had gone through the English channels to get to them, but the message had been clear enough. The ship was in Danish waters, hence the Danish police needed to come and make a decision, for a man was dead, presumably from an accident on board. A cause of death had to be ascertained before the body could be removed from the vessel. The Danish police had jurisdiction and were therefore the ones who needed to carry this out.

The Police Chief at Esbjerg had told his subordinate, Inspector Erland, it would be a simple matter: the police would do a formal find and see to it the body was shipped back to shore for an autopsy; end of story. Accidents in the North Sea oil fields were not unusual, though deaths were less common.

The tone of the helicopter engine changed while the pilot concentrated on putting them down in the middle of the 'H'. There was some wind, which buffeted the chopper as the pilot brought it down with a light bump and allowed the rotors to slow. He waited a few minutes, fiddling with the instruments, and waved his hand to the men in orange jump suits, standing on top of the steel steps leading down to the main deck.

One jumped up, ran in a crouch to come and open the passenger door, and gaped when he noticed Hedi Iversen as she prepared to leave the chopper. She wore blue overalls with a badge on the right breast of her anorak that read 'police', but as she climbed out there was no mistaking her well shaped figure. Erland tapped the pilot on the shoulder as he left the chopper.

"OK, we will radio you when it is time to come and pick us up. Thanks," he called over the sound of the engines.

The pilot nodded, gave the thumbs up, and watched them walk behind the orange clad oil man, who wore a dirty white safety helmet, toward the stairs. Hedi adjusted her cap as they walked. The pilot nodded in appreciation as he watched her, then, as they began to descend the stairs, he turned up the speed on the rotors. Soon he was in the air and made a sharp turn toward the east and the town of Esbjerg, sixty miles away on the coast of Jutland, the mainland of Denmark.

In the ensuing relative silence after the noisy departure of the chopper, Erland began to hear the sounds of a large vessel that worked a pipeline on the bottom of the sea. The ship shook as one of the huge cranes rumbled along the wooden deck below toward a group of orange clad men with safety helmets. He realized most of them were small, dark men who could have come from any number of Asian or South American countries. In some cases they were almost dwarfed by the larger, unmistakable North Americans, who were among them to direct operations. Even bearded, their faces could not hide the paleness of their skin.

The men who had met them on the helipad jogged down the steel steps with a speed developed from a lot of practice. Erland followed Hedi as she negotiated the several turns on each short deck they came to. She lifted her hand off the rough railing and showed him how filthy it had become. The rail was chipped and greasy, and from what he could see the whole ship was in dire need of a paint job.

When they came closer to the top deck of the vessel there was a loud roar. Some huge black tubes that came out of the deck, went around two huge reels, and disappeared over the back of the ship into the sea suddenly jerked and went taut. One of the men ahead of them noticed Hedi flinch and laughed.

"They've turned on the water pressure! We're goin' to work." He raised his voice over the rattle and rumble that engulfed them as they approached the main deck.

"This way, folks." He led them across the chipped and splintered boards of the deck, toward what seemed to be the bridge island on the right hand side—a large, steel structure that stood almost thirty feet above the main deck. Looking up, Erland could see there an array of antennae and a slowly turning radar disk. He glanced at the area behind the structure and had to look away as the blue glare of the welding shop blinded him. He looked around while the others began to enter the bridge structure and found, to his discomfort, he had a small bright spot interfering with his vision.

"Come along, Sorr. Don't go looking at the welders. That's a good way to get blinded," the lead man called and beckoned to him. "This way to the cabins."

He guided them through a steel door and held it open for Hedi with what Erland could only describe as a leer on his face. She took the combing with a cold nod and followed him as he scuttled down yet another set of steel steps into the warm interior of the ship.

They walked along a narrow corridor painted floor to ceiling in a beige color that had seen better days. Although the vessel was motionless, Erland held onto the rail that ran the entire length of the corridor. He hated being at sea. It was quiet here apart from the distant hum of machinery somewhere else on the ship, and their steps were loud in the confined space. The man leading the way opened a door on their right and waved them into a cabin.

"This cabin is normally for the inspectors, but we ain't got none at present. The super said y'all can use this place." His accent reminded Erland of an American film he'd once seen, in which everyone talked in the same manner.

Hedi ducked into the cabin, looked at the table and chairs and the curtained off section where the bunks must be, and glanced at Erland. "We'll need two cabins if we have to stay overnight," she said in English. Her voice was low but clear.

The man nodded and switched a wad of tobacco from one cheek to another.

"I reckon," he said slowly. "We weren't expecting a woman."

Hedi tossed her pony tail and looked as though she wanted to have a go at the man.

"We'll settle in and begin our investigation as soon as we've talked to the captain," Erland hurried to say.

"Ain't no captain here. He's the super. I'll go and tell him you're here. Want some coffee?" he asked.

"Yes, please," Erland said. He was ready for some, and after a glance at Hedi, who nodded, he added, "For both of us."

The man nodded and grinned at Hedi, showing off teeth darkened by tobacco, then left with the others, who had deposited their bags on the floor inside the cabin.

Hedi reached past Erland and retrieved her overnight bag. She put it on the table, opened it, and took out a notebook and some other items. She then pulled aside the curtain leading to the other section of the cabin and peered inside.

"A shower and two beds, how nice," she said, deadpan.

He had the grace to blush. "I'll ask for another cabin," he said, and left his own bag untouched on the floor.

"That guy gave me the creeps," Hedi said. "This isn't what I expected at all. Did you?" she spoke in Danish now they were alone.

"Not really. I ought to say I told you so, but I won't. It's a damned big ship. I thought it was some kind of rig, but someone told me it's called a barge. Maybe because it doesn't have any propellers?"

Before she could answer, a loud knock on the door interrupted them and a voice called, "Super here. Might Ah come in?"

Erland hastened to open the door to admit a man in clean orange overalls with the logo 'Santa Jose' on the top left breast. He was heavy, of medium height, and his belly protruded tight against the material of the overalls. His jowls overflowed his open-neck shirt. The full, round face showed a pair of beady eyes that never seemed to stop moving, set above a fleshy nose and small, rosebud mouth curled in a semblance of a friendly smile.

"Yes, come in. Who are you, please?" Erland asked.

"Ah'm Roger Stack, the super. Welcome to the *Cherokee*," the visitor said. He held out a huge hand to Erland and nodded as they shook, then he noticed Hedi, who had just come back from the bed section. His eyes roamed over her from top to bottom in silence and he gave a short bark of laughter.

"They said there was a woman in the party, but Ah didn't guess how pretty you was."

Hedi sat down on one of the chairs and regarded him cooly. "There are women in the police force in Denmark. Didn't you know?" Her topaz eyes challenged him to say anything stupid.

Roger closed his mouth and turned to Erland.

"You've come about the death, Ah presume. We have the body in the cooler, so whenever you're ready to check it out, let me know. If there's anything you want, just tell me."

Erland nodded. "We will, and thanks. I'm not sure how long this will take, but I suspect we'll be spending the night. If there's a second cabin we can use, I will be grateful."

Roger's small, dark eyes flicked to Hedi. "Yeah, I guess so. The cabin on the left of this one is unoccupied right now. It's the VIP cabin." He pronounced the letters as V-Ah-P. His accent was flat, and again Erland was reminded of films depicting the Deep South. He remembered *Easy Rider* and from what he could recall, it had not ended well for the heroes.

Roger continued. "You can use that. You're on the starboard side of the barge, that's the right side if you face the front." He looked at them as though he wasn't sure either of them had ever been on a boat before. "Ah'll have one of the riggers show you 'round so you don't git lost."

"Do you have time to answer a couple of questions, super?" Hedi asked him. Her voice was polite, but brisk and businesslike.

Roger glanced at Erland then back to her. "Why, yeah, I guess I have a few minutes before Ah go on the bridge."

Erland introduced her as Assistant Detective Hedi Iversen and himself as Detective Inspector Erland Knudson, knowing the Danish names would be confusing. Roger nodded in silence, pulled out the second chair, lowered his bulk carefully into it, and faced her across the table. Erland took the bench against the wall where he could see both their faces.

He knew what Hedi planned to do.

She asked the usual questions of time and place. Who had discovered the body and were there any photos of the corpse in the position it had died? There were none. She took notes of everything Roger said and it wasn't long before Roger looked defensive while Hedi asked simple but telling questions that established how the situation had occurred, but also cemented her position as the police officer doing the interrogation. Erland had sat in on one of her sessions in Esbjerg and liked the way she performed, which was why he had agreed in the end to have her come along.

The coffee arrived, black, and in polystyrene cups. Erland took one sip of his, grimaced, and put it down on the table. Hedi noticed and didn't even try hers.

"We will need a list of everyone who is on this ship... er, barge, as soon as possible, Mr. Stack," Erland interjected during a brief silence. "We would be grateful if you could tell us a bit about each person, so we know who they are when we interview them."

"Are yew goin' ta interview *all* the people on the barge?" Roger asked, surprised.

"Maybe," Hedi said, her tone noncommittal. "But we certainly need to meet the person who found the body and anyone else involved at the beginning.We'll take it from there."

Roger muttered, "M'a--aan! That's more than sixty men," in an undertone, and looked down at the table top with a disconcerted expression on his florid features.

"Is there a problem, Mr. Stack?" she asked with a cool stare.

"Er, no, Miss. Jest that when we're on the pipe we're busy and it's difficult to get men off, say, the anchors for any length of time. But we'll mange."

"Can you provide a list of names and backgrounds, Mr. Stack?" Erland asked.

"Yeah, Ah guess so. There are Americans and Brits and a bunch of Filipinos. Oh, yeah, a couple of Frenchies and one Hispanic guy, a welder."

"Do your crew all do two weeks on and two off like the rigs?" Hedi asked.

Roger laughed. "No way! It's three months on and three weeks off if the Brits and Americans are lucky, but the Filipinos are on-board for a year."

Both Erland and Hedi looked surprised, and Roger, mistaking Erland's expression, chuckled and said, "It's OK, they bring their women with them."

"They do?" Hedi asked, stunned.

"Yeah, you know, the blow up kind!" He laughed at his own joke. Neither of the police laughed with him. Hedi pursed her lips and gave him a cold stare.

"Can you take us to the body, Mr. Stack?" Hedi asked after an uncomfortable silence.

"Then we'll want to go where the accident took place," Erland added.

"Er, it's Roger to you, Miss. Call me Roger. OK, we can do that," he said, sounding relieved. He heaved himself to his feet. "Well, we might as well get that over with." He looked nervous, but Erland put it down to the fact there was a dead man on board and he was the super responsible for the smooth running of the barge.

Roger picked up the phone, pressed a button, and spoke over a tannoy: "Guillaume the medic, get down to the meat freezer, Ah'll meet you there." He put down the phone and led the way directly across the corridor to open a door, which admitted them into a large, low space with tanks against the back wall. He waddled towards what Erland thought might be another cabin, but when he opened the doors Erland realized this was the freezer. Roger paused and said, "We'll wait for the medic to come along."

They didn't wait long. A wide, bearded individual with dark eyes, dressed in blue overalls appeared from a door to their right and called across.

"Guillaume here, Roger. What's up?"

As soon as he noticed Hedi he stopped mid stride to stare wide-eyed before recovering himself and nodding to them.

"Danish po' lice, Guillaume. You can do the talking now. They want to see Charlie and ask some questions." He looked at them and pointed. "This is Detective Inspector Erland Knudson, and this is his assistant, Miz Iversen.

"If y'all will excuse me, Ah'll be on my way to the bridge. I'll send Skillet down first, as he's on shift. He's the one who notified me two days ago when Charlie was found. You can talk to the others when the next shift begins." He nodded and left, appearing to be in a hurry to get out of the room. Erland and Hedi watched him go and glanced at one another. Neither said anything, but it was clear to both there was much to discuss in the privacy of the cabin later.

Guillaume opened the doors of the freezer wide and walked into the cold, frost-covered room with steel shelves on either side, loaded with stores.

There was a gurney right in the middle of the chamber. He jerked the gurney and pulled it out of the room. On it lay a body covered with a sheet. A pair of dirt encrusted boots protruded from under the sheet at the far end of the gurney.

"You want gloves?" Guillaume asked. His tone was abrupt.

Hedi and Erland nodded.

"Wait here. I'll go get some." Guillaume left the room, leaving them with the body. Hedi stood over the gurney and lifted the sheet enough to see the face of the man called Charlie.

Her lips tightened as she peered down at the man. "He took a bad hit to the head." She lifted it higher for him to look.

Erland stared at the bloodstained face and the clotted blood and hair clinging to the back of the skull.

Just then Guillaume returned with the medical gloves and handed them over.

"Has anyone done anything to the body since it was found?" Hedi asked.

"We'll have to turn him over to get a better look," Erland said.

"No," Guillaume said. "We put it on the gurney and brought it straight here. No one's been in since, as far as I know," he added. "Don't think anyone wanted to come near Charlie once they heard he had the accident."

He stood back as they donned the gloves. Erland reached over and shifted the body so they could move the head and see the wound better. It was stiff and solid, so the whole corpse moved when he rolled it onto its side. Guillaume grabbed the legs to make sure the body didn't fall off the gurney as they rotated it. Finally it lay more or less on prone, with the entire back of the head exposed.

Hedi pushed the blood clotted graying hair aside and peered at the wound. She seemed unperturbed at the grisly sight, which further pleased Erland.

"It's deep," she murmured in Danish. Erland nodded and

peered at the crushed bone and gray ooze that smeared the hair and bone fragments. She pulled out a small camera and took some pictures. It was not one of those powerful cameras police photographers used, but it would be sufficient for a preliminary report.

"Must have tumbled quite a distance to get this. No safety hat?" Erland said. He probed with his fingers a little more. He worked from the head down to the boots. Hedi took notes. When he finished, he said, "The coroner will be able to make a clear statement about the head wound, but I wonder if there are any others. I can't find anything yet. It's difficult to say if any limbs might have been broken during the fall... assuming it was a fall. The clothing is in the way. We would have to undress the body to be sure." They were still speaking Danish.

He looked up at Guillaume. "There only appears to be one wound. What did they say happened?" he asked in English.

Guillaume looked uncomfortable. "Dunno, sir. All they did was tell me to make sure he was dead before we put 'im in 'ere. I check his pulse, just in case, and find nothing; check his breathing and eyes, nothing; so I report him dead. I wrote out the certificate of accident and time of death as estimated, which was around 10:00 am." He shrugged and flourished the document at Erland, who took it from him. "No one' talking about it as far as I can tell."

Erland didn't believe that. He was sure everyone was talking about it; the speculation as to how Charlie had his accident was probably the only thing they discussed anywhere on this vessel right now.

Just then two men entered the room. Erland turned to look at them. One was tall and rangy, well over six feet, while the other was less tall but compact. Both men looked wary and watchful.

Chapter 6

Questions

"Hello," Erland said.

"Hi, Ah'm Skillet. Chief rigger on the barge," said the taller one, who wore a mournful expression. "And this is Pat, ship's electronics engineer who found the... er, who found Charlie." He had a slight drawl. He glanced at Hedi, and his dark blue eyes registered approval before he snapped them back to Erland. Hedi and Erland stared at the other man.

Patrick didn't smile, he just nodded, glanced at Hedi, and said, "Forward port winch room is where I found him." His lean face was expressionless, his eyes watchful, but he seemed calm enough to Erland. Neither man seemed to be perturbed about being in the same room as their former dead associate.

Erland asked, "Can you take us to the location and show us exactly where you found the body?"

Patrick nodded, glanced at Skillet, and turned to lead the way out of the chamber without a word.

"Put it back in the freezer if you will, please." Erland said to Guillaume before he and Hedi hurried out after the two men in orange boiler suits and strode off down the corridor.

Hedi couldn't tell at this point which way they were going, but when they passed a large notice board on the wall she saw a map of the vessel with the various decks displayed. She resolved to ask for one.

Force 12 in German Bight

Patrick led the way along the corridor to the far end, opened a steel door, and ran down some steps, leaving Skillet to hold it open for Hedi and Erland.

The noise was horrendous. Hedi put both hands over her ears and looked smitten by the din. Skillet bellowed back at them to watch their step as he led them down to the floor of the huge chamber. There were two winches running, one let out the thick black steel cable at a terrific rate while the other moved slowly. The racket of the machinery was deafening. Skillet reached up to a steel cabinet and offered them some ear protectors. They gratefully donned them and followed Patrick as he guided them along the grating to the place where he'd found the body.

He crouched at the end of the gangway right next to the front winch, which worked slowly at bringing a thick, black, steel cable, still dripping sea water, in from the opening of a shaft at the end of the chamber. He waved them down and pointed to the grating.

"I found him against the housing of the winch," he shouted. "You can see there's no blood or anything on the rails." His expression was enigmatic but Hedi, who was closest to him and could see his eyes, felt he was trying to say something.

"I don't see where he could have fallen," she said and realized what he meant. Her eyes widened. She glanced up at Skillet and then Erland, who peered down at the grating near Patrick.

"There's blood there though," Erland said, pointing.

"Yep, there is. He was moved."

Patrick got up and moved around the two detectives to allow them space. Erland observed the grating and inspected the area thoroughly, even taking out a small flashlight and peering all over the area. He looked more and more puzzled as he worked.

He shouted at Hedi in Danish. "I can't see where he could have bashed his head. There's nothing I can see that could have caused that much damage. This seems to be the only place where he was lying. Yes there is dried blood here... but nowhere as much as if he had broken his head on something in a fall."

She nodded and glanced at the two men standing along the grating. Something about them bothered her. They seemed to be waiting for the police to come to some kind of conclusion.

"Those two know something. We need to talk to them, sir." She produced the camera and took pictures of the room, the winches and the grating, with a close up of the blood and mess on the metal of the grating.

Erland got up from his crouched position and signaled to the men that he wanted to leave. Just as he did so, the second winch sprang to life and the cable began to speed up as the winch hauled it in. Hedi flinched involuntarily; the noise in the steel chamber increased twofold. She eyed the black snaking cable and rotating drum with apprehension. She had never been so near to such large working machines before. Once they'd vacated the room and gained the relative quiet of the corridor, Erland said to Skillet, "We'll want to talk to you, now, if you don't mind."

Skillet nodded, but as he did the lights went out, plunging them into darkness for a few seconds before the emergency lights came on.

"Got to go," Patrick said and ran down the corridor. He disappeared through a door and vanished.

"He's the engineer. The generators are off again. He's the only one onboard who understands them. The lights will be on again in a few minutes," Skillet said as an explanation.

"Does this happen often?" Hedi asked.

"Yeah. This old tub is due for dry dock, but in the meantime we have to work with what we have. The generators and the radio are junk. Patrick and his pal Joel have their hands full."

He led the way along dark corridors back to their accommodation. On the way, Hedi asked for a map of the decks. Skillet said he would see what he could find.

They re-entered the cabin and Skillet took a seat. "What d'you want to know?"

Erland observed the lean features, two days growth of beard covering slightly mournful features, the dark blue eyes that seemed to not miss anything, and the strong frame with the big hands resting calmly on the table. His expression was bland, but not unfriendly.

Hedi took up her position in the chair opposite while Erland opted for the wall seat.

After taking down his name and where he was from, Texas, the questions began.

Force 12 in German Bight

"It was Patrick who found the body?" Hedi asked.

"Yep, that's him. Patrick's one of the Brits. Engineer. A really good one, too. He came and got me as soon as he found Charlie."

"I thought he said the body had been moved when you got back down there," Hedi said, watching his face.

Skillet nodded. "He told me he found the body in one place, but it was in another place when we got there."

"Are you saying that someone moved the body?" Erland asked in surprise.

Skillet turned to face him directly. "If Patrick says so then it happened. He don't f—I mean, he doesn't mess around."

"Was he upset when he came to see you?"

"Patrick? Nah, not really, he just told me to come as quickly as possible."

"His colleague had his head bashed in and his brains falling out, and he wasn't upset?" Hedi asked with a trace of skepticism in her tone.

"I think Patrick's seen worse," Skillet said calmly.

"What do you mean?" Erland asked, shifting in his seat. Skillet's eyes narrowed. "I've known him for two years now and there's no one else I'd trust myself to in a tight spot. He used to be in the army and while he don't talk about it much, I know it weren't easy. He was a Lurp."

"What's a Lurp?" Hedi asked.

"Long range patrols, stuff like that. You get to doing some serious soldiering when you play that game. Patrick's seen a thing or two, so this wouldn't have upset him. Surprised him perhaps, but not enough to make him lose his breakfast."

"Were you a soldier, too?" Hedi asked. She knew from her own father, who had been in the service, soldiers rarely talked about their lives to people outside the trade.

"Yep. Ah was in 'Nam. Patrick, now, is as hard as they come. May not look like Rambo, but I once set a couple of the riggers on him for fun, just to see what would happen."

"For fun? What happened?" Hedi asked.

"They grabbed both his arms, but man! In a blink of an eye he had them big lads down on their knees and was about to really hurt them when I told him to quit it. He shrugged and walked off. No one's tried anything with Pat since."

"Are there fights on board?" Hedi asked. Erland's mind had gone in the same direction and he nodded in approval.

"Yeah, sometimes. It's not often, but men get drunk and get mad and the sh—trouble starts. We usually get it under control fast enough. The men don't want to get fired, they make good money here."

"The wound is large and deep. I don't see how the victim could have fallen from high enough to do that much damage." Erland stared at Skillet for his reaction.

Skillet met his eyes, unblinking. "Yeah, that's what worries me and Pat."

The tannoy outside the cabin blared. "Skillet, report to the bridge asap! Skillet needed on the bridge!"

"I got to go. Sounds like Roger's having one of his panic attacks. Wants to hold hands and go out on the window sill, ready to jump. If y'all need me later, Ah can drop by."

"Could you send Patrick in later, too, please?" Erland asked.

"Sure." Skillet left them staring after him as the door shut.

*****

There was a long silence in the cabin when he'd gone. Erland dropped his gaze to the cold coffee on the table and drummed his fingers. The dim light of the emergency lamp above the table made the hollows under his eyes even darker. He'd pushed his fingers through his hair several times and made it unkempt.

"What are you thinking, sir?" Hedi asked as she watched him in the gloom.

The lights came back on and bathed the cabin in fluorescent light. Erland twitched.

"There's something wrong about this situation, Hedi. How could the accident have happened in that location? There's nowhere to fall other than into the winch well, and those men are clear the body was found where they showed us... and then moved, if Patrick is to be believed, along the grating above the winches."

"Do you think it was murder, sir?" Hedi asked. She was already on that path herself.

Erland stared back at her. "If you can explain it better.... Well, it's early days yet. Let's see what the engineer has to say."

They heard the tannoy calling for Patrick and a few minutes later there was a knock on the door.

"Come in," Erland said.

Patrick came in, smelling of grease and oil, and wiped his hands on a dirty cloth.

"Skillet told me to come and see you," he said.

"Yes. Patrick, isn't it? Please, have a seat," Erland said, and indicated the chair Skillet had vacated.

Patrick lowered himself into the seat. When his eyes met Hedi's they were steady and calm. She found herself unsettled by the penetrating hazel eyes that seemed to stare straight into her.

"Your name is Patrick McFarlane?"

"Yes."

"You know we're the police from Denmark, here to investigate the death of one of the men on board, and that we want to take a statement from you?"

"I understand."

They went through the formalities of establishing his name, profession, the fact he was British, and his home address in Scotland. They confirmed he'd been the first person to find the body and the fact he'd brought Skillet in to see it. Patrick described what they had then done, which was to get the medic, Guillaume, in to ascertain whether the man was dead and the estimated time of death.

"What do you do on this ship... barge,?" Erland asked.

"I'm responsible for one shift, the 6 am to 6 pm shift, for everything from the generators to the radio and the radar on the top of the bridge. All the electrics and electronics." He looked at the watch on his wrist. "It's almost time for the change."

"Skillet seems to like you."

"We get along."

"He said you were a soldier once, in the British army?"

"Yeah. I was a squaddie once, and so was he. Might be why we get along." His tone didn't encourage any further questions.

"Are there any other people here who were soldiers?" Erland asked. Hedi glanced at him as if to ask where his line of questions were going.

"Yeah, there's one more, other than Skillet that is, maybe two. One's a diver, a Brit like me, and the other's a Canadian who was once in the army."

"Why are there so many ex-soldiers out here in the North Sea?" Erland asked out of idle curiosity.

"They've been well trained and the money is good out here, even if the work sucks," Patrick told him.

"Why do you say the body was moved?" Hedi asked.

Patrick turned toward her. His lean, dark face was impassive. "I remember very clearly where I'd left him. You don't forget that kind of thing. He'd been moved as though someone was about to take him away when we showed up again."

"Did you see anyone?"

"No, but I heard a door shut on the other side of the chamber. Below the grating we were on is another doorway that leads to the laundry."

"But you neither saw nor heard anything else?" Erland pressed.

Patrick sighed and looked back at Hedi. He lowered his head and met her eyes from under his deep brows and rubbed his forehead with the tips of his fingers. "No, sir, nothing other than the door." Hedi almost grinned at the patient, long-suffering expression on his face.

Erland knew this was his only witness at present and resolved to find out all he could. He walked Patrick through the entire sequence of events several times to make sure the story didn't deviate and Patrick didn't trip over his own statement. The answers were precise and clipped, and remained the same, and he never raised his voice even when the interrogation became tiresomely repetitive.

Finally Erland came to the question he'd wanted to ask. "Did this happen during one of those "black outs" you seem to have on this ship? The generator problem?"

Patrick eyed him carefully. "Could be, but in that case I

couldn't have been there. Had we lost the lights while I was on shift, I wouldn't have been in the winch room. I would have been fixing the bloody things."

"Do your duties take you to the winch rooms on a regular basis?"

"No, not usually. It was a short cut to the laundry room. I wanted to collect my stuff from Henri-Pierre before I came off shift."

"Who's Henri-Pierre?"

"He's the French guy who does the laundry."

"Could he have seen anyone coming through from the winch room?"

"It's possible, but there's a corridor that takes you past the laundry room, so if he was doing other stuff anyone could walk by and he wouldn't notice."

Erland sat back on the couch, but left his hands on the table. His fingers drummed. Hedi glanced up from her note taking.

He asked Patrick, "Do you think this was an accident?"

Patrick sat back in his chair and stared back at both of them. After a pause he asked, "What did Skillet say?"

"I'm asking you." Erland said.

"OK, then. I don't know how it could have been an accident," Patrick said.

In the silence that followed, Hedi put her pen down. "So you think... the man was murdered, and someone tried to get the body out of there?"

Patrick nodded, but said nothing.

"Mr. McFarlane, you were all alone in the room, with no witnesses to verify your whereabouts when you say you found the man. Did you have any problems with Charlie?" Erland said.

Patrick hesitated for just a second then shook his head. "No, he was OK. I didn't see much of him. He spent his shift on deck with the other riggers."

Erland sensed something and pressed harder. "Could it be that perhaps it was you who murdered him? Skillet told us you're a dangerous man to get on the wrong side of."

Patrick's gaze became hard. "Skillet spoke out of turn. If I wanted to hurt someone, I wouldn't do it like that."

Hedi went still.

"Charlie was a stupid Cajun, but he didn't bother me. I had no reason to hurt him," Patrick added.

"What's a Cay-jun? Is that the name you used?" Hedi asked.

"Yeah, he's from Louisiana, a Cajun from the swamps. His French was terrible!"

Hedi suppressed a grin. "Did he have any enemies on the barge that you know of?" she asked.

"Could be." Patrick made to get up. "Have you finished with me?"

Erland stared hard at Patrick for a long moment before he motioned to the door. "Thank you very much, Mr. McFarlane, you may go. We'll probably want to talk to you again."

Patrick nodded, glanced at Hedi with a small smile in his eyes and said, "That's fine. I can't go anywhere."

Chapter 7

Conjecture

"Well that was interesting," Erland said in Danish.

"He hides it well, but I think he is dangerous," Hedi said. "I could swear I've seen him somewhere before." She rummaged in her mind as to where.

"You've met him before?"

"No, sir. I don't think so, but I feel like I have."

"Probably one of the villains you took off the streets of Esbjerg." Erland chuckled. "I don't like him, and I think he knows a lot more than he's saying. Bit too arrogant for my liking."

Hedi didn't think he was right about Patrick. Most of those 'villains' were drunks and petty thieves. They didn't have many real crooks she knew of in Esbjerg. Patrick didn't threaten, but his calm left her with the impression he was not a person with whom others picked quarrels. It wasn't arrogance, she decided, but a self confidence he carried with him. She kept her council, as Erland was likely to needle her if she let him. There was a mean streak to her boss.

"I'm hungry," she said to change the subject. Just then there was a knock on the door and Skillet poked his face in. "Y'all hungry?" he asked.

"Yes, I think we are," Erland said, standing up. "You've anticipated us."

Skillet grinned. "C'mon then, I'll take you to the galley. It's just over the way, but we'll have to go along the corridor to get there. They don't like it when we cut through the kitchens. Here is the map you asked for, Miss." He handed over a large roll of thick paper. "All there."

"Thank you, Mr. Skillet," Hedi said.

"Just Skillet, Miss." He smiled at her.

They strode down one of the featureless corridors which seemed to go on forever. Skillet didn't talk, which gave Hedi time to try and get her bearings. She knew Erland was probably lost already, even though they hadn't yet turned left nor right, but she herself wanted to know exactly where she was.

Finally, after two left turns and with the sound of many voices and the clang of pots and pans coming closer, Skillet led them into a large, brightly lit room, half full of men. It was painted in the same universal beige color, with tables and benches fixed to the floor in rows from one end to the other. They entered through a door that brought them alongside a stainless steel counter, behind a small queue of men in ubiquitous orange coveralls, who stood and waited for the cooks on the other side to bring the food. The cooks were sweating and calling out to one another in a language Hedi didn't understand. A strong smell of fried and grilled meat emanated from the kitchen area.

She became aware that she was drawing a lot of attention from the odd assortment of men waiting for their food. Men seated at long tables and benches paused their conversation and stared at the newcomers with interest before going back to their food.

The line moved and Hedi found herself confronted by the largest rib steak she'd ever seen, a choice of mashed potato, fries, and some beans in a red sauce. A stainless steel container full of green salad sat on the counter behind the vegetables. The men in front piled food on their plates in a manner that suggested they were starving, or that there was no tomorrow. Some spooned canned peaches and ice cream onto the same plates as their steak and potatoes, which appalled her.

She helped herself to a small amount of mashed potatoes and salad. A cook dumped a steak onto her plate without being asked and gave her a toothy grin. "Buenos dias, señorita," he said. She half smiled back and followed Erland and Skillet to an empty table. "You need something to drink?" Skillet asked.

What is there?" Hedi asked.

"Iced tea or coffee, whichever."

Remembering the coffee and Erland's reaction to it she said, "I would like some hot tea, please. Is that possible?"

Skillet looked doubtful but went over to the counter and negotiated with a large, fat man in dirty whites. He came back with a mug of hot water and a tea bag.

While he was gone, Hedi and Erland had a chance to look around. She noticed a man near the door on the other side of the room in clean orange overalls and dark glasses, which struck her as odd. The man worked at preparing a huge pile of sandwiches and stuffed several candy bars into his pockets.

When Skillet came back he noticed the direction of her look and said in a low tone, "He should be run off, but every one of them is on it."

"On what?" Erland asked.

"Don't you recognize when someone has the munchies? Just look at him. There won't be any damned peanut butter left for the rest of us by the time that bastard is finished," Skillet groused.

Hedi realized what he referred to. "Ah," she said. "Isn't that illegal?" She gave him a knowing half smile.

Skillet grinned. "You're the police. You going to arrest him?"

She focussed on the gigantic steak in front of her.

"How does this... barge work?" Erland asked, to change the subject. The man had left the room, leaving behind a mess.

"We dredge pipe. That means we move along the pipe, and blow sand and sea bed out of the way to allow the pipe to fall into it."

"That sounds complicated," Hedi mumbled while she chewed a piece of meat. To herself she had to admit it was probably the best she had ever eaten.

"I don't think I've ever tasted a steak as good as this!" Erland said, as he tucked into his meaty dish.

"That steak came all the way from Kansas," Skillet said, with a note of pride in his voice.

"Yeah, it can get tricky," he reverted to the other vein, "That's another of Patrick's pet peeves. This POS always breaks down and the Sled has to be brought up. He or Joel has to fix it pronto, and then we have to re-set it on the pipe with the divers and git goin' again. At sixty thousand an hour, any loss of time gets expensive right quick."

Hedi was surprised. "That's a lot of money."

"Sure is, but the owners won't invest in this tub, so things keep breaking and we keep having accidents." Skillet sounded frustrated.

What does this apparatus look like?" Hedi asked.

"You mean the sled? It's big, I'll show you if we come off the pipe; the radio guy talks about some bad weather north of us. It's a double pontoon like thing, with water jets. We drop it over the pipe and send down a lot of water pressure. Blows the sand and rocks off to the sides and makes a trench."

"What if you slide it the wrong way and damage the pipe?" Hedi asked.

Skillet gave her a hard look. "Then there's hell to pay and we have an oil crisis. Ain't happened yet, thank God. Big mess if it did."

*****

Later in the cabin they mulled over the incident. Erland seemed to have decided Patrick might be a prime culprit, and Hedi wondered why.

"What makes you so sure it could have been him, sir?" she asked, and had difficulty keeping the exasperation out of her voice.

He gave her a look that said she bordered on insubordination, but leaned forward and clasped his hands on the table. Instead of meeting her eyes, his own drifted down; she wasn't sure if he stared at her breasts or at the table.

"He claims to have found the man, and he was the only witness. Skillet said the body was still warm to the touch, even after he arrived, which means Patrick could have killed him and decided his best defense was to inform them the man was dead, before anyone else did."

"Why would he tell Skillet if he was the murderer? He could have just walked away, couldn't he?"Hedi asked. She wasn't fixed upon defending the man, but it didn't sound right to accuse him without proof. Also there was something he'd said. "He wouldn't have hurt Charles in that way if it was him."

She didn't realize she'd spoken out loud until Erland said, "What was that?"

"He said he wouldn't do it that way if it had been him."

"Well, who do you think might have done it?" Erland said, sounding truculent.

Just then there came a knock on the cabin door and Roger poked his head into the room.

"Ah heard you had dinner. Hope it was OK?"

"Very nice!" Erland said with a smile. "I've never eaten a steak that big before."

"We look after the men. They stay on this bathtub for three months, working twelve and seven, so they need to eat well," Roger said. "Ah don't know if y'all are still on duty, but Ah'm going off in a few minutes. It's nearly 6:30 pm. But... well, I brought something to ease the pain, you might say." He flourished a bottle of liquor.

"What's that?" Erland asked with interest.

Hedi sighed. This was shaping up to be a long night. Erland liked his drink.

"This is God and America's answer to whiskey," Roger said with a wet grin. "Wild Turkey is the invention of a genius." He produced some plastic cups and placed them on the table.

"I suppose we are now off duty?" Erland said with a glance at his watch. He grinned at the super. "We can have a small one before we have to turn in. Need to talk to you about other people who might have witnessed something."

"We can do that in the morning," Roger said as he poured three liberal drinks.

"Aren't the ships out on the oil fields supposed to be without alcohol?" she asked pointedly.

Roger grinned again. "This is a construction barge and Ah'm the one who says whether we can or cain't have alcohol on board."

Force 12 in German Bight

"I thought the oil fields forbade it," Hedi persisted.

"That's on the rigs, and that's reasonable, all that flammable stuff about. But Daryl, the other super, and me, we don't believe you need to keep men away from it for too long, and we don't have much in the way of problems because of it."

Erland took a sip of his drink. "Ahhh," he said. "Now that's as good as any schnapps!" He smacked his lips.

"I shall need to talk to my superior in Esbjerg," he said as an afterthought.

"Yeah, OK. Better get that out of the way first," Roger agreed. Hedi had barely touched hers while Roger had downed his in two gulps.

They went back through the corridor, up two flights of stairs, and arrived at two doorways. One was shut and the other open, displaying a well-lit room with two windows. Hedi realized they were inside the bridge island. Her eyes roamed quickly around the room and came to rest on the back of a man who listened intently to an English-sounding voice on the radio. He reached up, turned a knob, and exclaimed irritably.

"The fucking radio is on the blink again. Don't need this... do not fucking need this! Not now!"

"Ehem, Stan!" Roger said.

The man whirled about and noticed the two visitors, in particular Hedi.

"Oh, sorry!" he said sheepishly. "Hey, Roger, the radio's screwing up...again! Patrick got it working the other day when Joel couldn't, but now it's on its way out again. And we got trouble coming."

"What d'you mean?" Roger said.

"I'm listening to the shipping news right now, Boss. Storms everywhere, and some are coming this way, via Fisher and Dogger!"

"Then listen to what they say. We can wait," Roger said.

Stanley turned back to the radio and adjusted the volume.

The voice from the BBC shipping forecast came in loud and clear, in the clipped drone familiar to all who sail in the North Sea and far beyond.

"Dogger: Gale warning issued at 2100 hours. Storm: force ten, increasing to force eleven.Wind: North westerly backing northerly later, ten to eleven gale perhaps, severe later. Sea: rough to very rough. Squally showers and heavy rain later. Visibility: poor becoming very poor later." There was a pause then the voice resumed.

"German Bight."

'Thats us," Stanley interjected.

The calm English voice continued. "Gale warning issued at 2300 hours. Storm: force nine, increasing to ten gale. perhaps severe later. Wind: North Westerly, backing more Northerly later towards midnight. Sea: rough to very rough into midnight. Squalls and showers, and heavy rain later. Visibility: good, going to poor later."

The voice continued on to Fisher, which Stanley pointed to on a map of Great Britain and the surrounding European coast line, which he'd tacked to the notice board above his head.

"Fisher is north of us, on the coast of Denmark around Arlsberg," he explained. "We're here in German Bight, just below, and boy, are we in for it tonight!"

They heard heavy footsteps outside the door and another man pushed in.

"Ah, didn't know you had visitors."

"C'mon in, Hamesh," Roger said. "These are the Danish police. Detective Superintendent Erl..."

"Erland Knudson," Erland said for him. "Pleased to meet you. This is Detective Hedi Iversen, my assistant."

"I'll be finished in a couple of minutes, sir," Stanley said with a worried look at Roger.

"Go ahead, Stan. Get the report and bring it to me. I'll pass it along to Daryl as I'm off," Roger said. He turned to the detectives.

"We need to know the weather right up to the hour. It doesn't look good for this evening or later tonight. We'll have to get off the pipe for sure at this rate. No sleep for the wicked, Ah guess."

Stanley concluded listening and taking notes for a while, then turned down the volume and faced the detectives.

"Sorry about that. What can I do for you folks?" he asked. Hedi detected an English accent.

"I need to report to the police offices in Esbjerg. Can you arrange for me to call this number?" Erland produced a pen and wrote the Danish number on a pad Stanley handed him.

"Our calls are routed through the UK. Hope you don't mind, but it costs a guinea a minute. What account do I put it on, Roger?" he asked.

"Put it on the admin account. Ah imagine you'll want to be left alone with the radio, sir?" he suggested tactfully. "Stan, you set it up and then we'll leave."

"OK, Roger."

Stanley fiddled with the dials and spoke to someone in the UK. There was a delay while the station in the UK dialed the number in Denmark. A voice answered in Danish and the man in the UK office explained the call was from the barge called *Cherokee* in the North Sea.

The person in Denmark reverted to good English smoothly and asked whom they wished to contact.

"Chief of operations in Esbjerg: Kristian Vestergaard," Erland said. Within a few minutes another voice came over the line, and Kristian identified himself.

Erland asked Stanley in a whisper to give him their grid reference before he left. Stanley wrote it down on a note pad, explained how to use the microphone, and asked them to call him as soon as they finished. He would be upstairs on the bridge. Roger shepherded him and Hamesh out and shut the door behind them.

Erland hurriedly seated himself and motioned Hedi to do the same before he addressed the microphone.

"Hello, sir, Erland calling. This is a radio call and it's being routed via the British Isles. I don't know why and I don't know if it's secure."

"Hello, Erland. I wondered when you'd call. It's been a while. I presume you're staying on the ship for the night?" Kristian said.

"Yes, sir. It's too late for a helicopter so we'll stay." He glanced at Hedi, licked his lips, and continued.

"We've conducted a preliminary investigation, sir. We've seen the body and we've seen where it was found. It's kept in a deep freezer, awaiting an autopsy."

"What are your initial findings?" Kristian's tone was crisp. They spoke Danish, but even so Erland sent a reflexive glance toward the door. He also looked up at Hedi, who nodded.

"We have a body with a hole in its head and no good explanation as to how the hole got there, sir," he said.

There was a long silence at the other end, broken by the static on the radio, and then Kristian spoke. For some reason his voice was faint. "You don't think it was an accident?"

Erland and Hedi strained to hear but it was lost in static until the last words: "...back here in Esbjerg."

"Say that again, please, sir. You're breaking up."

"If you think it wasn't an accident we either need more people on that ship or you need to bring it into Esbjerg. Have you sealed off the location of the 'accident'?"

Erland looked at Hedi. "It happened in a winch room which is still operating. They're working on a pipe line at this time, sir. I cannot seal it off as it's critical to their operations."

Kristian was silent for a long moment. "If you suspect a crime took place, you have no choice but to shut down the operations, seal off that room, and bring the ship in. It is a ship, no? It's not an oil rig?"

"No, Sir, they call it a barge. It doesn't have its own power. I suppose they would have to be towed into Esbjerg. They have two large tugs working here."

"How far away is this ... barge? Where exactly are you on the map?" Kristian asked.

Hedi wrote down a number and showed it to him.

Erland gave him the grid reference and said, "About one hundred miles North by North West, sir."

"They're within Danish waters. Bring them in, Erland. Do you need more people?"

"Perhaps it would be good to have a few more policemen if you can spare them, sir."

"I'll see what I can do. I can send them out on a boat tonight, expect a Coast Guard vessel in a few hours," Kristian said.

"It would have to be soon; the weather is going to turn bad

tonight The radio operator told us," Erland said.

They discussed their findings for a few more minutes and then Erland signed off.

Chapter 8

Meeting Supers

Erland stood up; when his chair legs scrapped back on the linoleum floor Hedi could have sworn there was a hurried movement behind the door, but when they opened it there was no one outside. With a meaningful look at Hedi, Erland led the way up the next flight of stairs, which brought them to the bridge.

Stanley waited for them at the top of the stairs, and without more than a nod he brushed past them and headed for the radio room.

Erland detected a frosty atmosphere in the room and it wasn't just the temperature.

"We're done, thank you," he began, but Roger wasn't there. He'd been replaced by another fat man, who wore a peaked cap with a Santa Jose logo on it. He stood next to the front windows alongside a heavyset man. They both turned and stared at the detectives as they arrived at the top of the stairs. Their eyes were cold and flat.

The entire room was full of consoles lit up by lines of dials and lights. Hedi detected a low whistle from behind one of the consoles. The taller man, next to the one with the cap, snarled at someone out of sight: "Enough of that, pay attention to the line, Virgil. You break the line and I'll have you run off!"

A radar console was to the right of the two men, beside it was another, taller console with dials all over its face that twitched and paused then twitched again. A man sat at each of the consoles.

77

Force 12 in German Bight

"I thought Mr. Stack was up here," Erland said to the bridge at large.

"Off shift and probably drunk by now. I'm the one you need to talk to," a short, fat man man said without a smile. Then he remembered his manners and took off his cap, exposing a balding head. "Excuse me, M'am, Ah didn't know there was a lady on board." He smiled in an avuncular manner and addressed Erland.

"Ah'm the duty super, name's Daryl Galay, and this is my chief rigger, Richards. Whatever you need from here on, you just let me know."

"Thank you, Mr. Galay," Erland said. He extended his hand to Daryl, who shook it with a soft, pudgy hand, and then to Richards. Richards glowered at them both. No one offered to shake Hedi's hand.

"I urgently need to talk to you somewhere quiet, if possible," Erland said.

"Call me Daryl. OK, lets go to your cabin, more private there," Daryl said with a look at Richards, who shrugged and pretended to be watching the blips on the radar screen.

Daryl was a short, stocky, balding man with a paunch, who wheezed as he followed them down the steep steel steps past the radio shop, where Stanley hunched over the radio and another man paged someone called Joel. Two more levels down and they reached the corridor Hedi was now familiar with. They entered their cabin and Daryl lowered himself into the chair nearest the door with a sigh. He dragged out a large white handkerchief and wiped his brow and neck.

"What's so urgent you couldn't tell me up on the bridge, Mr. Knud..."

"Knudson, Erland," Erland said, knowing the man would never be able to pronounce even this simple name.

"I called my superior in Esbjerg and he wants you to bring the barge in to port. He's concerned this might not have been an accident," Erland said.

Hedi watched Daryl while Erland spoke and noticed his florid face and jowls seemed to lose some color. His eyes, almost buried in the puffy flesh, peered out at Erland with surprise and something else. She couldn't be sure what she saw, but his reaction was agitated. It took a couple of seconds, however, during which time he shifted a tobacco wad from one cheek to the other and back, then spat into one of the polystyrene cups on the table. Hedi wrinkled her nose in disgust.

"You can't do that!" Daryl said. "We stand to lose the contract if we quit the pipe. That's why we're out so late in the year to begin with. Only the weather can stop us, and that's legal. What you want to shut us down for? For an accident?" He sounded indignant and angry, but she thought he looked worried, too.

"We have come to the conclusion this might not have been an accident after all."

Daryl stared at them and swallowed. During the long pause he spat once more into the cup and seemed to collect himself.

"But you've only just gotten here," he said. "How do y'all know it wasn't an accident?" He wiped his sweaty brow again with the handkerchief he produced from his spotless blue overalls.

"It's not important how we know, but we are sure after the preliminary examination of the body and the location, it could not have happened as was first described to us." Again the awkward silence.

"I am under orders, sir," Erland said with a nervous glance at Hedi, who watchedDaryl.

"Well, your orders had better take into account we could lose this contract if we go back to port just because you *ain't* sure it was an accident. That's gonna cost our company millions. We have accidents all the time, this one was just worse than usual," Daryl said, the blood beginning to rise back up his neck. He lifted the cup and spat into it again. Hedi rolled her eyes.

"Do you have accidents all the time, sir? Is there a record of accidents on this vessel?" Hedi asked with an enquiring expression on her face.

He swung round to stare at her. "Well, not all the time, but you need to know this barge is a workin' vessel, Miss. Lot of things are goin' on at the same time when we're on the pipe, and accidents can an' do happen." His eyes darted back to Erland and they were not friendly.

"I don't think this was an accident, sir, and I must insist you pull up this... thing you use on the pipe and get us towed back to

Force 12 in German Bight

Esbjerg. It's now a police matter and you are in Danish waters. You must comply," Erland said as firmly as he could.

"Ah'm going to have to call the States to tell them about this," Daryl said. He sounded angry. "I can't get off the pipe till midnight, when you'll hear a lot of activity on deck. You stay here and out of the way while we do the hauling in. Don't go on deck while they're bringing in the anchors. You might get hurt, and we wouldn't want that now, would we?" he said with a pointed look at Erland. He got up with effort and made his way out of the cabin. Hedi was sure he almost slammed the door.

*****

Erland glanced at Hedi with a raised eyebrow as he poured himself another slug of bourbon.

"So, what do you think of *him*, sir?" she asked with a grimace. "The spitting is disgusting."

She reached for the cup and took it into the back of the room, looking for a trash can to place it in. Erland pointed to a plastic bin by the door. "Over there."

"I don't even know if he's going to comply with my instructions," Erland said unhappily. "I'm not even sure I can enforce them."

"I suppose he thinks the Danish police are not real policemen," she said with some scorn.

"Well, have you ever seen an American policeman? They look more like storm troopers than policemen to me."

"The others will be along within a couple of hours, which means you'll have the muscle to enforce the order. He gives me the creeps. There's something going on here, sir. I can feel it."

"Are you relying upon your woman's intuition, Detective?" Erland said with a wry grin.

Hedi bristled. "No, sir, but everyone is being very careful about what they say to us. No one, not that Patrick guy, nor Skillet, has offered anything beyond what we have directly asked them. This man is worried about something."

"I would be, too, if I'd been told to 'get off the pipe' as he puts it and sail all the way back to Esbjerg. They stand to lose a lot of

80

money. But Chief Inspector Vestergaard has given us an order, and we're ill equipped to deal with this situation now we think it's more than an accident."

"If it's murder then someone here committed the crime. They didn't just hop off onto the first ship that came by, so they're still here, and we don't know who nor why. I'm beginning to be certain there's a lot more to this," Hedi said, glancing at the door.

"You brought your hand gun?" Erland asked in a low tone. She could see that he was worried. She nodded and tapped her waist.

Hedi knew he was concerned, but now the man was drinking this ferocious bourbon, which she had tasted but decided she didn't like. She yawned. If Erland wanted to drink himself to sleep that was his problem. He had a reputation for liking the booze, but not for overdoing it.

Erland checked his watch and took the hint. It was close to 8 pm. "You might as well get some sleep. We'll be busy tomorrow; I want to interview as many people who have access to that area as I can. Lock your door."

"Goodnight, sir." She got up, took her overnight bag, and went next door. It was an identical cabin to the one she had just vacated.

She really was tired, but she also wanted to get away from Erland for a while. After locking the door behind her, she inspected the two bunks and decided the upper one was better. She undressed and climbed into bed with her hand gun, which she slipped under her pillow. She fell instantly asleep.

*****

Daryl made his way back to the bridge. Once he caught his breath at the top of the stairs, he motioned Richards, who was still there, to come to a dark corner of the room on the other side of the stair well. They stared down at the brightly lit deck and the large tug that was close to the port side of the bows. It had just come racing back with a buoy attached to its rear end and was about to leave again. A huge anchor was suspended beneath the buoy.

"Take her away, Joey!" Virgil, one of the control riggers, called into his radio. There was a brief squawk of acknowledgment, and the tug began to haul off into the night, all its lights blazing and a thick cable snaking out from its rear end, leading back to the barge.

Daryl and Richards registered what went on around them, but their preoccupation was with other matters.

Richards was aghast. "Shut down the work? Go back to Esbjerg? What are those fucking people talking about, boss? Besides, what about the... you know?"

"Yeah, well, they don't think it was an accident anymore, and we've got to haul in the sled and get going before midnight. Ah'm going to delay as much as I can, but Ah heard the weather's closing in anyway around then."

Richards swung his eyes around the dimly lit room and swore softly. "Fuck! Did you hear anything from Esbjerg?"

Daryl nodded. "Ah did, and they should be here around 1 am. Ah hoped it would be sooner."

"That's bad. We've got two po'lice on board now."

"Like Ah don't know that!" Daryl snarled. "We'll talk more below. Meanwhile, you better get preparations under way to haul in the sled at midnight. Stanley told me the weather's coming in real bad, so we don't have any choice about that. Ah'll discuss the police with you in ma cabin."

Chapter 9

Finding Allies

Patrick made his way up the stairs of the bridge well, then out onto the main deck. He paused there to see what was going on and to make sure neither of the huge cranes were anywhere near, then took a left towards the rear of the barge past the now silent welding bays. It had begun to rain and the deck was slippery. The thick planks of wood were torn and chipped, saturated with oil and grease, which made for slippery walking when it rained.

Within a couple of minutes he knocked on the steel door of the divers' cabin, placed on the port side among all the gantries and pumps that made up their work area.

The door opened to throw bright light out onto the deck where Patrick stood. The figure at the entrance waved him in.

Inside the cramped quarters of the four divers Patrick found Martin, who had let him in, and Leonard, the Canadian diver who had been humiliated in his cabin only a few days before.

Leonard was not effusive. "What the fuck do you want, Pat?" he said without wasting time.

"Where are Michael and Hansen?" Patrick asked, ignoring him.

"Sleeping back there in the decompression tank." Martin jerked his thumb upwards towards the large white tank on top of their cabin.

'Those two will get married one day, they spend so much time

83

Force 12 in German Bight

in there together," Patrick said.

"Why? what's the problem, Pat?" Martin asked him.

"He's probably come to ask for help with those generators, eh, Pat? Can't get them to stay on?" Leonard said with a sneer.

"Fuck you, Lenny. I didn't make them, I inherited them, and they're shit. At least I don't go poking Vicks up my nose hoping to get high. Only a moron would do that, so why would I be here asking for *your* help? Generators are too tricky for the likes of you," Patrick snapped back.

"OK, boys, knock it off. So what brings you to our palatial accommodation, Pat? You don't often come by and grace us with your august presence," Martin said.

Patrick glared at Leonard, who scratched his temple with his middle finger, grinned, and mouthed the words "Fuck you."

Patrick couldn't help but grin back, but then got serious.

"Listen you two, we have Charlie dead and the police from Denmark here. Any thoughts on what the hell is going on?"

"You tell us, Pat. You found him," Leonard said.

"What are the cops like?" Martin asked. "I hear one's a woman."

"Well ...she's a looker I can tell you that, but bright too. Cottoned onto the non accident part real quick. Her boss doesn't like me much." Patrick told them

"And yes, I did find Charlie, and I'm damned sure it wasn't an accident considering the size of that hole in his head. He'd have had to fall about thirty feet to get that by accident, and now I don't think the police think it was one either. That girl's sharp and picked up on what I was trying to show her in the winch room."

"But who would want to bash Charlie's head in?" Leonard said. "He was one of those weird riggers, they're all from the Deep South, which is spooky enough, but they stick to themselves most of the time and don't bother us much unless we're on the bottom with the sled. Maybe he pissed off someone in that crowd," he reflected.

Patrick wanted a drink, but he knew the boys in the divers' area weren't allowed to before they went down and contented himself with the coffee Martin offered him. It tasted like peat from an Irish bog.

"There's something going on I don't like," he said. "I wouldn't put it past either of those trolls that work on the same shift as Richards. I don't like him much either."

"What do you care if they're trolls, Pat? You don't have to run into them that often, do you?" Leonard asked reasonably.

"Pat's saying that paranoia is a healthy disease, Lenny." Martin said.

"Paranoia?"

Patrick rolled his eyes.

"We used that expression when we were in the mob; it helped to keep us on our toes. You know what I mean." Martin said.

"Yeah I guess so, but there isn't much to go on, and the police are here anyway so why the worry?" Leonard said.

"Because there are only two of them, and we are a long way from shore," Patrick said.

Just as he said this the lights went out.

"For fuck's sake! That's the third time today." Patrick bolted from the cabin and made his way to the after stair well, which he slid down, then raced along the corridors to the stairs leading down to the generator room.

He got there just as Joel arrived, and they both proceeded to take the rest of the generators offline before starting them up again one at a time. They ignored the loud calls from the bridge.

It only took a few minutes, as they were well practiced at this, but neither of them was happy. "I think we have a ground earth that's killing us, but the only place I can think of where the fault might be is in one of the lines of the sled cable," Patrick told Joel. "Have you noticed they only go off when we're on the pipe?"

"To find out would take us down for a whole day while we rung it out, and Daryl and Roger won't allow that. We'd really have to make a case," Joel said.

"What better fucking case do they need? These things go off at the drop of a hat, for Christ's sake," Patrick exclaimed.

They stayed in the generator room for a while to make sure all five of the engines came on without problems, and then Joel went off to deal with the pump that was playing up. Alistair, the mechanical engineer, was sure it was an electrical fault.

Force 12 in German Bight

"Stan's bitching at us about the radio. They lost signal while the cops were on the line."

"Tell Johnny to go up there and check it out. He knows what to do about the antenna," Patrick told him. "There's a storm coming, Joel. You'll have your work cut out for you by midnight. I'm going to the cabin. Just hope those techs aren't in there having another party."

The techs weren't in the cabin, but Larry and Ryan, the two 'trolls', as Patrick called them, were. Larry had commandeered the comfortable chair, and he leaned forward when Patrick came in. The lights were down but he knew who they were.

"Hi guys," he said casually. "What are you doing here?" He was conscious of his heartbeat rising.

Larry straightened up and Ryan spat into a polystyrene cup and shifted his wad of tobacco around in his mouth.

"What yer say, Patrick?" they said in unison.

"Not much, what's going on? To what do I owe the honor?" he said pleasantly enough.

Larry leaned over the desk and inhaled. Patrick was far enough into the room now to see that he had taken the mirror off the wall and used it to snort a line of some white powder. He did it with a hundred dollar bill.

"Shouldn't be doing that here, Larry. It's a run off if you're caught." Patrick knew full well Larry wasn't going to be run off by anyone, but it pissed him off Larry was doing this in his cabin. He wondered why they were here, and was sure it wasn't a good sign.

"Daryl wants to know what the cops were askin' you today." Ryan spoke from his position on the bunk nearest the desk.

Patrick sat down on the bunk opposite Ryan and decided not to offer them a drink.

"Usual things, I suppose. They wanted to know when, where and how."

"What you tell 'em?"

"I told them the when and the where but not the how, because I wasn't there when it happened," Patrick said, watching them. They exchanged glances.

"Just that? Nothin' more?" Ryan asked and spat again into his cup. His large, dark eyes bored into Patrick's as if he wanted to drag the truth out of him.

Patrick sighed to himself. Neither of these two were very tightly wrapped, but if Daryl sent them there might actually be something behind it. He didn't like the direction his thoughts were taking him. He shook his head and tried to appear bored.

"Nah, they just wanted to find out what happened, and what me and Skillet did after we found the body. They're just cops doing what cops do; getting in the way."

Larry had finished his snorting. He wiped his nose with the sleeve of his overalls and sniffed loudly.

"Well, they might be, but now they want Daryl to take the barge back to Denmark," he said, watching Patrick.

"What? Do they realize what that means for the contract?" Patrick nearly yelped. He now understood they were here to find out if he had put any ideas into the cop's heads. Well, he might have, but they weren't stupid; the girl had figured it out without much help from him.

"When do they want us to go there?" he asked. It wasn't hard to act pissed off.

"Right away, but Daryl ain't coming off the line before midnight, no matter what.

Patrick watched Larry. "Anything else, guys?"

Larry got up, followed by Ryan. "Nah, just wanted to see what the cops might have told you."

"Larry, this is an investigation into an accident Charlie had. The cops aren't going to talk to me now, are they?"

"No, s'pose not," Larry said, as he and Ryan left, leaving the door ajar.

Patrick shut the door with a kick from his boot, picked up the mirror, wiped it with his sleeve and replaced it on the wall. He sat down on the chair in the relative silence of the cabin. His ears automatically registered a generator going offline below. He tensed, but then another came online, so he relaxed.

He hated the off time while on the barge. In many ways he was glad there was so much maintenance on the old rust bucket; it prevented him from thinking about anything else, and when done he was usually too exhausted to want to. However he often wondered about the other men on the barge. Men like him with nowhere to be other than on this working prison at sea, earning pots of money. How many times had Joel reminded him?

"When you think you've had enough, just take out your calculator and do the numbers. You ain't any different from any of us, Pat. You'll stay for another three months!"

Many of the riggers were from the States. Almost to a man they came from the South, which he'd learned was a state of mind as much as a region in the USA. Three months on and three weeks off. The men would come back to the harsh conditions and the ever present risk of accidents. They went home with suitcases full of cash, so they wouldn't have to declare it on their tax forms. They would spend it all on whores, their wives, on booze and drugs or all four; then return to the barge for another three months, broke each time. Seven and twelve they called it. Seven days a week and twelve hours minimum on a good day. They did this year in and year out, except in winter.

He reached into the steel cabinet at the end of one of the beds, pulled out a bottle of Oban Malt from under a layer of books, and turned on his cassette player to play Fleetwood Mac's "You Make Loving Fun". He didn't enjoy much of anything any more, but it was probably better than being in an actual monastery, he supposed. At least here he made some money. He was engaged in sipping a small glass of the amber liquid and moodily half listening to the music when Johnny opened the door without knocking and sidled in.

"Hi, Pat," he said, eying the malt.

"Hi, Johnny. No! You cleaned me out of the last bottle and I'm not sharing this one."

Johnny sighed and sat himself on the bunk. "What's Daryl doing?" he asked.

"What do you mean? He's the Super or whatever." Patrick didn't like Daryl overmuch; whenever there was a problem he always rode Patrick and Joel hard, interfering when they needed all their concentration to fix the complex systems.

"Well, I was up in the radio box because Joel was off somewhere with Alistair, and Stan wanted to make sure the antenna tuning system was working. You know how flakey that is."

Patrick nodded. "Go on."

"Well, I'm still up there when Daryl comes in and tells Stan to get him a phone number in Denmark. Once he had it, he told Stan to scram, and I could hear him on the phone."

"Probably calling about the police telling him we have to take the barge back to Esbjerg," Patrick said.

"Ye what? They want us to go into *port*?" Johnny rolled his r's to make it sound like Porrt. His Scottish accent was strong. He wasn't the brightest spark on the barge, Patrick reflected, but he was a good techie.

"Wasn't that what he called about?"

"Noo, in fact he called about something completely different, but now you come to mention it, he did say something about it as well. He asked whoever was at the other end to cancel the delivery *because* the Danish police were here."

It was Patrick's turn to be surprised. He took a long sip of the malt and stared at Johnny. "Now that's interesting!" he said in a low voice.

He glanced at the door. "He didn't know you were up there?"

"Noo, nor was I going to be telling him neither. You know what a bastard Daryl can be. I guess Stan had forgotten me as he left, and I was still up above the radio set in the amp room."

Patrick had a mind's eye image of Daryl, hunched over the radio console and handling the microphone with earphones on his head, while Johnny crouched right up above in the small cramped room where the high power amplifiers and antenna tuning equipment were mounted.

"So what else did he say?" He pulled out another small glass and poured a finger of malt for Johnny, who smiled and nodded his gratitude.

"Way aye, but that's generous of ye, Pat," he crooned as he took a sip and closed his eyes in pleasure.

"Don't get any ideas. This is a *malt*, not the whisky pisswater you barbarians from Glasgow and the English drink. You don't have enough couth to appreciate it. Just the one." Patrick informed him.

Force 12 in German Bight

"Ye might be right, ye Highland bugger. I like it though, and I don't mind pot either. The pot pen ye made for me is the best thing while I'm on deck, but nothing can beat this malt," Johnny said as he wiped his mustache with the back of his sleeve.

Patrick nudged him. "What else did he say?"

"Oh, aye. Well, I couldn't hear the other side, as Daryl had the earphones on, but they must have said something he didn't like because the next thing he said was, "You have to stop it, call it back! Now is a really bad time," and he repeated the police were here. He nearly shouted."

Patrick prodded him again. "What else?"

"He listened for a while to someone at the other end and then he cussed like hell, low and angry like, and asked when it was due to arrive. He repeated the time, so I know when. A boat is going to come alongside at about one in the morning."

"Bugger me!" Patrick said. "I wonder what's coming in? That's in about five hour's time."

"All I know is Daryl was mad as hell and kept telling the people to contact the other boat and have it go back to port. He said several times the police were on board and he didn't want any more trouble than he had already. He said he wouldn't be held responsible if this all went to hell because they'd not listened to him.

"Soon after that he left, and before Stan could come back I cleared out of there."

Patrick said nothing. He thought hard. His instincts had been correct but he still didn't know why Charlie had been topped, and now a mysterious cargo would come aboard in the dead of night.

He turned to Johnny and said, "OK, Johnny, now pay attention. Do *not* say anything to anyone about what you told me. You haven't have you?"

Johnny looked worried but replied, "Noo and OK, I'll no say anything to anyone else."

"Johnny. There has already been one 'accident' on this barge and I don't want another. Don't go off blabbing to *anyone*. You don't know who to trust besides me. Let me deal with this."

Johnny looked startled, his eyes opened wide. "You think? OK, Pat, you're the boss. I'll keep quiet. You think it might not have been an accident then?"

"I'm almost sure of it. That's why the police have ordered us back to port," Patrick said. "Listen, Johnny, you're on shift now. Carry on with your work, but try to stay near the top deck as much as you can. There's always work to be done on the telephones at the aft end, near the sled. From there you'll be able to see anything that comes in from outside. You need to come and wake me up when and if it happens. In fact, wake me at about twelve thirty anyway. You clear about that?"

Johnny nodded, and his watery blue eyes regarded Patrick with a trace of fear in them.

Patrick hastened to reassure him. "You don't have to worry about anything, Johnny... unless you blab. Just keep your mouth shut and you'll be fine. Do as I say, and now get the hell out of my cabin and stop drinking my malt."

Johnny grinned and got up. He finished off the glass and left. "Goodnight, Pat."

Patrick sat for a long five minutes at the table with another shot of malt in his hand, thinking hard. Ever since he'd arrived on the barge this time there had been a change in the general atmosphere of the vessel. Only the Filipino riggers were no different; their normally cheerful faces were free of any guile that he could see.

However, there was a tension among the American riggers, especially on the night shift. It hadn't been there before, and the recent death of Charlie, who had been one of Galay's crew, disturbed him. Patrick had no doubt anymore it was murder. That hole was caused by a large spanner or similar tool, of that he was sure. The fact the body had been moved bothered him as well, but what he didn't understand was why Charlie had been killed.

Now the police were here in the form of a couple of detectives, and one of them was a woman, for Christ's sakes. This barge full of randy, sex-starved men was no place for a woman. But then, having spent just a little time with the Danish cop, he was pretty sure she could handle herself.

In any event, there was more. Why the visit by two of the trolls? He figured he could've dealt with them if they had come for some other reason, but in a cramped space that could have been difficult and the outcome uncertain.

He got up and hauled his duffel bag out from under one of the beds. He fumbled about for a while and pulled out a dark object. He slipped the curious looking knife out of its black leather sheath. Black all over and with a leather handle, the blade was long and thin, only an inch and a half wide at the hilt and a good eight inches long. He tested its slim, deadly blade with his thumb. It was as sharp as a razor. It wouldn't hurt to keep it handy, he reasoned as he brushed his teeth. That night he went to bed fully clothed with the knife on his belt. The issue Swiss knife he had owned since he left the army he slipped into his sock.

He briefly thought about paying the Danish police a visit but then realized they might be watched, and his visit would spill his hand to anyone who was keeping an eye on them. He went to sleep with the thought that Daryl and his trolls were behind something bad.

Chapter 10

Police Work

Detective Inspector Greenfield and Sergeant Toby Wilson made their way along the wet and darkened streets toward the welcoming sign of the Three Crowns pub. It was located in a dingy area, just to the south of Harrow Road off Edgewood Road.

Steven knew the pub was a hang out for the slightly more posh villains and thugs, but these same people rubbed shoulders with the locals and others who wanted a discreet night out.

They pushed through the crowd at the doorway and on into the smoke-filled pub itself. He immediately felt people were watching him, assessing him and placing him. He hadn't felt like this since he went into one of the Irish hangouts that dotted the city, where anyone who came in the door was suspect unless known by at least five people.

"We might find this fellow in the lounge, Toby. I'll check that out while you get a pint at the bar. I'll join you in a minute," he murmured.

His sergeant nodded and they separated. Steven pushed his way past miniskirted girls and their men, who eyed him warily as he went by. He was a cop and they knew it. Somehow they could smell it. Some of the girls had no business wearing miniskirts, he thought to himself as he squeezed through the crowd of women with large expanses of thigh and cheap, cloying perfume. It was difficult for a policeman to appear to be anything else to these people, he reflected.

Force 12 in German Bight

There was no one in the lounge that came close to the vague description Ben had given him, so he went to the bar and ordered a bitter from the harassed girl behind the counter. He watched the noisy crowd in the room while he sipped his beer, then decided to go back and talk to his sergeant.

He found Wilson with his back to the people in the bar nursing his beer, but something about the sergeant alerted Steven.

"What is it, Toby?" he asked as he joined him.

"Dunno, sir, but if I'm not mistaken I know that geezer over in that corner."

Steven glanced over to where his sergeant had indicated. A man sat at a table with his back to the window and leaned on his elbows. Even from this distance they could see his morose expression. He wore a leather bomber jacket and sported a pony tail of dirty-blond hair.

"I know 'im from some time back, guv. He was a small time thug then and seeing as he is not in the clanger my guess is he still is. His name is Nigel Spencer and he's a bad sort. Could Ben have been talking about him?"

"Bertie mentioned this guy, if he is Nigel, and the other one to to talk to is a former Royal Marine and might not even have a police record. Probably one that went bad. Happens now and again," Steven said, and sent a surreptitious glance over at the man in question. "That one doesn't seem like a military guy to me. Still, not a happy chap, is he?"

"No, but if I'm right about that guy over there he's got a rap sheet as long as your arm, guv. Might not hurt to take him in and ask a couple of questions."

"OK, we'll wait till he leaves and pick him up."

They waited for about twenty minutes before the man Toby thought was named Nigel finished his pint and got up to go. They hastily downed their pints and followed him out the door and along the short street toward Edgware Road.

They were just about to close in when a four door Jaguar pulled up alongside the curb, a window went down, and a man's voice called over to Nigel. He leaned down to look into the car, talked for a few seconds and got into the passenger seat. The car purred off along Edgware and disappeared into the traffic of the night.

"Did you get the number on the plate?" Steven asked Wilson.

"Yeah, I got it," his sergeant said.

They compared notes, as they had both instinctively done the same thing.

Steven was frustrated but not altogether surprised. These off chance encounters were frequently dead ends. Nevertheless, the next morning while he sat at his desk and braced for the visit from Scotland Yard officers, his sergeant knocked on the door and walked in with a lopsided grin on his face.

"Maybe a bingo, sir. The car belongs to one George Stanley. Got an address of sorts at Earls Court, not far from Cromwell Road."

"Seems a bit unlikely for someone who lives there to own a Jag," Steven said.

They drove around to the address that morning. Steven was even less impressed with the address when they got there. Earl's Court had rapidly fallen into decay after having been a place where young visitors to London often stayed in the not so grand hotels along the street. The cafes and cheap restaurants had definitely seen better days. In the grey of the morning the street looked even shabbier. Their destination was two floors up from a narrow stairway, wedged between a cigarette and magazine shop, which had porn magazines displayed in its grimy front window, and a shoe shop on the other side. That, too, looked as though it had known better days.

The woman who answered the door recoiled when she saw the two men standing there. Her expression was initially frightened, then wary. Her hair was in curlers and she was dressed in a worn and faded cotton house gown with wide sleeves. There was a television on in one of the rooms behind her that was far too loud, and a baby squalled somewhere else in the apartment.

"Wot yer want?" she said with a scowl. The door was on the chain.

"We need to talk to Mr. Stanley," Toby said.

"He ain't here."

"We're police, so if he is here please ask him to come to the door, Ma'am, or we'll have to come back with a search warrant," Steven said with a nice smile. They displayed their badges.

"Wait 'ere. I'll go and see if he's in," she said, her former unpleasantness replaced with wary civility.

There were low voices and then a man still in his pajamas came to the door. He was pasty faced, needed a shave, and the top of his head was headed for bald. His hair had once been black but now it was streaked with grey.

"Coppers is it? Wot is it? Wot yer want?" he said and peered out at them from behind the door.

"Is your name George Stanley?" Toby asked.

"Who wants to know?" he said.

Toby sighed. "The police, now are you going to let us in to ask some questions, or do we have to break in?"

Steven looked at Toby with approval.

"All right, all right, keep your hair on. Hold on, I'll open the door."

Stanley let them in but didn't invite them to the living room. He stood there in the foyer, if it could be called that, and stared up at them. He was a small man with mean little eyes, which now looked nervous."

"Do you own a Jaguar with this registration, sir?" Toby asked, showing him the number from his notebook in an official manner.

Stanley hesitated but then he nodded. "Er, yeah. I do, that's right... I own it."

"So could you please tell us where it was last night?"

Stanley looked worried, then shifty. "It was parked around the corner. I was 'ere in the house. You can ask the missus."

"So it wasn't missing or anything last night, and you were here? Hmm?"

Steven stepped forward to tower over Stanley. "You don't drive it, do you, Mr. Stanley? You had better find a better story for that Jag. I doubt if you could afford even one of the payments on it. So who's driving it around, and what is his name?"

"Perhaps we should take him down to the station, guv. We can keep him there for a while, till he decides to tell us something," Toby said, looking hard at Stanley.

Their victim began to look distressed. His former belligerence had gone and was replaced with a whine.

"I don't want any trouble, sirs." He wound his hands together as though washing them.

"OK, tell us who's driving it and who really owns it, Stanley, and we'll leave you alone."

He glanced behind him and then back up at Steven.

"It's a guy called Don Saunders. He paid me to buy the car and hand it and the papers over to him. That's all I know, and I don't want to know anything else."

"Where does he live?"

"I dunno." He seemed frightened. "He's a tough-looking fellah. Fit and well... he gave me the eye and told me I'd cop it if I told anyone."

"We were never here," Toby said.

As they went down the stairs Toby said, "He was bothered about something, guv."

"Frightened, you mean? Yes, I thought so, too. Well, now we have a name and it ties in with what Bertie said, but I'm not sure it's going anywhere, and my boss will give me a hard time for not being at the station to greet our friends from Scotland Yard."

Steven arrived back to find a note on his desk; one of his colleagues wanted to see him. He walked round to the desk of another detective, Barry Hawthorne, who handled petty crime in the Paddington area.

"Hello, mate," Barry said. "You might want to know a body turned up near Vauxhall today. The Met boys were talking about it, and I thought you might be interested."

"Bodies turn up all the time, what about it?"

"They dug a bullet out of the head, which tallied with the ones you mentioned for the train killing the other day. Thought you might like to know."

"Does it have a name? This body?" Steven asked him.

"Yeah." Barry rustled some paper. "Nigel Spencer, that's it. One shot to the head."

Steven blinked and stared at him. "You're sure?"

"Yes, that's him. Down by the river, under the bridge. Looked

Force 12 in German Bight

like he was dumped there."

Steven didn't stay. "Thanks. I owe you a pint for that," he said, then hurried back to his office. He called in Toby and told him the news. Toby was surprised but nodded his head.

"It would seem the rule that says not to get into cars with strangers still holds true, sir."

"In this case he knew the driver, Toby. I think if we can find the car we can find the killer, at least in this instance and my money is on Donald Saunders. What can this have to do with the murder at Paddington, I wonder? Put out an APB on the car and let's see what comes up. And bring in our friend George. I want an artist's impression of our man from him. Then we need to get to Military Records and see what turns up there," he said, and then he got up and went off to see if the Scotland Yard men had arrived.

*****

Later in the day, Sergeant Wilson knocked on Steven's door and came into his office holding two cups of coffee. He seemed pleased as he handed one to his boss.

"Thanks, Toby." Steven said as he sipped the brew. " Any news about the Jag? You're looking smug, so what is it?"

"Yes, there might be, sir. Customs at Harwich sent in a report of a Jaguar of the same cream color we noticed, with those number plates, leaving on the ferry to Denmark."

"Denmark? What town does the ferry go to over there?" Steven asked and looked up at the map of the British Isles and the coastline of Europe on his wall. It included Denmark and the Nordic countries of Norway and Sweden.

"That particular ferry goes to a town called Esbjerg, sir. Way up there." He pointed up the map to the west coast of Jutland.

"That's a bit off the beaten path, I'd say, but alright, now we'll have to notify the Danish police and Interpol. This is getting more and more murky by the minute," Steven said.

"Ok, I'll do that, sir," Toby said, but he didn't leave right away.

"What's on your mind, Toby?" Steven asked, knowing the signs.

"Well, sir. From the photos we saw today of the body, I'd say the last murder seemed more like an execution, don't you think?"

"Yes, that's possible. Your point being?"

"If you were going to top someone after giving them a ride, would you do it alone, sir? I mean, could the driver of the car have had an accomplice?"

"Yes... that's very possible, but we have no clues at this time. What I would like to do is to interview this Don Saunders when we find him, but in the meantime I'd also like to know if he's acting alone or for someone a bit higher on the food chain. Killings like this don't happen every day, and now we have what looks like two of them. Find out everything you can about this guy and get back to me, Toby."

"Yes, sir. Er, what about the people from the Yard, sir?"

They're getting set up in the spare lecture room and will be a while. We can help by starting this process, Toby. Oh, by the way, let's get a photo of the man from the train accident off to Interpol as well. Just a hunch," Steven said.

Chapter 11

Murder on the High Seas

A large container truck with a trailer behind it sped down the E20, which was the main artery between the port of Esbjerg on the west side of Jutland and Kolding on the east side of the peninsular. As it hissed along the wet autobahn in the pouring rain with the wipers working full on, the driver checked his dashboard clock and cast a worried look at the traffic on the road. He was late and the traffic was moving slower than it should.

He saw the flashing lights half a mile ahead of him and realized the police had a road block set up. For a brief moment of sheer panic he thought of turning off the road and abandoning the truck. In his present state of paranoia he felt sure the road block was for him, and he peered anxiously through the slashing rain, trying to work out what was going on.

But he could do nothing, stuck in the double row of cars headed for the red and blue police lights. To his relief he saw there had been an accident, and the police were directing traffic around the wrecks of two cars and a small truck parked on the side. He let out his breath in a low whistle as they waved him through. He continued driving along the highway until it petered out and he found himself guided by signs to a road marked number 24, and soon the signs said *Gammelby Ringvej*. He drove the truck along this ring road and searched for the turn off. He was near the port of Esbjerg.

After a few minutes he slowed and took the road marked

Force 12 in German Bight

Adgangsvejen, which led straight on past a left hand turn-off called *Dokvej,* which in turn led to the Harwich ferry wharf. The ferry docked in the harbor was lit up like a Christmas tree, all its lights on. Several lines of cars and trucks waited to be loaded,.

His road carried on for another half mile and brought him to a large roundabout. Here he consulted a piece of paper with a crude map drawn on it and began to look for Pier 2, which was at the northernmost point of the huge square basin of the harbor. Glancing off to his left he could see his destination was full of small craft of every type, from sailing yachts to seagoing tugs and small freighters.

As he drove up he noticed a large tug tied to the pier he was aiming for and began to relax. He'd arrived at his destination after a thousand mile journey, which would make him a lot of money.

Men waited for him on the dockside and waved flashlights, as the light was dim here and it still rained. He turned off his lights and stepped down from the cab to ease his legs, and was greeted by a curt remark, "You're late. What happened?"

"There was an accident along the highway back there." He gestured behind him. "All traffic slow down, police everywhere." His accent was eastern European.

The large man grunted and gave him instructions to move the truck so a small crane could access the trailer and his cargo.

Within a few minutes a tracked crane lumbered out of the darkness from behind some warehouses and parked between the truck and the ship. A couple of men hastily untied the straps of two containers on the flat top trailer. The half box container was quickly lifted off the trailer and swung in a wide arc to descend onto the open area of deck, behind the funnel and the bridge structure of the large tug.

The driver was handed a large package in a sealed envelope and told by one of the hard-faced men to leave the way he had come. He needed no second bidding; he hastily put the thick envelope into the inner pocket of his jacket and climbed into his cab. He drove off leaving the men to clear away the crane and board the vessel, which already had its engines running.

Before long the vessel pushed its way through the darkness of the harbor basin toward the entrance of the main sea walls. The boat then proceeded to speed up and head for the mainland entrance that provided Esbjerg with such a good haven from the storms of the North Sea.

Here the boat put on full power, the sound of its twin diesel engines increasing to a roar, and it pushed out into the now heavy seas west of Jutland.

*****

Chief Inspector Kristian Vestergaard leaned back in his chair and studied the coastal regions of Jutland. He pondered the phone call he had received at 1900 hours from this vessel they called a barge. As usual the indecisiveness of his subordinate, Erland Knudson, irritated him. He'd not been positive about the need to bring the barge into port. It was a murder investigation for Christ's sake; they had to bring it in and that was that.

All the same, perhaps there really was a need to send some back up. There were only the two of them there and one of them was the girl, Hedi Iversen. He already regretted having allowed her to go out with Erland. This was the oil field after all, and he didn't know how she would hold up. But the equal rights movement was getting involved even with the police in Denmark, and he didn't need that kind of pressure on top of all his other concerns.

He reached for the phone and called for his duty officer.

"Get me the Coast Guard, please, Eric," he said.

Within half an hour he had a cutter at his disposal and four men standing ready to go out with it to the barge. The last location he'd obtained from Erland was estimated to be slightly less than one hundred miles out in a line that cut North by North West from Esbjerg, in the area known as German Bight.

He had a few words with the men, who looked unhappy at going out in the worsening weather, but he insisted. The skipper of the cutter, a Lieutenant Asger, finally nodded and led the way out of the building.

*****

The police cutter went out at about eleven thirty that night and headed for the tumultuous seas beyond the island of Fane on their port bow and the marshlands to the North. As they drove out of the protection of the sheltering land mass, they were met by the full force of wind from the North West and the high seas.

The Coast Guard cutter was sturdy but light, and it wasn't long before the surging, pitching, and rolling of the craft had all the policemen vomiting up their last meals.

Up in the bridge the skipper and his subordinate officer grimaced as they listened to the ugly noises coming from below, but worse was the stink of vomit that began to permeate the boat.

"Get the windows open and some fresh air in here for Christ's sake," Lieutenant Asger called down to the other men. He was disgruntled because they were out in foul weather on what he considered a whim by the Police chief, to get more men onto a stationary ship somewhere out in the darkness. He had made plans with his girlfriend to go to the Library bar, which he'd had to cancel when he'd been called back to the station.

They'd been out for nearly half an hour and were making good time when his crewman pointed to the radar console and called over to him. He had to raise his voice to be heard above the noise of the huge turbines that drove the sleek vessel through the seas.

Asger shifted position so he could see what the screen.

"There's a vessel dead ahead that seems to be on the same course as we are, sir."

He watched the screen for a few minutes to verify they were indeed on the same course, but also that his vessel was gaining on the other. They would pass the other ship within fifteen minutes at this rate.

"Keep an eye open for that ship," he ordered. "It's unusual to find a boat headed out to sea in this kind of weather. Anyone with half a wit would be going in the opposite direction!"

His subordinate nodded in agreement and went below to see how the policemen were faring. He returned with a mug of cocoa for his chief and a wry grin on his young face. "They're not fit for anything, sir. Sick as dogs."

Asger grinned back as he took his mug and braced himself as the bows of their vessel seemed to head for the sky and then surged over the top of a wave to descend sickeningly into a well.

He checked the radar console again. They were gaining on the other ship quickly now. He peered through the storm screen and pointed.

"There, just off our port bow."

"I see it," said the crewman.

The night was black all around so he ordered the search lights turned on in order to see ahead of them. The beam cut through the rain and spume tossed up by their bows.

"We should pass them within a few minutes, I should think," said the skipper.

*****

In the boat ahead, the skipper of *Viking I*, a bearded man who knew the coast well, checked his radar console and swore. He made a substantial part of his livelihood smuggling things in and out, mainly drugs.

"Get the boss man up here now!" he bellowed at the crewman standing nearby.

The man disappeared and soon reemerged from the main cabin below with a strong looking man in tow. Donald Saunders was the worse for wear after only half an hour of rough seas. He was used to bigger ships; this tug, large though it was and with powerful engines, was being tossed about like a cork in these high waves.

The skipper motioned him over and pointed at the radar console; the rotating line that swirled around the screen showed the outline of land on the eastern side, but it also illuminated a blob near the center.

"We're being followed," the skipper rasped. "You said no one from Esbjerg knew about this operation!"

Fuckin' hell, how did this happen? Donald thought as he stared at the screen. There was no mistaking there was a blob, which meant a boat of some sort followed them.

"They're gaining on us, Don," the skipper added. "I'm not going to wait to be hauled in by the Coast Guard, if it's them. We're going to have to ditch the cargo and make a run for it."

Don stared at the man. "Are you bloody crazy? We don't ditch the cargo. You pile on the steam and let's see what happens."

Force 12 in German Bight

The skipper nodded and wiped his sweaty hands on his dirty blue coveralls. "OK, we might be able to show him our tail. What are you going to do if they keep chasing us?"

"Let me worry about that," Donald said with a grim set to his jaw. "Just pile on the gas and leave them behind. It might be just another boat on the same course as us by coincidence." He knew as soon as he said it, and from the skeptical snort from the skipper, this was wishful thinking.

"There ain't no one out in this shit who's in possession of his senses. Just the likes of us and the fucking Coast Guard, I'm sure of it," the skipper said.

He turned back to his instrument panel and pulled the throttles to full on. The diesel turbines that drove the tug changed their tone from a throaty growl to a fierce howl, and the tug surged. For a time they seemed to be getting away from the blob.

He waved a crewman over and told him to keep them on course while he went out the back of the bridge and stared back along their wake. In the distance a beam of light rose and fell, occasionally flashing into his eyes. A small craft was out there, and they had to be looking for him. No doubt they had radar as well. He almost yelled with frustration. Those bastard British had assured him that once the container was on board and they were out to sea, the operation was as good as over for him. All he had to do was deliver it to a vessel and go home. The weather couldn't be more perfect for smuggling, but there, right on his tail, was a fucking boat, and he was convinced it was the Coast Guard.

*****

On the Coast Guard vessel the second in command called over to the captain. "They are moving away from us, sir. I think they've picked up speed."

"Now why would they do that?" Lieutenant Asger inquired, glancing at the screen. "I really want to see what kind of ship that is. Try the usual shipping frequencies and see if you can get him to slow down."

"Yes, sir." The second in command went to the back of the bridge and began to dial several frequencies, searching for radio chatter that might come from the vessel ahead. He covered the standard frequencies every ship should have had open, but received no reply.

After several minutes he called over. "Nothing, sir. They're either shut down or they don't want to answer."

"More and more mysterious by the minute," Asger said. "Right then, we'll chase them and see what's what."

He ordered more power and the cutter surged forward.

It didn't take long before they could see the other vessel ahead of them. It kept appearing and disappearing as and when the searchlight passed over its rear. It appeared to be a large tug, with a cargo of one small container. The name on the back of it was the *Viking I.*

"Do you think they're smugglers, sir?" his second asked.

"If they are, they're going in the wrong direction," Asger said. "Tell those coppers below to hang on; this will be a bumpy ride."

They gained rapidly on the tug ahead, despite the fact that it wasn't slowing down, not even when they must have known they were being followed. Eventually the Coast Guard cutter took up position off the port bow. The captain reached for the loud speaker system switch and spoke into the microphone.

"Hello, *Viking I*, this is Denmark's Coast Guard. Slow down, we wish to come alongside."

A man standing in the bridge space waved and the tug boat slowed to a couple of knots, enough to keep position. The Coast Guard cutter approached with care. Both vessels were tossed about by the choppy seas, and the wind increased to the point where Asger worried they might even have to turn back if things got much worse, mission be damned. In the meantime, he had a strange vessel to check out.

There were several men standing on the afterdeck of the tug, watching them as they eased closer. The crewmen of the cutter threw lines to them, which one man caught and wound around a steel bollard. Then the second in command and a crewman from the cutter braced themselves to jump across the yard-wide gap between the two ships. Both were armed with stubby rifles, but they didn't expected any trouble, hence no one on the cutter was prepared when two men stood up from behind the side of the tug and opened fire with submachine guns.

Force 12 in German Bight

The harsh rattle of the firearms was barely heard in the bridge of the cutter, but the skipper could clearly see how his men twisted and jerked, their faces contorted in agony, before they fell out of sight in between the two vessels.

The two who had opened fired jumped across the gap, and while one of them went out of sight below, the other came up along the back deck, firing at the windows of the bridge as he came. The plexiglass shattered into a hundred shards which peppered the counter and Asger.

He had just enough time to duck out of sight and look around feverishly for a weapon when the shooting began again below him, in the well of the cutter. The noise deafened him as the machine gun fired into the small group of surprised and defenseless policemen. There were screams and cries that abruptly fell silent.

In the stunning silence that followed he reached for a 6.5cm rocket pistol placed next to the signals box. It was the only weapon in the cabin. He could hear more shouts of alarm below, followed by more shots. He couldn't see if his attacker was after him still, but the silence was ominous. He peered out over the shattered glass into the darkness but could see nothing, so he crept to the head of the stairs that led below, hoping one of the crew might have survived.

A man was about to mount the stairs, a sub machine gun in his hands He grinned malevolently up at the skipper as he took another step and raised the small stubby gun to a firing position.

Asger heard the small sound behind him far too late to do anything about it. Before he could turn to confront his attacker the bullets from the Uzi slammed into his back. In a reflexive movement his finger convulsively tightened on the trigger, and he fired the flare gun into the chest of the man in the cabin space below.

He never saw the result of his action, but the man at the bottom of the stairs was blown backwards, his Uzi flying. A huge, burning mass covered his chest and he writhed in silent agony for a couple of long seconds before going limp. The fire took hold of his clothes, expanded away from the inert body, and crept along the floor in a wave of bluish flame.

Donald stepped over the body of the skipper and peered down

into the blazing space below the bridge.

"Bugger!" he said as he looked at the mess below. He ran towards the doorway out onto the upper deck and passed a man in blue overalls lying dead on the steps. He nodded in approval; Mark knew his job. Too bad the fucking captain of the ship had topped him.

He jumped across the intervening space between the two vessels, landed, and ran back to the rear of the tug to cut the ropes that bound the two vessels together.

"What happened over there?" Hans, the leader of the Danish gangsters, asked. He stared at the flames reaching out of the windows of the vessel next to them.

"Mark copped it. We've got to go! Get rid of those lines and tell the skipper to make full speed. I want to be out of here, now!" Donald shouted.

He was exhilarated from the action, and even though Mark had died, he considered it a small price to pay for having taken out a boat full of Coast Guards with only two men.

"Never underestimate the value of surprise!" he said with a wide grin on his face as he walked into the bridge room with his Uzi still hot from the encounter.

The tug skipper regarded him with fear and awe. "Where did you learn to do that kind of thing?" he stammered.

Royal Marines, mate. Teach you all sorts of skullduggery, and I was a good student," Donald said. He was still on a rush.

"Well, put that thing away," the man said and eyed the weapon. "We won't need it any more."

They pulled away from the blazing wreck of the cutter. They had gone only a quarter of a mile when there was a bright flash that lit up the sky and an explosion that seemed to tear the night apart followed by darkness.

"Do you think it went down?" the skipper asked.

"Must have done! That was one big fire and one bloody big bang," Donald said with a fearsome grin.

Chapter 12

Nocturnal Visitors

Hedi woke in the darkness wondering for a moment where she was. Then it came back to her that she was still on the barge. She fumbled for the light switch above her head, and in the bright glow of the lamp looked at her watch. It was almost midnight; she realized the rumble of heavy machinery trundling about on the top deck had woken her, and now the proximity of other engines added to the noise.

She decided to go and see for herself what was going on. Perhaps the super, Daryl, was actually getting off the pipe and taking them back to Esbjerg. It dawned on her that she and Erland would probably have to remain on the ship until it docked safely and the forensics people and her colleagues could swarm all over it.

She hauled on her anorak and placed her small police issue automatic in the shoulder holster under her left arm out of habit. After giving herself a quick check in the mirror she opened the door to the corridor and went to the door of her superior, Erland. She knocked gently on the door and tried the handle. It opened into a dark room beyond.

Erland had clearly not followed his own instructions and locked the door. She listened and heard some heavy snores coming from the bunk alcove at the back of the cabin. The room smelt of alcohol. Evidently Erland had availed himself of the bourbon provided by Mr. Stack. She shook her head in disgust.

Force 12 in German Bight

Once she'd shut the door behind her she headed for the stairwell leading up to the bridge. As she came level with the main deck, the door crashed open and some men clumped in from outside. They wore bright yellow weather jackets that were streaming with water. One of them noticed her as he came in, nodded, and spoke.

"Wet out there, Miss." He used his elbow to get the attention of the other two, who stared at her as they went by. She walked past and began to climb the next set of stairs, which would take her to the radio room. There was a low whistle and some laughter as they clattered off down to the cabin deck.

She continued up the last flight of stairs, which brought her to the bridge where men with hand-held radios stood in every corner of the darkened room.

"You shouldn't be up here, Miss," a male voice said from over on the starboard side. She turned toward him and recognized him as Richards.

Hedi stared at him. "I've come to see if you're leaving the pipe."

"Yeah, we're leaving the pipe, but that's because there's a blow comin' in—" he didn't finish what he wanted to say, as the radio squawked and he was suddenly busy.

"Miss, you can stand over there by that doorway, out of the way?" suggested one of the men in a corner with a hand radio. "Just don't get in the way, as it's tricky business getting the anchors in and all, especially at night."

She nodded and positioned herself as indicated, which gave her a view out over the entire working deck below.

The deck was bathed in a blaze of light. Two huge cranes had swung their booms out over the water, and one of them lowered its hook to the crew of one of the huge tugs. The crew on board were attempting to catch a cable loop on one of the container-sized orange buoys that bobbed between the port bow of the barge and the rear end of the tug. The darkness was broken by many halogen arc lamps which lit up the entire deck, including the tug, so she could see everything going on.

She heard the man nearest her call into his radio, "Ease her back, Joey; we need you back just a little more. Should have come off the fuckin' pipe two hours ago. Now the sea's a bitch."

The radio crackled as a voice said, "Tell me about it! This is gettin' tight!"

She watched as the tug moved back and closed the gap between the buoy and the side of the barge. Waves were visible in the light beyond the tug; they were high and there were white crests on their dark, surging forms. One wave seemed to come out of nowhere; it washed over the small men who stood at the side of the barge rails, waiting to catch a cable loop with their long poles. They clung to the railing with desperate strength as the water rose over their knees to their waists and then receded. One of the men didn't pay close enough attention, and she watched with horror as his feet were swept out from under him and he was carried by the wash to tumble into the water between the buoy and the side of the ship.

It seemed as though he disappeared, to be crushed by the steel buoy closing in on him, when another surge brought him right back out of the water, to the point where he came level with the railing again. His mates seized him by his flailing arms and legs and hauled him without ceremony over the railing, where they were all doused again by another wave. The men struggled to get back on their feet and two of them led the survivor away at a run. Hedi realized she'd held her breath the entire time and let it out in a gasp.

"What the fuck is happening down there, Ryan?" Richards bellowed into his radio from the other side of the room.

The reply was muted and scratchy, but enough for Hedi to understand the man called Ryan had ordered one of the men taken below and needed backup.

Meanwhile, outside in the slanting rain that made slashes of light in the glare of the lamps, the crane had the buoy hooked and lifted it out of the water. The tug churned up the water as it headed back out in to the menacing darkness to bring in another buoy. The cable came out of the water and the buoy dangled over the deck, a massive anchor suspended beneath, like some huge creature of the sea. Water sluiced off it. The men on deck guided the crane driver as he lowered the huge assembly onto the deck, where it landed with a thump that shook the vessel. Men swarmed over the buoy to lash it down, and the crane trundled away to the starboard side for a repeat performance. The same activity took place at the rear of the vessel, but this work was hampered by all the other structures and equipment placed at the back end of the barge.

She noticed a huge, white apparatus sitting between the walkways at the very end of the barge. It hadn't been there when she arrived. She guessed this might be the sled Skillet had talked about.

The anchors were hauled out of the sea one by one and landed on the deck. The two tugs now took up station ahead of the barge and began to tow it in a North Westerly direction. She was watching, fascinated, when she felt a sharp tap on her shoulder.

"You... Miss, Ma'am, you need to get off the bridge before the super comes." Richard's tone did not brook any argument, so Hedi nodded and made for the stairs. She arrived at deck level, and on impulse she decided to go out onto the deck, which had quieted down as the last of the anchors had been brought in and the riggers were tidying up and lashing things down.

She was made instantly aware of the cold, the rain, and the wind when she exited the main doorway. She tucked her head deeper into her anorak collar and glanced around. Seeing the cover of the heli deck and the associated structures around that end of the barge, she hurried across the wide expanse of the main deck and gained the shelter of the steel structure overhead. The rain increased and the wind picked up so she had to make her way with care to avoid slipping on the wet and greasy wooden boards.

She peered through the rain and realized she was near the huge reels of hose that led to the apparatus at the back of the barge that Skillet had called the Sled. She could see it was suspended by a thick pair of cables from a gantry high above and understood what Skillet had meant. It looked like a huge pair of steel tubes, each sixteen feet long, spaced six feet apart, upon which sat a complex steel frame with vertical tubes and dozens of nozzles. Just behind this were two strange-looking objects that stuck out of either side, which looked like wide, hollow tubes.

She was gazing up at the enormous object when she became aware she wasn't alone. She turned and found Patrick standing only a couple of yards away. A cold feeling went down her back and she instinctively began to reach for her pistol. He spread both hands in a gesture of openness and smiled as if to reassure her.

"I heard someone moving about and came to investigate, it was you," he said, still keeping his hands in plain sight. He wore a dark green pair of coveralls and had a black woolen cap on his head.

"What are you doing here?" Hedi said more sharply than she'd intended.

"Well... I work here. What about you, what are you doing out here in this shitty weather?"

Hedi glanced around, aware she had only a yard between her and the railing and the dark seas rising and falling behind. It would be easy to fall overboard, or be pushed, she thought with the memory of the man who had gone overboard still fresh in her mind. Her hand stayed near her side.

"It's late and you should probably be in your cabin, Miss," the engineer said.

"I couldn't sleep, so I came out here to look around," Hedi said, trying to keep her voice steady and remain calm. Her heartbeat had risen, however.

"You might as well stay now," Patrick said. "I'm not working the shift; I'm here to see what that is all about," he pointed out to sea.

Hedi turned to look out overside of the barge, which had gone strangely quiet after all the previous activity. There was almost no one on the main deck now. The cranes were silent and the tugs had gone off to take up station ahead and drag the barge along with thick cables. All of which made her feel vulnerable, but Patrick didn't come any closer. She kept him in sight when she peered in the direction he had indicated all the same.

A couple of lights bobbed about in the agitated seas almost a mile off the starboard side. One was green, the other red. She supposed they were the running lights of a small fishing vessel perhaps, but nothing more.

"What's so strange about another ship?" she asked.

"Partly the time of night, but mainly because this one is not a scheduled supply vessel," Patrick said. "Listen, do me a favor and keep to the shadows. I don't want anyone on the bridge to see either of us."

Force 12 in German Bight

Hedi hesitated, but did as she was told and moved into the shadow of one of the huge hose barrels.

"I'm going to go up to that cabin below the helipad to see what's going on," Patrick told her and pointed upwards. "You're welcome to come along, it might be interesting, otherwise you should go back to your cabin."

Hedi made a decision. She didn't entirely trust this British man, but he hadn't done anything to threaten her. And her curiosity was piqued; perhaps something would shed light on the death she was here to investigate. "I'll come up with you," she said.

"Come on then. Keep to the dark places, and don't move fast or someone will notice."

He led the way along the after deck to the base of the same steel steps she'd descended earlier that day, and they climbed upward, with Patrick leading the way. She noticed he moved like a cat and made very little noise.

They arrived at the middle platform of the stairway up to the helipad, where a small cabin stood with some controls on a console inside. It had glass windows that gave a good view almost all round the barge. From this vantage point Hedi could see directly into the bridge, which was now fully lit, and they had an unobstructed view of the starboard side of the vessel.

Patrick moved slowly toward the small cabin and opened the door. He motioned her to follow and kept the door open to allow her into the cramped space. She moved past him, aware of how close they were. She took up a place in the far corner where she could both see the bridge and keep him in sight.

"Look!" Patrick said and pointed to the bridge. There seemed to be a lot of activity there as men stared off to the starboard and pointed toward the lights.

"I wonder who they're expecting?" he murmured. "All the trolls are there, and so is Daryl. I don't see the other riggers, though that is to be expected. This is down time and they'll have gone to their cabins. No one in his right mind would hang around the main deck on a night like this."

"I see no one on the deck at all," Hedi said. "You say they're expecting this ship?"

"Not a ship, a boat. Almost as big as the tugs up front by the look of it."

By this time they could see more clearly and hear the vessel that had been approaching the barge. It had come within about two hundred yards, churning the water as it lifted and dropped in the rising swell of the sea. Its skipper clearly planned to pull alongside, as its lights came on and flooded the waves between the two vessels with illumination. Someone went out onto the bridge gangway and waved an electric torch at them. One of the search lights on the approaching boat swung towards the bridge and stayed on the figure.

"That must be the police Erland asked for," Hedi said.

Patrick chuckled. "Now this could be interesting. If Daryl doesn't know it's the police he's going to be in for a surprise. But I don't see any police emblems on the boat though, do you?"

"No, I don't. Why would he be surprised?" Hedi asked.

"Because he's expecting something else, and most certainly not the police."

"What's going on, Mr. McFarlane?" Hedi said.

"That's what I'd like to know. It's why we're here right now. Don't move too much, they might notice us. I can't tell if it's your mates or someone else, and until I do know I'd rather not be seen."

Hedi complied and crouched so only her eyes were above the window sill. Patrick had done the same. They waited and watched the activity below and on the bridge.

The visiting boat now began to sidle closer to the barge, its high-powered engines rumbling as the skipper maneuvered the boat closer and closer. There were men on its decks, and several of the men from the barge bridge had exited the island, one of them making his way to the nearest crane. With practiced ease he swung himself into the cab and started the vehicle up with a roar. The crane began to trundle along the deck to a position where its boom could be used.

"They must have used the sailor radio to communicate. The main one is on the blink right now. I guess it isn't the police this time, Ma'am."

"It's Hedi, Mr. McFarlane," she said.

"OK... Hedi, then call me Patrick. Were you expecting a

Force 12 in German Bight

boatload of policemen then?" he asked her.

"Erland, my boss, asked for them when we were on the radio earlier this evening. They should be arriving before too long."

"Now why would he do that?"

"Because he's worried. There's something... not quite right on this, this barge of yours."

"Can't disagree with you there. Getting here should be interesting. The weather's going to be real shitty before long."

"What do you mean?"

"Force ten to eleven in this area of German Bight. Some big ones are coming down from the north. Earlier than usual for this time of year."

Patrick turned his attention back to the activity taking place below. The deck and the tug were bathed in bright lights from both ships, illuminating men as they moved about. The vessel was indeed a tug, only a little smaller than the two towing the barge. He could see the sea made it hard for the skipper to maintain his position alongside the barge without crashing into it. There was a real risk of damage to both ships if he miscalculated.

He noticed a small group of men standing on the tug's afterdeck, watching a basket drop out of the sky toward them. Four of them threw bags into the middle and climbed onto it. At a signal from another man on the deck, the crane roared and they were whisked up off the heaving deck and high into the air. The basket swung over the railings of the barge to be put down, none too gently, on the main deck next to one of the massive buoys.

The men scrambled off the net and retrieved their bags. The exercise was repeated, and three more men were lifted onto the deck. They were met by a shadowy figure—Patrick recognized Ryan—and, after a brief discussion, they were all shepherded towards the door of the bridge island which led below deck.

Someone, it looked like Larry, hastily released the net and the ball swung out again to come down just over a small, white half-sized container. The men on the tug's decks were quick. They hitched it up, and within moments the half sized container moved up into the air and away from the tug.

The skipper of the tug must have been talking to someone on the bridge, as he put his engines at full thrust and drew away from the barge as soon as the container was aloft, clearly not wanting to tarry too long. Within a few minutes the tug drove off into the ten foot waves and the rain-filled darkness, fountains of spray spreading out from its sharp bows as it disappeared into the night.

Patrick turned back to check on the progress of the container. The crane heaved it over to the fore end of the top deck and placed it among some other half sized containers, which held stores and spares for the barge. It was placed cleverly, so anyone who walked by wouldn't pay it much attention, but it could be seen clearly from the front of bridge. By the way the men on the deck were behaving this was an important piece of equipment.

The container was lashed down, the crane parked, and the men on deck disappeared. The lights on the bridge were dimmed and it was hard to see who was up there, but Patrick was sure the seven men who had come aboard were now talking to Daryl in the bridge.

The lights went out and the whole deck below was plunged into darkness. They could only just see one another's forms.

Patrick sat down on the floor with his back to the wall and waited until Hedi had done the same.

"What do you make of that?" he asked.

"Well, I don't think they're the police. There was no discussion of a container coming here."

"No, I don't think they were the police either, and I don't like what I saw there. Late night deliveries are not uncommon, but to have seven men come aboard as well? Something very odd about that."

"I need to go and wake Erland. We should head to the bridge and ask how long it's going to take to sail to Esbjerg," Hedi said.

"I don't think that'd be a good idea, Hedi."

"Why not?"

"Because at least one of those men carried a gun."

Chapter 13

Refuge

In the long silence that followed, Hedi stared at the dark figure sitting on the floor in front of her.

Finally she said in a whisper, "You're sure of this?"

"Yeah. I think ...those guys are baddies," he said slowly.

"You mean criminals? What would they want to do on this barge?"

"Hmm, its got something to do with that container for sure. Whenever I see weapons on civilians I get nervous," Patrick said.

"Why don't you want me to go back to my boss?"

"Because if they are what I think they might be, then they'll have taken care of him by now and will be looking for you."

Hedi's heart was beating faster. Erland might be in real danger, particularly as he was asleep and probably drunk too. There was an unpleasant feeling growing in the pit of her stomach.

"How... how do you know this?"

"Hmm, played around with the IRA a long time ago, and this has a familiar smell to it."

"What did you used to be before you came to this... this barge place?"

"I was a soldier."

"Skillet said you were more than just a soldier. He said you were... dangerous."

Force 12 in German Bight

"He's just having you on. But we need to think about where to put you until I've found out whether it's safe to get you back to your cabin. Come on." He pushed himself upright and cautiously opened the door while watching the bridge and the deck below for any signs of activity.

Hedi followed him out and they moved towards the steps. Just as they did so there was a screech, and a flurry of feathers passed very close to her. With a startled cry Hedi almost fell. Patrick's hand grabbed her and held her while she regained her balance and composure.

"What was that?" she demanded.

"That was Falcon. He lives here in these corners."

"A falcon? A bird of prey? Out here at sea? You're joking, no?"

Patrick chuckled. "Actually, he's a kestrel. Scared the living daylights out of you, didn't he? Yep, he lives here and takes out the sparrows when they come by on their immigration trips."

Hedi shook her head. This was a strange place, and if Patrick was to be believed it had just become dangerous too.

He led the way down the steps and across the after deck, keeping to the dark shadows, until he arrived at a low structure on the port side of the deck. It resembled a cabin.

He tapped on the door and as soon as it opened he hustled Hedi into the room and shut the door behind them. Leonard had been sipping a coffee and listening to a scratchy track of Emerson Lake and Palmer on an old cassette player. He stared at them both with his mouth open.

"What the..." he started to say. His jaw hung open.

"Where's Martin, Lenny?"

"I'm here. What's going on?" Martin said and ambled out from a back room in his underpants. "Shit!" he said, and beat a hasty retreat.

"What the hell's going on, Pat?" he said from behind the curtains.

"Hey, Lenny, turn the music down for a minute and you can close your mouth now. There's a problem, guys. Need you to look after the detective here while I do a recce."

"A recce? All right, mate, explain yourself, " Leonard said, and nodded to Hedi. "Miss."

"I'm Hedi Iversen with the Danish police," she said as she pushed aside a dirty pile of clothing and sat on one of the plastic chairs. The two divers were staring at this apparition that had appeared in their grubby lodgings.

"OK, you two can stop gawping now, its rude,"said Patrick. "Sit down and listen carefully. There are big problems out there," The two men dragged their eyes off Hedi looked at him expectantly.

Patrick gave them a quick run down on what he and Hedi had seen and who'd been involved as far as he could tell. He also mentioned the fact he'd seen at least one man carrying a submachine gun.

Their eyes widened.

"You're sure of this, Pat?" Leonard said and glanced at Hedi.

"Yeah, I am. We all know it's not so unusual to have a container come in at night, but not in this kind of weather. Then to bring seven men in, at least one of them armed, looks very bad to me. And, before you ask, they're not the police."

Martin glanced at Hedi. "Quite sure of this?"

"Yes." she responded shortly. "If they had been Coast Guard or even police on duty they would have been in uniform."

"Wonder what's going on?" Leonard asked rhetorically.

"Dunno, but I think Daryl is up to something. It was only him and his trolls out there tonight."

"No sign of Skillet and his gang?" Martin asked.

"No, I don't think Skillet knows about this caper or whatever it is."

Good, I hope not, because I like Skillet. He's good about it when we're down on the pipe," Martin said.

"Down on the pipe?" Hedi asked.

"Yep, we're the guys who go down and position the sled over the pipe when it's time to go to work. Dangerous as hell sometimes, because you can't see your hand in front of your face, let alone this whopping lump of iron hanging over your head," Martin told her.

"Sounds like dangerous work," she said.

"Oh, my God! You have no idea how dangerous! We lose

fingers all the time!" Leonard waved two fingers at Patrick, pretending to be missing the other three. It looked suspiciously like the universal British V sign to him.

"They're divers, and full of sh— too," he said by way of explanation, followed by a grin.

"Coffee?" Martin asked.

"Yes, please," Hedi said.

"You don't know what you've just asked for," Patrick sighed.

"OK, OK, don't get rude about our coffee or you won't be re-invited. Lenny here doesn't like you much for that Vicks trick anyway. I heard all about that performance. No way to treat a friend," Martin said.

"Sorry, Lenny, but you did walk into that one with both eyes open, mate," Patrick grinned. "Their coffee is awful but... Listen guys, can you keep her here for a while, with the doors shut and the lights out, while I check on something? Hedi, can you please explain what we think they're up to while I'm away?"

"Yes I... I'll try to."

She pushed a strand of her copper colored hair out of the way with slim fingers. He liked what he saw.

"Don't worry about these guys, your honor is safe with them. The two in the decompression tank over there are going to get married. This one," he indicated Martin, "has a running affair with ships' bottoms, he spent his entire military career looking up at them. And as for the Canuck," he pointed at Leonard, "he's deep into Vicks."

"Oi! He lies like cheap Chinese watch!" Martin said, pretending to sound indignant spreading his hands with a look of injured innocence on his face. "I wouldn't trust that fella with me granny!"

"You never had one," Patrick said, but then said soberly, "No one needs to know she's here, Marti. It's that serious. Remember the trolls? Good idea for all of you to get some sleep. We might not get much tomorrow. And lock your door."

Martin nodded, as did Leonard, and Patrick slipped out of the door into the night.

As he left he heard Hedi ask, "Who *are* you people?"

"Have you got a gun?" Martin asked her. Patrick moved off

into the shadows feeling better, Martin was taking him seriously. He didn't hear her response.

*****

Patrick made his way down the port side-stairs to the second level, where the pumps were located, and saw Joel and Alistair hunched over some diagrams near one of the pump engines. Neither of them noticed him, and he guessed that they weren't aware of the nocturnal goings on above deck.

He hurried along the corridor to the starboard aft winch room where it had all started. The pump engines, which normally ran at full power while they were on the pipe, were silent. The only sound came from the distant roar of the generators, which had decided for the time being not to go offline and plunge the barge into darkness.

He encountered no one along the way as he made his way up the next set of stairs, which would lead him to the cabins. He opened the steel door carefully and peered out along the corridor.

It wouldn't be a good idea to be caught skulking, he decided. He was, after all, the engineer on the vessel and had legitimate access to every single nook and cranny on the barge. His curiosity nagged at him to go and find out who had come aboard, but he knew it would incur the suspicion of Daryl and the trolls if he were to appear on the bridge right in the middle of Joel's shift. He was supposed to be tucked up in bed.

He opened the door wide and walked through; after closing it, he walked casually down the corridor as though heading for his own cabin, which was located close to the barge hospital. All was quiet, so he assumed the visitors were still on the bridge.

He was about to check on Erland when he heard voices in the stair well above him. There was just enough time to move to the very end of the corridor and get out of sight. He peered around the corner and saw Ryan arrive, followed by several men he'd never seen before. He guessed these were the visitors. Even in this light they looked like hard cases. Larry trailed behind them looking shaky. Probably needed a hit, Patrick decided unkindly.

They walked past the two police cabins, but as they did, Larry indicated Hedi's. He said something and there were grins and snickers from the men. He heard the words, "Not going anywhere, can deal with them tomorrow."

Patrick knew he'd made the right decision to stop Hedi from going back to her cabin. The men continued along the corridor to the vacant captain and chief engineer's cabins. "Y'all can sleep in here, gents. Your bags are already in the cabins," Ryan said. They grunted good night, disappeared into the rooms, and closed the doors in the two rigger's faces. The two men began to walk back toward Patrick. He had no choice but to vanish into his own cabin and listen to them going by. He was relieved there wasn't another party in his cabin; he needed sleep badly.

****

When Patrick had gone, Hedi examined the two men who sat facing her with mugs of coffee in their hands. Both were strong men who regarded her back with frank approval.

"So you are divers?" she asked as she smoothed her hair and adjusted the pony tail.

"Yup, we are," Martin said, "and despite what that bigoted sod Pat may have told you, we're quite good at what we do."

"He said you liked looking at ship's... bottoms?" she asked, keeping her face straight.

"His sort are envious of our sort. We're the elite of the elite and he's just jealous, is all."

She smiled. "How long have you known each other? I think he trusts you, even though you insult each other."

Martin and Leonard grinned. "Yeah, I suppose that's right. He's all right, is Pat." Leonard said. "He did some hard time in the Middle East a while ago. Him and Martin were in Ireland together, and Martin and I have been diving for about four years now."

"He's all right, Hedi," Martin chimed in. "Pat keeps to himself most of the time. Bit morose, something went very bad over there somewhere. After he left he went to college, and now he's here. Not much to tell beyond that."

Hedi was certain there was probably a lot to tell, but she refrained from pressing.

James Boschert

"Why did you ask if I have a gun?" she asked Martin to change the subject.

"Because if Pat says there's a problem out there, then there is one, and it's always good to know where all the weapons are. You're a policeman, er, woman, and if you're in the Danish police then you possess a weapon, right?"

She patted her side to indicate she was armed.

"What kind is it?" Leonard asked.

"H&K 9mm, and yes I do know how to shoot. Were you also in the army?" she asked.

"Yeah, some time ago. Lenny here was in the Canadian army, Special Forces, and I was in the British army."

"You're here to investigate the death, right?" Leonard asked her and hunched his broad shoulders under the red check flannel shirt he wore.

"Yes. It's still in the early stages."

"Pat doesn't think it was an accident," Martin said, watching her.

She didn't mind the scrutiny. Somehow in the last half hour she had begun to trust these odd people.

"We have to wait before we make that decision, but it would be nice to be able to eliminate some people from the list of potential suspects." She gave them an arched look.

"You mean us? Where we were when it happened?" Martin asked with a grin.

"It would help to know," she responded with a smile, then a grimace. "Ugh, your friend is right! This coffee is really terrible; don't you know that?"

"I won't take offense at your remark, young lady, but know that it wounds me deeply," Martin said, pretending to be hurt. "We were both down on the pipe that day because we had some problems with the sled and had to go down and fix it. Some trouble with the sensors, if I recall. Skillet was on the bridge at the time."

"There are two other divers, no?"

"Mike and Hansen" Martin jerked his thumb behind him. "They're in decompression right now. Both were working the gas system to keep us going down there as it was our turn. They wouldn't have had the time to go off and do anything that daft," Martin told her.

"Did you two know Charlie?" she asked.

"Oh, yeah, but not more than a nodding acquaintance. He was one of the deck riggers in charge of a gang of Filipinos."

"He wasn't too friendly. Came from Louisiana and called himself a Cajun," Leonard said. "His French was terrible. At least, Patrick says so."

Hedi bit back a smile. "Did he drink? What made him unfriendly?"

The two men exchanged a glance. "Everyone on this barge drinks like a fish, Hedi. We divers can't unless the barge is off the line for a couple of days. Most smoke pot, at some time or another. Some even try Vicks," Martin said with a grin at Leonard, who scowled.

"I think he was on the powder. Rumor had it, in this ship full of rumors, several of the anchor control men were on the white stuff," Leonard said.

"You mean, coke, heroin?" she asked.

"Yeah, I think so. If he was mainlining you'd find out fast enough." Leonard pointed to the inside of his arm. "Otherwise the coroner will uncover it, won't he?"

"I should arrest everyone on this ship!" she said with a wan smile.

"Ooooh hoo, yes, please!" Leonard leered. "Cuff me now, Miss!"

"Shaddap, you nit wit," Martin said to him. "You must be tired, Miss Hedi?"

She nodded, yawned, and glanced at her watch. It was well past two in the morning. "Patrick said I should stay here."

Yeah, I think he's probably right to be careful." Leonard said.

"Can I sleep somewhere? It's been a long day."

"Oh, yeah, sure," Leonard said. "Er, it isn't very tidy, but you'll be left alone."

"We should check our inventory of useful weapons, Lenny," said Martin matter-of-factly, after Leonard came back from showing Hedi into the cabin's back room.

Leonard nodded soberly, "Yeah. All I have is a big knife. Better tell those two in the tank as well, so there are no surprises. They're due out in an hour. Might want to check out the portable radios, too. "

"Tell them not to come out bollock naked like they usually do, we have a lady with us right now," Martin said, while he stacked some loose Playboy and Penthouse magazines and slipped them under a trash bag in the corner.

Chapter 14

Visitors

Donald and his men followed the big Americans, who had introduced themselves as Larry and Ryan, as they headed down the stairs from the windy, rain soaked deck above. The sudden warmth of the interior of the barge was welcome after the cold, wet ride on the tug. The excitement of the encounter with the police boat had worn off and he felt tired. His companions also seemed glad to be out of the foul weather.

They were led along a quiet corridor with cabins on the right hand side. Larry pointed to one of the first in the line and told him the police were in there. Donald registered this with keen interest. That was a problem they'd have to deal with sooner rather than later.

Larry opened the fifth door along and stood back to wave them in.

"This will take two of y'all, and the next one to the left will take three," he said. "You can have this one here, boss. Ya'll make yourselves comfortable. Ryan, go and get some coffee, would ya?"

Ryan nodded and left the men to enter their cabins. The two Danish men, Toke and Willie, took the next door cabin. Donald took the first with Hans as company, and the three Brits took the last one along the line.

Donald shrugged out of the bright yellow all-weather jacket and handed it to Hans, who hung it along with his own on a hook on the back of the door.

Larry was gone a few minutes but soon returned with a man whom Donald recognized.

"Hi, Daryl," he said. He didn't offer to shake hands but motioned to Daryl to take a seat and watched as Larry left. Hans stayed, as he was part of the Danish group Charlie had commissioned to help with the operation.

"Can't say I'm happy to see y'all," Daryl said and moved the wad of tobacco around in his mouth. "I sent a message back to Esbjerg asking you to stay there. We have a problem on board."

"Firstly, why are the Police on this ship?" Donald interrupted him.

"That's what I mean. 'Cause we had an accident and they came out to investigate it. I tried to tell those pricks in Esbjerg, but they told me you was on your way. The police have told me we have to go into port for further investigation."

"What do you mean by investigation? Why do the police need to be here at all?" Donald demanded.

"'Cause the man died. They told me they had to have a full investigation and the only way they could do that was to have us back in port."

"How the hell did this happen?" Donald said.

"Charlie threatened to rat on us unless he got a larger share," Daryl told him.

"Are we going back to port now?" Hans asked. He sounded very concerned.

"Na, I had to pull up off the pipe 'cause the weather's too bad, but we're just going to cruise around until it blows over, and then we go back on the pipe."

"What about the cops? Didn't you just tell me that they had ordered you back to port?"

"I'm delaying until we have the cargo on its way. Should be soon, right? You promised me it wouldn't be on board for long."

"I need to get to a radio as soon as possible and tell them to get going. It will take them about six hours to get here from what Hans here told me," Donald said with a glance at Hans, who nodded his head. He was a large man who kept in shape and had his light blonde hair bound up in a pony tail that made him look even more rugged. Donald figured the man could handle himself; at least he gave that impression.

Daryl looked from one to the other. "OK, I'll take you up to the radio room now. I've got our latest coordinates. Let's get this done and then you all can go to your bunks. I'm still on shift."

He led the way up to the radio room and asked Hamesh, who stood in for Stanley on the night shift, if the radio worked.

"Yeah, kinda, Daryl. What do you need?" Hamesh had been nodding off, but he came wide awake when he saw the men behind Daryl.

"Get us started with this phone number, Hamesh," Daryl said, handing him a piece of paper, "and then skedaddle while we make the call. I'll take the cost, put it on my account."

Hamesh wrote the number down on his pad and began the process of contacting the people in the UK who acted as the exchange for calls from the sea. Within a few minutes they had a phone ringing and soon a sleepy voice answered.

"Call from the Barge *Cherokee*, North Sea," the operator said.

"OK, thanks," the voice said.

Hamesh left and Donald took the seat while Daryl and Hans stood by.

"Hello, Stuart? It's Don," he said.

"Hey, Don, what's up? D'you know what time it is?" the voice was querulous.

"I don't care what time it is; you have work to do, Stuart, remember?" Donald said. The tone of his voice, even on the radio, brooked no more complaints.

"OK, Don, OK. What's the news?" Stuart responded making more of an effort to sound accommodating.

"News is we have a location. Here are the coordinates." Donald read out the numbers that indicated their position. "Get yourself out here ASAP, the weather is closing in and I'd like to have the transfer complete before it really gets going."

"It's gale force ten to eleven out there right now, Don," Stuart said.

"You bet it is, but it's nothing compared to what kind of gale will come your way if you don't get going, mate," Donald said.

There was a long silence.

"OK, Don, we're on our way. I'll call in when we're near the location. I need frequencies."

Donald looked up at Daryl, who wrote down two of the standard frequencies the barge people listened to. He gave them to Stuart and shut the conversation down with a warning.

"Remember, Stuart. Be here on time. This is important. No cock ups and no excuses."

Donald turned to Daryl and said, "He'll be here, just make sure we are, too."

He yawned and stretched his arms. "I'm tired. Let's go below. There's one last thing we need to talk about."

They trooped back into his cabin where someone, probably Larry, had left a bottle of bourbon on the table with some stacked plastic cups.

"Nice hospitality!" Hans said as he grabbed a cup.

When they were seated Donald squinted at Daryl. "The cops here are a liability."

Daryl spat his tobacco into one cup and reached for the other, which was half full of bourbon, and took a swig.

"What d'you mean, Don?"

"We can't have them poking around the ship while we're waiting for the ride, now can we?"

Daryl was nervous. "We can keep them occupied with their enquiry, Don. No need for them to know what else is going on."

"And when the other ship comes by to pick up the goods? Don't you think they'll be suspicious? They're might notice our people, who weren't here when they arrived. All sorts of things can go wrong when cops are about, Daryl."

"We have stuff come and go all the time. They wouldn't know the difference, Don. What have you got in mind anyway?"

Donald sent a look at Hans, who shrugged. "We were chased by the cops when we left Esbjerg, Daryl."

"You were *what*?" he gargled on his bourbon he was so surprised.

"A ship load of cops chased us and stopped us. You wouldn't

know anything about that, would you, mate?" Donald spoke the words softly, but there was a menace in them that made Daryl flinch.

"Jesus, Don! How could I? We were here with our own problems. How the hell did they know to follow you?"

Donald watched him hard and didn't detect any guilt, so he let it rest for the moment, but he couldn't resist telling him the outcome of their meeting with the Coast Guard.

Before Daryl could ask he said, "Do you know what happened when they stopped us?"

Daryl shook his head and his jowls wobbled as he did. He looked scared.

"We took them down, Daryl. Every last one of them, and blew their boat up. You should have seen the explosion. Like a Guy Fawkes night." He chuckled and took a deep sip of his bourbon.

Daryl gasped. "Jesus Christ!" he said in a horrified whispered. "You killed them all?"

Hans chuckled, "It was like a commando raid. Went like clockwork. He's good!" He jerked his thumb at Donald, who smiled. It was a smile that terrified Daryl.

"You never told me there would be killings," Daryl mumbled and tried not to look at Donald.

"So you see, Daryl, me old mate, those cops knew something and might have been coming here to find out more. I can't take the risk of having these two finding out anything either."

"What... what are you going to do?" Daryl asked, but he could guess.

"No choice. Leave it to me though, you can go back to whatever it is you do up there on the bridge. Me and Hans will deal with it. No one'll know and we can all get on with the operation."

He watched fear and uncertainty switch back and forth on Daryl's face.

"You're in this up to your neck now. You'd better get used to it and work with me. Now get the fuck out of the cabin; we want to get some shut eye."

Daryl shambled off without a word.

When he had gone, Hans turned to Donald and said, "You

trust him? He might go to the police yet."

"Nah, I don't trust him, but he won't dare go to the police. Of that I'm certain. But then I don't trust anyone, not even you." He clapped a hand on Hans' shoulder.

"Bring your shooter, let's get on with it." He led the way out and down to the last cabin on their left.

Donald knocked gently on the door but got no response. He tried a little harder and tested the door knob. It gave and they were in the room within a second. The lights were still on, but there was no one in the main room. With a finger to his lips Donald crept over to the curtained alcove and peered in. He glanced back at Hans and nodded. Hans stepped over to the door and locked it. He waited while Donald disappeared into the back cabin where the bunks were located. There was a brief scuffle and a dull, crunching sound. A few minutes later Donald backed out of the alcove.

He nodded to Hans, who opened the door, and they slipped out. Hans demonstrated that the door was now locked. Donald nodded his head approvingly. They moved to the next cabin where the girl was located.

Once again the door wasn't locked and they slid in without a sound. The main cabin area was in darkness, but a light was on in the alcove above a bunk. Donald searched the alcove thoroughly, even the toilet, but this time he backed out with a puzzled expression on his face. He shook his head at the enquiring look Hans gave him.

"Nobody here!" Donald whispered. He indicated the bunk, which someone had recently slept in.

"Shit! We'd better get out then. We can deal with her tomorrow. I'd like to do the dealing, too," Hans said with a leer.

The two men exited and returned to their cabin, where they went to bed. Donald spent some time wondering where the policewoman might be at a time like this before he fell asleep.

*****

Daryl summoned his men to his cabin as dawn was about to appear in the east. Ryan had to stay on the bridge to remain in contact with the tug boat captains, who were both complaining about the fact that they needed fuel.

When the other two, Richards and Larry, came in, they were alarmed by the state of their super.

Daryl was no longer the self confident boss of a large construction barge with senior responsibility, instead he was haggard and pale.

"What's up, boss? You look like you're comin' down with somethin'," Larry asked him. Richards, who had a good idea as to why Daryl was this way, said nothing. He took a swig straight from the open bottle of bourbon and prepared a wad of tobacco for himself while Daryl pulled himself together.

"You've met them now, so Ah won't waste your time boys. Them's real dangerous folks. They just told me they killed the entire crew of a po'lice boat that came after them when they was on their way out here."

"Oh, mah Lord!" Richards gasped and dropped his tobacco on the floor.

"Holy shit! You mean they killed them *all*? Fuck me! How many was there?" Larry asked, squinting at him.

Richards scowled at Larry and said, "Y'all needs to keep the blasphemy down."

"How the hell would I know, you idiot?" Daryl said, ignoring Richards. "Those guys scare the heck out of me, 'specially that Brit guy!" He took another swig of bourbon.

A cold chill settled over the atmosphere in the cabin, and there was silence as all three men in the cabin realized control of the barge had spiraled out of Daryl's grip and was now firmly in the hands of a ruthless Brit who was probably mad.

"What I want to know is how did the police know to come after them?" Richards asked after a while. He didn't bother to clean up the mess on the floor; he re opened his tobacco tin and started again.

"Ah have no adea, but if those po'lice got back into the radio cabin, Hamesh or Stan would know of it. You need to ask tomorrow if they did," Daryl told Richards.

"OK, so they whacked a bunch of po'lice," Larry said. "That

means no cops coming here to bother us, don't it, boss?"

"They want to take care of the ones we have on board," Daryl whispered, as though the walls had ears.

Both the other men stopped what they were doing and stared at him.

Richards was the first to recover. "Perhaps," he said slowly, "that's for the best, boss. We can't afford loose ends. Not with this much at stake. Ah know we'll pay for this sometime, though."

"Shaddup, Richie. Ah don't want none of that holy shit from you right now!" Daryl said.

"Yeah, but he's right, boss." Larry said. "About there bein' too much at stake here, I mean. Remember Charlie? He was askin' for too much or he'd go tell."

"All the same, I should have overruled that asshole Hamesh and Gey'om, and not permitted them to call the accident in to the god damned police," Daryl said. "I should have waited until this was all over."

"You didn't have much choice, boss. Besides it was Roger who called it in, not you. You couldn't say no now, could you? They would have thought it pretty strange if you had. They was within their jurisdiction to notify the company and the po'lice at a minimum," Larry told him.

"Ah know, Larry, but you *should* have done a better job of gettin' Charlie out of sight. Then we wouldn't be in this situation."

Larry managed to appear indignant and defensive at the same time. "How was we to know that fuckin' engineer would show up, Boss?"

"You two idiots were hiding in the other room when he left but still you couldn't git the body out the way and overboard!" Richards snarled at him.

Larry, who was desperate for a snort of coke to help him through the rest of the shift, regarded Richards with active dislike.

"There wasn't no time. Ryan'll tell you the same. Listen, boss, Ah did as I was told, but we were nearly caught when Pat showed up. We had to get out of there in a hurry. Pat came back with Skillet real quick, and there was *nothing* we could do after that." Larry, glowered at Richards from under his brows.

Daryl regarded Larry with jaundiced eyes. "Well, now the

po'lice are here. But there are only two of them. We'll have to keep them out of the way until this job is taken care of. Ah just don't like the idea of whacking them, which is what that crazy Brit wants to do."

"Nor me, but if that's what we have to do then so be it. This is going to make us all rich. We can get away from all this shit, and I for one can't wait," Richards said as he closed the lid of his tobacco tin.

Daryl lumbered to his feet. "Rich, you need to get Virgil and Bobby up to speed with this situation."

Richards nodded.

"Did you two clowns have the sense to get rid of the weapon? Tell me you did that at least, Larry," Daryl said to the rigger.

"I dumped it over board soon as we got onto the deck," Larry assured him.

"No one saw you?" Richards asked.

"Sure of it, boss."

Chapter 15

The Flying Dutchman

Patrick woke when Joel came into his cabin and pulled the curtains of his bunk aside.

"Hey, Pat. It's time to get up and greet the bright sunny day with all your heart!"

"Fuck off, Joel. Leave me alone."

He sensed the sea outside must have become worse, as he heard a creaking sound and there was a mild roll to the barge.

"The radio's misbehaving again, me old mate, and Alistair and I have found the problem with pump number six."

"Bravo for you." He swung his legs off the bunk and stood up.

"What's that for?" Joel pointed at the knife on his belt.

"Oh, that's nothing. I just forgot to take it off last night."

"Are you expecting any trouble, Pat? You've been acting a little strange since you found Charlie."

"No, but if I am I'll let you know, Joel." He left it at that and wore the knife under his overalls when he left for breakfast.

"Hey, be careful on the top deck, Pat. The sea's pretty bad today, and my guess is it's going to get worse," Joel called after him.

He found Skillet in the galley as well as Mike, one of the divers, who sidled up to him while he was in line for an omelette. "Hey, Pat, I'm getting some breakfast for the... you know," he said.

Force 12 in German Bight

Patrick nodded. "Good, but don't make it too obvious."

He watched while Mike took a pile of toast and stacked jam, several eggs, and bacon on a huge plate, along with enough peanut butter to clog an elephant's arteries. That done, he disappeared.

"That Mikey, is he smoking pot or something? Looks like he's got the munchies. If we have to dive he's not going down, that's for sure," Skillet said to Patrick when he sat down alongside him at a deserted table. They had their backs to the rest of the room, which wasn't what Patrick normally did, but this time it suited him well enough.

"Hey, you got a minute?" he asked.

"Yeah, what's up?"

"Skillet, level with me now, will you?"

Skillet frowned and stared sideways at Patrick.

"Always have, haven't we? What's going on, Pat? You don't seem like a happy camper. Homesick already?" Skillet grinned.

"Did you know about the shipment that came in last night?" Patrick said, ignoring his friend's friendly gibe.

Skillet turned to face Patrick. "What's that? A shipment came in? When?"

"About one am. A half container."

"You serious, Pat, or have you been snorting somethin', too? God knows there's enough of the stuff around. Just ask that junkie, Larry."

"No, Skillet, I'm not, and again I'm asking you."

"No, I do not, and I will be asking Daryl what the fuck is going on when Ah have finished breakfast."

"I'd be careful about doing that. It isn't so much the container, although it's a bit unusual. That's not what's bothering me. There are seven men on this barge who are armed, and not just with pistols. They came with it." He talked in a low voice to avoid being overheard by others at the table behind them.

Skillet went very still for a moment, his head lowered as he regarded Patrick out of the corner of his narrowed eyes.

"You look serious, Pat. Are they more cops?" he asked.

"I was with the girl last night, and no, not like that." He grinned. "She came on deck just as the boat arrived and we

142

watched it together. She's quite sure they're not the cops, and I verified it later last night. They're in the captain's cabins right now, along the starboard side, right next to the police quarters."

"Fuck!" Skillet murmured. "So there's more to this than just Charlie, it would seem."

"We're both meant to be on duty, so we can go anywhere we like. But I'm really worried about the other cop," Patrick told him.

"Why's that?" Skillet said and then, "Oh, yeah. If they're goons and run into the police it could be a problem."

"Only him, the girl is elsewhere. Got her stashed in a safe place. Seemed crazy to let her go back to her cabin with those guys right next door. If they're baddies it could go badly."

Skillet stared at him. "You've been busy, Pat. But we can't just make the cops disappear; they'll wonder what's going on and get suspicious. Could make things worse. Wonder what the hell is going on?"

Patrick yawned. "I think we need to alert him at least, don't you?"

"Yeah, we can do that, but then I have to get onto the bridge. Richie is like a bitch on the rags when it's time to change over. Let's go."

They got up, sauntered out of the galley, and made their way to the starboard corridor where the Inspector's cabin, the last in the row, was located.

Skillet knocked gently on the door and tried the handle. There was no reply so he tried again, and both men watched the other cabin doors to see if they'd woken anyone else. The corridor was deserted. Skillet glanced at Patrick, who shrugged, and then Skillet turned the handle and put his shoulder to the door. It was a flimsy cabin door, made of plywood, and the lock gave easily and they stumbled in. Patrick hit the switch near the door and they looked around. He shut the door carefully after them.

"Try the bunk section," Skillet said.

They moved quietly to the area and pulled the curtain back to expose the two bunks behind.

Both stared. Erland lay on the lower bed bunk fully clothed, sprawled on his back, and with his head at an unnatural angle. His eyes were half open and his mouth gaped, and his skin was as white as the sheets on the bed.

Patrick quickly knelt and tested the neck to check for a pulse, but there was none. He looked up at Skillet and shook his head. Skillet jerked his head toward the other room. He pulled the curtain closed and they left the dead man behind.

"Neck's broken, but he'd been boozing, that's for sure," Skillet said in a whisper as he jerked his head at the half empty bottle of bourbon."

"This must have happened last night when they came aboard. A couple of those men were big lads and must have done this, although I'm not sure why just yet."

"They're the baddies sure enough, though, Pat. You were right," Skillet said.

Patrick remembered something and slipped back into the bed section. He rummaged about on the bed and then very quickly felt in the duffel bag on the floor nearby. There it was. He grabbed the hand gun in its leather holster along with the harness and slipped it into the leg pocket of his overalls before he joined Skillet in the other room.

"What kept you?" Skillet asked.

"I was checking to see, er... if I could tell when he died. I think it was about five hours ago."

"Huh, did you get his gun?" Skillet grinned. "I know you, Pat."

Patrick had the grace to grin back. "Yeah, thought it might be useful. Do you have any iron?"

"Just so happens..." Skillet said. "Small 38 automatic."

"How in the hell did you manage to smuggle that on board, Skillet?" Patrick asked, genuinely surprised.

"Don't ask an' I won't lie. Ah'm from Texas, buddy. Feel naked without one."

Patrick chuckled. "We have to leave him here and get out. Got to behave as though nothing's happened and find out what the hell's going on," he said.

"You have to get that radio going, Pat; I think we're going to need it."

They cautiously opened the door and looked out. No one was

around, so they eased out and closed the door behind them. It shut, but not as well as it might have had they not broken it when they went in.

Together they walked up the stairs toward the bridge. There were few people about, as they weren't on the pipe but on tow, which was one of those times when the riggers went to their cabins and either partied, watched movies by the dozen, or simply went to sleep.

"You sure the girl is OK, Pat?" Skillet asked him as they came level with the radio room.

"For the moment, but I don't know for how long," Patrick murmured as he turned into the doorway. Skillet carried on up to change out with Richards on the Bridge.

*****

"Where the fuck have you been, Pat? I've been calling for you!"

"Good morning to you, too, Stan. What's your problem now?" Patrick said as he walked in and closed the door.

He glanced out of the window. It was the first time this morning he'd had a chance to see out, as the only windows that gave a view outside the ship were in the bridge structure and started with the radio room.

The sea was very agitated, with spume coming off the tops of the waves and flying high, indicating a very strong wind. He estimated the crests were about fifteen to twenty feet, and in some cases more. He always found it odd the barge never seemed to feel the sea very much, even up to this level. Other ships would be rolling and pitching with half the crew sick as dogs.

"Did you get the forecast, Stan?"

"No, and I need it badly."

"OK, OK, keep your shirt on. I'll see what I can do."

In fact there was not much he had to do other than ask Stan to find the frequency and lock it manually while up in the cabin.

"Let's hear the news then," he said as he clambered down.

"I don't know how you do it, Pat. Joel can't fix that shit, nor can Johnny. OK, here we go."

Force 12 in German Bight

The clock was about to turn seven, so Stan tuned in to the shipping news, and the welcome sound of the announcer for BBC 4 filled the room.

He worked his way around the grid of locations in the area around the United Kingdom and the European coastlines, until he came to those that mattered to the two men listening. The names were Fisher, Dogger, Forties and German Bight.

Their vessel was in the middle of German Bight, but the information from the other three areas, which were all to the north and west of them, was just as important.

This morning it was all bad news.

"Forties: gale warning issued. Southwesterly force ten going to force eleven later," the voice said.

"Wind: south ten to eleven, backing ten to severe storm eleven, perhaps severe gale eleven later in the day. Seas: rough with waves in excess of forty feet. Rain: squalls and storms. Visibility: low to poor."

Patrick and Stan exchanged looks and bent their heads to listen to the rest of the report. The voice continued.

"Fisher. Wind: south ten to eleven, backing ten to severe gale eleven, perhaps severe gale twelve later in the day. Seas: rough with waves in excess of forty feet or more. Rain: squalls and storms. Visibility: low to poor. German Bight. Wind: south nine to ten, backing ten to gale eleven, perhaps severe gale twelve later in the day. Seas: rough with waves in excess of forty-five or more. Rain: squalls and storms, possible hail. Visibility: low to poor."

The voice carried on with the forecast but the two men were no longer listening.

"Shit! This sounds really bad, Pat. I'll need to tell Roger. Those tug skippers will want to know."

"Yeah, I hope they've got everything battened down on the main deck." Patrick said.

"I've got to go upstairs and report the good news," Stan said and left.

Patrick hastily looked for the number Stan had written down for Erland the night before. It was buried under some other pieces of paper on the notebook. He wrote it down and checked the same pad for any other numbers with the same area code. There was one, so he wrote that down too. Afterward he pretended to fiddle with the dials of the radio. He noticed the system had drifted again.

Just to see what might be going on he decided to climb onto the roof of the bridge and check if there was anything loose. The only people on the bridge at this time were Skillet, Roger and Stan. The consoles were deserted because they were on tow.

Patrick peered out of the front windows, which were angled back at the base to help keep rain from obscuring the glass. There was just a spattering of rain at present. The blunt bows of the barge rose and fell with slow deliberation, smashing waves down in a billow of spray and rising again, streaming with water that swept over the front upper deck. He looked further forward along the two huge towing cables to the tugs about a quarter of a mile ahead. Large though they were, they were being tossed about by the high waves, corkscrewing their way forward.

"How fast are we going?" he asked the room in general.

Roger glanced over. "Oh, hi, Pat. Barely five knots by my reckoning. We're going to turn and head for port. This is no weather for the barge, nor the tugs. Stan just gave me the news. With force eleven or even a possible twelve we're deep in the shit if we stay out here."

"How far are we from port?" Patrick asked.

"About fifty miles or so now, I'd guess," Skillet said. He had a chart on the table which he and Roger had been looking at.

"If we can make it to the island of Fane we can shelter there and tow around till the storm blows itself out. We could be there in about six or eight hours if we go round now."

Roger spoke into his radio to the two tugs ahead of them and got a squawk in reply. Patrick noticed the two vessels began to change course in one large, slow curve.

He nodded to the men, opened the door to exit the bridge, and immediately found himself buffeted by a strong wind that howled around the bridge and tore at him as he climbed the short ladder to gain access to the top. He had to hang onto the rails tightly as he checked out the equipment. Nothing looked as though it had broken out of its multiple layers of paint for a half century, which was more or less as he'd expected. He was sure it was the paint

Force 12 in German Bight

and not the bolts that held the base of the antennae in place. While he was up there he happened to glance westward.

There was one, wide black unbroken bar of storm cloud ahead of them that looked ominous, but it wasn't so much the black menace of the storms to come that arrested him and made him squint hard. He noticed a fleck of white on the horizon. At first he dismissed it as a wave crest, but as he stared harder he realized it was something quite different.

The hair on his neck began to rise and he felt a cold chill pass through him, because what he saw was a ship. Not a modern steam ship but a sailing ship of pure white with all sails set, and it came straight at them. *Shit! The"Flying Dutchman"!*

He shivered and shook his head. "Oh God I promise I'll never fucking smoke pot again!" he swore under his breath as he shivered and watched, frozen to the rails while the apparition came closer and closer. There was no doubt it was a large, all white, three masted sailing ship with all sails set. He could see nothing on board to tell him there might be anyone on board and this scared him silly.

The ship flew towards them in eerie silence while he clutched the rails. He remembered what the legend said: The Flying Dutchman was a portent of disaster for ships and sailors who beheld it in a storm, for when they did their ship was in grave peril and would go down with all hands.

He watched, mesmerized, as the large sailing ship closed in on them. Then he began to see movement on its deck. The ship was entirely white from stem to stern, and with the white sails it looked ghostly, but the crew were ordinary men outfitted in ordinary, modern storm gear, yellow safety jackets and hats. He realized he was holding his breath and let it out in an explosive gasp. Although he'd thought he'd witnessed a deadly apparition it was a beautiful sight.

Dear God, but I must really be losing it, he thought. *That's a flicking training ship, and she's running from that black mass over there.*

The ship reminded him of one of the famous clippers that sailed the seas, famous for speed and grace. It didn't pause as it approached, but when it came within half a mile of them Patrick

148

had an idea.

He clambered down the ladder, ignoring the wind that tore at him, and rushed down the flight of stairs to the radio room. He grabbed a flashlight from a corner and ran back up. The others stood at the starboard windows and admired the magnificent apparition as it fled past their side in total silence, but he scrambled up the stairs again, laid flat on the deck, and began to flash the ship.

During his army training he'd been taught Morse code, the people who trained him had told him it was useful. On one or two occasions it had been. Now might be the time to find out if he could remember any of it. He flashed the ship going by.

"Can you see me?"

He repeated this message three times and held his breath again, wondering if they could see his flashlight at all.

Then there was a response. He had to focus, as it was rapid and indicated the user knew his business.

"We see you. What message?"

Patrick flashed back, "SOS, SOS. Bandits on board. Call Danish police Esbjerg."

He waited.

Then came a message with a frequency they wanted him to use.

"Cannot use. Danger. Contact Esbjerg police. Urgent."

Then the white ship was past and headed away from them. It was doing a good ten knots, he estimated, perhaps more.

The last message back from the ship was "Wilco." He knew it meant "Will cooperate."

He scrambled off the top of the bridge to find the others still watching the clipper's passage. Roger had his binoculars aimed at the departing ship.

"Man, Ah don't think I've ever seen such a bee'utiful sight in ma whole life. Will you look at that? Hey, Skillet, they've been signaling us. Can anyone read what they're tryin' to say?"

Stanley had watched the signal, but just as he opened his mouth to reply Skillet put a hand on his shoulder, gripped it hard, and shook his head slightly. He motioned Stanley to leave the bridge.

"No one here. I guess it might have been Morse code, but none of us know that old stuff," Skillet said with a hard look at Patrick.

Patrick walked to the top of the stairs and gave Skillet the thumbs up sign. "I'll talk to you later," he said cheerfully and disappeared downstairs.

*****

He was half way down the stairs when he heard men's voices at the base, where the corridor began. He continued down and encountered Larry and Ryan, accompanied by two men he didn't recognize.

"Hey there, Pat! What d'yer say?" Ryan called out. Larry nodded but said nothing.

"Hi, guys," Patrick said and gave them room to pass. He tried to observe the newcomers without being too obvious. The leader looked as though he could handle himself; he had heavy shoulders and was light of step with a cold, expressionless face. Patrick had met his kind before. The other was skinny by comparison but had one of those pointed faces that could produce a vicious expression. Like a rat, Patrick decided; he also had a terrible acne problem that had followed him into his late twenties. There were red volcanoes all over his face. Patrick, who had a habit of giving simple labels to people he didn't like, chose to call him Zitty.

"Hey, Pat, you haven't seen the police girl, have ya?" Ryan asked casually.

Patrick took his gaze off the zitty man and looked puzzled. "Nah, probably too early for them right now. Want me to bring them breakfast in bed?"

"Prick," Ryan muttered under his breath. "Well, if you see the girl, tell her Daryl wants to see her about somethin'," he told Patrick.

"Sure, I bet I'll bump into them down in the engine rooms. It's just the place to find a policeman," Patrick said.

"Ship's engineer. Real smart ass. He's a Brit, too," Larry said to the larger man, who stared at Patrick as he went by. No words, just a nod, and then he was past.

James Boschert

Patrick looked back with a bland expression on his face, hoping the man wouldn't see how intensely Patrick was evaluating him. He was left with the impression this man was a hard case, as was his companion, and they appeared to be tough. Patrick watched them climb the stairs and wondered what Skillet would make of them, now he knew more about the situation. He hurried off towards the divers' hut at the back of the barge.

He made the top of the stairs that led out onto the rear of the port side of the barge and paused at the opening onto the deck, just inside the combing. The wind keened through the cables and pipes overhead, playing them like a giant's hand on a diabolical harp. The waves were now breaking level with the main deck,leaving hissing ripples of water that washed over his boots where he stepped.

It was as though the storm showing its hand slowly, biding its time, but was certainly about to demonstrate its awesome power. He watched the water for a few seconds, noting that he could step off the railing right into the heaving, green sea. Then the barge dipped at the front end and he felt himself being lifted away from the roiling waters as though on a see saw. He clutched at a rail on the side of the divers' hut. Then the water on deck changed direction and swept back towards the bows, surging past the anchors and buoys. Far down the length of the barge he saw the bows buried in the mass of a wave.

The cabin where the divers were housed groaned on its mountings. That sound boded ill for the structure if things got much worse. They might have to find other accommodations.

Within seconds he'd crossed the short distance to the cabin door. He banged urgently. Martin opened the door, which the wind immediately tried to pull off its hinges.

"Get in here, Patrick, quick!" Martin yelled as he hung onto it.

Patrick dived in and Martin hauled the door shut with both hands before he turned and greeted him.

"What? The land lubber doesn't like a little bad weather?" he joked, but then he noticed Patrick's expression.

"OK, what's up out there, Pat?" he asked, and indicated the coffee pot and a mug.

"Where is she?" Patrick asked while he helped himself to the

151

noxious brew and checked the room. Hedi wasn't present, but Mike and Hansen were seated at the table playing cards.

"I'll get her," Mike said. "She just went back there." He jerked his thumb towards the back of the cabin.

"Hold on a minute, guys," Patrick said in a low voice and waved Mike back. "You need to know something, and I have to tell you quickly, while she's out."

He explained what Skillet and he had found in the police inspector's cabin. They looked stunned, all except Martin, who nodded slowly and said, "So it looks like they're going to try and take over the ship. I wonder what the hell is in that container. Did you get a look at any of them?"

"Yeah, one of them is a serious hard case. Ryan said he was a Brit. The other got his face from an Indonesian island. More volcanoes on it than anyone should have. I think he's a Danish baddy."

Just at that moment Hedi came in, looking as though she had slept in her clothes. Her reddish hair was unbrushed, but Patrick still liked what he saw.

"What's this about the container?" she asked. Her eyes landed on Patrick and she smiled. He felt warm and caught himself smiling back like an idiot.

"Hi, Hedi, good morning. Is this gang of hoods taking care of you OK?" he asked with false cheerfulness.

"Good morning, Patrick. Yes, they've been very good to me. What can you tell me about things going on out there? I'm impatient to know, and do you know if Erland is up yet?"

The other men in the room shuffled uncomfortably. Patrick had told them, but now he hesitated. Hedi noticed. "You look worried, Patrick, what is it?"

Patrick rubbed the space between his eyebrows with the fingers of his left hand as though he was trying to wipe something off.

"Um, have a seat, Hedi." Martin said, and pulled out one of the plastic chairs.

Chapter 16

Esbjerg

Chief Inspector Kristian Vestergaard found a piece of paper on his desk the next morning from assistant Police Chief Balder.

The report was a curious one. Nothing had been heard from the Coast Guard cutter sent out to sea the night before with his police men on board. It had gone completely quiet. Normal procedures were not being observed, whereby the commander of the ship would report in on a regular basis, and even after several attempts had been made to reach them on a variety of frequencies, there was no response. The captain of the cutter was in serious trouble for not adhering to standard operating procedures.

The Assistant Chief was perturbed, as the Coast Guard were asking the police what had happened to their cutter. Why hadn't it reported in after so much time? Its time of departure was 22:30 the night before, it had still not reported in, and it was already mid morning.

"They were going out to this 'barge' thing to assist Erland Knudson, who felt he needed backup," he reminded Kristian when he walked in to ask for more news.

"Yes, that's right. Four of our men, and the crew of what, four of them on their boat? A Lieutenant Asger commanded the boat, didn't he?"

"Yes, sir."

"Keep trying to find them. We need to know if we can get

through to that vessel and find out if they have arrived."

"We can't raise the ship, sir. I've had the radio operator try to go through the UK. They tell me there's no response. They've had problems with their radio in the past."

Kristian sighed with exasperation. "Can we send out a chopper to have a look at them?"

"Not in this weather, sir. It's getting worse, too. Last night it went from a force seven to eight, and now it's going up even further. The whole of German Bight, Fisher and Dogger are under a severe storm watch with rain and low visibility right now and well into tomorrow."

"I have to know what's going on out there, Chief."

"We could send out an aircraft to find out what's happening, but it won't be able to tell us very much, sir. Other than to check whether the ship is still there or on its way back here."

"What's the Coast Guard thinking?"

'They have begun to get very worried, sir. The weather is going down the toilet and it would be risky to send out another cutter, but I suspect they would if you wanted them to."

Kristen nodded. He had an uneasy feeling about this, which only increased when a report from Interpol landed on his desk to inform him a man named Donald Saunders had landed in Esbjerg off the ferry from Harwich, England the evening before. The man was wanted by the British police for information relating to a murder, and he was possibly armed and dangerous.

A description of the car was provided. Jaguars weren't that common in Jutland or even Europe, so this one would have stood out if seen on the Autobahn, he reasoned. He stared at the artist's impression. The man had a short haircut, not quite military, and had a face like a boxer. His nose might have been broken before. The eyes were deep set under heavy brows, over high cheekbones. The mouth was a slash set in a heavy jaw. It wasn't a lot to go on.

He instructed his chief to put out a notice to the Esbjerg harbor police and widen the net to the area around the town. His jurisdiction didn't go much beyond that, but he made sure the information went out to all the neighboring stations. If someone drove the cream-colored Jaguar on the roads, he would be found easily.

James Boschert

He was contemplating lunch when his chief knocked on the door.

"A report's in from Interpol, sir. Apparently the German police have been keeping an eye on a large container truck with a trailer they think might have been carrying drugs. Heroin. Came in from Yugoslavia three days ago. It crossed the border last night into Jutland, but after that it was lost in traffic. The highway police think it was on E20 coming west because it didn't go to Copenhagen. Details here, sir. I put out an alert to our people to check for this kind of Mercedes truck and the number plate the Germans gave us, but I think the trail might have gone cold, sir."

Kristian rubbed his forehead from side to side. This whole thing was becoming complicated, and there were no answers from anywhere as yet.

It could just be a coincidence the wanted man arrived when a truck carrying drugs was suspected of being in the vicinity, but what were the odds? He went to lunch still pondering the situation.

The chief shrugged and rang up the Coast Guard to tell them a decision wasn't going to be made before two pm. He got an earful for his troubles, as they didn't want to send boats out to sea in the dark a second time.

He put the phone down with a sigh and opened the sandwich box provided by his wife. It was going to be liverwurst today, he surmised unhappily, peering into the box.

*****

Later that day a curious message arrived from the Danish naval training ship that had been working out of Esbjerg for the last year. It had just arrived within the confines of the island of Fane and the mainland, where it was relatively safe. They'd been flying back from the ferocious storms, which had beset the North Sea much earlier than normal for this time of year, when they had sailed past a large vessel accompanied by two sea going tug boats. They had tried to call the vessel and received no answer, but then something very strange had occurred. The information made Chief Inspector Balder stand up and head for his boss's office with some urgency.

155

Force 12 in German Bight

Balder walked the short distance and knocked on the door before pushing it open. Kristian Vestergaard glanced up from the papers on his desk and regarded him with a marked lack of enthusiasm. "What is it, Chief?" he said.

"You know that naval training ship we have on our books, sir?"

Kristian nodded somewhat impatiently.

"We have a message from the captain of the ship, which has just arrived. They got a message from the vessel Erland and Iversen have been on."

"Oh, what kind of message?"

"Well, sir. They were sailing past the vessel when one of the seamen up on the rigging told them there was a lamp flashing from the top of the vessel's bridge. Although the flashing lamp was very dim, it clearly spelt out the words, 'SOS, SOS. Bandits on board. Call Danish police Esbjerg.' This message was repeated several times until they responded.

"The captain of the training ship reported that they had asked for a frequency but the flashing lamp told them, "Cannot use. Danger. Contact Esbjerg police. Urgent." Here, I have it all in the message, sir." He placed the paper in front of Kristian, who now sat up and showed more interest.

"That's odd. Very odd, indeed. I presume it was in English?"

"Yes, sir."

"Have we had any signals from the vessel since I last spoke to them?"

"No, sir, and that was nearly twenty-four hours ago."

"Nothing from the police cutter we sent out there either? The sailing ship didn't mention that in passing?" Kristian was beginning to sound perturbed.

Chief Balder shifted his balance from one foot to the other uncomfortably. "No, sir, and the Coast Guard is wondering about that, too."

"They haven't heard anything either?" Kristian sounded incredulous.

"No, sir. The weather is closing in rapidly. We're hearing of a force twelve gale in our area."

"We can't send another boat out there in a force twelve, Chief!"

Kristian exclaimed. "I wonder if that message was serious?"

"It's possible, sir. In which case our people might be in danger."

"You don't have to remind me, Chief, but the weather isn't helping. Do you have anything on the driver we were searching for?"

"Ah, yes, sir. A man driving a lorry that matched our description was apprehended in Kupfermühle. You know, the German border. They searched his vehicle and the trailer but didn't find anything incriminating. They did, however, find an awful lot of cash on him, which he had a problem explaining."

"Get him back here. I don't care if they found nothing, he knows something!" Kristian said. "Get him back here," he repeated. "We need to question him. If he knows anything at all we have to hear about it. There must be something that connects some of these dots. The car showed up in the early hours from what your boys tell us, on the docks near Pier Two. Have we found out if there was a boat there yesterday?"

"Not yet, sir, but the shifts have changed and we need to find out from the records if there was a registered boat alongside last night."

"Hurry that along, will you? The British are very interested in this man."

"Yes, sir. I'll take care of it right away. What about that ship out there, sir? Everyone at the station is concerned."

"I'm well aware of that, Chief!" Vestergaard snapped. Then he rubbed his eyes and glanced up. "Sorry, Chief. I am, too. Very worried. But we're stuck for the moment, unless the Coast Guard can get a chopper out there. In a force twelve? I don't think so. It's worrying they haven't communicated with us. That's routine procedure. Won't do at all. Stay on it, please. Oh, and have we heard anything more from our English friends?"

*****

At that moment, in London, Inspector Greenfield was worrying a problem around in his mind as he sat in his damp and badly heated office.

157

Force 12 in German Bight

Why had the man called Don Saunders gone over to Denmark? The Danish police had just informed him they'd found the car parked alongside a pier named Pier Two in the harbor of Esbjerg. No one had seen the man in the town. His mind wrestled with the question of why the car was where it was.

Had Mr. Saunders left the harbor in a boat for somewhere else? There was also a cryptic message from the customs and excise in Harwich who'd been asked earlier to inform him of any untoward activity from known villains in the area.

A certain Stuart Higgins had left the harbor during the night, in a fierce gale, on his large, sea-going tug. Customs had viewed Higgins with disfavor for some time as a suspected smuggler, but so far they'd never been able to pin anything on him. Not many boats went out in a force nine with the weather deteriorating quickly, so they had pricked up their ears.

Steven couldn't put the pieces together yet, but he knew there might be a connection. For the moment he dismissed the report and focussed back on the railway murder. There was probably another man involved in the murder of the man from Yugoslavia. This kind of thing wasn't a lone gunman's gig, he reasoned. Two men with a single gun, perhaps, but not just one man. He wondered how he was going to find the other man.

Perhaps the street might know? This kind of execution was rare and might well scare some people into talking. He reached for his hat and collected Sergeant Wilson on his way out.

"Let's try Bertie again," he said as they drove to the cafe.

Both men waited in the cafe for over half an hour for Bert to arrive. The rain came down in sheets outside and the coffee in the place was horrible.

Even Toby winced as he took a sip of the brown mixture of watery coffee laced with sweetener. "Ugh, they don't pay us well enough to drink this swill, do they, sir?" he said.

"We're getting it on expenses, Toby, don't complain too much. Our Illustrious Leader was in the army, ate broken glass, and drank Ganges water for breakfast, so who are we to complain?"

Toby snickered.

"Ah, here's our man."

Bert came into the cafe and did his usual look around to check who might be there. His rheumy eyes settled on the two men in a booth well away from the window, and he shuffled towards them warily.

"'Ello, Bert. Nice day for a visit," Steven said.

"If you say so, guv," Bert replied. He was clearly unhappy at having been called in without much notice.

"So, Bert. You know what happened to Nigel, right?" Steven said in a low voice.

Bert looked frightened. "Yeah, I heard."

"What's the word out there, Bert? This isn't normal. Did Nigel piss off the big boys?"

Bert hunched deeper into his worn rain coat. He smelled of fish and chips and other less definable odors. The fug inside the cafe had misted up the glass windows. Steven found he wanted some fresh air.

"Nigel was topped for fucking up. From what I could tell, anyway," Bert said.

"He fucked up what? He wasn't alone, Bert, now was he? We both know what he fucked up, don't we? The job at the railway station, right?"

Bert's features became shifty. A ten pound note crossed the table and vanished into his raincoat.

"I want more, Bert. Something is going down, my nose tells me so, but I need more from the street."

"Dunno much more, guv," Bert said. "But 'is mate should have gone to ground after this one."

"His mate? What do you mean, Bert? Who's his mate and where can we find 'im?" Toby asked. His voice was stern.

Bert looked very unhappy. "Nigel used to hang out with a skinny guy called Pete, not sure of his surname. Pete's disappeared since Nigel got topped."

"Really? And where do you think we can find him?"

"No idea, guv." A stubborn expression stayed on Bert's unshaven face.

Steven leaned across the table and tapped Bert on his chest. "Now you listen to me, Bertie. I need help and I need it fast. I don't like murders like this in or around my bailiwick. The Yard is

Force 12 in German Bight

involved now, and you know how heavy they can get. If they get a whiff of you, you'll be grilled till you don't know what time of day it is. Wouldn't you prefer to talk to me and Toby here?"

Bert sagged. "Yeah, well, the last time I saw Pete he was at the Gyngleboy pub. He was with that Don fella. I wasn't huntin' for anything, I just noticed them. Maybe he's back there; one of the bar girls was talking to 'im like he was the best thing since sliced bread. Gawd knows why."

"What does she look like? Does she have a name?" Toby asked.

"Yeah... Gretchen, I think. Can I go now?"

"Yeah, bugger off, but stay available," Steven said.

After Bert had shambled off, Toby commented, "Not a lot to go on there, guv."

"No, but it's all we have. Certain people are markers and they need to be used effectively. They give off hints we need to listen to, Toby. Bert is one of them. Well... It's late enough, let's go there now and see if we can't get Gretchen to tell us anything."

The Gynglboy pub turned out to be a pretty decent place on the corner of Spring Street. Steven still felt conspicuous in his standard grey raincoat and cap, which he'd substituted for his walker's hat. This was a working man's pub and many a suspicious eye roved his way as he walked to the bar, where he ordered a pint from a blonde slip of a girl.

Toby joined him after checking out the lounge bar. He shook his head when he sidled up to Steven. "I suspect I'll have met this boy before, guv," he murmured. "Nothing here as yet, though."

Steven leaned over the bar as the girl went by. "Your name Gretchen by any chance?"

She glanced at him suspiciously. "Who's asking? Perhaps it is."

Steven took a chance. "Looking for Pete; I hear you're his squeeze," he said.

The girl stopped in her tracks and stared, and there was real fear in her eyes, but her gaze was not at the two men at the bar. Toby and Steven whirled just in time to see a slim man get up and make for the entrance of the pub. He stared at the girl, they exchanged a meaningful glance and then he moved swiftly.

Toby was the first to react. He dove after the man and slammed out of the doorway with Steven right behind him. The

160

man sprinted down the road as fast as he could go on the wet road, with Toby right behind him yelling, "Police, stop! Police, stop, you bugger!"

Steven made a mental note to talk about his sergeant's unsuitable language next time they were in the office.

Toby was a fit man, who played rugby for the local club, and he quickly gained on the slimmer but less speedy quarry. They collided in a rugby tackle just in front of a bus stop where people were waiting. They smashed into a group of young people headed out for the evening and some of the older generation who were going home, taking several of the men and women down with them in a sprawling, undignified heap. There were yells of surprise and anger from everyone at the sudden shock to their lives.

Steven arrived just in time to sort out the tangle of angry and indignant people, who were loud in voicing their disapproval of wet roads, scrimmages, and the police in particular. Their clothing was now wet and filthy from the roadway.

"Sorry, Police. Sorry... sorry." He flashed his badge and backed away, leaving the people to commiserate with one another and glare at them.

"Bloody cops! Throwin' their weight around all the time!" Some one grumbled.

Toby had regained his feet and now had a firm grip on their quarry, whom he hauled to his feet.

Steven apologized to all and sundry again and joined Toby as he rammed his victim up against the black cast iron railings behind the bus stop. A pair of hand cuffs appeared like magic and snapped into place over their man's wrists.

"You just ruined my best trousers, mate," Toby said as he turned the man around and they got a good look at him in the lamplight.

"Your name Pete?" Steven asked.

"Wot's it to you?" the man asked.

"We're police." He flashed his ID. "You're a suspect in a murder case. You're coming down to the station with us."

The man tried to bluff it out. "Wot murder? Wot are you talking about? I don't know nuffin' 'bout no murder!"

Force 12 in German Bight

"No, I am sure you don't, but we want to talk to you anyway. Why did you run if you have nuffin' to worry about?" Steven mimicked him.

"Check him just in case he's got a lock pick or some other dastardly weapon on him. Never know with villains these days," he told Toby, who frisked the man efficiently and then exclaimed. "My, oh, my! What *do* we have here! You're such a bad boy, Mr. Pete. Very bad indeed. Where did you get this from?" He waved the automatic under Pete's nose and placed it in his pocket. The people at the bus stop were beginning to take in interest in the goings on behind them.

Steven nodded in approval.

"Good work there, Sergeant. He might have used it if you hadn't nailed him so fast."

"Time to leave, boss," Toby said glancing at the crowd that was beginning to form.

Chapter 17

Strike One

Hedi sat at the table and tried to compose herself. She glanced across the table at Patrick, who wore a concerned expression as he watched her react to the death of her colleague. She swallowed as she thought of Erland lying below. She stared down at the table and shook her head, determined not to show any emotion to these men seated awkwardly next to her.

"You're sure, Patrick?" she asked, knowing the answer beforehand.

Patrick's mouth was a tight line. His hazel eyes were cold. "I checked carefully. Someone who knows how to did him in, Hedi."

He rubbed the stubble on his chin. "I'm very glad you weren't there...." He left the rest unsaid.

He exchanged a glance with Martin. "You were right, these guys have taken over the barge. No idea why, but I'm sure it has to do with that container."

"Any way we can check what's inside?"

"It's filthy outside right now, even dangerous," Mike said. He was the youngest diver present. This was only his second tour on the barge.

No sooner had he said this than the speakers opened up and Roger's voice came over.

"All hands, all hands. This is super Stack speaking. Due to increased bad weather no one, repeat, *no one* is allowed on the main deck until further notice. The galley will be closed until further notice. Stay in your cabins as much as possible." The speakers clicked off.

"Well, that takes care of that for the moment," Martin said.

"Those bastards murdered her colleague, guys. What are we going to do about it?" Leonard said.

"Oh, we're going to do something, all right," Patrick said, staring into Hedi's eyes as she lifted her head again. She nodded uncertainly.

"OK, Martin, I guess you've already done an inventory of weapons?" Patrick asked.

Martin nodded. "Yeah, me and the boys came up with four knives and a couple of fishing spears."

"Fishing spears? Bugger me! Were you thinking of going whaling while out here?" Patrick's tone dripped with sarcasm.

"No one thought there'd be a turf war, Pat. Anyway, what's wrong with a whale once in a while?" Martin turned the corners of his mouth down, pretending to be hurt.

Hedi smiled despite herself; these men were tough and apparently not frightened by a situation rapidly spinning out of control. She was relieved that she wasn't alone.

"Yeah, well, Hansen wanted to go spear fishing if we got some shore leave. Not sure what he thought he could shoot here in Denmark," Leonard explained.

"Nothing without a license," Hedi commented, trying to lighten her mood.

"Do you think the present circumstances merit a license, Officer?" Martin grinned at her with approval.

"Then we have your hand gun, Hedi, and I have the one that belonged to your friend," Patrick told her, and opened his overall top to show them the pistol nestled under his left arm.

Hedi stared at him. He seemed to be very composed, but if what the others had said was true he'd done something like this before. His demeanor and the quiet confidence he and Martin displayed went a long way to reassure her.

"We have one more advantage, if it can be called that. Skillet has a piece with him. Don't ask me how he got it on board but, well... he's a Texan, and by the way, I'm now quite sure he's one of the good guys. I don't want to involve him until it's really necessary, but I'm sure we can depend upon him if things get rough."

"Things have already gotten rough, mate," Martin said.

"I agree, but one of the first things we need to do is to find a safe place for Hedi here," Patrick said.

"What's wrong with this place?" Martin said.

The sea is going to get much worse; we're in for a force eleven within a few hours, which is why we're heading for Esbjerg. If it does get bad, you guys are going to have to get below the main deck, because this place is going to take a beating."

Hedi showed her surprise. "They're actually taking us back?" She felt a great sense of relief at the news.

Patrick nodded. "Yeah. Roger decided to take us back to port because of the weather report. Should be there in about eight hours, if all goes well."

Hedi sighed. "I wonder where the boat with the police Erland asked for is."

"You mentioned that last night. They should have been here by now if they were still coming, shouldn't they?" Martin asked.

"They would have come in a Coast Guard cutter, which is powerful and would have—or should have—arrived around the same time as the other boat," she said. Then her eyes widened as she stared at Patrick, who met her gaze with an odd look.

"You don't think? It... couldn't possible be... could it?" The room seemed colder. Her eyes opened wide, then she put her face onto her hands.

Patrick tried to reassure her. "We don't know, Hedi. Perhaps your boss in Esbjerg didn't follow through with it? Many possibilities there, so don't fret about it right now." He turned to the others. "What we have to do is figure out how to keep her hidden and pretend we know nothing."

"We could hide her in the sewage treatment area, they'll never think to search for her there if they are out hunting," Martin said with a grin on his face.

"Will you all please stop this silly joking?" Hedi's composure threatened to fall apart faced with this other, horrible possibility.

Martin was instantly contrite. "Sorry, Hedi, I'll behave."

Mike sat up. "But you know, although he's a right twit, he might be on to something. There's a space up front of there. Patrick, you know, it's your work area. It's a good hiding place."

"That's where the techies hang out and smoke pot when there's work to be done elsewhere," Patrick agreed. "OK, we can try for that, but we have to figure out how to get her down below without attracting any attention."

"Shouldn't be too hard. Everyone's asleep or in their cabins when we're on the tow," Hansen spoke up for the first time. He nodded to Hedi. "We could dress her up in an orange coverall and safety hat and walk her back there."

Just as he said this the speakers came on again. "Will the Danish policewoman please go to the captain's cabin? Danish policewoman needed in the captain's cabin." It was Larry's voice.

"Well, now we know two things. One, they know about Erland, or they would have included his name, and two, they don't know where you are. Which is a good thing, because I think that visit would be terminal," Martin said.

"It's time to move," Patrick said with a nod at Hedi. "You go and get into one of those coveralls hanging back there, and then we can all head out. You guys need to get a hold of one of those empty cabins on the port side and move your stuff there. I really don't like what's coming down, and this is too flimsy a place if it gets really rough."

As if to emphasize his point the cabin shook and creaked as the wind increased in savagery. Hedi wondered how bad it would get.

The others all stood up with Hedi, who followed Mike back into the other rooms to get dressed. When she left she heard him say, "Get some gear together boys, and don't forget to bring the weapons."

*****

They left the shelter of the divers' cabin to slosh through the ankle deep water deposited on the deck by the last wave. They were clawed at by the howling, tearing wind that seemed intent on

166

throwing them into the grey, heaving sea. It took only a few moments to reach the shelter of the stairway, but what Hedi witnessed in that short time terrified her. The barge had begun to plunge and the rolling had started. She slipped on the greasy deck and would have fallen, but a strong hand came out of nowhere and caught her arm in a vice like grip. It pushed her on to where Patrick grabbed her hand and pulled her into the stairwell. She was grateful for his firm grip. The others followed in a rush, and they all made their way down cold, wet stairs.

"So far, so good. Now we have to get below and onto the engine deck. Come on." He led the way down the two flights of deserted steps until they came to a short passage. In front of them was a compartment with some large consoles.

"Engine room controls for the pumps. I see even Alistair has gone to bed. He's normally here," Patrick said, when he saw the question in her eyes. It was empty, so they crossed the room to a doorway that opened into another chamber, one that stank of diesel and oil, in which stood two of the largest engines Hedi had ever seen. They squatted in the room like great monsters in captivity, silent and still.

Patrick and the others hurried her through to a door on their left, which led into another room with more enormous engines in it, again silent. Across this chamber to another, full of smaller machinery that hummed to itself. They could now hear the sound of other engines in the distance more clearly, which Hedi took to be the generators. The noise got louder each time they crossed a threshold.

Martin, who had been leading the way, had just opened the bulkhead door a crack when he stopped and put his finger on his lips. Hedi wondered why; even with most of the machinery not working, the generators alone made a huge amount of noise.

Martin beckoned Patrick over. "Listen," he whispered.

Patrick pressed his ear against the crack. Voices came from the other side.

Cautiously, he moved back to Hedi and the others. "Trouble. Ryan has one of the visitors on the other side."

"What do we do if they come this way?" she asked. His expression was enough to frighten her.

Force 12 in German Bight

"No choice. Don't forget what they did to your mate," he whispered to her.

She saw Martin take out a nasty looking knife and stand just inside the door where Patrick joined him, holding another slim black blade similar to the one Martin held. The rest of them made themselves scarce among the small machines. She noticed all of them were armed with knives, but Mike and Hansen also had their fishing spears ready and pointed at the door. She took out her pistol and checked it. It wasn't cocked, but she decided not to make any noise and just held it ready. Her heart began to beat faster.

She glanced at Mike. He seemed to be nervous; his fishing spear wobbled about. Hansen seemed calm enough, while the other three were a study in stoicism. Somehow that allowed her to relax and pay attention to the door.

Ryan's voice came closer, the door was pushed open, and two men came through the doorway. Ryan was talking and was the slower of the two to realize they were in trouble. The man with him noticed, however, and stopped in his tracks with one foot over the combing of the doorway. He glanced wildly about and was about to back up in a hurry when Martin kicked the back of Ryan's knee, sending him sprawling, and Patrick seized the man by his collar and heaved him over the rest of the way. But the man was quick; his hand dived for something inside his leather jacket. Patrick was exposed with only the knife. He was too far away to reach him without taking a step, and the man was already drawing a weapon. Patrick braced himself to close with his knife held in front of him when there was a sudden, loud snap and the man fell over backwards with a spear sticking out of his chest.

There was complete silence while they registered what had just happened. Ryan stared aghast at his late companion lying on the floor.

Patrick continued his forward momentum, came down on one knee next to the man, his knife at his throat. He stopped and felt for a pulse, and then stood up to look down on the dead man. A bright red stain began to bloom where the spear protruded from his vest.

Martin wasted no time. He shut the door, pulled the levers down to lock it, and joined Hansen, who towered over Ryan, trying to look threatening. Mike gaped at the damage he'd wrought.

"I... I didn't know it would go off like that!" he said.

"Patrick barked a short laugh. "What do you know, Marti, we've just had an accidental discharge of a firearm. That can get you time where we come from."

"Twenty eight days field punishment, to be precise," Martin said.

Hedi was still stunned by what had happened. "Is he dead?"

"'Fraid so, Hedi. We'll have to call it self defense, right?" Patrick said. "Here's what he reached for. Bloody hell, it's an Uzi! *And* he's got a handgun! We've got three handguns and an MG, now, and no doubt about that self-defense plea."

He tossed the Uzi to Martin, who checked it automatically. Patrick tossed the handgun to Leonard, who picked it out of the air and checked its magazine, then verified there was a bullet in the chamber.

"He had one up the spout, Miss. This is a Browning 9mm. I'm used to these," he said, as he stuck it in his pocket.

She nodded slowly. This was one of the men who had killed Erland. She glanced down at Ryan, crouched next to a blue pump motor with his hands on his head. He appeared to be shocked and frightened.

"Please d-don't do anythin', folks. I was jest showin' the guy around. He's from the UK, Miss."

"Shut up, Ryan. You're in a world of trouble, so stop whining and shut up," Patrick said.

"Do you know who killed my partner?" she asked, advancing on Ryan.

"Hold on, Hedi. We have a couple of problems to deal with before we interrogate him, which we will, I promise," Patrick said, standing over Ryan. "Some one find some rope or straps; we need to immobilize him. There should be some in the machine shop on the other side of the control room."

Mike was still in shock and barely heard him, but Hansen, who seemed more composed, opened the door and hurried off. He came back soon after with several long nylon straps and some rope and shut the door behind him.

Force 12 in German Bight

"See anyone?" Martin asked.

"No one," Hansen said.

"Lenny, you and Hansen tie him up and get a gag on him. Hurry," Patrick said. He and Martin exchanged meaningful glances.

"I'll go ahead and check on things...." Martin said.

"Are you all right, Hedi?" Patrick asked, and put his hand on her upper arm.

She nodded. She couldn't understand how the men, in particular Martin and Patrick, could remain so calm. "Yes, yes, I'm OK." But there was a tiny tremor in her voice and she remained shaken.

"They wanted to kill you, Hedi. Remember that, won't you?" he said in a low voice.

She nodded again and sat on one of the pumps while they tied Ryan up tight despite his protests and shoved a rag into his mouth, held in place by a torn off strip from his shirt.

He continued to make sounds, but they were unintelligible, and people ignored him as they stared down at the dead man.

He was dressed in a leather bomber jacket and vest, with blue jeans and expensive, light leather boots. He'd carried his pistol in a harness. Patrick removed it and tossed the harness over to Leonard, who strapped it on.

"We need to get rid of him, and fast," Patrick said.

Leonard stepped forward. "Overboard?"

"What do you want us to do, Hedi? You're the police." Patrick watched her.

Hedi swallowed and cleared her throat. "If it's possible, can you please put him somewhere for the moment? For identification later," she said.

"I know just the place," Leonard said. First he bent down and yanked the spear out of the man's chest. It didn't come out easily, and when it did there was a small flood of blood. "You got him right in the heart, Mike, me old buddy. Good shooting, man," he said and handed the spear back to Mike, who looked ill. Seconds later he was abruptly sick over one of the small pumps off to the side. His retching didn't help Hedi, who also felt sick, but was determined not to vomit. She clenched her teeth and looked away.

"You'll never get him to the freezer without someone noticing, Lenny," Martin said.

"No, we'll stick him in the pressure tanks. Come along, Mike, Hansen, let's get this done."

Mike had come back from where he'd been retching, and he and Hansen helped Leonard lug the body back the way they'd come.

"It's not likely anyone will know to look for that guy in there," Martin assured Hedi as they left.

"Hey, you two, quit the chatter. We're still not where we want to be, and there's still Ryan to deal with," Patrick said.

Patrick and Martin hauled Ryan to his feet and peered through the doorway once again. The room beyond was deserted, so while Patrick skipped ahead to check for danger the other two held Ryan by his arms and more or less dragged him along with them. He stopped resisting when Martin punched him in the kidney region. The pain brought a choking sound from him and tears to his eyes, but he saw the grim determination of his two captors and came along docilely enough afterward.

Patrick's destination was the electrician's work shop at the other end of the next chamber. The first room they crossed was full of square machines, about waist high, with many steel pipes running in and out of them. They hummed quietly to themselves. To their right was a glass-fronted control room, which Martin told Hedi was the generator room. The roar they made was deafening now. Patrick peered through yet another door that opened into a stair well. Under the stairs was a small door. He slipped across and opened it cautiously before he signaled for them to follow.

They had to stop and pull Ryan into a corner when they heard someone walking the corridor above them. Martin pulled out his knife and held it against his throat with a fierce look at their prisoner. Ryan was wide eyed with fear and did not move. The steps came closer to the top of the stairs, but the person walked on without stopping, and they were able to continue without meeting anyone else.

"That's the sewage treatment room on our right," Martin said with a grin at Hedi. "Still want to hide in there?"

Force 12 in German Bight

She shook her head with a weak smile. A distinct smell emanated from the room. The barge lurched, the metal walls groaned, and the floor tilted to an angle of about ten degrees for a long moment. Then it slowly returned to center before it continued to tilt in the opposite direction.

"Storm's getting worse," Martin observed to Patrick.

Patrick led them to a metal grating with a locked door. On the other side was another enclosed room. He reached up, took down a small key, and opened the grating door.

"Come inside, quickly," he said as he pushed it open. He went to the other door and opened it with another key that he brought out from his pocket.

"Here it is: the Hilton Hotel for all our guests," he said and waved his hand about in a grand gesture.

Hedi didn't think much of it. There were some old leather office chairs and a bench along the wall, which was covered in wires, tools and electrical instruments. A small, narrow window opened out onto the front of the enclosed grating, providing a view of the door they'd just entered.

There was a recliner at the far end of the room with a dirty cushion on it and a dubious blanket. There was also a distinct, stale aroma. Patrick noticed her sniff and said, "This is where the techies hide when there's work to do. They won't come down here while we're on tow, because they'll be drunk in their cabins instead." His expression was somewhat embarrassed.

Hedi began to wonder how this enormous ship functioned if everyone was either drunk or high on pot, or worse. But these men seemed to know what they were doing.

They put Ryan on a stool, tied his feet to the legs, and wedged him into the furthest corner to counteract the increasing motion of the barge. Then they moved across the listing floor to the other side for a conference.

"I don't know how long it'll take them to find out they have two men missing, Hedi, but when they do, shit's going to hit the fan, and they'll search this ship from stem to stern. We're going to have to move you around if they do and try to stay one step ahead of them. One of us will stay with you and him all the time," Patrick told her.

172

She nodded and glanced back at Ryan, who appeared to be very sorry for himself. "Do you think he's involved with these... gangsters?" she asked.

Martin nodded. "He's part of Daryl's shift, and works for him. I'm willing to bet he's up to his neck in it. Why don't you and Pat here interrogate him, while I go and see if I can get some food and join up with Lenny and the boys at the same time?"

"Good idea, Marti. While you're at it, tell Skillet what happened if you get the chance."

"Will do, Pat. I'll get all the maps off the walls too."

"Now you're thinking, mate."

Martin disappeared and Patrick locked the door behind him. Hedi became aware of the motion of the barge once more. The rolling was much more pronounced than before, and the pitch had increased to the point where items were rolling off tables onto the floor and she had to brace herself.

The place and area they had just traversed had been empty. From the activity she'd witnessed on the decks the day before, the amount of machinery they'd passed, and the number of men, Stack had mentioned over fifty. Where had all the men gone?

"Where is everyone, Patrick?" she asked.

"One deck up. That's where all the cabins are, and the movie room, the gym, and the galley. They're all up there stuffing themselves, watching movies or screwing off in their cabins getting high. Why?"

"It... it seems... what's that word... *spooky* down here with no one about."

He grinned. "Yeah, spooky is right. Wait till you've spent three months on this rust bucket. It runs itself most of the time, or should do, but this old barge is ready for the scrap heap."

The barge lurched again, almost as though it resented the slanderous description, and threw her into his arms. For one brief moment she looked into his eyes and saw concern. He held her arms at the elbows for just a moment. Without thinking she gripped his forearms back.

"It's warming up out there, Hedi. Hold onto something."

A warm flush rose on her cheeks, but he seemed not to notice. He began walking over towards Ryan with his knife out, and Ryan leaned back, away from the approaching menace with wide, fearful eyes.

Chapter 18

Change of Course

After he sent Ryan away with Jonah, one of his men, Donald stayed on the bridge for a while longer. He was worried. The weather outside was seriously shitty, and from what Roger Stack and his taciturn assistant with the odd name, Skillet, had told him, it was about to get worse, much worse. This had definitely not been planned for.

Donald was used to being at sea; his time in the Royal Marines had been spent on one or another of the HM ships, including destroyers, and even the air craft carrier HMS *Ark Royal*, so the motion of the 'barge', as these weird people from America called it, was not a problem for him. What bothered him was the sight of the tugs, which were large boats, being tossed about like corks. These vessels, tied to the barge by huge cables, were at the mercy of the spume-covered waves, which lifted and dropped them like toys in clouds of spray as they rose and fell. How the hell was the boat from Harwich going to get to the rendezvous in this kind of sea? And, just as importantly, how were they ever going to transfer the container to that boat? His experience told him these waves had to be at least thirty feet high, maybe even higher.

He stared down at the half container, hidden amongst the supplies, with a pensive expression on his hard features. That container represented his future. If he managed to get it into the UK he was assured of riches beyond his imagining, and while he trusted Charlie, Donald had no doubt in his mind what would happen to him if he failed to deliver.

He turned back to the bridge to find the man Skillet watching him. He didn't like the cool stare of the large, rangy man with watchful, blue eyes. In another place and time he would have challenged the arrogance of the Yank and beaten some manners into him. Now, however, he depended upon these people to make sure he got what he needed, so he gave Skillet a nasty look and left the deck.

He went down to the almost deserted galley and obtained a large mug of coffee and a sandwich. While he was there he noticed a couple of men in bright red overalls making piles of sandwiches. One of them wore dark glasses and giggled as he smeared peanut butter all over the bread.

Donald shook his head in disgust. These people spent far too much time at sea. The signs were all there. He made his way back to his cabin to see if Hans was up. They would get with Daryl and rehash the plans. It couldn't be long now before they were contacted by the boat from Harwich.

He found Hans sitting at the table in the front room, a worried expression on his usually bland features. He had a coffee sitting on the table in front of him and seemed glad to see Donald.

"What's up, Hans? You look like your grandma died."

Hans got up. "Come with me, Don. I have something to show you." Like all Danes his English was good even though there was a slight accent.

They exited their cabin and Hans led the way down the corridor towards the end cabin where the policeman had died. He still carried his coffee. Donald followed, puzzled.

Hans stopped in front of the last room in the line and gestured towards the door lock. "Do you see this, Donald?" he said. "Do you see that lock?"

Donald bent down and stared at the door lock. It had been broken. He turned the handle and the door opened without difficulty. "You locked this last night, didn't you?" he asked Hans, who now stood back and drank his coffee, an odd expression on his unshaven features. He nodded in grim silence, his pony tail flopping over his shoulder.

Donald eased himself back into the cabin and Hans followed.

176

The lights were still on and nothing in the front room seemed to have been disturbed. They peered into the back cabin and saw the still body of Erland sprawled on the bed, just where Donald had left him, but Donald noticed something amiss. He stepped closer to the body and stared. The man's shirt collar was disturbed, as though someone had checked the body for signs of life.

They checked around the cabin for any other signs of a visitor, but found none. They missed the carry bag that Patrick had shoved under the lower bunk. Donald waved them back to their own cabin. Once there, they sat with their coffee cups in front of them on the table.

"Someone broke into the cabin last night. Someone knows about the policeman," Hans said.

"I doubt very much if it was any of those mutts that work for Daryl. They'd have been told to stay away. By the way, we still haven't found the police woman, have we?" Donald asked. "Wonder where she is? Maybe she broke the lock and found him. Maybe that's why she's not showing. We have to find her, we'll get some answers."

"We should find her before the rendezvous. No loose ends, Don." Hans was worried.

"The first thing we need is a map of this place," Donald said. "I noticed one on the wall outside. Go and get it while I think about things for a moment."

Hans disappeared, only to reappear with a puzzled expression on his face. "I can't find the map."

Donald gave an exasperated sigh and went to look for himself. He saw the space where the map had been the night before, but it wasn't there now.

"Someone's playing games," he said in a low, menacing voice. "Well, two can play at that. Wake that idiot Daryl, Hans. I want to see him on the bridge. That guy Skillet knows more than he's letting on. He watched me oddly when I was up there. Bring the Uzis. I think he might know something. Bring the other three guys with you, too. I reckon the gloves are off as of now."

*****

Force 12 in German Bight

Donald arrived on the bridge to find Stack still there, but Skillet had gone on some errand, which pissed him off. He wanted to have a little chat with that cocky Texan. Daryl came puffing up the stairs and paused at the top to catch his breath. Hans arrived just behind him, accompanied by the other Brit, Sammy and Hans' other two men, Toke and Willie. Don wondered where Jonah and Bill were. The men now carried submachine guns, but they kept them concealed from Roger, who stood at the other end of the bridge and did not notice them.

"I don't know where Jonah has gone to. Bill is still in a cabin, I think," Hans told Donald in a low voice. "I think Jonah went to look around with one of those men called a rigger."

"Hey, Daryl. What d'ya say?" Roger asked him when he caught sight of the men. "Who are you guys?" he asked, staring at Daryl as though he should provide an explanation. "Never seen you before, and why are you all up here on the bridge?"

Daryl had collected his breath by now and was less red about the gills. He nodded to Stack and said, "Hi there, Roger. These gentlemen arrived last night."

He wheezed and walked over to the radar to check for company, but they appeared to be alone in the sea. He peered out the front windows of the bridge and watched the tugs performing their gyrations on the agitated seas. He shook his head and peered at the compass for a moment, looked up, and then peered at it again.

"You more of the po'lice? " Roger asked.

Donald was just about to answer when an angry exclamation from Daryl stopped him. "What the hell!" he said. "Hey, Roger, what course are we on?" He almost yelled it.

Roger walked over. "I'm taking us back to port, Daryl. The po'lice want us there, and we have a force eleven, maybe worse, coming in. Need to get into the shel-"

Donald grabbed him by the throat. Roger was choking and gurgling when they heard the rattle of someone else coming up the steps.

"It's that fella Skillet. Grab him," he told the hoods.

He had not relaxed his grip on Roger, who looked as though he needed air by now. His hands were wrapped around Donald's thick forearm but were having no effect whatsoever. Donald released him and shoved him back into the main room, where he came up against the rear counter of the bridge.

"How long have we been on this course?" Donald asked him with a glance at Daryl, who stood by the compass, his normally reddish face white with rage. His wad of tobacco was still in his left cheek, and his mouth was turned downwards in a steep 'U'.

"What the fuck is going on?" Roger shouted as he staggered backwards against the rear shelves of the bridge, holding his throat. "You can't come up here and tell me what to do!"

"Shut the fuck up and answer the question, asshole," Daryl shouted back at him.

"About six hours, we're... we're only an hour out of Esbjerg now," Roger stammered and stared at him with a shocked expression on his face.

"You asshole! What have you done, and why didn't you tell me, you stupid bastard?" Daryl yelled. His jowls shook and an unhealthy, bright red color now showed on his features. His eyes had almost disappeared into the folds of fat around them.

At that moment Skillet made an appearance. He'd just arrived at the top of the stairs when Hans leaned over the railing and pointed a submachine gun at him.

Skillet froze. Hans smiled at him and motioned for him to come all the way up. "Keep your hands where I can see them," he told Skillet with a cheerful grin, and then waved him over to the corner where Roger stood, looking very frightened and wide eyed.

"Who...who are you people?" Roger stammered clearly shaken by the treatment from Donald.

"None of your damned business, so shut the hell up and start doing as you're told. Don't make any more mistakes, or my boys will take care of you," Donald called over.

"We have to go back!" Donald told Daryl. "That boat was given coordinates, and if we can't reach him by radio he's going to be hanging around out there. We need to get 'round now!" He spoke in a low intense voice so the others couldn't hear him.

"Yeah, OK. I'll make the call," Daryl said. He reached for one of the radios.

Force 12 in German Bight

"You're mad!" Roger shouted. "We're in for a force eleven, maybe even a twelve! Look out there, you stupid bastards, it's madness to turn round now!"

Donald didn't say anything. A pistol appeared in his hand as if from nowhere, and he pointed it at Roger. There was one shot. Roger staggered back against Skillet and crumpled to the floor. He was dead with a bullet between his eyes.

Skillet knelt by Roger and stared up at Donald. "You didn't have to do that, you bastard," he said with quiet venom.

Donald pointed the gun at him, and laughed. "You're expendable, mate. We have another crew, so don't piss me off or you'll join that fella." He turned to Hans. "Take him below and lock him in one of the more secure cabins. I'll stay up here with Willie and Daryl. Where is Jonah and that other rigger of yours?" he asked Daryl.

"I dunno," Daryl said. He was visibly shaken by what had happened right in front of him. "I'll... I'll page him." He picked up the tannoy microphone and called for Ryan. No one answered him, so he called again. Still no answer. He sent a worried glance at Donald and called Richards to come to the bridge.

Hans and Sammy came over and hauled Skillet to his feet. "Come on you," Sammy said, brandishing the Uzi at him. "Don't get wise and you won't get hurt."

"Find Bill and send him up to the bridge while you are at it, Hans," Donald told him.

Skillet shrugged Hans off and led the way out of the bridge. They clattered down the steps and out of sight. They passed Hamesh on the landing by the radio room; he watched them going by with wide, scared eyes.

"What's going on, Skillet?" he asked, but then he saw the weapons and his mouth clamped shut.

"Go back in the radio room and shut up. You won't get hurt if you stay there, you hear?" Hans said with a smile as they went by. "Toke, stand guard over this room," he ordered.

Hamesh disappeared into the room and Toke took up position just outside the door.

*****

180

James Boschert

Skillet continued down the stairs, very conscious of the two men behind him with their weapons trained on his back. As the barge swayed and rolled in the rising seas he wondered if he could take advantage of the situation, but a glance behind him told him Hans and his friend were taking no chances. There was no way he could jump aside, as the corridors were too narrow. The only thing he might be able to do was jump through a door, perhaps, but the man Hans seemed as though he knew how to use the weapon, and he hadn't come close enough for Skillet to try to strike him yet.

They emerged into the long corridor that passed the cabins for the visitors and the Supers. As they did, he saw Leonard walking towards them.

Leonard raised his hand and called out. "Skillet, hold up! Need to talk to you." Then he noticed that Skillet had his hands in the air and paused.

He was only about twenty feet away when he said this, and Skillet used his eyes to tell Leonard all was not well. In one swift motion Leonard reached inside his coveralls and pulled out his pistol; Skillet dropped suddenly to his knees, rolled over, and reached for his own weapon.

He heard two shots come from Leonard's handgun and a gasp from the man directly behind him, who stumbled forward. Hans, however, reacted far faster than either had anticipated. He fired almost as the man in front of him collapsed. Leonard was right in front of Hans when he fired.

The bullets took Leonard in the side of the chest and abdomen, and he fell back against the wall with a grimace of agony on his face and blood spurting out of his wounds. The pistol dropped on the floor. He looked over at Skillet and tried to speak, but blood welled out of his mouth and his eyes rolled up before he followed the man called Sammy to the floor with a dull thump.

Skillet looked up in shock. Hans checked Sammy for life, but the still smoking Uzi was pointed directly at him. "Make my day, mister!" Hans said with a grin. "You remember Dirty Harry, yes?"

Skillet said nothing, he just waited. Hans was unnerved by the cold, unemotional stare. He motioned Skillet to get to his feet. Skiller prayed that the man would not search him. He had feigned

181

surprise and taken his hand away very quickly when he had realized that Hans would shoot him out of hand if he moved.

Doors were beginning to open along the corridor at the far end and confused men called out, but Hans stood up and shouted. "Go back to your rooms. Nothing to worry about. Go back to your rooms, stay there, and no one will be hurt."

A couple of the more daring men came to the corner at the end of the corridor, but a quick deafening burst from Hans's Uzi sent splinters flying from the walls all down the corridor and they vanished. There was a deathly hush as the men in the corridor looked at one another and at the two bodies lying in widening pools of blood.

"Get up and come this way," Hans said. He moved over to the inert body of Leonard and stooped to pick up his gun. "Goodness me! Where did he get this gun?" he said as he placed it in his pocket.

He motioned Skillet to get up and move along the corridor, back the way they'd come. "Open that door there," he ordered Skillet, who complied. It was a small room filled with cleaning products. "This should do. Get in." He stood back and let Skillet move past him. That was a mistake.

Skillet threw his right arm out and smacked Hans across the eye, jerking him backwards. In that brief second when Hans reflexively reached for his stinging face and as he turned to fire, Skillet dived through a doorway on the other side of the corridor behind him and disappeared. Hans fired at the closing door trying to hit him, but all he succeeded in doing was to send splinters of wood in all directions and the door was nearly torn off its hinges.

He followed through the door and stared down the steps Skillet had just slid down. He just caught a glimpse of him as he vanished behind the next corner.

The radio on Hans's belt squawked. "What's going on down there? We can hear shots," Donald said.

"We have a problem down here," Hans said while he peered into the gloom below.

*****

Up in the bridge they heard the muted but unmistakable sound of gunfire. Daryl cast worried looks towards the stairwell, but Donald said, "Concentrate on the boats, mate. Willie, stay here. I'll go and take a look see." He raced down the stairs to the cabin deck and cautiously opened the door leading out into the corridor. Hans was there to greet him with the other man, Bill, who had heard the shooting and came running with his Uzi at the ready.

"Go and get Don's uzi. Hurry!" Hans said. Bill ran off.

Don still held onto his pistol as he stared down the corridor at the two bullet-riddled bodies. "What the fuck happened here?" he said.

"We ran into that guy over there. He had a gun and nailed Sammy before he could even react, but I got him. "

"How in hell's name did he know? What happened to that other guy, the Yank?" Donald said.

"He got away in the confusion. He's down there somewhere. " Hans said and indicated the door Skillet had disappeared through.

"OK, where does that lead?" Donald asked, hanging onto his patience with a great effort.

"I don't know. I think it's to the engines?" Hans said. "I need back up if I have to go down there."

Donald stared at him with contempt."Take Bill with you and take care of that guy, he's dangerous."

At that moment, Richards came running down the corridor, closely followed by Larry and Virgil. All three stopped the other side of the carnage and stared, shock written on their faces.

"What're you lot staring at?" Donald said loudly. Then he made a decision. "Hey, Richards, get one of those two to go with Hans, to make sure they don't get lost. Put these bodies," he nudged the body of Sammy with the toe of his boot, "into one of the cabins here. Then you and the rest of us are going up to the bridge. I want the radio room secured, and the bridge."

Richards recovered and commandeered Virgil. "Go down to the engine deck with these two and see if you can find Ryan. I dunno where the hell he's gotten to, the lazy bastard."

"The last I knew he went below with one of your men, Don," Hans said. "They should still be somewhere down there."

Force 12 in German Bight

"OK, get the bastards back up here. Get going and find the Yank then get rid of him."

"Who are we talking about?" Richards asked.

"Skull... something or other "

"Shit! You mean Skillet? What did he do?"

"He tried to shoot me. I got that one over there." Han pointed to Leonard's body.

"That's Leonard, one of the divers. What the hell happened here?" Richards shook with fear.

"That fella tried to kill me, too. He shot my man, but I got him just in time." Hans smirked.

"Fuckin' hell, what the hell have you bastards done?" Larry gasped.

"Come on, come on. We don't have all day!" Donald said, and then staggered as the barge lurched in a slow corkscrew motion. The corridor seemed to take on a life of its own as it twisted out of line, and he felt seasick.

"Bloody 'ell, what's going on out there?" he demanded.

"We're going into some bad seas from what I can tell," Richards said, clearly worried, and hurried up the stairs. Larry, who had been silent with a shocked expression on his face, chased after him.

*****

Patrick had just finished prodding Ryan for one last piece of information when he stopped and held up his hand for silence. Ryan didn't notice and continued to moan, so he slapped him gently on his cheek and put his finger to his lips. "Shut up," he mouthed. There it was again, an alien sound, not one you normally heard on the barge.

"I just heard gunshots!" he said to Hedi, who had been watching with horrified fascination as Patrick persuaded Ryan to talk with the point of his knife.

Martin appeared at the doorway, looking concerned. "I think they've topped old Lenny, Pat."

"Bloddy hell. How so?"

"I was in the corridor upstairs, hunting for Skillet, as was

Lenny, who was way ahead of me, when I heard shooting on the starboard side where the toff cabins are. I poked my head around the corridor and saw Lenny down and Skillet lying on the floor, too. I didn't have time to do much else, as one of the bastards sent some bullets down the corridor, and we had to scarper. I heard more shots. When I checked again a bunch of them were standing around talking, but I'm sure of one thing: they're coming downstairs."

Hedi clenched her fists. "Who are these people?" she asked.

"No bloody idea, luv. But they mean business, that's for sure," Martin said.

"Which way?" Patrick asked.

"If they're going to come down it will be the galley stairs, which puts them in the pump room. Oh, shit, that's where we left the other guy."

"Well, it might scare them a bit when they find him. Where's Skillet now?'

They heard a sound and Martin put his finger to his lips. He glanced at Ryan, who was still tied up but not gagged, and clearly interested in what was going on. "You too," he whispered, and flicked his fingers across this throat in a theatrical gesture with an ugly grimace to emphasize his point.

Ryan's eyes went wide and he clamped his jaw shut. He was sweating. Patrick hastily tore off a strip of masking tape and wrapped it around his mouth, patting it into place with exaggerated care.

Martin slid out of the cage and vanished around a corner. He reappeared a few moments later, assisting Skillet, who limped.

"Hang on, mate. We'll have you right soon enough," Martin assured him as he helped him into the room.

Skillet was bleeding from his left calf. The leg of his coveralls was soaked with blood.

"Nothing serious, but we need to get it covered. I might have left a trail," he grunted and nodded to Patrick and Hedi.

"Afternoon, Miss," he said, as he thankfully took one of the work stools. Martin busied himself with some torn pieces of cloth. "Flesh wound. Lucky it wasn't a bone or an artery; you'll live."

185

Force 12 in German Bight

"Hi, Skillet. What happened up there?" Patrick said.

'They killed Roger, Pat. Right up there in front of me on the bridge, and then Leonard down in the corridor. Not before Lenny managed to take out one of them, though. They really mean business, that crowd. Their boss is one nasty piece of Brit work."

Patrick wore a somber expression and Hedi put her hand to her mouth. "They just killed them?" she demanded.

Skillet nodded. He'd just noticed Ryan, tied up with a gag. He, too, was bleeding from a couple of pricks that had been administered earlier.

"What have you been doing to him, Pat? You tell me what he told you, but I think we have to hurry. They're comin' after me."

"Oh, you know... just a little info gathering. Ryan was most cooperative. Weren't you, mate?" He waved airily to Ryan, who nodded; his eyes were frightened.

"What did he tell you?"

"That Daryl and the goons upstairs are involved in a scurrilous plot to overthrow our barge and transport drugs to a bunch of villains from the UK. Can you imagine? Who, by the way, are going to show up any time now."

Skillet turned to Hedi. "Do you understand these two Brits? Ah never could."

She shook her head. "Their English is terrible. I think I understand you Americans better."

He grinned. "Then Ah'm yore man." He winced. "Ouch! Will you go easy there, Mr. Martin? I'm a wounded man!"

"Sorry, Skillet. I got lost listening to your flirting just now."

"OK, listen, I think we have to take the fight to them. We're short of the right tools. I presume he took your shooter, Skillet?" Patrick said in an attempt to get them back on track.

Skillet shook his head. "No the idiot didn't even think of checking.".

"I have one, Martin has the Uzi, and Hedi here has one," Patrick said.

"We're a multi-gender assault team!" Martin exclaimed, looking pleased. Hedi pretended to frown but not very seriously. She seemed scared, but dealt with it well, Patrick noted with approval.

"Shut up, you twit!" Patrick said, but not unkindly. "We've got to ambush them somehow. You and I have to try to remember our killing room training, Marti. Where do you think they might be right now, Skillet?"

"Don't know, Pat, but we will be trapped if we stay here," Skillet said. The barge lurched and tilted, then settled back and tilted the other way with a slight roll. "I would love to be able to see what the hell is going on out there. Doesn't feel good at all to me," he said.

"OK, we'll keep Ryan locked up in that cabinet over there and scarper out of here. I think we should draw them into some kind of killing zone."

Both Martin and Skillet nodded enthusiastically. "Where did you leave the other two divers, Martin?" Patrick asked.

They're up in the port side cabin, just behind the cinema. Not much we can do about them right now, though."

"Then we have to manage on our own. I think we should try for the food storage room."

"Where's that?" Hedi asked.

"One door over from here, but we should hurry. They could already be down here searching for Skillet."

Chapter 19

To Catch a Cable

Donald had to hold onto both rails as he climbed the two sets of stairs to the bridge. At one point the barge lurched, as though trying to throw him back down, and he had to hang on tight to prevent falling.

When he gained the opening to the bridge he heard shouts. Richards and Larry were over by the dead body of Roger, which was now surrounded by a pool of blood.

"What the hell is going on?" Richards shouted at Daryl. "You never said it would come to this!"

"I didn't know..." Daryl didn't finish as Donald crossed the slanting floor with his automatic out, pointing it at Richards.

"If you don't want to go the same way as this guy here, you'll shut the fuck up and do what you're told. Dump the body out on the cat walk outside and clean up the mess, *now!*"

Richards and Larry didn't protest; they took Roger by the shoulders and legs, and while the grinning Willie held the door open against the tearing wind they staggered outside into the rain with the body and dropped it unceremoniously onto the catwalk outside before returning. Willie barely managed to shut the door as the screaming wind threatened to tear it off its hinges.

"Bloody 'ell, this isn't getting any better," he said and wiped the rain water off his face. His accent was stronger than that of Hans. "Go on then," he ordered the two riggers. "Clean it up and be quick about it."

Donald went to the front of the bridge and peered out through the hurling rain. He could just see the two tugs, several hundred yards ahead of their blunt bows. Both vessels were making heavy work of it in the now raging sea. The cables coming out behind them appeared and disappeared into the water between the tugs and the barge.

"What have you done about changing course?" he demanded of Daryl, who stood nearby and stared fixedly out of the windows.

"We're changing course right now, but it's a slow business. It'll take several miles of turn before we're back on our original heading," he said tonelessly.

"They don't look as though they're turning to me," Donald said.

"Have a look on the radar then. For Christ's sake, why did you have to kill him?" Daryl asked in a low voice.

"He played the fool, and it's done, so shut up and make sure we get where we are supposed to," Donald said with a glare.

"If we try a sharp turn we could lose the cables. In these seas I don't know what can happen." Daryl sounded nervous.

He picked up a large hand-radio lying on the counter in front of him and clicked it. "Louisiana, you listening?" he said.

The set squawked. "Yeah, I'm here."

"How long before we're back on course?"

"Another hour if that Italian gets his act together."

"OK. Giuomo, stay parallel with Louisiana and don't get left behind, you hear now?"

"I hear. You people is all mad! My radio tells me this is going to get worse, not better! We should be looking for shelter, not focking about in these sheet!"

As if to punctuate his words there was a great jagged streak of lightning to the north.

"Just remember who pays your wages, Giuomo, and get on with it!" Daryl said and clicked off.

Donald didn't like what he saw out in front of them. The tugs seemed to be moving slowly to port, but it was hard to tell in the worsening visibility. He felt a slight chill as he watched the waves break over the bows, sending in huge billows of spray high into the air, high enough to splatter the windows of the bridge. He estimated they were at least twenty-five feet above the main deck, which now seemed level with the raging sea. He stared at the radar, hoping to see their contact, but so far there was nothing, no other ship in their vicinity. Up here in the bridge they were swaying about much more than below.

There was another great flash of lightning that lit up the sea for a moment, giving it a metallic color like agitated mercury. The crash of thunder that followed was so loud that the steel walls of the bridge shook.

Donald decided that watching the seas wasn't going to make the situation any better, so he turned away and nodded to Willie, who kept an eye on the two riggers cleaning up the now congealed blood on the lino floor. Donald walked down the stairs to the radio room. He had to hang onto the rails as he slid down the steps.

He opened the door to find one of Hans' men, Toke, sitting and drinking coffee with the operator. He nodded to the Danish thug and said to the operator, "What do they say about the weather now? Getting any better?"

Hamesh, who looked frightened and subdued, ducked his head and clicked on the wireless. There was a period of silence and some humming. He turned a dial and the English voice of the BBC Met office announcer filled the room.

He had just reached the area known as Viking when they came online.

"Gale warnings—Southeasterly storm force 10 continuing. Wind: southeasterly 9 to severe gale 10, increasing storm 11 at times. Sea: very rough or high. Rain at times. Visibility: moderate or poor."

"Where's that?" Donald nodded to the radio.

Stanley pointed to a chart on the notice board above the table. It was an area well to the north of their own position as he estimated it.

The men listened intently as the announcer worked his way through Fisher and Dogger, which were both in a bad way with gale forces in eleven to twelve. Finally he came to German Bight, which Stanley pointed to as he named it. "That's where we are," he added unnecessarily. "This is beginning to sound like a wind storm."

"What's a wind storm?" Donald asked him.

"Its a big bugger, like a hurricane." Stanley said. "Not common at all."

The voice continued. "German Bight: Gale warnings—Southeasterly storm force 11 continuing. Wind: southeasterly 10 to severe gale 11, increasing storm 12. Sea: very rough and very high. Rain squalls continuous. Visibility: poor to very poor."

Hamesh sounded worried. "Bloody 'el. That's us! I bet there isn't another ship in the whole of German Bight right now. They'll have scarpered for cover wherever they can find it!"

"I need to get in touch with this number. Here's the frequency. Give it a try," Donald said. He read out the numbers and Hamesh wrote them down. "What's his call sign?"

"*Penguin 454.*" Donald checked his piece of paper. "Daft name."

Hamesh put on the earphones and fiddled with the tuning dial for a while. When he thought he had the right frequency he began to call.

"Hello, *Penguin 454*, this is *Cherokee* calling. Do you read me?"

The radio crackled. He tried again on a side band. "Hello, *Penguin 454*, this is *Cherokee* calling. Do you read me?"

The radio dials stared back at them. It crackled with static again and then it went quiet, and a faint voice came back.

"Calling *Cherokee*, *Penguin 454*. Reading poor, you are very faint."

Hamesh was concerned. "We've got fifteen hundred watts on this piece of crap. We should be booming." He thumbed the microphone again.

"Hello, *Penguin 454*, what's your location?"

"I'm at the rendezvous, where the hell are you?" came the curt reply.

Donald snatched the microphone from Hamesh, who sat back in surprise.

"We're on our way, Stu. Hold station and wait until we give you a new bearing."

"Can't wait much longer... We're in the middle of a gale force eleven and it looks like it's getting worse."

"You stay on station!" Donald yelled. "Wait it out!" Angrily he tossed the microphone to Toke.

"You can keep listening for any call back. Watch him," Donald said, indicating Hamesh. "Don't let him use the radio unless one of us is here."

He left the room and climbed the stairs. The bridge was dimly lit now and the instruments glowed.

"Our contact is waiting for us at the RV," Donald informed Daryl, who nodded. Larry and Richards were standing near the radar, confused and frightened.

Daryl thumbed the speaker of the radio. "Hey, Louisiana, what knots are you doing?"

"Maybe four," came the laconic reply.

"Bugger, it's going to take the rest of the day at this rate," Donald muttered.

"Can you put some more steam on it?" Daryl said.

"Are you nuts?" Captain Joey called back.

Just as he said this a huge wave rose out of the sea ahead of his tug. It seemed to move in slow motion, and for a moment or two Donald wondered if his imagination was going wild, but the dark monster rising out of the sea ahead of them was for real. It just seemed to keep on rising, far above the other waves.

There was a horrified gasp from Richards. "Oh, my Lord God! Oh fuck! It's a rogue!"

Larry's jaw hung open as he fixated on the monster climbing up to tower over the tug boats, which reached its base, and then began to climb a seemingly impossible slope towards the top. For an insane moment Don had the impression he was staring directly up at the vessels, as if they were floating above them. Then the two huge tugs bobbed over the top of the spume-covered wave like rubber ducks and disappeared from view, briefly showing their undersides and their propellers. The cables cut their way through the water behind them as though slicing butter.

The monster wave slid inexorably towards the barge, which

slowly, so very slowly, began to rise. But the combination of its deadweight and the cables prevented the bows from climbing the way they might have without the tow lines. The cables from the bows went taut as bow strings, cutting into the wall of water. It looked as though the barge would be hauled directly into the wave.

The horrified people on the bridge gaped up at the awful monster that towered over them, its crest trembling as though it were some watery creature about to pounce upon them. They gasped as the bows disappeared into the cliff of water. The rogue wave surged forward, engulfed the bows and swept over the main deck in one vast tumble of raging seawater. Metal screaming and groaning, the barge tilted to a fifteen degree angle under the incredible weight of the wave, which roared along the front deck to slam against the front of the bridge, shaking the tower and rattling the windows. For a seemingly endless moment they could see nothing except a brown, foaming maelstrom of water as the huge crest obscured the windows, and then swept by in a foaming mass past them.

The men inside the bridge were tossed about, clutching at anything for their balance, while their massive steel vessel staggered under the weight of thousands of tons of water. For long seconds it seemed they were about to go completely under. Then, like some kind of enormous submarine, the barge slowly began to resurface, water streaming off its deck in rushing waterfalls. It shuddered and shook, then righted itself and regained stability. The men stared at one another, too shaken to speak. They were all bruised and shaken. Willie had to go over to the other side of the bridge to retrieve his weapon which he had lost and which had slid across the floor to hammer into the cabinets. While Larry had garnered a cut on his cheek.

The silence was broken by Larry, who peered down at the main deck as he dabbed at the blood on his cheek bone. "Holy shit! Do you see that mess down there?" he asked in awed tones.

The rest of the men hastened over to the port side. They were shocked by what they saw. The huge orange buoys, eight of them, formerly tied down securely with chains, had broken their bindings and been swept in all directions. One even hung off the port side, having destroyed the railings on its way over. Its anchor cable was all that connected it to the barge. One of the 50 ton cranes was lying on its side.

"Jesus!" Larry exclaimed. "How high d'you think that monster was, Rich?"

"I dunno, but easily sixty-five feet, I'd say. " Richards voice was awed and frightened.

"Ah'm gettin' a bad case of religion after seeing that!" Larry said. "If we ever git out of here Ah'm *never* going to sea again!"

To Donald it looked like Richards already had a bad case of religion. The man was muttering and looked up at the sky. "Oh, God, forgive us our sins. We're going under. God save us!"

"Shut the fuck up, you whining bastard!" Donald shouted at him with a glare. Truth was he was scared, too, but he didn't want some pious babbling idiot to make him even more unnerved than he already was. He exchanged looks with Willie, who was as shaken as he. The scar on his cheek twitched badly.

"Where in the hell do these silly buggers all come from?" he asked Willie. "They're all so..." He searched for the right word. "Fucking... dysfunctional!" He liked the sound of the word and used it again. "They're dysfunctional!"

Willie cackled with laughter and shrugged. "Be damned if I'd work out here, Don," he said. "You'd have to be seriously screwed up to do this for a living."

The wave, carrying a buoy with it, had smashed the divers' cabin to matchwood and the decompression tanks were lying at odd angles on the main deck, having been torn off their mountings.

One of the massive reels for the water tubing wasn't there anymore, and the wreckage at the very back indicated the huge steel sled was probably smashed beyond repair. The welding shop behind the bridge had simply disappeared.

All the riggers, who knew how sturdy the equipment was, were badly shaken. They were taking stock of the damage, but every one of them knew the barge would have to be towed into port for repairs no matter what happened now.

Donald was stunned. He'd been to sea before and knew a little about storms, but this horrified him. He simply couldn't grasp the enormity of the monster that had risen out of the depths and almost swamped the vessel. The sense of malevolence from the wave as it reared up in front of them unnerved even him. What had that prayer mat Richards called it? A Rogue wave? He hoped he never saw another one again.

But worse was to come.

Richards, who had been checking the forward part of the barge, shouted something and pointed, which brought the spectators back in a rush to stare out of the front windows.

"We've lost the cables!" Richards yelled. "Oh, my God! We've lost both the cables!" His eyes were wild with fear. "Oh, my God, this is punishment for our sins, Ah know it!" he babbled.

Donald swore and ran to the front to look out through the hissing rain. The wipers did little to help with the visibility. The tugs had disappeared... completely. He grabbed Richards by the arm, making him wince.

"Get a hold of yourself, man. Are you sure? Are you bloody sure?" Donald almost yelled.

"Let go of me!" Richards tore his arm free. "Yeah, I'm fucking sure. We're dead men walkin'! God help us now!" he wailed.

Donald had to hold himself back. All he wanted to do was punch the man in the face and get him to straighten up. Shooting the whining bastard would make him feel much better, but they probably needed him.

"Call the tugs, right now!" he snarled at Daryl, who looked as though he also might be losing it, he was so pale and shaken.

Daryl took the radio in shaking hands, and after a brief fumble he managed to make a call.

The radio hissed for a few moments so he called again. "Where the heck are you, Joey, Giuomo? Answer me!" he shouted.

"Ah'm here... keep yore shorts on," Joey called back.

The relief on the bridge was enormous.

"You know we've lost the cables?" Daryl said. "Come on."

"Yeah, I know. I can see you on the radar but not much else right now. That was one big motherfuckin' wave. Goddam near shit ma self! C'mon."

"Tell me about it! Where is Giuomo? Giuomo, where the hell are you? Come on."

There was no reply.

"Ah cain't see him from where I am neither. Don't know if he's pissed off or went under," Joey called back.

In the silence that ensued the men on the bridge contemplated Giuomo's possible fate. Larry looked as though he was about to faint and fumbled a small package out of his pocket. He snorted its contents right in front of everyone. He wiped his nose and mouth and went back to staring down at the wreckage of the deck. His fingers drummed on the counter and his foot tapped the floor while he whistled tunelessly. Richards muttered something to himself. Donald wondered if he was praying. No one seemed to know what to do.

"How the hell do you manage to keep this rust bucket afloat?" Donald asked Daryl. Then he pointed at Larry. "Look at that junkie over there! Does he really operate something on this heap of tin?"

Daryl glared at him. "We know our jobs," he said.

Donald gave a derisive snort.

The radio crackled. "Ah can come backward if you can fire me a line."

Donald snatched the radio off Daryl and called back. "What do you need from us?"

"Well, Ah need you folks to get off your asses and out on that there deck. Fire lines to me so we can haul in a new cable."

Donald, who had no idea as to how this might be accomplished, turned to Daryl.

Daryl had recovered somewhat. He took the radio back from Donald and turned to Richards. "Get that group of Filipino anchor riggers together, and git hold of Steve and Bobby. You're all goin' on deck, and you're goin' to shoot lines to Joey when he comes back within range."

"Hell no!" Richards said and Larry looked as though he might argue, but Donald drew out his automatic and pointed it at them. "Get going, boys. We don't stand a chance as we are. Willie, go with them to see they don't fuck off and hide in some rust hole. I don't trust either one of them."

Willie nodded. No one could tell if he grinned or if the scar on his cheek twitched, but his eyes were cold when he waved the two riggers ahead of him down the ladder with his Uzi. After they'd clattered down the ladder and out of sight, Donald looked back down at the mess of the main deck. The anchors had stayed where they were for the most part, as they were very heavy lumps of deadweight iron, but anything else that hadn't been lashed down was either strewn across the deck or gone altogether. He had a brief moment of panic and strode to the front where he could see down at the deck right in front of the bridge.

To his enormous relief the containers were still there, but they had all shifted. His container was a few yards closer to the side of the vessel, but otherwise it seemed to be in one piece. But the lifeboat was gone, its davit bent at a very odd angle. Now they had no way of getting off this tub anyway, he thought. He fervently hoped the boat they were trying to meet with could help, although with a crane on its side he wasn't sure how they would get the container off the barge. The small crane sticking out of the front of the bridge might be OK. He hoped it would still work.

He waited for the action to begin on the foredeck. He could see the tug now, heaving up and down in the huge waves as it drove slowly back toward them in reverse. Sea water broke against its bows in huge walls of spray higher than its bridge, while the low rear end seemed to spend a lot of time under water.

He estimated the waves were now well over forty feet high. Now that it had no headway at all, the barge wallowed like a log of wood. In his opinion it was in real danger of turning sideways to the sea, which would be the end, he reckoned. He stared back behind him and realized they might be spared that particular fate. He stared up at the massive helicopter deck that towered over the bridge. It could be the deck up there acted as a kind of sail, but that meant they were going backward, even if slowly, away from their rendezvous and toward land. The wind came in, as far as he could tell, almost directly from the west.

"How far did that fella say we were from Esbjerg?" he demanded of Daryl, who peered at the radar.

"Ah'm damned sure I can see that bastard Italian. Right there! Bastard's running away!" His finger stabbed at a blob of light headed away from them in an easterly direction.

Donald repeated his question.

"About an hour out from the coast," Daryl said. His tone was both wary and resentful.

"Have we made any progress since we turned?"

"Not much," Daryl said. His eyes flicked to Donald and away.

"Can you calculate how far we are from land?"

Daryl didn't say anything. He turned a switch on the radar and the scale was enlarged. He didn't look happy at what he could see.

"What's the problem?" Donald said.

"We're closer than I thought. That's the land there." His pudgy finger pointed to the outline of the Danish coast line. "We're less than twenty miles out, God dammit."

They both stopped what they were doing when the radio crackled. It was Richards.

"How far away is Joey right now?" he asked.

"Ah'm about two hundred yards off your port bow," Joey responded.

"You all in the bridge can make yourselves useful by watching the waves," he called to them. "When there's a big one coming in they need to git below, and no waiting."

"Roger that," Daryl replied. Now that he had something to do he was more assertive.

"You got that Rich? You keep listening. When I yell, you guys get below, you hear me?"

"I hear you."

"Not long now. Are your men ready?"

"We're ready."

The tug boat was suddenly close. It rose and fell, nose down one minute with its propellers showing, and then standing on its tail. Donald had to admire the seamanship and courage of this man from Louisiana. His boat had only to be driven against the barge and it could be sunk in a minute.

"Go! Go, men, go!" Daryl yelled into the radio. The forward hatch sprung open and men, bulky in yellow waterproofs from head to foot and bright red safety jackets, poured out. They ran to the railing at the front of the raised foredeck overlooking the V shaped wave guard, and aimed wide mouthed pistols at the tug. They fired lines towards it and ducked out of the way, and three men behind them did the same. The men on the bridge could see how the wind tore at their clothing and unbalanced them, but they clung to railings and fired off their pistols. Even on the bridge they could see there was an air of desperate urgency to what the men on the bow were doing. White lines arched out from the bows of the barge. Some went straight into the sea but others landed on the heaving back deck of the tug. Men who had been waiting there rushed out of their shelter, seized hold of he lines, and began to pull on them urgently, trying to tie them off to a winch.

Just then Donald noticed the sea beginning to rise ominously again. "Get them below!" he shouted.

"Git below! Git below!" Daryl screamed into the mike.

They could see someone, presumably Richards, yelling and waving his arms at the men on the foredeck, who abandoned what they'd been doing and raced for the hatch. They tumbled out of sight and slammed the hatch shut just as a huge wave swept in to lift the tug up even higher than the barge foredeck. The wave swept over the bows of the barge, which lurched, and buried the place where the men had just been under seven feet of green-brown seawater.

"Jesus!" Donald breathed. "Why is it so brown?"

"You don't know?" Daryl gave a grim laugh. "This is a shallow sea. It's only a hundred and fifty feet deep, maybe not even that right here. We're seeing the sand from the bottom. This is one of the worst in the world for high waves."

Donald scowled.

Daryl thumbed the radio, "You all right down there, Rich?" he enquired.

"Yeah, we're good. Good call. Did any of the lines hold?"

"Hey, Joey. Did you get a line to hold?"

"Nope. Gotta try again."

Daryl sighed. "Rich, you've got to get out there again."

"OK. We got a couple of injuries down here. Men falling about."

"We'll all be injured if you don't get off your ass and out there, mister," Daryl called back.

"Ready when I say. Joey, let me know when yo'r ready?"

"You bet." Joey had managed to avoid a collision, and now he once again moved in reverse toward the solid bows of the barge.

James Boschert

He came dangerously close this time and shouted, "Get out here, Rich, I'm waiting for you! Ain't got all day!"

The hatch sprang open again and the same men clad in yellow clambered out and ran forward, trailing lines behind them. In quick succession the men fired their lines. One after the other the lines snaked out over the boiling waters between the two vessels, and once again the men on the tug rushed out to grab the lines that fell across their deck. They succeeded in catching hold of several cables, which they wound around winch wheels in frantic haste and then started the winch slowly to draw on the cables. They managed to draw in a line followed by a thicker cable about the size of a man's wrist, followed by an even larger one. It was slowly snaking across the intervening sea when the men on the bridge screamed for the men on the foredeck to get under cover once more.

Again Donald and Daryl witnessed the frantic rush for the hatch, and once more the front of the deck was buried under tons of seawater. Donald felt a sinking in his gut as he watched the cable snap like a piece of string and the tug vanish into the waves ahead of them.

"I don't know if we can do this!" Daryl exclaimed. His features were a mask of fear and his hands were shaking.

"No choice, mate. It's that or we go under. We nearly had it that time. Get them out again. Third try's always the best." Donald tried to sound optimistic, but he, too, had a sick feeling this task was a hopeless one. Nature wasn't about to let it happen, but for him there was too much at stake to give up now.

"You guys OK down there?"

"Yeah, we're OK. We can hear shooting. What the hell is going on?"

"Forget about that. Concentrate on the job for Christ's sake," Donald said.

Daryl keyed the mic. "Stay on the job, Rich. Get a line to Joey, that's all we need right now."

"The Filipinos are getting nervous."

"Shut the fuck up and get out there when I tell you!" Daryl screamed.

"What's goin' on over there?" Joey called.

201

Force 12 in German Bight

"Get yourself back here and we can try again, Joey." Daryl said, ignoring the question.

"Coming in," Joey snapped. They saw a small plume of smoke from the stack, which was torn away by the wind in the blink of an eye as the engines were revved.

They waited a few minutes and called Richards and the crew to go out once again. While they waited Donald had the distinct impression the sea was getting worse, if that were possible. The sound of the wind had taken on a manic howl that penetrated even the thick steel walls of the bridge.

"Get out! Get out there, Rich," Daryl called urgently.

They watched as the tug came perilously close again, one moment showing its rear end, and the next its bows high in the air. The men rushed out, and this time they were more practiced and took their time sending lines over to the tug, even though the wind tore at them savagely. More than ten lines landed on the deck and were seized as a bundle and wound around the winch. The men who had fired the lines disappeared one by one, leaving only three as the cable took again and the long process of feeding the larger cables began.

The process went well, in spite of the tearing wind, the gyrations of the tug and the heaving deck of the barge. The three men leaned over the front and shouted to the men on the short deck below, who were feeding out the larger cable using the small winches in the bow. Slowly, painfully slowly, the cable began to snake out towards the tug.

Donald and Daryl watched the process from above, barely daring to hope this time it might work. To his immense relief Donald noticed the huge, full cable, about the size of a man's thigh, start to feed out and be captured by the tug. He watched intently as the men secured it to their own vessel.

It might have been because everyone was preoccupied with the success of the cable transfer, but their attention had not been on the waves.

Suddenly Daryl screamed into his microphone. "Get below! Get below!"

The three men turned and made for the hatch. The tug rose into the sky above them and a monster wave reared up right in front of the bows. Two of the men tumbled into the hatchway, but the third man fell. He tripped or slipped, but it didn't really matter what had happened; it spelled his death. They could see him reach for the combing of the hatch from his prone position as the wave towered over him.

The men on the bridge watched in horror as the wall of water slid over the rails of the bow. It picked up the yellow clad figure and swept him along in a welter of foam and spray. The hatch closed just as the wave struck. There was no hope for the man left behind. He was carried at great speed over the back rail of the bow deck, to be thrown against the solid surface of the fallen crane cab, and then tossed like a rag doll against one of the anchors on the deck nearby. He disappeared in the tumbling foam and bore of water that roared down the length of the deck, and they did not see his yellow clothed body again, not even when the water cascaded back out over the sides of the barge.

There was an awful silence on the bridge for a few long moments before Daryl reacted.

"Rich, Rich! What happened? Who did we lose?" Daryl shouted into the microphone.

"We lost Larry. Why the fuck weren't you watching? I fuckin' hate you bastards," the man shouted back over the radio.

Donald could almost hear him stamping his foot as he said it.

"Petulant bastard, isn't he?" he said.

Daryl keyed the mic but didn't say anything. He stared helplessly at Donald, but his anger was not so easily contained.

"I didn't see you out there risking your life for the boat, you bastard." He glared at Donald with real hate in his eyes.

"Stay on focus, Daryl," Donald said. He tried to make his tone calming, but it came out as threatening. He didn't want Daryl to fall apart, and it was clear he was almost ready to do so.

"Christ! Larry."

"Call Joey and find out if he has the cable tied in," Donald said, but Daryl didn't hear him.

He snatched the radio off Daryl and did it himself.

"Hey, Joey. Everything holding over there?"

He could see the men on the back of the tug laboring to anchor

203

the thick cable to their winches. To the people watching on the bridge it seemed as though the men were on a roller coaster. Donald felt a grudging admiration for these men of the sea.

"Who's this?" Joey asked.

"It's Don. Daryl's indisposed right now. We lost one of the men."

"Ah, shit! Who was it?"

"A man called Larry."

There was a long pause. "Sorry, man. Yeah, the boys tell me it's holding, but I don't know for how long. We're getting into shallow water."

"You just hold us till this blows over and then get us out to the location."

"If, and I say if, I can hold you, then when this is over I'm taking us all into Esbjerg, mister. No fuckin' arguments."

Donald wanted to shoot him.

Chapter 20

Engagement

Patrick opened the door to the food storage area with great care. The levers on either side squeaked as he pulled them down, making them all wince and hold their breath. He used his left hand to push it open and peered into the brightly lit chamber. The view of the whole room was blocked by the wall of the actual food storage cabinets. He slipped into the short corridor and peered around the right hand corner of the longer corridor, which led out towards the generator rooms.

Just as he did so, he noticed a man with an Uzi stepping into view at the far end. The man walked stealthily through the doorway, and Patrick could see others behind him. There was no time. The man saw him, raised his Uzi, and sent a long burst of fire down the length of the room. The noise in the confined space was deafening. Bullets zipped and whined as they ricocheted off the steel walls in between.

Patrick dived back out of sight, but the moment the barrage stopped he leaned out with his hand gun and sent a double tap back down the corridor. He had the satisfaction of hearing a sharp cry.

"Come on. They're already here. No ambush this time. Skillet, we have to get out and up to the cabin decks or we'll be cornered and have to go out on the main deck. Don't want that!"

They scrambled back through the entrance to the electronic

and electrical workshops, and then out into the narrow corridor which led off to the laundry and another, large storage room. They heard the blast of another burst of firing and the racket the bullets made, but by then they were well away.

"This way!" Martin called and led the way up some steel steps at a run, Hedi right behind. Just as they passed the door to the laundry it opened, and Patrick nearly shot Henri-Pierre as he peered out. His eyes went wide and he threw his hands into the air.

"Don' shoot, Pat!" he cried.

"Get out of sight and stay there, Henri. There's trouble," Skillet said. He vanished and the door slammed shut.

Patrick and Skillet chased after Hedi, who bounded up the steps two at a time. Skillet was limping but keeping up. They reached the top and turned left, skipping around the corner that led to the rear of the barge. On the right hand side were the crew cabins and on the left the galley. There were men in the galley, but not many. Patrick was glad no one was wandering about. It would be bad timing and dangerous, given the mood of the men who were after them.

The crew might have gone to their cabins, but most had not gone to bed. There were several parties going on. Patrick could hear music blasting away from his own cabin and the noise of laughter and shouting. Just they passed Patrick's cabin the door opened.

Johnny stepped out. He didn't see Patrick at first, but he did see Hedi and let out a whoop.

"Bloody hell, lads! Ah've just seen my angel. Ah have to be hallucinatin'! That's a woman, by God!" he slurred and made to go after her. There was a clamor of voices inside the cabin and the distinct smell of marihuana and whisky. The sound of Fleetwood Mac blared out of the cabin. Patrick grabbed Johnny by the shoulder and hauled him back.

The boys were getting high on the best Danish Gold and swilling his malt, he was sure of it. The bastards.

"Oy!" Johnny shouted in surprise and turned on him, but then he noticed the weapon in Patrick's hands and stopped, his jaw hanging open.

"Shut up and go back in there, and close the door behind you, Johnny. Do it!" Patrick commanded.

"OK, Pat... you the boss, man. What's with the... thing?"

"Never you mind, and tell the others to stay put or they might get hurt. I'm serious, Johnny."

Johnny nodded his head up and down. His eyes where beginning to focus better, and he started to look scared.

"If you're all drinking my best malt there will be hell to pay, Johnny. Tell Joel to stay put, too."

"Noo, Noo, Pat. It's Pete's whiskey, and well... ye know where the pot comes from." He giggled and staggered as the barge lurched.

Patrick pushed him back down the very short space between cabins and he went through the door. Patrick watched as it slammed shut, and then he scampered after Skillet.

They passed two more cabins where there was music and partying in process. At the end of the corridor just before the main bulkhead doorway the loud sounds of a movie could be heard. Skillet opened the door and peered into the darkness. It showed a western. John Wayne played a ranger out in the Arizona desert with the cavalry. The strong smell of pot wafted out.

He shook his head with a grimace. "At least if they hear shootin' they'll think it's the movie," he said.

They heard a shout, followed by a blast of machine gun fire. Bullets smashed into woodwork and whined through the air. Patrick dived over the combing of the doorway held open by Martin. Hedi was on one knee on the left hand edge of the doorway, and she had her hand gun pointing back along the corridor.

"Come on, you slow buggers!" Martin said as bullets tore into the soft walls of the corridor, throwing chips and smashing notice boards to pieces. Glass shards flew in a shower to the floor.

Patrick heard four sharp reports, two from Hedi and two from Skillet. The shooting stopped at the far end.

"Help!" Hedi called. "Skillet is hit!" She holstered her pistol and reached for Skillet.

He'd fallen backwards, his head only a foot away from the

combing.

"Get him through, I'll cover you!" Patrick yelled and leaned out with his own handgun to send several double taps back up the corridor towards the figures at the other end. He didn't have much ammo and wanted to conserve what he had.

Martin and Hedi wasted no time; they grabbed Skillet by his coverall shoulders and hauled him through the opening. He gasped as he bounced over the combing but otherwise said nothing.

"This is totally unacceptable!" Martin said loudly. "They're making a mess of the living quarters. There'll be a hell of a bill to pay!"

"Would you *please* fucking concentrate, Marti?" Patrick said.

"OK, chum. Skillet, how yer doing?" Martin asked the rigger lying on the grating next to him.

"Ah'll live, I guess." Skillet grunted with pain as he tried to sit up.

Patrick caught a glimpse of one of the figures lying prone in the middle of the corridor before the door was slammed shut and the levers were thrown by Martin.

"You guys got one of them, I think," Patrick said as he turned to see Hedi cradling Skillet on her knees. There was a lot of blood around his shoulder, and he clenched his teeth with the pain.

"OK, Pat, you do rear guard and we'll carry him. Where too?" Martin said. They were at the top of the stairs leading down to the after winches. The huge room was quiet, as the machines were still.

"We need to circle back around behind them if we can, Marti. Make for the pump rooms, we'll have some cover there. I'll be right behind you." He watched as Hedi tore open the coverall and exposed a nasty hole in Skillet's left shoulder.

"It didn't hit the lung, I think," she said calmly enough. "But I must stop the bleeding, and he'll need treatment at once!"

Skillet reached into his pocket with his right hand and pulled out a clean handkerchief. He looked pale, but not as though he was about to pass out. Martin passed along a not-so-clean cloth he found in his pocket.

Hedi quickly placed the cloths in a tight wad over the wound and told Skillet to hold it there. He did so with a nod of thanks. They lifted him to his feet, and while Martin and Hedi supported him down the steps Patrick stayed near to the door.

"Come on, Skillet, me old mate," Martin said. "Pat thinks we got one of them."

"I recon it was Hedi here." Skillet gave Hedi a wan smile. "She's a cool one, this chick."

Hedi looked embarrassed but pleased.

Patric opened the door a crack, just enough to allow him to see down the corridor. Two men were creeping along close to the walls. He sent another two rounds down towards them, knowing that the pistol didn't amount to much beyond a few dozen feet. It still had the effect of making the men dive for doorways nearby. They returned fire, which was what he wanted. He didn't want them to figure out they could go around as well. He wanted them to keep coming. The figure at the far end of the corridor stayed where it had fallen. He wished he could have hit one of these two, but they were quick and much more careful now.

He shut the door, closed the latches, and hastened down the steps to the base of he winch room. If he did this right he had them trapped, as there was only one other way out.

Just as he reached the floor Martin showed up. "You go with those two and get Skillet taken care of, Patrick. I'll deal with these guys."

Patrick was about to protest but Martin said, "Look, Pat, I've got the big gun and someone needs to turn off the generators and even the odds a little. I can lead these guys around a bit, and I can do it in the dark, but you need to take care of Skillet and the generators. I don't know how to muck about with all that electrical stuff. How many are there out in the corridor, by the way?"

"There's two left of this lot. The rest might be up on the bridge for all I know. You be careful, Martin. Give me five minutes to get Skillet to the infirmary. We can hide him in there if we get lucky, and then I'll turn off the generators."

The barge gave a huge lurch. Both men were thrown against the railing overlooking the winch well and had to hang on tight while the barge seemed to tip upwards at an angle and twist in a strange manner they'd never experienced before. Eventually it began to move back towards level, and then, as though on a pivot, the front of the barge began to tip at an alarming angle. The whole vessel groaned and settled slowly back to its normal roll and slight pitch.

"Bloody hell! What's going on out there?" Martin said and glanced up at the ceiling of the huge chamber as though it could provide answers.

"No idea, but they said the weather would come in hard. Come on, mate, find some good cover and make sure you can get out. Don't get trapped, that's for them. See you in a little bit."

He rushed off to the entrance Hedi and Skillet had taken and met up with them in the jetting pump room right next door.

Hedi had tied a crude bandage around Skillet's shoulder and fashioned it as a kind of sling. He looked pale but aware.

"Where's Martin?" he asked.

"He wanted to play the hero. Told me to turn off the generators, which I think is a good idea. Wish I'd thought of that before," he said. "Hedi, you're doing OK there, thanks. Now we've got to go."

They hastened across the second jetting room area and turned left into the starboard pump room. Skillet, limping, leaned on Hedi as they traversed the pump room to find themselves back in the generator room where the noise of the diesels stifled any other. The huge machines were doing well, Patrick noted absently. They hadn't gone off for hours, which meant it was when they were on the pipe the problem resurfaced. His mind wanted to chew on that but there were more urgent things to attend to now.

There was a stairway that led up to the starboard cabins from the generator room. Patrick went up first to make sure none of the goons lurked about in that particular corridor, and when he saw no one at all he motioned the two at the bottom of the stairs to get up with him as quickly as they could. He noticed a large stain on the floor and guessed that this had been where the shootout had occurred. The bodies of Leonard and the downed goon had been moved out of sight. He was worried about Martin but knew he shouldn't be. Martin was a tough, former SBS diver who had learned his trade well and knew how to look after himself.

The hospital was right across from the stairwell and it only took a moment to get across the corridor and into the darkness of the room. It smelt of antiseptic. Patrick stayed near the door and turned on the light switch.

A figure stirred in the corner. In an instant Patrick and Hedi pointed guns in its direction. Guillaume sat up on one of the gurneys and rubbed his eyes.

"Who's that? Holy shit! What's going on?" he asked in a raspy, sleep-laden voice.

Patrick heaved a deep breath. "Gilly, Skillet is hurt. It's bad. You need to fix him up until we can get a chopper out here to medivac him off."

Guillaume landed on his feet next to the gurney. He was in his pajamas, which were covered in small teddy bear prints. He didn't seem in the least embarrassed by his attire, but there was surprise and concern written all over his face.

"What happened, Skillet?"

"It's a gunshot wound. Can you help?" Hedi wasted no time with introductions, but he recognized her, gaped and nodded, too stunned to speak.

"Better get him onto the table over there," he said. Based on his thick voice Patrick figured Guillaume had been drinking the night before. Who didn't on this floating steel prison full of lost souls?

Hedi and Guillaume helped Skillet onto the thin mattress that covered a steel gurney. Skillet laid back, clearly exhausted from the effort to get here. Hedi hovered about him watchfully. Guillaume leaned over him and lifted the crude dressing with care to expose the wound. "It looks like a gunshot wound!" he exclaimed.

"Well duh! She just told you that, you nit-wit!" Patrick said. "Can you fix him up? By the way, he's a collector. He has another wound on his leg."

"Bloody 'ell! I 'ave never done this kind of thing before," Guillaume said, his French accent stronger than before. He looked nervously at Skillet.

"Well, now's your chance, buddy. You'll need to get it out before it goes bad," Skillet said in a weak voice.

Guillaume went back to examining the wound. "OK," he

muttered. "I think I might be able to do this, but I'll need help."

"I can help you," Hedi said.

Patrick and Hedi's eyes met. He nodded.

Suddenly he hissed, "Shut up, everyone!"

They all went motionless, and they heard the pounding of boots outside. The sound receded and a door further along the corridor slammed, followed by silence.

Patrick continued to listen and after a while he opened the door to peer out.

He shook his head. "Nothing there. Keep the door locked when I'm gone. Three knocks and then two. No one comes in other than me. Get the job done, Gilly, then get him out of sight. Never know... they might come searching," he told them

Guillaume looked frightened. "Come back? 'ere?" he asked.

"There are some bad men out there, and they shot Skillet. You must hurry, but don't make a mistake," Hedi said.

"I'm going down to the generator room. The lights will go off in a couple of minutes. You have emergency lighting here, don't you, Gilly?"

"Yes, it's there," Guillaume pointed. He turned on a switch which lit up several other lights in the room. "Move him under that one over there while I get prepared," he said to Hedi.

"I'm off then," Patrick said. "Skillet, don't go wandering off now, your angel is right there with you, mate."

He grinned as Skillet gave him the surreptitious finger, and then leered up at Hedi who ignored him and said, "Please be careful, Patrick."

He liked the tone in her voice.

*****

After Patrick had gone Hedi locked the door behind him and returned to Skillet.

"We need to get you out of this clothing and into something clean," she said while she pushed his gurney under the light Guillaume had indicated. Skillet glanced up at her nervously.

Hedi grinned despite her own exhaustion and worry. "It's all right, I've seen a naked man before."

Skillet sighed and said." Hmm I guess, put my gun somewhere Ah can reach it will you Hedi?"

Guillaume arrived with a medical smock on over his pajamas and medical gloves on his hands. "I will help him change while you go and get one of these smocks and clean your hands, Miss." His tone was prim as he pointed to the corner he'd just come from. She nodded and went off to do as she was told.

Hedi smiled to herself at the discomfited plea in Skillet's eyes when she passed him and turned her back on the two men. She could hear the injured man grunt with pain as they took off Skillet's coveralls and boots, which landed with a thump on the floor. The room seemed to be a small haven of sanity in a ship full of weird, dangerous people and awful weather conditions outside. She shivered, feeling tired and frightened. Her hands were trembling with reaction from the shooting earlier. She'd never fired her personal weapon other than in practice before.

It was one thing to go through her training as a policewoman, but this was well outside her experience. All the same, she was determined not to show any weakness to these slightly insane men who were trying to protect her. She took a deep breath and held it for a few, long seconds and then let it out. She felt better.

By the time she'd donned a smock, scrubbed her hands, and put on gloves she felt calmer, and Skillet was ready. He lay back with his head on a clean pillow, wearing a fresh set of orange coveralls that were rolled down to his stomach, exposing his chest and the bloody area of his shoulder. Guillaume had examined his leg and pronounced it a flesh wound; the bullet had passed right through. He had expertly cleaned and dressed it, having just finished when Hedi came back.

"You will need a stitch or two later, Skillet," he told his patient, "but right now I 'ave to deal with the other one." Then he turned to Hedi.

"I've never done this before, Miss, but if you can 'elp I think we might be OK," he told her.

"Does he get an anesthetic?" she asked.

"I can only give a local, so we'll clean it first and then I can go to work." Guillaume seemed to be more confident now that he had a purely medical problem to deal with.

"You can just hold ma hand while he's at work, Miss Hedi." Skillet attempted a leer at her.

She laughed despite herself. "Are you people never serious?" she enquired. "Those two, Patrick and Martin. They're always joking... even when it's dangerous."

"Oh, yeah, well, it gets to be like that, Miss. Those two Brits? They're real nice guys, but a little crazy, too. We're lucky to have them on our side, so don't worry and come and hold ma hand while Gilly gets to work."

"You will have to wait for the hand holding, mister," Guillaume grunted as he prepped the area around the wound. "She's going to be needed with me."

Skillet gave an exaggerated sigh, Hedi grinned, and then the lights went off.

*****

Patrick slipped out of the hospital room and across the corridor without encountering anyone. He sped down the steps into the warmth of the generator room. At first he thought he was alone when he cautiously moved into the control room overlooking the roaring machines. A small movement made him whirl about, and he found himself pointing his gun at Joel's head.

Joel was wide eyed with shock as he regarded his colleague from near the console.

"Christ, Patrick! What the fuck's going on?"

"What do you mean?" Patrick asked, feigning stupidity.

"You've got a gun pointed at me for Christ's sake, and we, me and the techs, heard shots earlier. In fact the corridor outside our cabin sounded like a shooting range and looks like it was. And Virgil is lying dead up there. Has everyone gone crazy?"

"OK, Joel. It's gotten really dangerous, and you need to go back to the cabin and stay there till this is done."

Whatcha mean done? Hey, mate, it's Joel you're talking to. There's a bunch of guys up there who are bloody terrified, and all you can say is go back to the cabin? What are you doing here anyway? You could at least explain what's going on, Pat." Joel looked angry and frightened.

Patrick sighed. He wished he could simply go back to his cabin with Joel and finish the bottle of Jura he'd hidden.

"Did you bastards drink my malt?" he asked without thinking.

Joel threw his hands in the air. "For Christ's sake, Pat. We're having some kind of gun fight at the O.K. Corral here and you're worried about your fuckin' whisky!" he said, his tone was incredulous. "I hid it, OK? Not even Johnny will find it. Now will you tell me what the fuck is goin' on?"

"You just don't understand, you silly bugger. It's not whiskey, it's malt. Some malts are like the Holy Grail. You're an ignoramus!" Patrick glanced out the control window at the generators to make sure no one had appeared, and then explained in a few short sentences what had been going on since Charlie died. He omitted to mention where Skillet was and where Martin might be, and stuck to the facts about the Brits upstairs, and Daryl and his trolls.

"Did Ryan and Larry really kill him?"

Yeah, I got Ryan to confess to that, at least. Larry did the actual dirty deed. Charlie got greedy and threatened to rat on them, that's why he met with an accident. But it's much larger than just these twits on the barge. The guy leading this mob isn't coy about topping people. First the other cop, and now they're after the girl and Skillet."

Joel seemed to make up his mind. "I like you, Pat. Everyone says you are a dark horse, but I'd never have thought you were up to this. Brit Special Forces or something, were you?"

Patrick nodded. "Or something, yeah. Long time ago."

"What can I do to help, mate?" Joel said, but he was clearly nervous.

Patrick thought about it as he regarded Joel closely. Finally he nodded. "OK," he said. "Here's what I want you to do for me."

*****

Patrick made his way aft to find out how Martin fared with the hoods in the winch room. He wished he'd thought of the small Motorola handsets, which were in racks here and there. There had been one in the control room for the generators, and Joel had pointed this out. They'd picked a channel that seemed unoccupied and tested four of the sets. He now had three in his possession: one for himself, one for Martin and one for Hedi.

He'd told Joel to wait for his signal and then turn off the generators. Afterward he was to stay in the control room, pretending to try and fix them if anyone came to investigate. He told him his prime suspects on the barge crew were Daryl, Larry and Ryan, but there could be others, including perhaps even Roger, the other super. Joel's eyes had widened at this information. Clearly he'd had no idea what had been going on.

Patrick made his way along the side of the control room where he could see Joel waiting nervously by the main switches, and then he was in the pump room starboard side, moving carefully through the myriad of small pumps that kept the barge systems going. These were humming and gurgling away to themselves and were a pleasant respite from the roar of the huge diesels that drove the generators next door.

Very cautiously he opened the door to the jetting pump room where he'd been only fifteen minutes before. Nothing moved. The massive engines were silent and still, the smell of grease and diesel was rank, but there did not appear to be anything alive in the echoing chamber. He moved to his right, toward the port side, where he'd left Martin in his ambush.

He eased himself through the last door where he had last seen his friend. Again there was no movement, and as his eyes swiftly scanned the room his alarm grew. Then he saw a dark figure draped over the railing above him, on the grating at the top of the stairs that led to the cabins. Patrick was himself motionless, but he watched the figure carefully for any signs of movement. There was none; the figure on the grating was dead. His eyes flicked around the chamber for signs of activity.

A slight sound from the back of the chamber made him freeze. He lifted his pistol to the ready and crept slowly towards the sound, every nerve screaming alarm. He peered around the drive motor of one of the two winches in the room and saw a figure on the floor covered in blood. It was Martin.

Patrick went cold. He glanced back behind him to check nothing threatened him and knelt beside his friend. At first he thought Martin might be dead; there was so much blood and he was very still. Then he felt a slow pulse at his friend's neck and his relief was huge.

"Christ! What happened to you, yer silly bugger?" he said in a soft tone. "How did they catch you out?" He had a hard time with his emotions.

Martin stirred and opened eyes in a a dead-white face. "'Lo, Pat... It jammed, fucking thing jammed, Pat. Wish I'd had a Stirling, they never jam." He sighed and shut his eyes.

For a desperate moment Patrick thought Martin had gone, but again there was a persistent slow pulse. Despite the fact he'd lost a lot of blood, Martin was holding on.

Patrick used his knife to cut up their clothing so he could stem the bleeding. The urgency of getting Martin to the hospital was paramount. There were two wounds. One to the abdomen, and one to the upper chest. He put his ear to Martin's chest and listened, but to his relief there were no alarming sounds of bubbling breathing going on. He could only guess what a mess the bullet had made of his guts.

He would have to heave his friend onto his shoulders, or figure out how to carry him and climb the steps with every chance the killer was around somewhere, but there was no other choice.

"Come on, me old mate. Let's get you up there," he said. "Joel," he called on his radio. "Turn off the generators."

Chapter 21

Mayday

Hedi was shaken out of her worried thoughts by the urgent knock. She almost ran to the door, but then remembered and waited with her gun ready. The three knocks were followed by two more. She opened the the door a tiny bit, but as soon as she saw Patrick in the gloomy corridor outside, supporting Martin, she gasped, opened it wide, and assisted him with Martin, who was limp and unconscious. She caught her breath; even in this poor light she could see their clothing was covered with blood, and it looked like it was all his.

They half-ran Martin to a gurney, and she watched as Patrick heaved his friend as gently as he could onto the surface and laid him down. He turned to her. "He's been shot twice, once in the chest and once in the abdomen."

His look of anguish told her he didn't think there was much hope for his friend, and she blinked away the tears. She brushed irritably at them, trying not to let him see. The last thing he needed right now was a weeping girl when their world was coming down about their ears.

Guillaume hastened over and helped them get Martin settled. "Jesu!" he muttered. "This looks bad."

"It is bad, Gilly. You have to do what you can to save him," Patrick said, and his tone was grim. "I have to get out of here and find out what's going on upstairs."

Force 12 in German Bight

"Do you need help?" Hedi asked.

"Yes, you need to stay here and guard these guys for the moment, Hedi. I have to find the other two and get them sorted out. I'll bring them back here."

She nodded, tense and worried, and tried hard to keep the panic from rising out of control.

"Both these men need hospital care. Martin is critical," Guillaume said. His tone was fearful as he pried the overalls off Martin to get to the wounds. "Miss, need your help. Got to stop the bleeding, or we'll lose him." He grunted as he swabbed at the still leaking holes in Martin's torso. "He has a very low pulse. I might be able to improve things if I can get an IV into him."

Hedi gave Patrick a quick glance. "Be careful, Patrick," she said as she turned.

He nodded. "I need clean overalls," he said and went to the back of the room to hunt for some. His were soaked in blood. She marveled at how much blood Martin had lost and the fact he was still alive.

Once in a clean pair of orange overalls, Patrick made for the door. "Don't let anyone in unless you hear the signal," he repeated.

Hedi hurried over and let him out. Their faces were close, and for the briefest moment she wondered if she should kiss him. Then he was gone.

*****

Feeling ridiculously pleased to hear her say his name, Patrick hurried along the darkened corridor and gained the base of the stairway. He glanced at the luminous dial of his watch. It showed six thirty in the evening. He yawned; the lack of sleep and the fighting had tired him out, but there was no chance of any rest anytime soon. He had to find out what was going on outside the barge and on the bridge. The barge behaved as though it was in very rough seas, and he wasted to know just how bad.

He knew he was taking a risk, as he might have been recognized at any one of the shooting exchanges, but that was a chance he would have to take.

He gained the level of the radio shack without encountering

220

anyone, which made him wonder, but he didn't have time to worry about that right now. He climbed up the last set of stairs and reached the bridge.

The thug from England he had met on the stairs met him at the top, standing in his way.

"What do you want?" he demanded. Patrick noticed his hand was in the pocket of his leather jacket and was sure a pistol pointed at him.

"Hello, mate," he said. "I always come up here when I'm starting a new shift. Got to check the instruments and make sure they're all in working order."

He pretended not to notice the gun pointing at him and continued up the stairs when he heard the unmistakeable voice of Daryl on the bridge say, "It's OK, Don. He's the ship's engineer. C'mon up, Patrick."

The hard man stepped back, but kept cold eyes on Patrick, who nodded to him and peered around the now gloomy bridge area. Patrick scanned for any other strangers and saw two more, standing near the back of the bridge.

Daryl stood at the front and stared out at something ahead of the barge. Patrick's eyes swept around the room, missing nothing, including the freshly cleaned floor where Skillet had told him Rogers had died. Richards was there, standing next to Daryl. They both looked up at him with worried expressions.

The men seemed to Patrick to be frightened, exhausted and cowed. He'd never seen Daryl's normally florid features so pale. There was another man at the back of the room, who had a blond mustache and long blond hair in a pony tail. He seemed tough, and Patrick recognized him from their brief encounter below. He prayed the man wouldn't do the same for him. His right hand was in the pocket of his padded wind cheater, holding something which was pointed at him. Next to him was a shorter man, who also had something pointing at him. Again he pretended not to notice and played the dumb engineer, concerned only with his machines. It made no difference, he wasn't going to get away with anything up here.

He nodded to the stranger and walked as casually as he could to the front and stared out at the raging seas. He gasped. The waves outside were enormous and he could only see one tug in the spray filled area of sea ahead of the barge.

"What happened to the other tug? Where's Giuomo?" he asked.

"Bastard ran out on us when we lost the cables," Richards growled. He took a swig of bourbon from a bottle on the counter in front of him. He was clearly half drunk.

"We lost the cables?" Patrick was incredulous.

"Yeah. Joey stayed behind, and Rich here and Larry got a crew to tie us up again. Never seen sea like this before," Daryl said. "This is more like a hurricane than a gale." He sounded frightened. He reached for the bottle of Wild Turkey and without wiping the top he took a healthy swig. Patrick only just managed to restrain himself from asking for a swig himself; what he saw outside terrified him.

He stared out at the monstrous waves and listened to the keening wind as it tore at the bridge structure. All the while the men below were totally unaware of the peril they faced. It was getting dark fast, so visibility was going to be down to nothing before long. He assumed Joey would keep his lights on so they could see him, but it would be of little help.

"Bloody hell," he muttered. "That must have taken some doing. Good work, Rich," he complemented him. He could smell the drink on Richards' breath.

"All the while we were sleeping the sleep of babes below deck. Never knew a thing!" he said in feigned awe. In fact he was stunned. It must have been incredibly dangerous work and had taken a kind of courage he hadn't credited to these riggers. He took a casual look at the radar and noticed they were close to the Danish coast line. Too close, he would have thought. Then he noticed the wind meter dial. Incredulous, he stared at it again. It read 45 knots. He did the mental math and realized that was almost 85 miles an hour winds, and the instrument flicked up to 50 knots now and again as gusts shook the frame of the bridge tower.

He didn't say anything, but he did wonder how long this situation had lasted, or could last for that matter. It seemed to him as though they might be in serious trouble from the bad weather as well as this gang of thugs.

Patrick wanted to know where everyone was. Larry wasn't on the bridge. "Where's Larry now?" he asked. "Resting up?"

Richards threw him an unfriendly glance that told him not to ask too many questions. There had never any love lost between the two, but now his glare was full of antipathy.

"He bought it... out there. A fucking huge wave just... took him, and he vanished, poor bastard," Richards said. Patrick could have sworn the man was near to crying.

"Bloody hell. I'm sorry, Rich," he said and tried to sound consoling. Inside he breathed a sigh of relief. One more down, but how many more to go? Three up here, and there had been more on the tug when it arrived. He and his crew had killed one of them, captured Ryan, and apparently killed Virgil as well, and then Martin had finished another off in the engine room. How many did that leave behind? he wondered. One way or the other he was hopelessly outnumbered.

"Y'all need to check on the radio, Pat. It's not working right... again. And when are you and Joel going to fix the generators? They've been down for almost half an hour," Daryl said.

"Yeah, see if you can fix something so it lasts, will yer?" Richards said, his tone full of spite.

Patrick held his peace but nodded and made for the stair well. During the time he'd spent on the bridge he'd assessed the man Daryl called Don, the other large man he decided to call Ponytail, and his sidekick, a swarthy hard case, he dubbed Tonto.

Don appeared to be strong and lithe. Not prone to saying much, but watchful and never turned his back. Patrick could have sworn he could see a submachine gun lying casually on the counter just behind him. No chance of getting to that, he decided.

"OK, I'll go and check on it. You'll recall we ordered parts months ago, but none have shown up, so..." He left the rest unsaid, but it was a dig at Richards, who was responsible for supplies of the technical kind. The look he got for that sally was venomous.

He clattered down the stairs making as much noise as he could and knocked on the door of the radio room, which was uncharacteristically closed.

"Patrick here, Let me in, you skiving bugger. Wake up, Stan. Time to go to work," he called.

Force 12 in German Bight

The door was opened by Hamesh, who appeared to be frightened and subdued. "Oh, hi, Patrick. Did Daryl send you? No one's allowed in here unless he says so."

"Yeah and guess what for, me old matey."

Hamesh gave a wan grin. "Stan is off, I'm on. Come in."

Patrick strode in and stopped. He could have spit. Zitty, the youth with the bad acne stood there, staring back at him with a look of deep suspicion on his cratered features.

"It's OK. The guys on the bridge sent him," Hamesh said.

He nodded and backed away from his position in the middle of the cluttered room to allow Patrick space to take a look.

Patrick's mind raced. How many more of these bloody people were there on the barge? If he could take down this one, would that leave only the three up above, or were there more below, the ones who had hunted Skillet and taken out Martin? He was sure it wouldn't be that hard to take this guy down. In one glance Patrick had decided he wasn't in the same class as the other three hoods upstairs.

In the meantime, however, he needed to see if he could get a Mayday out. That might bring the cavalry. He knew it was dangerous, but unless they got some kind of signal out to the Danish, or even the British authorities, there was no telling what these men might do next. They had proved they weren't coy about shooting people. Not only that, he had an ominous feeling about the weather and what it might bring during the night.

He sat down at the radio and motioned Hamesh to come and sit close, while he pretended to work the dials and asked silly questions.

"You'd better turn that knob over there and get the inductive capacitive network and resistor mesh on the servo shaft to move a micron or two to the right," he said aloud. "I've always said it was the filters and their servo systems that were up the chute."

Hamesh, who wasn't even a radio specialist and was spelling Stanley at the radio, nodded wisely, although he was totally bewildered as Patrick as he went through his nonsense speak.

"What d'you say, Hamesh?" he said, keeping his tone light and ignoring the other man in the room.

"Not much, Patrick," Hamesh said in a low tone. "They need

the radio. Trying to get hold of a boat out there."

"In this shit? Jesus!" Patrick tried to sound incredulous and simple at the same time. "Well, this old POS isn't doing well, is it now?" He tuned in to a frequency he and Stanley knew was linked to the UK telegraph system and listened to the yowling of the tuner. They glanced at one another. Patrick put on a frown of worry for the benefit of their guard and said.

"It's so low I can't hear a thing." He put the earphones on. Hamesh's glance told him that the man had come closer.

Patrick listened and turned the fine tune knob just a fraction. He got a station in the UK very clearly over the background static, which faded completely when he made one small adjustment. He locked the system onto this frequency and turned to Hamesh.

"It's not working, we'll have to check with the transmitter up there," he jerked his head upwards to the small cubby hole above them.

Hamesh nodded, but then gasped as Patrick reared up out of his seat and swung around to slam the edge of his left hand into the exposed neck of the guard. The blow was sufficient to make Zitty reel back, but not enough to knock him down. However, he was choking and leaned back, holding his neck with one hand, while he fumbled with something in his jacket. His face wore an agonized expression as he tried to get his gun out and point it at Patrick.

Patrick danced in front of the gasping man and delivered a ferocious snap kick to his crotch, which elicited a groan of agony from Zitty; his eyes rolled up in his head as he began to fall forward. When he did, Patrick slammed the point of his other boot directly into the man's solar plexus. Zitty jerked upward then slumped, and as he did so Patrick reached behind his head with one hand and gave a tremendous heave to smash his head onto the counter right next to where Hamesh sat. Zitty's jaw hit the edge of the table with an audible crack, some broken teeth shot out of his mouth to rattle on the side of the radio and then he slid off to the floor where he lay in a crumpled heap, his head at an unnatural angle. Patrick knelt quickly and felt his pulse. There was none.

"Dead, now that's a surprise," he said in a low voice to Hamesh, who was frozen in his seat, his eyes wide with shock.

Force 12 in German Bight

"J-Jesus, Patrick. Where did you learn to do that kind of thing?" he stammered.

"Never mind, Hamesh. We have to get rid of him one way or the other.

"You stay here while I take him below. He can't weigh very much." He retrieved the handgun from the jacket pocket of the body and slid it into his coveralls.

"There's always the window," Hamesh said, recovering enough to be useful.

"Good idea," Patrick said. He didn't relish the prospect of being discovered carrying the body by any of the other thugs. "Open it then, and hurry; we have a message to get out."

The window was narrow and stiff with paint. It creaked loudly when they pulled it open. Both men glanced upwards towards the bridge hoping no one had heard anything. Patrick doubted it had been opened in years, but eventually Hamesh got it opened wide enough for them to push Zitty out, head first. The wind outside howled and screamed at the opening, and they had to push hard to get the rest of him out, but his hips refused to squeeze through the narrow opening. The belt of the jeans got stuck on a catch. Patrick dragged out his knife and cut the belt, whereupon the body moved some more.

They both heaved at the legs and the rest of the body slid out a little more. Finally Patrick had to twist the legs so that the hips would shift, and Hamesh put his shoulder to the buttocks of the body, which farted. Hamesh grimaced with disgust and smacked angrily at the body, which shifted, then began to slide out, leaving the pants bunched around the ankles. Patrick shoved, and then gravity took over and the legs began to follow. A boot got stuck and refused to budge. Both men heard movement on the stairs leading to the radio shack level, they stared at one another wide eyed. Hamesh let out a small moan of fear and gave the foot an exasperated twist. The body disappeared into the gloom. Patrick assumed it would fall onto the deck below, where the sea should take care of the rest. No one was likely to see anything from the bridge, as the grating all around would have obscured the body being pushed out of the window. Hamesh hastily slammed the window shut and fastened the bolts that held it tight.

"Wipe up the water and blood with something, and hide those teeth or they will suspect us of doing evil things," Patrick said.

Hamesh's face was still frozen in shock, but he did as he was told while Patrick hurriedly checked the frequency, made a small adjustment, and then called out,

"Hello, this is the *Cherokee* in zone German Bight. Need to send message urgently to Danish police in Esbjerg. Anyone there?"

He repeated his call and listened with his eyes on the door. Hamesh wrung his hands.

Finally they got an answer. "Hello, vessel *Cherokee,* repeat your location." The British voice was calm but curious.

Patrick called in their rough location, but added, "You need to get the British police to send a message for the Danish police in Esbjerg. This vessel has been pirated and we need urgent assistance. Repeat urgent assistance. Mayday. Mayday. Mayday!"

"What are our coordinates, Hamesh?"

Hamesh looked vacant for a moment and said, "Roughly twenty miles out from Esbjerg, due west?"

"Twenty miles out from Esbjerg, got that? Esbjerg, Denmark, due west. We have badly injured people on board from gunshot wounds. We need urgent medical attention from Esbjerg as well as police support. Out."

He shut down the radio and was glad he had. There was a noise outside and the door slammed open. The man with the ponytail stood there, snapping his eyes around, but this time there was no pretense. He leveled a submachine gun at the two men innocently seated by the radio, who stared back up at him with what appeared to be surprise at the intrusion that changed to fear. Both stared at the gun as though it was some kind of snake.

"Where is my man?" he said. The gun was steady and pointed straight at them. Both men raised their hands in the air.

"Where is my man?" Ponytail repeated louder and jerked the weapon at them.

"He... he went to the bog, sir," Patrick quavered. "Said he was also going for a sandwich?"

Hans glared at them in disbelief. "What is this... 'bog'?"

"Er, the toilet, sir. Sorry, sir."

"You are certain of this?" he asked. "And he is also going for a sandwich, you say?"

"Look, mister, would you please stop pointing that thing at us? I... I'm trying to fix this radio, and you're making me very nervous. He told us he was going to the bog and then asked for directions to the galley. That's all I know, right, Hamesh?" he turned to Hamesh, whose arms shook as he stared at the weapon in Hans' hands. His nod was spastic.

Hans said something that sounded like an expletive in Danish, and then said, "What are you doing to the radio?"

"I'm trying to fix the bloody thing. Daryl, up there, said you needed it."

"Yes, that is so. Have you done so?"

"No, not yet. There are... problems, and I need to keep working on it."

Patrick watched Ponytail carefully even while pretending to be afraid. The gunman had a crude bandage on his right arm that was stained with blood. One of them had at least winged the guy.

"You will hurry up and then you will leave." Hans pointed the gun at Patrick who nodded obedience. "You will stay and run the radio when it's fixed," Hans told Hamesh.

At that moment the sailor radio squawked and Patrick knew time was up. "This is Stuart calling *Cherokee*. Is anyone there?"

Patrick leaned back pretending to be pleased. "Well, one of them is working anyway. Who is Stuart?"

"Never you mind that." Hans waved the gun at him. "Answer the radio."

Hamesh picked up the microphone for the sailor and responded.

"This is *Cherokee*, you are four by five, come in. Who are you?"

"This is Stuart. I need to talk to Don," came the curt reply.

Just then all the men in the room had to reach for something to hang onto as the barge heaved first in one direction and then the other. "Bloody hell," Hamesh said. "That was bad."

"You. Go and get the British man called Don," Hans said. "And no funny business."

Patrick got up and made his way past the gunman and called

228

up the stairs.

"Sailor radio is working. A man called Stuart wants to talk to Don?"

There was a murmur and the large Brit came to the head of the steps. "Radio working, then?"

"No, but the 'sailor' is, and there is a guy who wants to talk to you," Patrick told him.

"OK, I'm coming," Donald said and stamped down the steps. Even as he came closer Patrick could tell he wasn't going to be surprised. "Go on in there ahead of me," Donald told him pleasantly enough.

Patrick did as he was told and Donald followed him into the room.

"Ask him where he is," Donald told Hamesh.

Stanley repeated the question to the other vessel and soon there was a reply.

"I have you on my radar. Must be about two miles away to your north. You look like you might be drifting."

Donald cursed. He took the microphone off Hamesh and said, "Yeah, we could be, but you did good, Stuart. You need to come and take us off. We have some cargo with us. Over."

"Roger that. I'll come alongside. Do you have the means to transfer it?"

"Might have, if the sea settles for long enough, but it'll have to be quick."

"Sea is very bad from what the met is telling me."

"Just get your ass over here and take us off!" Donald said.

Patrick wanted to get out of there, but the man called Don seemed to be watching him, so he pretended to be casual about getting up and saying. "The generators are down. I need to go below and see if I can get them going again. Can't have the emergency jenny running for too long."

Donald stared hard at him. "OK... deal with it, but don't be blabbing off to all and sundry about what's going on up here. Do you hear me?" he said.

Patrick nearly laughed, the statement sounded so absurd. All the gun fire below had told everyone there was a big problem on board, and most likely that the barge had been taken over by pirates. They were staying in their cabins, hoping no one would notice them.

He knew by now this man had spent some time in the military. He didn't think it was the SAS, but you could never be sure; he had known ex SAS men to go bad.

"OK, I'll keep my mouth shut," he said and left the room. The temptation to run up onto the bridge was strong, but he didn't think he had the firepower to take the other one and hold off these two determined hoods, and besides, Don followed him out to make sure he went down instead of up. Better get below and find out how Martin was doing, he decided. Also, if he could get anyone else of the gang on his own below, he might even the odds some.

He clattered noisily down the heaving steps, wondering at the strength of the gale forces outside. He wanted to check out the diving station to see if it was still a viable place to stay for the night.

Running now, he raced down the two levels and ran the length of the corridor along the port side, and then charged through the end door to drop down into the winch room where the gangster still lay draped over the rails. He checked the body for weapons and found only a knife which he pocketed. His pal must have taken the gun.

He ran into the back room and up the two flights of stairs, hanging on tight to the railings to stop himself being thrown about as the barge groaned and twisted, and then the after part of the vessel began to move downwards. He found it hard to keep climbing while the barge was performing like this, but then it slowed and began to move upwards again. He marveled at how much movement up and down there was for such a huge craft.

Patrick forced the door at the after part open and immediately regretted doing so. Four feet of water poured in. It swept him backward and slammed him against the railing. There was so much water he had to hang on for dear life while it tried to tear him away and throw him down two flights of stairs. Then the after end of the barge rose high enough for the tide to ebb and the water level abruptly subsided, draining back out, although the combing of the door prevented it all from leaving. The water remaining in the chamber poured down the steps to form a small lake below.

He dragged himself to the door and stared out into the evening gloom. He heard a heavy thumping sound that shook the deck around him; he peered around the corner toward where the diving shack should have been. There was almost nothing left, and what little there was of it was a tangled wreck strewn over the deck. The heavy thumping sound came from the compression chamber rising and falling with the water level. It hung on its side and seemed about ready to tear loose. There would be no refuge in that place tonight. Patrick retreated back into the shelter of the after chamber, slammed the heavy door shut with a clang and bolted it as the rear of the barge began to sag into the seas. In a few minutes the deck would be under about six feet of water and he didn't want a repeat of the last incident.

He leaned against the rails, drenched and numb with cold and weariness, and for the first time he felt a sense of despair. Their two best men were out of action, one of them perhaps dead by now, and he didn't know how many more of the thugs he might have to deal with. These people played for keeps, which meant the cargo they had in that container must be very, very important. He suspected it was full of drugs.

There was no way he could get to it in these seas without being seen; he would go the same way as Larry if he tried. Not for the first time he wished he could at least see out from the barge, but the only windows on the entire vessel were in the bridge tower, the radio room, and the bridge itself. He felt like he was on some kind of submarine, and it was no comfort.

He shook his head to dispel the black mood that threatened to overwhelm him. He realized that he was shaking and not just with the cold and wet. The temptation to find a cabin and sit it out was very strong and he longed for a dram.

"Fuck me. Get a hold of yourself you silly bugger. You don't just give up!" he grated through chattering teeth. He shook his head again forcing himself to regain control. He couldn't just let it happen, others depended on him. He was soaked to the skin and very cold and could have killed for a drink. Turning away, he hurried back the way he had come to find the two other divers. He banged on the door where he thought Mike and Hansen were supposed to be. The door opened a tiny crack and Mike peered out. Patrick pushed past him and found Hansen sitting on one of the bunks, holding one of the spear guns, and it was pointed right at him.

"Whoa there, mate. Point that thing somewhere else, will you?" Patrick said.

"Sorry, Pat. Didn't know who it was," Hansen said, with a sheepish grin.

"What happened to you?"Mike asked staring at the bedraggled and soaked figure standing in front of them.

"Your old home on the top deck is no more, lads. Any spare overalls here I'm as cold as a witch's tit!"

"What d'you mean?" They both asked in unison, eyes wide with surprise.

"It's gone. Something swept it away, and the compression chamber is gone, too."

They looked stunned. "Jesus, that's got to be some wild sea out there to do that!" Hansen said with awe in his voice.

"Right, and it is. Do either of you two mugs know how to use a hand gun?" Patrick asked without preamble.

Hansen raised his hand. "Since I was a kid," he said.

Patrick sighed. He'd heard this before from his American acquaintances, nonetheless he dragged out one of the handguns he possessed and tossed it to Hansen, who sensibly checked the magazine and whether it was full. Then he cocked it and glanced up at Patrick. Patrick nodded approval. Hansen might do. Neither of the weapons they possessed was a remarkable piece of work. Italian factory made, but they would work at close range.

They looked for some dry clothing but there was nothing in the bare cabin.

"OK, both of you come with me." Patrick ordered. "Mike, bring the spears; we might still need them." He led the way back along the corridor at a lope, watching to see if there was anyone who looked dangerous along the way. No one came out of the cabins to investigate. The former shoot out must have scared most of them into a funk in their cabins, where they were safest. The entire length of the corridor walls were shredded from the machine gun fire.

After giving the signal at the door to the hospital room they were admitted by a surprised Hedi, who backed out of the way to allow them all to slip in, shut the door firmly, and locked it again. Patrick noted her hand gun was at the ready.

She seemed to be relieved he was there and smiled. The former chill from being wet disappeared, replaced by a warmth all over. He grinned at her. Then she noticed he was soaked.

"What happened to you?" she asked with concern in her voice.

"Went to check something out and got wet for my trouble," he said.

Mike and Hansen stared at the two men lying on gurneys with shock on their faces. "Christ! What happened here?" Mike asked.

Skillet tried to sit up. "Glad you could make it, boys. What's goin' on out there, Patrick?"

"It's a mess, Skillet. We lost the cables. Richards and Larry took a gang out and managed to get a line to Joey, who stayed, but the Italian buggered off. The divers' cabin has disappeared and the compression chamber's been trashed. We're in a force eleven or maybe worse, with only one cable."

"Jesus!" Skillet said. "Who's in charge up there?" He referred to the bridge.

"Not Daryl or Richards, that's for sure. They're getting drunk. Larry was swept away and we have a really rough night ahead. It's getting dark outside, too, so there's no telling what's going to happen next. I don't see this storm improving any time soon." He shivered. "I've got to change out of this stuff."

"How many of them are there, Patrick?" Skillet asked the question on all their minds.

Patrick answered from the other end of the room where he was peeling off the soaking coveralls and drying himself off.

"Well, we got that guy below, and Ryan's still locked up, I guess. I told Joel to keep the generators off until I said otherwise. Then we nailed Virgil in the corridor, that makes two down. Martin got one of them in the winch room before they nailed him, and I took care of one up in the radio room. That's four of them, but I don't have a clue as to how many others there are."

"Don't forget the one that Lenny got in the corridor." Skillet reminded him.

Patrick nodded. "That's right, five."

Force 12 in German Bight

There was silence in the room when he finished. He changed into a dry set of overalls as he talked. "Damn, but I could do with a nice cup of tea and a dram!" he muttered to himself.

"Who does that leave?" Skillet coughed and Hedi stooped over him.

"Skillet, you are badly hurt and need to lie back." She began to fuss over him and pulled the blanket up over his chest. He clearly enjoyed the attention.

Patrick knew a moment of jealousy as he watched, but he answered the question as best he could. "I really don't know, Skillet. I have to go and find out who might still be lurking about below decks, but there are only three of them on the bridge now. I think they're the leaders of the gang."

"What now, Patrick?" Skillet asked from his prone position. Patrick glanced at Guillaume. "How is Martin doing, doc?"

"He's still alive if that's what you mean, but only just, and I don't know for 'ow much longer, Patrick. He needs serious medical attention, and I cannot provide that for this kind of thing. I don' know 'ow much internal bleeding there is, but I'm sure there is some."

Patrick bowed his head. Poor Martin, he had survived the campaign in Oman only to get it here. That sucked. He wondered if his radio message had been passed along. He glanced up at Hedi and caught her look of concern. He tried to smile, but it didn't come out very well.

"I did get a message out, but I've no idea as to whether anyone paid attention and passed it along," he said.

"No many of us left to do the fighting," Skillet said from his gurney.

Patrick nodded, acutely aware of the odds against them.

"You all stay here while I do a recce," he said and prepared to leave.

"This time I'm coming with you, Patrick," Hedi said. "I am in the Danish police, and it's time for me to do something besides hang out here."

He stared at her. "I was planning on taking Hansen with me."

"Does he know how to use a gun?" she asked with a hard stare at him that challenged him to object to her wish.

"Er... yeah, I can use this," Hansen said and pulled it out to show them.

"We've got the Uzi Martin was using, but he told me it jammed, so that doesn't help much," Patrick said. "Skillet can show you guys how to fix it, perhaps, then Mike gets a gun, too." He shrugged. Hedi had a set to her jaw and had a determined look in her eyes that brooked no arguments.

"Come on then, we can go and find Joel and see if he can swell our numbers. Mike, you stay here and guard the fort with Hansen. I might need you both later."

Chapter 22

Force 12 in German Bight

The weather forecast mentioned a large storm cell moving across the eastern seaboard of the UK, but Inspector Steven Greenfield paid it little attention. He had problems of his own to deal with. Besides, it rained endlessly in October, so what was new?

The Scotland Yard detectives had arrived and made demands upon his time and that of his sergeant Toby. The two of them had to walk the detectives through the incident of the train death, the subsequent death of the man called Nigel, and their conclusions as to how the events were connected. It was all very routine, except now they had a man in custody and Steven wanted dibs on him first. Both he and Toby forgot to tell the Yard boys about Pete, who was safely locked in a cell below.

He had to endure the scathing remarks of his boss, who seemed to think he'd been doing nothing all day. Again he didn't want to say anything until he'd had a chance to grill Pete, so he held his peace and let Commander Pollock rant away. Finally his chief grew tired of the lack of response and stomped out.

While he waited for the detectives to leave, he checked out a file Sergeant Wilson had obtained for him. It contained more information on the man called Donald Saunders. He'd been in the Royal Marines and had done some time in Malaysia and Borneo, followed by a spell in Northern Ireland. He'd had a good record of service, but with a consistent pattern of charges for violence on his record. Otherwise he would have been considered good material for further special training. However, in 1978 when he was a corporal, he got busted to private for using a bayonet on one of his room mates in the barracks at Portsmouth. The man was only slightly wounded or the charges could have been far worse. The Royal Marines took a dim view of the incident, and he went to jail to await his fate. The subsequent court martial had him dismissed with a dishonorable discharge after serving one hundred and twenty days in the military prison. After that he'd disappeared until he surfaced again in London.

When he finished reading the report Steven concluded the guy was a hard case and should be considered dangerous.

He glanced over at the map on the wall and the chalkboard across the room. A piece of string connected two pins, one jabbed into London and the other in Harwich, on the east coast of England. Another string stretched across the North Sea to Esbjerg in Denmark. Why would the man go there, and so soon after topping one of his own, too?

Was he on the run or was it something else? On the board Donald Saunders topped the suspect list, but he'd added Nigel, the dead man, and connected the two with dots. He had little else to go on, but now he had Pete in the cell. Pete might be the key. He did have a shooter on him after all, and it was likely the daft bastard had forgotten to throw it into the Thames after the botched job.

Not for the first time Steven wondered what might have happened, and why Donald had gone out of the country.

Steven was used to taking an unconventional approach to cases, and this time was no exception. He didn't inform the detectives of his catch, preferring to wait them out till they decided to leave for the day. Once they did, he called Toby and the two of them went down to the cell where Pete had spent the last few hours. The night shift had begun, but the desk sergeant knew better than to disturb Inspector Greenfield when he worked late. Pete looked up when they arrived; he was pinched and cold. His jacket had been taken from him by an unsympathetic Toby, who would have preferred to be at home with his wife and children on this blustery, wet evening.

They handcuffed him, moved him to an interrogation room,

and closed the door on the outside world.

"I want a coffee and my lawyer. You can't just keep me here for no reason," he said. He rubbed his upper arms when they released him from the cuffs.

"You'll get time in the big house when we're done with you, mate," Toby said.

"Well, now," Steven said as he took a seat on one of the plastic chairs opposite Pete. "What do you have to say to being in possession of a firearm, Petey?"

Pete glowered at him. "I want me lawyer," he said, trying to sound determined.

Steven glanced up at Toby, who remained standing. It was an intimidating stance, and Pete kept nervously glancing up at him and then back at Steven, who calmly fished a pack of cigarettes out of his pocket. Steven didn't smoke, but he knew Pete did. For some reason most of the low life crowd in London smoked.

"Did you hear that? He wants his lawyer. Want one?" he said and offered one to Pete, who seized it and waited for a light.

Steven took his time finding the lighter. "Tell us a bit about your mate, Nigel. Sad story, that. How come he got topped? Know anything about that?"

Pete shook his head. "Nuffin', guv. Nigel?" He put the cigarette to his mean, thin lips and waited with wide, blue eyes. "Never heard of 'im."

"Hmm, tell you what, Pete. You shouldn't get smart with us. We're tired and grumpy... bit like badgers, you know? Don't piss us off tonight or we'll bite you. We have you on a gun charge. Could get you two to five if we push hard. Dear me, but you have a rap sheet a yard long! No judge will take kindly to you having a shooter on you. What evil things were you plotting?

"Then there's the matter of a murder on the rails by Paddington, which we can charge you with. The ballistics people will tell us what we need to know in the morning and then you're done for, my lad. Need a fall guy for that case, and you'll do as well as anyone I know."

He watched Pete go pale and start biting his nails, which were already ragged.

Force 12 in German Bight

"That's first degree. Another twenty on top of the five. You'll be an old man when you get out, Pete. What d'you think?" He flipped the cap on the lighter and Pete leaned forward.

Pete was clearly uncomfortable. He shivered and scratched his crotch while he took a drag on the cigarette.

"Why're you picking on me, guv? I don't know anything," he said in a whiny voice and blew smoke across the table. Steven wanted to choke him to death.

"We're not very interested in you, Pete," He said, and forced himself to make his tone reassuring. "It's that fella Don, who we think topped Nigel, who we want, and anyone above him."

He saw the flash of fear in Pete's eyes and pounced. "His name's Don, isn't it? Donald Saunders." Pete reacted like a trapped animal even as he tried to pretend nonchalance. The scratching continued. Steven wished he would stop it.

"You know we have his record with us, and he's not a nice man, Pete. Likes to use bayonets on people. Bad habit he picked up in the Marines. He topped your mate, and you can be sure he'll come after you if we don't get him first. You know too much about something, don't you?"

The interrogation went on for several hours until all of them were yawning. Both policemen wished they were home in bed. Pete looked haggard and cast envious looks at their coffee.

Toby, who hadn't spoken much up to this point, said, "Hey, Petey, you look a little peaky, want a coffee?" He filled a polystyrene cup and held it out to the man, who reached for it eagerly. Toby moved it out of reach and drank the coffee down. Pete looked as though he wanted to weep.

"OK, let's go over this one more time, Pete," Steven said. "You've told us where you were the night of the train incident, but it doesn't hold up. We have your car spotted in the area of the railway siding at eleven o'clock. Just doesn't add up, me old shiner." He proceeded to pick holes in Pete's alibi, one by one.

Finally he leaned back in his chair and said, "Toby, I think we'll just charge him and lock him up for the night. You know, Pete, you're a marked man from now on, because people know you were nabbed. That means when your 'lawyer' comes along you'll be on your own on the street, and guess what? Tiger Don is out there, looking for you. Got somewhere to crawl into, have you? I doubt if he'll take long to find you, mate. His record is impressive. He's one hard case, that one."

Pete tried to look defiant and failed. He was close to exhaustion by now, but both policemen knew they were coming to the limit of own their powers, too, and were frustrated. They had nothing much to show for it.

Steven decided to switch tack and asked, casually, "Know anything about a job in Denmark, Pete?"

He knew he'd hit the mark. Pete sagged and seemed to come to some kind of decision. He pulled on the remains of a cigarette and blew out a long stream of smoke. "What if I do know? What do I get in return?" Pete looked more and more like a cornered rat.

Steven gave an inward sigh of relief.

"Well, then give us what we want to know!" His tone had gone up an octave. "Names! We know all about Mr. Donald Saunders, and if you're good we can grab him before he gets to you, but there are others in this, right?"

Pete nodded reluctantly. The fight seemed to have gone out of him.

"Yeah... there is. He's big. Don works for him."

There was a knock on the door and Steven glanced up. Toby slipped out.

He came back with a piece of paper in his hand. "It's a message from Scotland Yard for the boys who are here. But they've left for the night. So they brought it to you as the senior bod here. Some bright spark thought there might be a connection with that guy Don. Someone sent out a Mayday from a ship called the *Cherokee,* asking for the police in the UK to contact the Danish police about some piracy going on on the North Sea. About twenty miles out of a town called Esbjerg. Same place Don went."

Steven forgot how tired he was in an instant. "Go on, what else does it say?" he asked, barely able to contain his excitement.

They left Pete alone in the locked room while they checked the rest of the message, verified it, and began to call Denmark.

When they were done it was late, but Steven had a couple of things still to discuss with Pete. He walked into the damp, cold room and said, "Now, Pete, have you ever heard of the witness protection program?"

"Like those films the Yanks do?"

"Yep. Now... Let's talk about that, and discuss those names you're going to give me. Especially the big man you mentioned."

*****

The town of Esbjerg shut down early for the night. The the impending storms and gale warnings over the Danish radio had convinced even the most determined drinkers it would be foolish to go too far afield. Factories that might have worked through the night shut down, and even the supermarkets closed. The streets were devoid of people and almost empty of cars. The few still out hissed their way along the wet streets, their wipers working furiously in the pelting rain as they headed for home.

The hanging traffic lights swayed and dipped as the wind from the west tore at them and made them look more like swaying lanterns at a drunken party. There were already reports of trees falling and tiles flying off roofs. People huddled in their warm homes and listened to the storm outside rattle their windows. Because this was a town of sailors and fishermen, the more pious prayed those at sea would be protected from the worst of the huge storm.

The Harwich ferry remained in port for the night, waiting until the weather improved. The Coast Guard had put out an order for all ships in the area to head for harbor, and forbade any boats to leave. Not that there was anyone interested in doing so. The last windstorm of 1981 was memorable for the number of small boats wrecked, and the fact it had destroyed many sea dykes in Jutland and done a huge amount of damage. This one promised to be every bit as bad.

In the Esbjerg police station there was an atmosphere of tension and worry. Nothing whatsoever had been heard from the police cutter sent out the night before, and now the weather was so bad not even the Coast Guard ventured to send out a search team.

Police Chief Balder knocked on the door of Kristian's office and walked in without waiting for a response.

"We've received something odd from the British police, sir," he said. He sounded excited.

"What is it?" Kristian said wearily. There were with deep lines between his eyes .

"Apparently a call came to the telegraph office in the UK, where ships often send messages. Someone called and told them to get in touch with the British police, but there was also a message for the Danish police. The caller, who didn't give his name, said it was the ship *Cherokee*."

"Isn't that the one we're interested in?" Kristian asked and sat up.

"Yes, it is, sir, but the message says the vessel had been taken over by pirates and there were people on board in need of urgent medical attention."

Kristian blinked. "That ties in with the message the training ship gave us, doesn't it?"

"Yes sir, but they also gave a rough position, which is only twenty miles out from Esbjerg!"

"Christ! In this weather? The met office says there's a massive gale out there. But twenty miles isn't that much. Could we send a boat out there, or perhaps a chopper, to get the injured out?"

"I'll ask the Coast Guard again, sir, but they've told me the winds are at well over sixty knots now; too great for even a rescue chopper to go out. They tell me it's gusting at about a hundred and ten to a hundred and thirty kilometers per hour. Unbelievable! They say this is a severe windstorm, and any ship out in this will be in serious trouble."

Kristian looked stricken. "So we cannot help them. But what about the pirate thing? Could the man we've been looking for be on the ship? He must have had help to take over the ship, but what on earth for? What would they want with a *barge*?"

*****

Hedi followed Patrick out of the door, which closed firmly behind them. He had his handgun out and pointed down the corridor. This was the most dangerous moment, as they had no corners to duck behind. "Stay close," he told her. "Remember your training and you'll be fine. Don't forget to breathe, will you?" He grinned at her, eliciting a tentative smile back.

"We need to check these cabins before we go anywhere. That one was Roger's, and the one behind it belongs to Daryl. I know he's up on the bridge, and I'm pretty sure Roger is dead."

She stared at his back in silence, then nodded, holding her gun up with both hands while she tried to remember to breathe the way her instructor had told her. She remembered to check behind them, leaving Patrick to focus on their front.

Pat moved carefully along the gloomy corridor, but he was also swift. He knocked on the first cabin and eased the door handle down. He opened the door slowly and peered in. The cabin was identical to the two they'd just passed, and while there were carry-on bags on the floor there was no one in the main room.

The emergency lights were on. Patrick tip-toed over to the alcove where the bunks were located, but there was no one there either.

They left the cabin and checked two more before they came to the one she'd used.

"Not this one, I was here. Erland's is the next one along," she whispered. He nodded. "I checked out his cabin with Skillet. That's how we knew."

Just then the generators came back on and the corridor blazed with light. "Damn!" Patrick muttered. "Joel was supposed to keep them off."

She shifted her feet. After a very long day she was tired, but alert enough to hear something. "Get into the cabin, *now!*" she whispered.

Patrick shoved the door open and they dived into Erland's cabin. Hedi had her gun trained on the door while Pat closed it silently. He left a gap just wide enough to see down the corridor. They heard hurried footsteps and low voices go past.

Hedi noticed him start then and blink with surprise. Then there was silence. Not even the muted sounds of normal life in the galley could be heard, which told Hedi the crew had gone to ground.

"What is it, Patrick?" she asked.

"There were two men. One of them was Joel... but the other was Ryan!" Pat stood back with a very pensive expression on his face.

"You mean Ryan got away?"

"I doubt it. Joel must have released him, which means... we have more problems to deal with. Didn't think Joel would be involved." He shook his head. "Well, now we don't have to go below. I think they're all up there now." He jerked his head upwards.

"Come on," he said. "We need to go and make sure there are no more guns around for them to play with in their cabins."

"Where is Erland?" she asked, although she knew.

"In there," Patrick said, and his tone indicated he was reluctant to let her see

She clenched her teeth and pulled the curtain aside.

Although Hedi had seen dead people before, in accidents and at the morgue, she was still shocked at the sight of her former boss. He lay sprawled on the bed, on his back, quite dead. She jerked away and glanced at Pat.

"You're OK, Hedi. I'll give you that," he said with his wry smile. He allowed her time to sit down at the table in the front part of the cabin and recover from the shock.

She shook her head and put her hands on her temples. "These people are evil," she said unnecessarily and shook her head again. "We mustn't let them get away with it, Patrick." She gave him a stricken look.

"Yep, they are," he said. He wanted to move. "Come on, they might return soon."

They checked the other cabins and rifled them for any weapons that might have been lying about. There were no guns, but they did find several clips of ammunition and a box of loose 9mm shells which Pat put in his pocket.

They heard some banging noises coming from above and a loud crash against the walls of the cabins, so harsh that Hedi held her hands over her ears.

Patrick and Hedi stared at one another. "I wonder what they're up to now?" he asked out loud. She wondered, too, but they couldn't just go up there and ask.

Hedi took her hands off her ears and listened. "I think I heard shooting, Patrick," she said.

He nodded in a somber way. "I heard it, too. Let's hope it's thieves falling out."

They made their way into the deserted galley with caution and helped themselves to some tins of spam, peanut butter sandwiches and candy bars. No one was there to stop them or ask them what they were doing, which suited Hedi nicely. She was starving and stuffed her mouth with bread and peanut butter. Patrick grinned and pointed at her face.

"What is it?" she asked.

He leaned over to wipe the corner of her mouth with a paper napkin.

"You had something... There. Gone. You must like peanut butter," he said with the wry smile she'd come to like. She would have wanted him to touch her again, but the barge gave huge lurch that threw them against one another. He stared into her eyes as he steadied her, and she wondered for a mad moment if he might try to kiss her. She didn't think she would mind at all.

Chapter 23

Rendezvous

Up on the bridge an intense discussion was taking place. Joel and Ryan had arrived and told Ryan's story. He showed them the wounds inflicted by Patrick while he'd 'interrogated' him. "When I get him he's a dead man!" Ryan said, full of bravado now he was among his own.

"Not if I get him first, Yank," Hans said. "He killed my friends, I'm sure of it. Bill got it, and now Toke has disappeared."

When they finished Daryl, told Joel to go down to the radio room and check on the status of the communications system.

"Now we know what he's up to, Ah don't trust Pat at all, an Ah don't want him up here neither. God knows what he's been doing with the radios. Ah don't trust that limey Hamesh either. Make sure he don't do anything stupid, Joel, but take it easy. We still need him."

Joel nodded and left.

"I wondered what was going on," Hans said with a vicious punch into the air. "Where the hell is that idiot Toke?"

"That Pat is a dangerous guy, and so is Skillet. He was in the special forces in 'Nam," Ryan said.

"Pat was in something like the Rangers, but with the Brits," Richards said. "I heard rumors about him from the techies."

Donald's interest was piqued. "D'you mean the SAS?" he said. *No wonder they're fighting back,* he thought. "You morons," he muttered to himself. "I've got to get off this thing as soon as I can."

"Well at least we got two of them," Hans said with a satisfied smirk. "I got the last one in that big room at the back of the barge when he got Bill."

"Know who it was?" Richards asked with a slurred voice. He was getting drunk.

"No, but he had one of the Uzis."

Donald waved his hand for silence. "Shut up, you lot. Someone's calling."

They all listened. It was Joel shouting from below. "Radio call!. Someone get down here please!"

Just then Daryl, who had been watching the bows and the spectacular performance of the waves in the gloom, called out.

"Hey, I think it might be easing off! The wind is dropping. Yeah, and I can see a light off to the starboard side. It ain't Joey neither!" Daryl shouted. He, too, was half drunk.

They rushed over to the starboard side of the bridge and stared off into the rain. All that could be seen were some riding lights that waved about in crazy loops around a quarter of a mile away.

"I need someone down here, right now!" Joel called.

"I'll go. You guys keep an eye on that boat," Donald said.

He ran downstairs and into the radio shack and snatched the Sailor microphone off Hamesh, who had been talking to Stuart.

"Where the fuck have you been?" he said over the radio.

"What d'you mean? That you, Don? I'll tell you where I've been, motherfucker. I've been sailing my goddamned boat all the way out here in the middle of a goddamned hurricane to pick up some goods. That's what I've been doing!" Stuart shouted back at him.

"OK, OK, Stuart. Calm down and tell me what you want to do. It's pretty rough out there."

"Last chance, my friend," Stuart called back. Even over the radio his voice seemed slurred and Donald knew Stuart had been at the whiskey.

He sighed.

"Listen you prick. Stay off the whisky and get this job done. I'm surrounded by half wits on this tub, they're not even half wits

James Boschert

they're quarter wits so I need you to be sober and not sink your own fuckin' boat!"Donald yelled. He slammed down the microphone.

He was surrounded by drunks and junkies out in the middle of a killer storm. What else could he want? He'd watched the elaborate plan to evade the Danish and British customs and excise fall to pieces almost from the moment they'd come aboard. He cursed the man called Patrick, giving him most of the credit for everything that had gone wrong. It did occur to him the weather had contributed to their problems as well, and he cursed his luck. It could have gone so smoothly. Off one boat and onto another, after a short wait on this rust bucket. He shook his head as if to get rid of the unsettling feeling that threatened to swamp him.

"OK, then we've got some work to do," he said. "You," he said to Joel. "There's a crane just below the bridge. Know how to operate it?"

"Yeah, I know how. I have to get into the emergency generator room, and I can operate it from there."

"Come up stairs with me, I'll show you what we need."

When they got to the bridge Donald shoved Richards aside and pointed down to the half container illuminated by the remaining deck lamps, which shone light over the wreckage of the deck and the containers just below the bridge.

"We need to hoist that small container down there onto the boat that's coming in," he said.

Joel looked down at the arm, and then at the raging seas and distant lights. "I can't do that!" he said with a wild look at Donald.

Donald took out his pistol and pointed it at Joel's head. "Yes you can," he said softly.

Joel started to sweat and swallowed hard. "Listen... er, Don. I'm just an engineer, but Ryan's a rigger, and he's a wizard at this kind of thing. If anyone can do this, it has to be him."

Donald stared at him for a long, dangerous moment before he lowered his pistol and called over to Ryan. "Get over here... Ryan."

Ryan had been in a huddle with Richards, but he came over and stood in front of Donald. "What yer say, mate?" he said, mimicking the English accent.

Force 12 in German Bight

Donald gave him a glare and said, "I hear you're magic with the crane at the base of the bridge here. You're going to lift that container down there," he pointed to it, "and then you're going to drop it on the back of the boat that's coming alongside."

Ryan paled, but Donald casually pointed the pistol at him. Ryan had already heard a thing or two about Donald, so he swallowed and nodded at the same time. "OK, I'll give it a try," he said.

"Do more than try... *mate*," Donald said, and his expression made Ryan's adam's apple jerk.

Donald went below to the radio room again, where he and Stuart talked for a while, and then Donald told Ryan and Joel to get into the cab of the small crane. It was accessed from the cabin across the walkway from the radio shack.

"Get in there, Ryan, and start it up. You, Joel, is it? You get down on deck and grab the straps, and then you two hook it up. Be ready for my call to get it over to the boat. It's coming in now, so move it!"

Joel was aghast. "You want me to go out *there* in *this*?" he asked. His tone was incredulous and his eyes wide and fearful.

"Yeah, you didn't want to be the crane operator, so now you're the man on the ropes. Get going, *buddy*," Donald said with a nasty grin.

Joel hesitated, trying desperately to find a reason not to go and risk his life, but Donald wasn't in the mood for rebellion. "Get out there, you bastard. I'll shoot you if you don't, you know I will," he said. "Then you can kiss your share of that box goodbye."

The two men were frightened, especially Joel, who now had to go out onto the deck, get on top of the box, and hook it up to the ball from the crane.

There was no doubt the wind had fallen off; the wind meter now only read 45 knots, but there were still rushes of water flowing across the top deck. Joel was scared silly about going out onto the deck, but Donald gave him no choice. He donned a life vest and the yellow waterproofs and clumped down the stairs to the main doorway out.

After he'd disappeared Ryan got into the small cab of the crane. Donald noticed that it was not a large boom and probably wasn't designed to lift more than a life boat.

Ryan had popped a couple of speed pills but didn't consider the effects serious enough to get in the way. He fancied he could do the job. With the electric system up and running and the arc lamps focussed on the deck in front of the bridge, he proceeded to turn the crane so the boom was poised just over the top of the box.

Donald saw Joel run out into the lamp light and clamber up the ladder welded to the side of the box, and then scramble onto the top, hanging onto whatever he could to prevent himself from being blown off. He didn't get to his feet; he couldn't, the wind was too strong for him and tore at his clothing while he struggled with the straps and the dangerously waving ball and hook just over his head. It was a good thing he'd made it to the top when he did, as a wave swept over the deck that would have taken him off his feet had he still been on it. Although the wave was nowhere near as high as the former ones, it still could have swept him overboard.

It took Joel far longer than the impatient men on the bridge had anticipated as he tried to catch the wildly swaying hook and ball, which threatened to bash his brains out if he got in the way. Finally, while they held their breath, he got the straps onto the hook and gave the thumbs up sign to Ryan.

Ryan, who was by now as high as a kite, began to lift the box before Joel got off the container. Joel gave a scream of terror and tumbled off onto the deck, where he lay for a few moments in a crumpled heap while the box began to climb into the air.

Ryan let out a cackle of laughter before he concentrated on getting the box positioned above the boat. Daryl and Richards were too drunk to do anything but watch with stupid expressions on their faces as Joel picked himself up and staggered back towards the main doorway. Willie and Hans were preoccupied with watching the boat as its skipper negotiated the waves to get into position.

Stuart's boat appeared in the full light of the starboard arc lamps. It was a sea going tug, much like the one Joey had out in front. It rose and fell at a far faster rate than the barge. Donald could see the tug and how close it was. It was going to come within a few meters of the barge and might even hit it, but he didn't care if the tug holed the barge. Good riddance. The tug's steel ribbed sides were designed to take a lot of punishment.

He wanted off this crazed barge full of drunks, junkies and a dangerous former SAS man. Where the fuck had he come from? Donald was no coward, but the container was his preoccupation, not quelling the restless natives on a ship full of dysfunctional imbeciles. It was probably going to sink anyway, given what a rust bucket it was. This was a mother of a storm, and he hoped it would claim the barge; that would take care of all the witnesses.

A crazy idea began to form in his head. There was no way he could risk a jump, but there was another way, although it was as daft an idea as any he'd ever had. What the hell. Life was full of risks, and this crate was worth it, all or nothing!

Without saying anything to anyone he ran back down to the crane room and told Ryan to put the box down on the deck, and only lift it when he told him to.

Ryan wanted to object. "Just do it!" Donald yelled at him waving the gun, and then ran out and down the stairs.

Hardly pausing, he slung his Uzi on his shoulder and raced down to the main deck door and ran out into the howling gale. He nearly knocked an already dazed Joel off his feet, but paid him no attention as he ran by, around the corner, and up to the container, praying a wave wouldn't catch him by surprise. He scrambled up the iron ladder and onto the top of the container, where he crouched just as Joel had, hanging onto the straps of the lift with one hand. He waved frantically up at the window at Ryan, who he could not see, in the hopes the stupid bastard hadn't passed out. He was rewarded with a lurch of the box and it began to rise.

At the same time he heard the roar of the tug over the howl of the wind, which was tearing at him trying to throw him into the sea. There was a screech of steel on steel as the boat crashed into the side of the barge, scraped it clean of paint, and buckled some of the plates when it rose with a wave

"That mad bastard is really drunk!" Donald said to himself as he grit his teeth and prayed he hadn't made a very stupid mistake. He soared into the air, hanging onto the straps for dear life.

On the bridge Richards blinked and rubbed his eyes. "Ah could swear that Joel got off the box, but he seems to have gotten back on again," he said and took another swig.

Daryl peered owlishly past him at the container, which was now in the air just below their vantage point and about to fly over the top of the tug boat. The tug was rising and falling alongside, busy bashing the plates of his barge into scrap.

"What the ferck!" he said. "That ain't Joel, it's Don fer Christ's sake. What the hell is he doing, the mad fucking bastard?"

"What did you say?" Hans said as he stumbled over from where he'd been checking out the back of the bridge. He thought he'd seen something move there.

When he got to the front and stared out into the driving rain he gasped and realized what Donald planned to do.

"The focking bastard! He's leaving us behind, Willie. Don't let him get away, no by God!" he roared in Danish while he ran to the door leading to the outside grating that ran all the way around the bridge, with his Uzi at the ready. It took a few seconds for him to wrench the door open on the port side and run around on the outside, fighting the tearing wind all the way. Willie took one incredulous glance outside, swore in his own language, and pounded out after him, cocking his Uzi as he ran.

By the time Hans got to where he could look down on the tug it was about to pull away. Ryan had dropped the container onto its back deck, right where he should have, with Donald hanging on for dear life.

"There, motherfucker! How's that for the champ!" Ryan yelled with glee.

He was so busy congratulating himself he forgot to give some slack to the cable. Don was shaken off the container and fell onto the deck, where he lay for a moment on the steel plates, stunned, with sea water sloshing around him. Stuart, on the bridge of the tug, saw the container descend and heard it land with a crash.

Thinking he'd spent long enough gouging the sides of the barge, he pulled the throttles back, the engines roared, and he turned the steering wheel hard over to starboard. The tug began to pull away.

Just as the tug started to accelerate away, Hans and Willie, both swearing and yelling with rage and frustration at their evident betrayal, leaned over the railing and began to shoot at anything they could see on the tug's decks. The chatter of the

Force 12 in German Bight

machine guns was almost lost in the screaming wind. They sprayed the back deck and made Donald roll out of sight, and Hans sprayed the bridge for good measure. Stuart heard the gunfire even in his inebriated condition, and then bullets shattered his bridge windows. He dropped to his knees for cover from the flying splinters and glass shards, but he instinctively pulled the throttles further back as he did so. The tug lurched and roared, churning up the already spume-topped water. It began to rise with a huge swell, putting its bridge almost level with the radio room but well below the maddened men who continued to fire their guns. Willie ran out of ammunition and paused to fumble for a new magazine.

Donald recovered and picked up his machine gun. He crouched behind the cover of the container, quite forgetting it hadn't been unslung from the ball and hook, and began to return fire. The tug moved so erratically, and the lights beaming down on the tug half-blinded him, making it impossible for him to see Hans or Willie properly. Hans ducked and scrambled backward as bullets whined and shattered windows just above his head.

While the duel took place, Joel had made it to the crane cabin. He was mad as hell and the first thing he did was to punch Ryan hard on the back of his head. "You bastard, you didn't even let me get off the fuckin' box!" he yelled and looked around for something harder with which to hit Ryan.

Ryan cried out with surprise, although the blow hadn't hurt much. Joel wasn't a big man, in fact he was quite skinny, and Ryan was large enough to make any seat he sat on seem small.

He lashed out in return with a snarl. Joel fell forwards onto the levers, which made the crane begin to haul in the cable. For a short while the cable obediently ran in. Joel tumbled onto the floor and Ryan rubbed his neck, swearing. Neither noticed for a few long seconds what was happening as they glared at one another, ready for another encounter. Then Ryan noticed the tension gauge had gone to its limits, and without thinking he applied the brakes.

Down on the barge Stuart panicked and had the throttles of the tug at full on, which drove the vessel further away from the huge bulk of the barge and the dangers lurking thereon. The cable still holding the container tightened and began to drag it across the deck toward the transom.

Donald was taken unawares for a moment, but he quickly realized with horror what was about to happen. Sixty million pounds worth of heroin was headed for the sea. He didn't have a knife, and Hans and Willie had started shooting at the tug again. Bullets howled and screeched as they ricocheted about the steel deck and machinery, making life hazardous on the back deck.

The crew of the tug had vanished the moment the container arrived, and now as it scraped along the short deck he didn't have anything to cut the straps with. The container smashed into a winch motor and demolished it in a shower of sparks from the heavy duty cable as the machine tore away. Then the container stopped, wedged into something. Donald couldn't see what it was, but an ominous creaking sound hinted the cable was tightening.

The tug drove away, the cable stretched taut, and when he peered around the corner of the container he saw the crane on the barge sag downwards and break away from its mountings. For Donald this was enough. He turned his Uzi onto the straps and shot at them, shredding them. The cable made a loud tearing and popping sound, which could easily be heard over the wind, when it tore away and leapt back out of sight behind the lights. The tug jumped off like a hound released from a leash and bored off into the raging seas and the darkest night. Donald laughed wildly and fired a parting burst at the lights receding behind him, and then staggered off to find Stuart.

Willie stiffened, dropped his weapon, and stumbled back against the wall of the bridge to sit on the grating. He held his chest for a few seconds and coughed out some blood before he fell over onto his side.

*****

In the crane cabin Joel stood over Ryan, who was slumped against the frame. The cable had lashed back like a bullwhip and all but demolished the cabin; there was no glass left, and the frame was distorted out of shape. Ryan had died when the strands of the cable tore away half of his face and neck. One eye was open and this glared up at Joel balefully. There was blood everywhere, but the rain swept in through the openings and began to wash it away.

Joel vomited into the wreckage then staggered out of the cabin across the space of the emergency generator and into the radio room, wiping his mouth on his sleeve. Hamesh sat frozen to his seat. He'd heard the shouting and then the loud smash mingled with the screech of tearing metal and shattering glass.

"What happened?" he asked, as Joel, soaked to the skin and covered with Ryan's blood, staggered in and fell into a seat.

"Stupid fuckin' idiot Ryan was high as a kite and didn't release the cable. Tore the crane right off the walls," he said. He ran his fingers over his wet hair and covered his face with his hands. "Dear God, what am I going to do now?" he groaned. "The bastard Brit, Don, has pissed off and left us behind."

"Were... were you one of them, then?" Hamesh asked.

"You're a stupid Brit git, Hamesh. Yeah, I was. We were going to be rich, and I could say goodbye to all this unspeakable shit in this floating toilet." Joel groaned to himself in a tired voice. "Ah well, I'd better go up there and tell Hans and Willie." He heaved himself to his feet and clumped out of the room.

Just as he did the barge lurched in a corkscrew manner and seemed to stagger. Joel kept moving, but the radio squawked and Joey came on. For the first time there was a tinge of panic in the Louisiana captain's voice.

"We've lost the cable! We've lost the cable! Do you hear me over there? Hello? Anyone at home at all? Fuckin' potheads! What was all that stuff happening on your starboard side? Come on, fer Christ's sake."

Hamesh reached for the microphone. "Hello, hello, Joey. Say all again?" he sounded incredulous.

"You all are adrift, pal. That's what I said." Joey sound resigned.

Hamesh looked up at Joel, who had turned pale and come back into the room with anguished eyes.

"Oh, God, it can't be happening!" Hamesh all but whimpered. "Not again!"

Joel was stunned and rooted to the floor. He took a deep breath and picked up the microphone.

"I'll get Daryl on the radio, Joey. Stay with us."

"Sure. Ah ain't goin' nowhere right now, but we're gettin' close to shore. We've been losing ground for hours now."

Joel ran out of the room and raced up the stairs. No one on the bridge seemed to have realized they were adrift.

"Joey says we've lost the cable!" Joel said breathlessly as he charged onto the bridge. Daryl and Richards were huddled over the chart, and the bottle of Wild Turkey was now only a third full. They turned bleary eyes on him.

Joel noticed Hans stood apart, tapping his foot and pounding his fist onto the counter while he stared vacantly out into the night. He hadn't even seen the cable break and he'd been looking straight at the bows.

"The bastard fucks off and kills Willie! Bastard! When I get him I'll... I'll kill him!" he roared. Joel flinched. Was the world going mad all around him? He wanted to slink into a hole and hide.

He glanced over at the radar and noticed they were less than ten miles from land. He blanched. They were in deep trouble and no one seemed to be in charge!

"What you say?" Richards asked him.

"We lost the cable, Rich. Joey just called it in. Didn't you guys notice anything?"

Richards didn't reply. He leaned against the wall of the counter, put his head in his hands, and clutched the sides of his face, which wore an expression of hopeless terror.

Suddenly he seemed to lose it completely. He pushed himself back from the counter and waved his arms in the air. "We're all goin' to die!" he wailed. "God's punishment is on us, we're all going to die."

"You shut your stupid, stupid mouth!" Hans yelled from the front of the bridge. "You're all so... fucked up I can't believe you! I can't believe you are seamen, for God's sake." He spluttered in his rage.

"Excuse me! Did anyone hear me?" Joel said louder than he'd intended. "Ah, fuck," he said as he peered out of the windows. There was no way they could get a cable back to the tug in this darkness or in these seas. Even he could see that. He went back down the stairs to the radio room.

He picked up the microphone. "Joey, I think we're screwed. I'm goin' to send out a Mayday."

Force 12 in German Bight

"Where's Daryl and Rich?" Joey asked.

"They're shit faced and out of it right now."

"Jesus! I knew you were all fuckin' nuts on that boat, but this is really bad. Irresponsible bastards. Yeah, you'd better do that, Joel," he said. "I'll try to stick around as long as Ah can."

Chapter 24

Retribution

"Something serious is up. We'd better go up and find out what it is," Patrick said with some urgency. "Come on, I know how to get onto the deck without being seen from the bridge." He disengaged himself. Hedi was reluctant to let him go, and it didn't appear to her as though he wanted to either.

He led the way at a run along the corridor on the starboard side, down through the winch room, and raced up the stairs at the other end. They opened the rear hatch door carefully, and Hedi was glad to see the waves outside weren't as bad as she'd seen before. The wind still keened and tore at them when they exited, and she hung onto his arm when a small wave topped the deck and slapped their legs. She shivered; it was frightening out here in the cold, with the sea a moving, ominous threat appearing level with the deck.

"Look! Look over there, Hedi!" Patrick seized her arm and pointed with his pistol out to the starboard side of the vessel. "That's a large boat and it's not coming this way, it's leaving. That might mean the bridge is clear."

"Perhaps you're right, but I think we should be very careful, Patrick," she said and stared up at the windows of the bridge, which were only dimly lit.

"Look up there. I see someone, and I'm sure he is carrying a weapon."

259

Force 12 in German Bight

Patrick stared up to where she indicated. "Yeah, I see. You might be right. OK, we have to figure this one out. We *must* get control of that bridge, and the radio room. Come on, let's go downstairs and think this through."

They made their way back to the galley to collect the sandwiches and were thus engaged when the door to the corridor on the port side slammed open and men poured in. The sound of them opening doors and calling to one another reminded them of the fact there were other people on the barge, men who were confused and frightened.

Hedi had shed her overalls, and when the men came running into the galley they paused at the sight of a woman in police uniform and Patrick, both holding weapons at the ready, by the sandwich counter.

"What the hell is going on, Pat?" One of the technicians demanded as they trotted into the room. In a very short space of time the galley began to fill up with men in a variety of clothing, from underwear to orange overalls. All of them crowded together and demanded in three different languages to know what was going on. Everyone was nervous and desperate to know what had been going on.

"What was with all the shootin', Pat" One yelled

"Are they pirates?" another asked.

"Who would want this piece of shit for Christ's sakes?" yet another demanded.

"Listen! Listen up all of you!" Pat shouted at the top of his voice. The excited babble died to a murmur.

"There are men on the bridge who have guns, and they've been shooting at us. This lady," he indicated Hedi, "is a policewoman from Denmark, and she's helping. He partner is dead, as are several others. Skillet is badly hurt and so is Martin. These men are dangerous as hell, they're not fooling around, guys. All of you should go back to your cabins and not hang around here. I don't want hostages taken, so stay out of sight and out of the corridors. We don't want anyone else to get hurt."

There were astonished murmurs of surprise and anger at the news. "Bastards!" someone exclaimed out loud.

"Who are they? What do they want with this old heap of rust?"

Johnny, one of the electricians, called over from the back.

There was so much excitement that for one, crazy moment Patrick wondered if he could lead a rush on the bridge. But then common sense kicked in; he knew full well men with machine guns at the top of the stairs would always win against a rabble at the bottom.

"Keep it down, lads. I don't want them coming to check on us. They brought a cargo on board and have been using us as a staging place, Johnny. We were just on deck and noticed a boat leaving. Could be it's taking them all away, but we're not sure. You have to let us check it out. Then we can tell everyone the all clear on the tannoy. OK, lads? Give us some time. Grab some food and and drink then get out of sight."

There were murmurs of agreement and some even offered to help, but Pat told them unless they had a gun in their possession they couldn't. A good few of them cast curious and approving eyes at Hedi, who despite the fact she was tousled and her uniform was rumpled and stained, looked like a vision to men who hadn't seen a woman other than a pin up or a blow up for months on end.

The men began to help themselves to the remainder of the bread, while others went into the kitchen to see what they could plunder from the fridges.

"Don't hang around too long, lads," Patrick said, as he and Hedi left out the door that led to the hospital, with their arms loaded with food and bottles of Coca Cola.

They tapped the code and the door was cautiously opened by Hansen, who had his pistol at the ready. He let them past, shut the door behind them, and rapidly locked it before taking up post next to it while they placed their loot on a medical counter.

"Food for the crew," Patrick said and raised an eyebrow in enquiry to Guillaume. Martin lay under a blanket with an oxygen mask over his face and a drip going into his arm. He was as pale as death and his breathing was shallow.

"He's stable for the moment, but I don't know for how long. We need help, Pat!" Guillaume wrung his hands.

"We saw a boat leaving, I think it might have been what made all that noise on this side of the ship," Hedi said. "We don't know if all of them left with it, so we must still be careful."

Force 12 in German Bight

"She's right," Patrick said. "I think I have a way to find out but... it's going to be risky, and we need to time it just right."

Skillet, hungrily munching on a sandwich, looked up expectantly and the others clustered around. "Don't tell me, Pat. You're goin' to storm the bridge? Why don't you set up a decoy first?"

Patrick nodded and seemed amused at how Skillet had divined his plan. He glanced over his unlikely crew of fighters and wondered if he was doing the right thing, but it was paramount in his mind to gain control of the bridge and the radio room.

"We must get help from the Danish Coast Guard, but the only way to do that is to storm the bridge, just as Skillet said. No one can help us out here unless we do it ourselves. If, and I say if, one or two of them are still there, it's going to be tricky."

"What are you going to do, Patrick? You can't just charge up the stairs!" Hedi said.

"No, not quite, but I could try to lure them down, and then you and Hansen can get up there and take it over while I give them the run around below decks."

Hedi stopped chewing and stared at him aghast. "You're mad, you know? You're quite mad!" She turned to the others. "Tell him he's mad!" she pleaded in a strangled tone, almost on the point of tears.

"You're right, Hedi. I agree, I think he's nuts, too, but then I've always figured he was crazy," Skillet said. "But he's right, we have to have the radio room, and we really do need help. Down here we've no idea where we are, what's going on up there, or outside, and Ah hear it's real bad."

"The more important thing is... can you and Hansen do your part of the job?" Patrick demanded.

She glanced over at Hansen, who nodded, although he looked scared. She nodded reluctantly. "What is it you want us to do?"

Patrick grinned at her and outlined his plan.

Before they left he made everyone check they had a full magazine and took a spare for himself.

*****

James Boschert

Patrick eased open the doorway that led up to the bridge from the lower deck and peered up the lighted shaft, listening for noises. He glanced back down the corridor to assure himself Hedi and Hansen were out of sight, and then crept up the stairs. He arrived at the main deck level without incident and noticed the door to the outside was only half shut. Someone had been out and forgot to close it, so rain and sea water had come in and made everything sopping wet.

He heard voices and listened hard. They shouted about something, but he couldn't tell what or whether the voices came from the radio room or further up.

He was halfway up the stairs when someone came to the door of the radio room, still shouting. Patrick slid down the stairs to get out of sight but wasn't quick enough.

The blond man with the ponytail caught a glimpse of him and reacted by sending a burst of fire in his general direction. The noise in the confined space was deafening, and the whine and howl of bullets ricocheting against the steel walls made him curl into a ball before letting himself tumble to the bottom of the stairs and out of the direct line of fire.

He remembered to shout when he landed. "You! Hey, you shithead up there. Can't hit someone even this close!" He was shaking and his mouth was dry but he forced himself to shout more taunts about Ponytail's worthless existence and bad aim while he crept towards the head of the other stairs. He loosed off a couple of rounds and was gratified to have a noisy response from above. Once again a burst of fire rattled all around him. He was relieved no random bullets hit him, although it was terrifying in the confined space.

Ponytail shouted, "Are you that Mr. Patrick shit?"

"That's me, stupid git," Patrick yelled back up.

"Then, Mr. Patrick, I'm coming to get you and take care of you for killing my friends. Did you kill Toke as well? He's disappeared."

"Yep, Ah sure di-id." Patrick tried to imitate Skillet and failed dismally. "Come and get me then, you silly bugger!" he yelled and fired another couple of rounds. The empty shells bounced off the wall nearby and hissed when they landed in the water.

Force 12 in German Bight

"You! You're coming with me." Patrick heard him shout at someone out of sight.

The more the merrier, he thought. He wondered how many there might be left.

Then he heard Ponytail clatter down the stairs, and fast. Patrick raced around the rail, slid all the way down, and landed just as Ponytail gained the top. Bullets followed him down, ricochetting off steel rails and steps and whining into corners as he dove through the doorway and rolled into the deserted corridor. He picked himself up to race toward the doorway that led to the winch room below. This was the most dangerous part, as there was no cover whatsoever in the long corridor. He made it to the door just as Hans dived through the doorway he'd just left, shouting to someone behind him as he came out.

"Get down here or I will shoot you myself! Take the left and cut him off if he tries to come around behind us! I will follow him. *Bastaard!*" Hans shouted as he spotted Patrick, who had just wrenched his door open and dived though. The Uzi chattered, sending bullets tearing into the soft walls of the corridor and clanging off the steel door as it closed.

Hans took off at a run, leaving Joel to stagger through the stairwell doorway and start to hesitantly make his way along the corridor to his left. He held a pistol in both hands but appeared to be very nervous to the watchers behind the door, as though he wished he was anywhere but where he was. Hans wrestled the distant doorway open, cursing all the while, and disappeared. He slammed the door behind him, leaving the corridor in relative silence.

*****

Joel walked slowly past the cabin where Hedi and Hansen hid. They had the door open a small crack and had witnessed Patrick's not so elegant return to the corridor, and the subsequent chase. Hedi's mouth was dry, but she waited until Joel had just passed them. Then she opened the door fully to allow both of them to exit and stand behind Joel.

"Police! Put your hands up and don't move!" Hedi said in a loud voice. She could see her handgun wobble at the front, and her hands were sweaty. Her finger tightened on the trigger. Would he try it she wondered.

Joel froze. "Do as she says, Joel," Hansen called out. "As high as you can, buster. There are two guns pointin' at you. Damn, I didn't think *you* were involved, asshole."

Joel's hands went into the air. Hedi glanced at Hansen, nodded, and walked up behind Joel, making sure Hansen could still get a clear shot if Joel tried something.

"Put the gun on the floor very, very slowly, by the barrel behind you, and don't do anything stupid." She told him.

Joel let the gun down gently. When it clattered to the floor Hedi kicked it back towards Hansen, and then reached behind her under her blue jacket and pulled out the handcuffs that were in a small pouch on her police belt.

"You're under arrest, so don't resist and shut up," she said. Joel glanced back at her with frightened eyes and said nothing.

She snapped the cuffs on one wrist then dragged the other around behind him and cuffed his wrists together behind his back. Hansen had picked up the pistol and put it in his pocket. He pushed past Joel and Hedi and knocked on the hospital door. "Mikey, open up!" he called. "Hurry!"

Mike opened the door a crack and Hansen shoved the pistol into his hand. "Know how to use it?" he asked. Mike nodded. "Ask Skillet if you don't. OK, stand by on the hand radio; we're going up the stairs now."

"Good luck!" Mike said and shut the door.

Hansen trotted after Hedi and Joel, who made for the doorway and the stairs.

"I'll go first with this man as my shield; will you cover our back?" she said.

He nodded. "Yep. Lead the way."

They went through the door. Hedi pushed the silent Joel into the well and turned him to face them.

"Who's up there? And how many of them are there?" she asked and pushed her pistol into his neck.

"Just... just Daryl and Richards now, and Hamesh," he said.

"Who is Hamesh?" She demanded.

"He's the relief radio man Miss." Hansen provided.

"No one else?"

"That fella who came down the stairs ahead of me was the last of them."

"Where are all the others?" she asked, suspecting a trap.

"The last one, Don, is gone. He left about twenty minutes ago on a boat."

"Who's Don?"

"He's... he's the leader."

"What happened to all the others? You'd better be telling the truth."

"I... I think they're all dead," Joel said.

Hedi looked at Hansen, who was as surprised as she was. He pointed with his chin up the stairs. "Push him ahead of us and then he can take it if he's lying," he said.

She nodded back, although her mouth was dry as she peered up the stairs towards the top.

"Come along, you," she said to Joel and shoved him ahead of them. "Walk up ahead of me, and no silly business." She hoped she sounded threatening enough.

Joel's shoulders slumped, but he did as he was told and they went slowly up the stairs with Hedi right behind him, grasping onto his collar with her left hand and with her gun resting on his his right shoulder. They reached the top of the stairs where they paused. Hansen slipped past them and opened the door with his gun at the ready.

A surprised and scared Hamesh looked up from the radio where he'd been trying to send a message.

"I was only going to send out the Mayday again. D-Don't shoot me!" he stammered when he saw the gun pointed at him.

"It's OK, Hamesh. We're on your side. Who's up there?" Hansen said.

"Richards and Daryl, as far as I know."

"No one else?"

"Nah, Don scarpered on the boat not long ago. Jesus, that Hans feller! He's is so bent out of shape over it! I thought he would kill all of us just because..." Hamesh said.

"OK, stay here and wait for us. Keep calling in the Mayday. Tell them what you know, and I'll be back as soon as possible," Hansen said.

He left Hamesh staring after him and shut the door. "He's on his own, Miss. He said the same thing as Joel here. Just two of them: the super, Daryl and the senior rigger, Richards."

"Come on then, let's take the bridge from them," she said with a determined glance up the stair well and shoved Joel ahead of her.

They arrived at the top of the stairs where it was much colder and noisier, since some of the windows were shattered. The wind keened outside and tore at the open window spaces. They didn't have to worry about making any noise, but could just hear the two men talking. Richards and Daryl were hunched over the front counter, seated on elevated office stools and leaning on their elbows with a bottle of whiskey in front of them. Another empty bottle rolled about on the floor in a corner.

"Freeze! Police! Don't move! You're under arrest!" Hedi shouted over the din of the wind.

They both turned their heads and gaped at her with bleary eyes. Neither moved from their positions.

"Where you been, girl?" Daryl slurred.

Richards glowered, "Women bring bad luck to a ship..." his voice trailed off.

"You're under arrest," she said.

"Ah'm in charge of this ship an' you cain't arrest me," Daryl said loudly.

Hedi flicked a look at Hansen, who nodded and waved his left hand toward her. "Go on," he said.

She took a deep breath. "No. I represent the Danish police and I am in charge here now. You're not. You'll do as you are told," she said with more conviction. Hansen grinned.

"We're going to sink. It's God's judgement!" Richards mumbled.

Daryl turned angry eyes on her and muttered something, but otherwise he sat still. He appeared to be weary and defeated.

Hedi glanced out at the patch of lighted sea, saw how it

writhed and surged, and felt a shiver. The waves seemed enormous even from this vantage point. There were running lights ahead of them, which indicated a boat out there.

"What's he talking about?" she asked Joel, who had slumped against the counter.

"We've lost our tow and are drifting backward toward Jutland," he said and nodded towards the radar screen, which showed a lighted coast line on one side.

"How far are we off the coast?" Hansen asked with a horrified look at Daryl.

"I'd guess about six miles, maybe a little less now," Joel said.

"Is that right, Daryl?" Hansen asked.

"Yep, I'd say it was right. No hope of getting off neither. No life boats, nor rafts." His voice was slurred and then he cackled with laughter like it was some kind of joke.

"What?" Hansen exclaimed in real alarm now. "Where are they?"

"Waves took them! Took it all! We've been in a force twelve for Christ's sake, didn't you know that? We got hit by at least two rogues. Biggest Ah'v ever seen!" Daryl said. He took another drink of bourbon and shook his head. "Maybe Rich is right, the stupid asshole's got religion real bad this time."

"We're all going to drown!" Richards wailed. He glared at Hedi and muttered something. Hedi wished he would shut up.

Hansen produced a piece of cord from the electrical cabinet under the sled console and went behind both men, tied their hands behind them, and made them get off their stools to sit on the floor alongside Joel.

"I must send a message to Denmark," she said in an urgent undertone.

"Yeah. You do that, Miss. We're in a world of shit. Excuse my French, but this is bloody serious. I'll stand guard at the top of the stairs to make sure that guy doesn't come back. I hope Patrick knows what he's doing down there."

Hedi turned away and leaned on the railing, feeling weak from the tension, and wondered how he was doing. She clenched her teeth with worry as she walked down the stairs on wobbly legs. She hadn't realized how wound up she'd been.

James Boschert

*****

Patrick fled down the steps of the winch room, knowing he was only just ahead of the maddened man behind him. He threw himself around the rail at the bottom of the steps and ran through the jetting pump room and into the generator room, where he waited. It wasn't long before he heard the sound of running feet and Ponytail dived past the door he'd just come through.

Patrick loosed off a round to assist him with his sense of direction and popped behind a large, steel cabinet just before another doorway.

Hans peered around the opening and Patrick sent another round his way, which made him duck out of sight. The reprieve lasted only a moment before the Uzi came back and a long burst of bullets was sent in his general direction. Once again the air, already dense with the roar of the huge caterpillar engines that drove the generators, was full of even more noise as the lead flew off walls of steel and punctured steel cabinets, including the one Patrick hid behind. He jumped when one went right past his backside; he actually felt the wind of its passing. He decided it was time to vacate the room.

The automatic jerked in his hands as he loosed off a couple to get Ponytail to stay out of sight and dived into the generator room proper. Here it was deafening and he wished he had ear protectors, but it was so full of machinery it was easy to find a place to duck behind. He'd expected Ponytail to charge into the room, but somehow the man figured out he could access the room from another quarter. The first Patrick knew was bullets were flying all over the place, but not from where he'd thought they would. It was time to leave in a hurry. He fled past two generators with bullets buzzing by and threw himself onto the grating to avoid more. The grating in this room was serrated and tore at his coveralls, but he didn't feel it. He rolled and shot as he scrambled back, trying to get out of sight.

He heard the gratings clank as Ponytail charged toward him, and he rolled out from under a roaring engine to send a couple at his opponent, who noticed just in time and vanished before the two bullets slammed into the space where he'd just been.

"That guy's good!" Patrick said to himself. This was going to be harder than he'd thought.

"You there, Mr Patrick? You know I'm going to kill you!" Ponytail shouted over the din. "Might as well get it over with quickly, no?"

"Fuck you, Jimmy!" Patrick shouted back and stood up to fire two more rounds before he dashed for the entrance nearby. He got through, hearing bullets slam into the wall behind, and then he had to decide which way to go: up or left. He took the left, not wanting to bring more noise and fright to the boys upstairs. This meant the passage took him to the laundry and at the far end of that room the gym.

He skipped behind a corner and fired back at the glimpse he got of Ponytail, who ducked out of the way but pushed his Uzi around the corner and let a small burst loose at him. Patrick ran down the short stairway to the laundry room and across the space between the double row of washing machines. He wondered briefly if he could hide in one and ambush Ponytail, but decided that might be terminal and ran on. He slipped his magazine out to check how many bullets he had left and saw only four. He reached for the spare magazine and found to his consternation it wasn't in the pocket he'd placed it in.

"Oh fuck!" he muttered to himself. "Must have lost it on the bluddy gratings!" He raced up the short stairs that led to the forward compartments and slid into cover where he could see the laundry room floor, but not the other entrance. He might be lucky here, he decided, as he lay panting behind a huge drying machine.

There was a light clatter and he saw his magazine slide toward him along the linoleum floor. It was empty of course.

"Bogger," he muttered.

"Missing something, Mr. Patrick?" Ponytail asked in a friendly shout.

"What are you so pissed about, mate?" Patrick shouted back. "Really bent out of shape you are."

There was a pause before Ponytail shouted back. "You would be, too, if your comrade deserts you like that bastard British, Donald. Never trust an Englishman!"

"Oh dear! Leave you behind, did he? That wasn't friendly at all, by golly gosh! Serves you bloody right anyway, you toad," Patrick called back. By now he knew it was a pointless exercise to keep annoying the man, but it kept his own spirits up to do so.

"I am not a... what did you call me? A Toad? What's that?

"It's a badly made frog!"

"Ha ha! You know, Mr. Patrick, you cannot insult me. I think under other... what do you call it, circumstances, I could actually like you, but... I am a Viking and in a very short time I shall prove it to you."

Patrick said nothing. His mind worked feverishly on how he could get away.

"Before I find a way to escape I intend to settle with you, Mr. Patrick. You've done a lot of damage."

"Come on then, mate. I'm waiting." Patrick waited. He hoped fervently Hedi and Hansen had managed to take the bridge, or all of this would be for nothing.

He heard a shuffle and a bag of clothes flew through the air, then another, and another, and suddenly Ponytail was there, shooting up at him, and the place became untenable. Patrick couldn't get a bead on his opponent because of the hornets that flew all around his shelter, so he loosed off a couple of rounds in the hope he might connect, but then it was time to leave. Once again he had to flee, and while the thought of holing up in the weight room was tempting, he realized it would be a trap. This left him with the short corridor leading out onto the deck and nowhere else to go. He could hear Ponytail running up the stairs behind him and knew he had no time left. Ponytail saw him and let out a yell of triumph, but before he could shoot Patrick turned at bay and fired his last two bullets at him.

His luck was out. Ponytail ducked out of the way and the bullets howled past into the opening near his head. Patrick threw his own gun back at the doorway in frustration. Now he had nothing to fight with other than his knife. Did this guy have an endless supply of bullets?

He wrenched the clamps of the doorway open and skidded through into the open deck, just below the main deck right up at the bows behind the water barrier, which acted as a baffle for waves coming aboard. The door slammed shut behind him. The short deck was lit by one remaining arc lamp, which allowed him to see the deck around him and the seething turmoil of the sea ahead in a dim light. Enough to make him feel very scared. It seemed as though the barge sailed into a canyon of water; on all sides the seas towered over the vessel, dwarfing it. We're like a rubber duck in a whirlpool, he thought, and glanced around wildly looking for an escape route.

He staggered against the terrible tug of the screaming wind that tore at him and threatened to throw him over board, but his greatest fear was the looming waves he knew could pick him up and carry him off into the sea where he wouldn't survive for a minute. He scrambled towards the stairs that let up to the main deck. There was nowhere else to go. The door behind him opened and Ponytail fired in his general direction. There were only two shots this time, which made Patrick pause for a second. At the back of his mind he registered there was no cable snaking out into the sea towards a tug boat, instead it drooped over the bows, clearly severed.

He glanced back, waiting for shots, but none came. Ponytail braced against the steel walls and wrestled with the gun. It looked as though it had either jammed or run out of bullets. Without thinking, Patrick reached down and hauled his knife out then sidled, crouched like a crab, toward Ponytail, who angrily hammered on the cocking mechanism. His ponytail had come undone and his hair whipped around his face, making him look like a crazed berserker from some legendary horror story.

He glanced up as Patrick shambled towards him. There was no running about on this deck with the wind and the sea sloshing around their ankles. Hans laughed and threw the gun at Patrick, who dodged. It bounced off the rail and disappeared into the sea without even making a splash. Then Ponytail reached down to his boot, took out a long knife, and waved it at Patrick.

"Ha ha, now we see who is a man!" he bellowed over the awful noise all around. Both men were already soaked to the skin, but neither paid any attention to the elements now. They shambled closer to one another and waved their knives threateningly at one another. Abruptly Ponytail stabbed forward and up at Patrick, who stumped backward and parried. He felt the strength of his opponent along the blades and knew it was going to be very close.

He slid his knife free and lunged at Ponytail's face. The man dodged back and used his left hand to wave him off, lunged again, and managed to cut Patrick across the chest before he could step back in time. He grinned; clearly he expected to finish it soon. The pain of the cut sharpened Patrick's senses.

Then, out of the corner of his eye, he saw a strange sight. The sea seemed to be moving away from them, but it was a smooth wall of water receding out there. He knew what that meant: they had seconds to live. It was a wave wall, and the barge would go into it nose first. They would be under tons of water within a few seconds if they stayed on deck.

He pretended to stumble and Ponytail fell for it. He came forward with a slashing move, his knife blade tucked alongside his forearm and his other hand ahead of him like a claw. Patrick slid to one knee, which wasn't hard it was so wet, and shot his left hand up for Ponytail's wrist. He only managed a tenuous grip, but it was enough. He pulled as hard as he could across himself, which turned the man just enough away from him to stab hard with his own knife into Ponytail's side. His opponent let out a startled yell of surprise and then an agonized scream as the blade penetrated.

Patrick didn't wait to see what Ponytail would do next. He shambled past the staggering man, who sank to his knees with an agonized expression on his face. Patrick wrenched the door open and dived in. He just had time to slam the locks in place before he heard a muffled scream and the heavy thud as tons of water slammed against the door. It shook the whole area of the bows. Patrick leaned against the steel walls, gasped for breath, and slid down onto the floor with his knees up and let his forehead drop onto them. "That was for Martin and Lenny, you bastard!" he muttered. "God, but I need a drink."

Chapter 25

Abandon Ship

Hedi managed with help from Hamesh to reach Joey with the Sailor radio, and from there he was able to patch them through to Denmark where the Coast Guard took the message.

"We're adrift and only miles from the coast off Esbjerg," she said. "This is Assistant Detective Hedi Iversen speaking. We are the *Cherokee* oil vessel and need immediate assistance."

"We have you on our radar now, *Cherokee*. We can see you're far too close to the shore. Are your engines not operational? What do you need?" the operator at the Coast Guard called back.

"We do not have propulsion. We've lost our tow and we have wounded people on board. We need emergency medical treatment. Can you send a helicopter?"

The operator told her to wait on the frequency while they notified the right people.

*****

Back in Esbjerg there was surprise mixed with consternation when the call came in from the Coast Guard. Chief Balder almost ran into the office of his chief with the note.

"They've been picked up on the Coast Guard radar. It seems they're adrift and headed for the coast, sir," he said.

"Can the Coast Guard do anything about it, Chief? Has the

wind dropped enough to get a chopper out there and find out what the hell's been going on?" Kristian asked.

"They said they were working on it, sir. The wind has dropped to less than forty knots, so they are pretty sure they can get to the ship with a helicopter. They apparently have no life boats, nor any safe means to abandon ship. It was all swept away by huge waves that broke their cables and set them adrift."

"Jesus, I bet the seas are still very high. So they're just drifting?"

"The ship is expected to drift just to the north of Esbjerg and ground at about dawn. It's nearly four o'clock right now, sir,"

Kristian gave startled grunt. "Where has the time gone?" he said. "This has been a storm for the record books, I'd say. Did you hear it blew part of the roof off the palace in Copenhagen, Chief?"

Chief Balder nodded. He'd brought the news to the office an hour ago.

"There is other news, sir."

"What is it, Chief?"

"Assistant detective Iversen reported that Inspector Erland was killed on board. Murdered, actually, and there's been a lot of shooting."

"Dear God. What were they doing out there? Weren't our men there to support them?"

"Er, no, sir. She reported they never showed up."

"I beg your pardon, Chief? Never showed up?" Kristian repeated stupidly.

"No sir. She says the only help she had was from members of the crew, who assisted her in regaining control of the vessel. There seems to have been quite a lot going on, but our men never appeared. They still haven't reported in."

"We must find out what happened to that cutter," Kristian said with a shocked expression on his face. "They can't just have disappeared into thin air!"

Chief Balder said nothing; he'd been a policeman in Esbjerg for a long time and knew the North Sea. In storms like this, small boats *did* disappear. They both knew what the answer might be, but weren't ready to discuss it.

"There is more, sir."

Kristian rubbed his forehead with both hands. "OK, let me have it."

"Iversen reported a large tug boat type vessel picked up a cargo during the night. It left with one of the men who'd been directing the operation by the... pirates."

"Then we must put out an alert for all ports along the Jutland coast and alert the Coast Guard immediately," Kristian said.

"The man was named Donald, sir. You remember the man wanted in Britain for possible murder? His name was Donald Saunders. The man with the Jaguar?"

"Yes , yes. What's your point, Chief?" Kristian asked impatiently.

'Well sir. The man is British and knew the captain of the boat, who he called Stuart. That means the boat might have been British, don't you think?"

"I suppose it's a possibility, yes. What on earth were they doing out there in any case?"

"Remember the driver of the truck broke down and told us about a tug taking a container out to sea?"

"Yes... Ah, do you think it went to the barge?"

"A very good possibility, sir. We're still looking for the tug that left here, but I'm almost sure it's not the one that came to take the cargo off. I suspect that one is headed for the UK."

"All right, then. Notify Scotland Yard there's a boat coming in, and to alert their Coast Guard it's carrying a container, so it's a large kind of sea tug? That should work, Chief."

Balder agreed and went off to talk to the Coast Guard some more and send a message to the British police.

*****

Hedi leaned on the counter at the front of the bridge and stared out into the night. Joey had called and told them if there was one thing they could be grateful for it was the fact the huge heli pad on the back of the barge acted as a sail, and helped keep them from turning around and risk being rolled. If that happened it was all over. The bad news was they were being pushed backward in high seas toward land, and nothing could stop them. Hansen had gone down to the radio room to help with the radio, leaving her on her own with the three prisoners.

She was so preoccupied with watching the sea and her own thoughts that she didn't notice that Richards had scrambled to his feet. The first she knew was his big hands seizing her around her throat.

She gave a startled gurgle and twisted hard trying to turn and face him. She only succeeded partially but she kicked out desperately. Her shoe connected with his shin, causing him to slip. But he managed to drag her down onto the floor with him and fell on top of her. This time she was on her back but she was pinned under his weight, and he was a big man. He still had one hand on her throat causing her to choke while the other rested on her chest pinning her down. She caught the stink of alcohol on his breath as he leaned over her.

"You brought this on us! If you... if you hadn't come on board this would never have happened! Women bring bad luck to a ship!" he roared. "Ahm goin' te kill yew, woman!"

Hedi couldn't breath properly. She choked and flailed with her hands, scratching and trying to kick back; then with a desperate heave she managed to shift him enough to enable her to reach for her pistol. She couldn't remember if it had a round in the breach or not, but there was no way she could cock it. She was on the edge of passing out, there was a red haze in front of her eyes. She drove the barrel into Richard's side, prayed and pulled the trigger. The explosion drove Richards off to the side where he rolled over, choking and jerking for some long seconds before lying still.

Hedi rolled over, watching him and drawing in great breaths, "This is *not* a ship!" she gurgled, holding her throat with her left hand while she waved the pistol angrily at the two men crouched in the corner where they had been earlier.

"Do you two want to join him?Hah?Hah?" she demanded. Her throat hurt and she was very frightened but mad enough to let loose if they even twitched.

Their eyes were wide with shock, but neither showed any interest in more resistance.

"Always was a bit crazy, was Rich. Never did like women. Don't think he liked anyone, really, since his third wife left him," Daryl muttered, more to himself than anyone in particular.

There was a clatter as Hansen rushed up the stairs.

"What happened! Miss, are you all right?" he called out. Then he saw Richards lying on his back in the middle of a growing pool of blood and gasped. "Oh Shit! How... how did he get loose?" he stammered.

"I don't know, but he tried to kill me all the same." Hedi had climbed to her feet and holstered her pistol.

"Please check the other two again, Hansen. I don't want to repeat that again." She pushed back a strand of hair with a trembling hand and leaned on the counter near the radar with both arms outstretched and her head lowered. She found that she was shaking.

"How far are we away from land now?" she asked Hansen, trying to regain her composure.

He glanced up at her from where he was checking Daryl and Joel. Satisfied they were secure he stood up and joined her at the radar.

"Real sorry, Miss. Don't know how he did it. I tied him up tight." He turned to peer at the instruments.

"I can see by the radar it's only about four miles. I think I can even see lights, but I'm not sure," he continued.

"Do you know what's happened below?" she asked him.

"No, Miss, I don't, and I wish I did. That Hans feller was a dangerous type from what Joel told me. He said he wasn't as bad as the Brit, but very nearly so. Don't know if Pat can deal with that, especially up against a machine gun." He gazed out of the window with Hedi. Both of them were apprehensive as they watched the riding lights of Joeys' tug, which had held station a quarter of a mile off on their port side since the loss of the cable.

'That Joey, one of the best," he said. "Most people would have pissed off in this weather and left us to our fate, but he stuck around even if there isn't much he can do."

"Yes, I agree. I'd like to meet Joey one day," Hedi said, but her mind was on Patrick. Where was he? They'd left Mike at the head of the stairs by the radio room to make sure if things went badly wrong he could warn them, and they could at least defend the bridge.

She glanced at the two disconsolate men seated on the floor and her eyes flicked over the still form of Richards lying where he had died. They'd been complicit in this whole thing. Her jaw tightened. They were responsible for the death of several men, including Erland, and the wounding of others, one of whom might not survive. She glanced back behind the bridge toward Jutland. When would the Coast Guard come and rescue them? she wondered. She'd told them it was urgent several times, but each time they'd called off.

Both of them heard voices below and glanced at one another with wide eyes. They snatched up their guns and made for the head of the stairs, prepared for trouble. Then she recognized the voice coming up the stairs. It was Patrick. He was soaked from head to foot again; his boots squelched when he climbed the stairs. He had a crude bandage wrapped around his chest and appeared to be exhausted. He still managed that wry smile for her, and she thought her chest would explode. It took an act of serious will power not to embrace him.

"What happened to you, mate?" Hansen asked with both relief and concern in his voice.

"Had a small altercation with our Ponytail man and the sea," Patrick said. His eyes were still on Hedi, who wore a smile to light the bridge.

He glanced around quickly and then stopped as he saw Richards' corpse. "What happened here?" he asked her.

"He managed to get free and then attacked me. I had no choice," she said, lowering her head so that he couldn't see the tears of tension and relief in her eyes.

"So, what... where is he, Hans I mean, now?" she asked to get herself back together. She felt his hand on her arm and felt a lot better.

"It was the only thing you could do Hedi. You'll do OK."he said in a low voice. Then he continued.

"Well, that fella is out at sea now, I imagine. We were on the foredeck when that big wave came on board. I got in just in time. He didn't."

Hedi remembered that wave. It had reared up over the bows and the barge had simply nosed into it. Watching the wave come in with the lights on it, she'd known no one could survive this kind of thing. It was as though nature had wanted to demonstrate its power and had left her paralyzed with fright at the sight of it. This was what they'd been talking about, she realized. These were the tall waves that did so much damage. She was desperate to be on dry land and away from this uncontrollable world of wind and sea.

"Yes, I remember seeing it. You were on the very front?"

He nodded, sat down on one of the chairs with a soggy squelch, and pushed his hand through his wet hair.

'Tell me what happened up here?" he asked. He glanced at the men on the floor, but while his face went grim he said nothing. Joel looked up and then away again.

She told him what had happened and how they'd taken back the bridge after he'd been chased off by Hans. Then she gave him a terse description of the incident with Richards. His eyes never left her face while she talked. She also explained that they were off the tow again, as the cable had gone for the second time. He nodded.

"So it *had* gone. I wondered," he said. "So we are drifting back towards Denmark now. We'll have you home for breakfast yet, missy." He grinned at her.

She nodded and couldn't hide her smile, although there wasn't much to smile about. Then she told him she'd been in touch with the Danish Coast Guard, who had promised help, but it was slow in coming.

"They probably have a lot of preparation to do, so don't be too hard on them. It's crazy outside, even though I think the wind's dying down a bit," he told her with a glance at the wind meter, which read 40 knots. "They might just be able to get a chopper out here, even in this."

Hamesh shouted up that a message was coming in and would someone help him deal with it.

"I'll go," Patrick said. "Perhaps we can get the big radio going, too." He rubbed the middle of his forehead with the fingers of his left hand as though wiping the tiredness away.

He got up painfully and left with a tired smile in her direction.

Force 12 in German Bight

*****

It was Joey on the Sailor. "Y'all are about three miles off shore now, Pat. You'll be grounded soon, and then the real problems will start. You need to drop your anchors when you get within a mile of shore. Yours is a flat bottom so you'll slide up the sand, but if you stick there the sea might turn you around and roll you over."

"You can keep us honest then, Joey. I don't really trust our depth sounder to tell us exactly when."

"Sure, I can do that, but it's soon time to take people off that ship, Pat. I can come alongside and start when the wind drops a bit more. It's dropping fast, at least from what Ah can tell. The sea is still high right now, but I can chance it."

"I hear you, Joey. We need to start preparing for it. I'll talk to the crew. Hey Joey!"

"Yeah Pat?"

"Thanks for sticking around. We appreciate that, mate."

"Y'or welcome." Joey said and clicked off.

Patrick went upstairs and made the promised call over the Tannoy to the crew and told them to prepare to abandon ship. Afterward he went over and checked the console, where the instruments for the ship's anchors were located. He tried the on switch for the starboard anchor and noticed the green light didn't come on. He checked both port and starboard anchor and found that only the port side worked.

He sighed, thoroughly pissed off at the thought of what that entailed. This wasn't what he wanted. With only one anchor they might still turn, and there was a good chance of dragging, in which case, with the waves as high as they were, they could still be rolled.

As he worked on the anchors, too preoccupied to pay attention to the goings on around him, he didn't initially notice the excitement.

"There are lights coming this way from the land!" Hansen shouted. "Hey, Hamesh!" he called below. "Are they on the radio?"

"Yeah, they are. It's the cavalry. It's the Coast Guard, and they said they're coming to pick up the injured people. Who's that, Hansen?"

"Martin and Skillet! We've got to get them to where they can be picked up!" He peered out of the window down at the deck. "Hey, Pat, can we use that patch out there on the deck near the crane?"

Patrick walked over to the side of the bridge and cast a look up the deck towards the bows. Although the sea was still very high and waves were breaking over the bows, they weren't sending six foot bores of water to rush down the length of the deck.

"We've got to try. Never know when the chance will come again. Hedi, can you go off with those two? The Danish police need to know what's been going on as soon as possible so they can deal with that Don guy."

She nodded and glanced at the two men still seated on the deck. Daryl had talked. He was angry and bitter at the desertion of Donald, and had told her he thought the destination would have been Harwich. He'd hoped to go off with the boat, but now his world had crashed about his head.

The Coast Guard chopper appeared out of the night like some huge dark insect as it came closer, its lights flashing with a large spotlight shining in their faces. While Mike went down to the deck to wave it in, Hansen and Patrick went down to the hospital and organized the crew to get Skillet and Martin moved through the corridor and up the stairs. There were more than enough men to assist with carrying them now.

They took the gurneys with them. When they arrived on deck the two men were placed on them while the helicopter negotiated the landing. It had first headed towards the heli pad, but the wind was too strong and the pilot informed Stan, who was now at the radio, he would try to land on the open spaces on deck. They couldn't haul Martin up in his condition.

Using its own lights, the huge craft made a good landing, despite the wind, and men jumped out and ran over to the two gurneys. Guillaume explained the situation and the condition of Martin and Skillet. Skillet gave Patrick a salute and a grin as they lifted him aboard and placed him alongside Martin, who was still unconscious. Patrick waved. He hoped Martin would survive but wasn't optimistic. Skillet would be just fine. Someone touched his arm.

"I leave now, Patrick," Hedi said. "You'll come off soon?"

The two prisoners, Joel and Daryl, were hustled along by

unsympathetic men who had heard the story of their involvement with the gangsters. Two of the technicians, Johnny and Pete, went with them as an escort.

"We need to get everyone off the ship as soon as possible, Hedi. Joey's going to help, but the Coast Guard needs to know we have more than fifty men on board who have to be taken off one way or another. I don't think Joey can take us all. See what you can do?"

"OK, I'll tell them."

He smiled at her. "Get going, love."

"Take care, Patrick. You will, right?" she shouted over the din of the wind and the rotors, and shoved a piece of paper into the top pocket of his coveralls.

"I will. Just have to get the anchors down, then I can leave. Take care of those two."

She waved and climbed aboard the machine, which lifted off almost immediately. It rose above them, wobbled as the wind beat on it, and swept away into the darkness.

Hansen and Patrick ran back up to the bridge and watched it leave. Joey called and told them he was about ready to come alongside. They could try to rig a bosun's chair, he suggested. Patrick didn't like the idea, as he considered it to be too slow; the alternative was a net, which men could climb down. Then Dana suggested the second crane.

"It's still on its tracks, Pat. I could get it running, and if Joey comes to the port side we can get them onto it five at a time."

"That's a good idea, Dana. Where's Matt? He can help you get set up. Get going, mate," Pat said. Dana and Matt ran off to start the crane. "Wear safety harness and life jackets, you guys!" he called after them.

"Hey, Hansen," he said. "The starboard anchor isn't responding. We need to drop the port side anchor in a few minutes and I'll go down and use the local power unit to get the starboard side anchor down. We need both."

Alistair had come up onto the bridge. "I'll come with you, Pat. It's been tricky in the past, so you might need some help."

"Nice of you to offer, Alistair, but I think you should stay here and operate the port one so we can do it at the same time," Patrick said and switched on the port side anchor winch. He glanced over at the radar and could see they were now very close to shore. The waves were still high but nowhere near as awful as they had been. Even so, it would be a difficult job for the riggers to get the men off using the crane and the net.

He watched as Joey maneuvered his tug alongside and kept just enough distance to avoid running into the side of the barge. At one point a surge of waves did drive him into contact, and the shriek of metal on metal plate was heard even up in the bridge.

Joey quickly gunned his engines and moved the tug further away. Men were now running out on deck as the riggers got their Filipino teams together and told them what was happening. They clearly didn't like what they would have to do, but the alternative wasn't a good one either; the barge could sink and they would go down with it.

The crane roared into action and trundled towards the middle of the deck. Its boom came down, and the crew hooked up one of the round net devices used to bring people on and off the barge when at sea.

The first batch of men took off to soar into the darkness, and then descended at what seemed to be a dangerous speed towards the heaving deck of the tug. Just at the last moment Matt put the brakes on and they landed with a thump. The men spilled off and disappeared into the guts of the tug, while the net rose swiftly into the air to land once more on the deck.

Another batch of men ran out in their yellow waterproofs and red life jackets. They jumped onto the round platform and clung to the net while it lifted into the sky.

Patrick turned away and called Alistair over. "We're going to ground any moment. I'd like to get the anchors down as soon as we can. Before we ground, if possible. You stay here, and when I call on the radio, you let it down so they both go down at the same time. I wonder how deep it is here?"

He hurried down the steps and pushed through the press of men when he came to the main deck, and then went on down to an empty corridor. Trotting now, as there was no one left on this deck, he hurried along the same short corridor he'd been in not long ago, trying to get away from the man called Hans. It was silent in this area, other than the groan of stressed metal and the thump of waves on the blunt bows. He opened the door off the corridor that led into the small winch room, where the main ship's anchor winch was located.

The chamber smelt of oil and paint and had only a storm lamp on the wall that barely lit the winch, which filled the room. People didn't come here often, as it was generally simpler to operate from the bridge, but like everything else on the barge it was old and didn't always work properly. He focussed on the small console in front of him and called up to Alistair using the Motorola hand set.

"Give me a second and I'll turn it on here, Alistair," he called up.

"Roger that, Pat." came the reply.

He pressed the red button for the power and was gratified to see the green light come on.

"OK, Alistair, let her go!" he called and turned the winch switch hard. He heard the rattle of the cable outside and felt the rumble of the port side cable as it roared through the hole in the bows. Both anchors dove into the sea and within seconds they were on the ground. The barge pulled hard against them and for a brief moment he thought they might slip and drag.

"They're holding, Pat. We're stationary," Alistair called from the bridge. Even over the radio he could tell Alistair was excited at how well the idea had worked. "Well, at least something's gone right for a change," he muttered to himself.

"Grand. Get as many onto Joey's boat as possible, and then we can hope for some help from the Danes. I'll see you on land," Patrick said and switched off the radio.

He was about to leave, having turned off the console, when he became aware of the fact he wasn't alone. He barely saw the shadow in time to dodge, and the blow that landed on his left shoulder knocked him to his knees.

He gasped with pain and swiveled his head to stare up at the apparition towering above him in horror. He couldn't believe his eyes. Hans stood right over him, and he looked as though he'd been raised from the dead. His blond hair hung in wet strands around his neck and shoulders, his face was battered almost beyond recognition, and his clothes were in shreds. He had an insane look in his eyes, which stared unblinking out of a face that was dead white and almost devoid of blood.

Hans gave a crazed laugh and shouted, "I sooo wanted you to come back!" He cackled. "I prayed I could have a chance to kill you before I died. You bastard, you've killed me anyway."

"But, but, you were outside when the wave came. How...how did you survive?" Patrick quavered wildly, quite sure he was seeing a ghost, but his shoulder told him it was no ghost that had struck him. He felt as though his collar bone was broken. He searched for his knife with his right hand while he desperately stalled for time and gaped up a Hans.

"It takes more than a little wave to kill a Viking, you pig," the ghost shouted. "I got into a corner and lived, and then I came back in. Now it's your turn to die."

Patrick rolled out of the way of the iron bar that came down toward him in a vicious arc. It missed and clanged against the winch covering. Hans staggered, but he regained his balance too fast for Patrick to strike him and swung the bar high again. Patrick no longer watched the bar. He dived straight at Hans with a fearful yell of his own and drove his knife straight into his heart. Then his world went black.

*****

Hedi was exhausted. She'd spent the day at the police station, where she'd been treated by her colleagues like a returning heroine. Chief Balder finally extracted her from the excited group who had been clustered about her belaboring her with questions, and had taken her to Chief Inspector Kristian Vestergaard. He'd greeted her with a tired smile of welcome, sat her down with a strong Danish coffee that tasted like black nectar, and demanded to know everything that had happened on board.

It took a long time to give them the whole story. They in turn told her what they knew of the gang. The boat had indeed arrived at Harwich, but customs and excise, having been tipped off by the Danes, were waiting for it. They'd arrested all on board, but no one had seen the man called Donald Saunders nor the container that was supposed to be on the tug.

It seemed he'd slipped past them, but the encouraging news was he'd made it onto a most wanted list and a high level arrest of

Force 12 in German Bight

several men had been made in London. She listened gravely to the two men, but the entire time she'd wondered where Patrick was.

After Kristian had congratulated her and asked for a report, which she typed out slowly on an ancient typewriter, she left the police station. It was already dusk when she departed and made her way in her small car to the place where the men of the barge had been brought. She thought she would fall asleep at the wheel, she was so tired.

The men from the barge were housed in a school gymnasium, where they'd been placed under police guard until someone could be reached who knew what to do with them. The company agent had been found and dragged out of bed early that morning by two policemen, and set to work on their future accommodation and flights out of Esbjerg. Hedi asked as many of the men as possible if they'd seen Patrick. Not even Hansen knew, and a man called Alistair told her the last he'd seen of Patrick was when he left the bridge to take care of the winch. No one seemed to know where he was since then.

She finally drove to the hospital and paid a visit to the ward where Skillet lay. He greeted her with a grin and raised his hand to hold hers.

He hung onto her hand for far too long, of course, and in the end she had to pull it gently away. They chatted about his condition, which was stable, and about Martin, who was in critical care. The doctors had told him there was a good chance of Martin making it. When she mentioned she hadn't seen Patrick and no one else seemed to have either, he became serious.

"You mean he didn't get off the barge?" he asked.

"Skillet, I'm worried. No one has seen him since he went below again to fix an anchor something or other. I don't know what it's called," she said.

"Probably an anchor winch. That starboard winch has been giving us trouble for some time. Pat is one of the few people I know who could keep the old tub working at all. Best engineer Ah have met out there."

"So what could have happened to him, Skillet? I'm worried."

"Have they checked the barge all over? Did it sink?" he asked.

"No... no, it didn't sink. They say it grounded, but not very hard because it had its anchors out, so the Coast Guard think it will not sink. I don't think they've made a full inspection of it yet because some bodies are unaccounted for," she said and fidgeted with the edge of the coverlet. "They will probably send the Coast

James Boschert

Guard out there to check it out tomorrow when the sea is calmer."

She was clearly very upset, he took her hand in his two huge paws and tried to be encouraging, even though he couldn't imagine what might have happened to his friend. He knew enough about Pat as a survivor, but he, too, was distressed to hear he was missing.

"Go home, Miss Hedi. You've sure got to be tired after all the excitement out there, and Ah'm sure they'll find him. That Pat is a pretty tough guy, I reckon. Try to get some sleep and don't worry too much," he said without conviction. His Texas accent was strong and he regarded her with sympathetic eyes.

"You like him, don't ya?" Skillet asked kindly and with not a little regret in his tone.

She nodded in silence, and with her head down tears began to trickle. She rubbed them away angrily with a fist, but he smiled and said, "Lucky bastard, Ah'm envious."

She smiled and withdrew her hand again to pat his. "He got under my skin, as you say in English." she gave him an affectionate peck on the cheek. I will see you soon.

She left him to a nurse, who came in to fuss about him, which Skillet made the most of. She peeked in on Martin, who was lying in a clean white bed with tubes coming out of his nose and drips into his arm. He looked bruised, but appeared to be sleeping quietly enough. He was surrounded by machines that beeped and squeaked, which she guessed was a good sign. The nurse on duty told her they had operated and removed the bullets, but he would be in the emergency ward for a good week before he was pronounced out of danger. The wound in his abdomen had been severe.

Hedi drove away, parked her car and dragged herself across the wet street and up the open stairs to the entrance of her apartment. She lived on the second floor, where her apartment door opened out onto a small balcony. She was so preoccupied with her thoughts she didn't notice the dark shadow at first, and when it moved she jumped with a gasp. She was so startled she gave a small cry of alarm and instinctively reached for her weapon.

"Hey. It's only me," said Patrick.

Hedi choked back a sob of relief.

"Where have you been!" she demanded so accusingly she almost shouted. But her heart made a jump into her throat and she dived into his arms.

289

"I, er, got... delayed," he said, his voice muffled in her anorak. "Ouch! Careful there, I'm one of the walking wounded, now." All the same he held her tight in his good arm.

She noticed the sling and the bandage on the side of his head, and realized he looked terrible.

"What happened to you, Patrick? Are you all right?" She asked.

"I bumped into Hans again." He rubbed the center of his forehead with the fingers of his good hand, in a by now very familiar gesture.

She jerked her head back to stare up at his face, "Dear God! What happened?" Hedi said, but continued to clutch at his arms.

"It felt like I was fighting a zombie. He came back from the dead! No one should have survived that wave, but he did. This time though, he *is* dead."

He smiled that slightly lopsided smile again. She drew in a big breath of relief.

For an inexplicable reason the kestrel popped into her mind.

"Will the kestrel be all right, Patrick?" she asked.

He chuckled. "Kind of you to ask. He should be fine. Land is only four kilometers away, and I am sure he can see it and fly off. He'll leave when he's ready."

Then she noticed the two carry bags on the floor next to him. One of them looked very like her own.

"What are those doing here?" she asked.

"If you are going to abandon ship at least do it in style," he said pretending to sound pompous. "I wasn't going to leave my malt behind for those thirsty vikings in the Coast Guard to drink, and you forgot your bag, so here we are!" He grinned disarmingly in the gloom.

She laughed. "You are quite, quite crazy, you know?" There was a brief silence while they smiled at one another; their faces were very close. He leaned forward and kissed her. It lasted a long moment and she enjoyed every second of it.

When they finally parted she whispered."Hmm. I think you better come in," and opened the door to her apartment.

The End

Author's Note
The North Sea

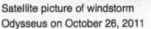
Satellite picture of windstorm
Odysseus on October 26, 2011

The North Sea has a well deserved reputation for being one of the most deadly spaces of water in the world. It is rarely a mill pond of calm, and within a matter of hours can become a raging, mountainous sea that is terrifying, dangerous and often deadly.

Generations of men and women who have sailed on its surface, all around the British isles, Denmark, as well as Norway and Sweden, have been doing so for well over three thousand years. The incredible thing is that in the very early days they did it in open boats made of wood. It takes courage and determination to make a living on that sea, but people still go out in all weathers to earn their bread, many of whom have paid for it with their ships and their lives.

The Shipping forecast has gained a well deserved reputation for both reliability and comfort to the people at sea. All of whom are very familiar with the British voice of either a woman or a man who calmly reads out the regions in the vicinity of the British Isles and provides the necessary details. The area of German Bight is hard up against the coast of Jutland, Denmark.

Rogue waves have been around for ever but have only fairly recently acquired that name, and it too is well deserved. Men who are witness to the horrifying spectacle of a rogue wave rising out of the already very high seas will never forget what they have seen and few ever want to again. It is probably only because ships are that much more buoyant and well designed that they survive encounters with these monster waves today, but in the past it was usually terminal. The ships simply could not survive the crushing weight of a wave if it crashed down upon their decks, burying the vessel under hundreds of tons of raging water, nor could they climb its almost sheer sides. They simply perished, and no one on shore ever knew why. "They died at sea in that awful storm of ..."

There is a phenomena called the "Wind Storm" that is becoming well known in the same regions I have mentioned above. These localized storms are really hurricanes on a small scale, and winds have been recorded of over 117 knots (217 km/h). Waves of over 90 feet, or 30 meters, have been recorded and photographed. A wave of 100 ft has recently been recorded by a ship at sea.

Although this book is fiction, several of the events of the storm really did happen. The vessel was struck by a rogue wave of well over sixty-five feet, which tore loose the tow cables, then swept aboard and wrecked just about everything that was not welded to the decks. And yes, brave men really did risk their lives to go out in those awful conditions and reattach one of the cables to a sea-going tug. I was standing on the bridge when it all happened and witnessed the courage of those crazy riggers, and no, I cannot forget that wave and several others that struck our vessel one afternoon in 1983.

An illustration of what they can look like is below. This is a large ship:

A rogue wave is any ocean wave larger than those around it at any given time. Often they come from a different direction than the rest of the swells. Researcher Thomas Adcock of the University of Oxford suggests that it is a perpendicular angle between swells that creates a bulge, forcing the waves' energy into one place and making a wave several times larger than those around it.

For further information on these frightening phenomena, go to Google and find 'Ships and Rogue waves' or 'North Sea Storms'. It will give you the chills!

James Boschert

Severe European windstorms between 1975 and 1999 [edit]

Event	Date	Notes
Gale of January 1976 ("Capella storm")	January 2-5, 1976	Central UK windspeed gusts of 105 mph (169 km/h) were measured at RAF Wittering. Middlesbrough saw winds of 114 mph (183 km/h).[18] Widespread wind damage was reported across Europe from Ireland to Central Europe. Coastal flooding of 400 homes occurred in Cleethorpes, United Kingdom. In Ruisbroek, Antwerp Belgium dike failures and floods on the Scheldt estuary led to the adoption of the Sigmaplan (the Belgian equivalent of the Dutch Delta Works)[19][20] The highest storm surge of the 20th Century was recorded on the German North Sea coast, with some flooding of coastal marshes.
Fastnet Disaster Storm	August 13-14, 1979	An unusual storm during the 1979 Fastnet yachting race resulted in 24 yachts being disabled or lost and 15 fatalities.
1981 Storm series	November and December 1981	• November 23-24 A severe storm affected Denmark and southern Sweden, killing two, with a storm surge breaking sea dikes along the Jutland coast.[21] • 1981 December storm in England, high tides combined with a storm surge resulted in extensive flooding and £6 million worth of damage along the Somerset coast of the Bristol Channel, with the highest water recorded in the Channel since the start of the century.[22][23] In France, the storm caused widespread flooding in the south west, causing considerable damage in the river basins of the Garonne and Adour and flooding Bordeaux.[24] • December 19, Another storm leads to the Penlee lifeboat disaster.
Southwest France and Spain windstorm	Early November 1982	A windstorm swept through Iberia and killed 21 on its path.[25]
Christiansborg storm	January 18, 1983	A windstorm affected Denmark, blowing a roof off Christiansborg Palace in Copenhagen which killed two.[5][26]
Ex-Hurricane Charley	August 25, 1986	Rainfall records were broken in Ireland (e.g. 200mm in Kippure) with consequent flooding, up to 2.4 metres in Dublin, and the storm also caused flooding in Wales and England. At least seven people were killed in Ireland and Britain.
Great Storm of 1987	October 15-16, 1987	This storm mainly affected southeastern England and northern France. In England maximum mean wind speeds of 70 knots (an average over 10 minutes) were recorded. The highest gust of 117 knots (217 km/h) was recorded at Pointe du Raz in Brittany. In all, 19 people were killed in England and 4 in France. 15 million trees were uprooted in England. This storm received much media attention, not so much because of its severity, but because these storms do not usually track so far south, the trees and buildings are not used to such winds (indeed, in mid-October most deciduous trees still have their leaves and were therefore more susceptible to windstorm damage and, following weeks of wet weather, the ground was sodden, providing little grip for the trees' roots), the severity of the storm was not forecast until approximately 3 hrs before it hit and it struck after midnight, meaning few people had advance warning.[citation needed]
Scottish windstorm	February 13, 1989	During this storm, a gust of 123 knots (228 km/h) was recorded at the Kinnaird Lighthouse (Fraserburgh) on the north-east coast of Scotland. This broke the highest low-level wind speed record for the British Isles. Much higher (unofficial) windspeeds have been recorded on the summit of Cairn Gorm and on Unst in Shetland.

James Boschert

James Boschert grew up in the then colony of Malaya in the early fifties. He learned first hand about terrorism while there, as the Communist insurgency was in full swing. His school was burnt down and the family, while traveling, narrowly survived an ambush, saved by a Gurkha patrol, which drove off the insurgents.

He went on to join the British Army serving in remote places like Borneo and Oman. Later he spent five years in Iran before the revolution, where he played polo with the Iranian Army, developed a passion for the remote Assassin castles found in the high mountains to the north, and learned to understand and speak the Farsi language.

Escaping Iran during the revolution, he went on to become an engineer and now lives in Arizona on a small ranch with his family and animals.

If You Enjoyed This Book

Please visit the website of

PENMORE PRESS

www.penmorepress.com

All Penmore Press books are available directly through our website, amazon.com, Barnes and Noble and Nook, Sony Reader, Apple iTunes, Kobo books and via leading bookshops across the United States, Canada, the UK, Australia and Europe.

More books by James Boschert

www.jamesboschert .com

https://www.facebook.com/pages/James-Boschert-Author/

ASSASSINS OF ALAMUT
BY
JAMES BOSCHERT

An Epic Novel of Persia and Palestine in the Time of the Crusades

The Assassins of Alamut is a riveting tale, painted on the vast canvas of life in Palestine and Persia during the 12th century.

On one hand, it's a tale of the crusades—as told from the Islamic side—where Shi'a and Sunni are as intent on killing Ismaili Muslims as crusaders. In self-defense, the Ismailis develop an elite band of highly trained killers called Hashshashin whose missions are launched from their mountain fortress of Alamut.

But it's also the story of a French boy, Talon, captured and forced into the alien world of the assassins. Forbidden love for a princess is intertwined with sinister plots and self-sacrifice, as the hero and his two companions discover treachery and then attempt to evade the ruthless assassins of Alamut who are sent to hunt them down.

It's a sweeping saga that takes you over vast snow-covered mountains, through the frozen wastes of the winter plateau, and into the fabulous cites of Hamadan, Isfahan, and the Kingdom of Jerusalem.

"A brilliant first novel, worthy of Bernard Cornwell at his best."—Tom Grundner

PENMORE PRESS
www.penmorepress.com

Historical fiction and nonfiction
Paperback available for order on line
and as Ebook with all major distributers

Knight Assassin
The second book of Talon
by
James Boschert

A joyous homecoming turns into a nightmare as a Talon must do the one thing that he didn't want to - become an assassin again.

Talon, a young Frank, returns to France to be reunited with his family who lost him to the Assassins of Alamut when he was just a boy. But when he arrives, he finds a sinister threat hanging like a pall over the joyous reunion. A ruthless man is challenging his father's inheritance, aided by powerful churchmen who also stand to profit by his father's fall. When Talon's young brother is taken hostage, Talon has no recourse but to take the fight to his enemies.

All is not warfare, however; Talon's uncle Philip, a Templar knight, brings him to the court of Carcassonne, where Queen Eleanor has introduced ideals of romance and chivalry. And there Talon is pressed into the service of a lion-hearted prince of Britain named Richard.

Knight assassin is a story of treachery, greed, love and heroism set in the Middle Ages.

PENMORE PRESS
www.penmorepress.com

Historical fiction and nonfiction
Paperback available for order on line
and as Ebook with all major distributers

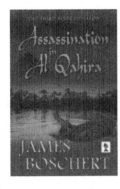

Assassination

in

Al Qahira
James Boschert

Talon, a young Knight of the Order of Templars is finally returning to the Holy Land to search for his lost friend, but Fate as other plans for him.

He and his companions find themselves shipwrecked on Egypt's shore. In that hostile land they face the constant threat of imprisonment, slavery and execution.

When Talon thwarts an attempted murder, he finds out that a good deed can lead to even greater danger. Soon Talon becomes a pawn in a political game within a society that is seething with old enmities, intrigues and treachery at the highest levels. To save the lives of two children and a beautiful widow he is now oath-sworn to protect he must call upon all of his skills as an assassin.

A page turner that you will not be able to put down. It grips you from the very beginning

Review:

PENMORE PRESS
www.penmorepress.com

Historical fiction and nonfiction
Paperback available for order on line
and as Ebook with all major distributers

GREEK FIRE
BY
JAMES BOSCHERT

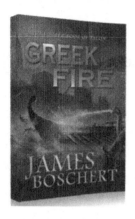

In the fourth book of Talon, James Boschert delivers fast-paced adventures, packed with violent confrontations and intrepid heroes up against hard odds.

Imprisoned for brawling in Acre, a coastal city in the Kingdom of Jerusalem, Talon and his longtime friend Max are freed by an old mentor from the Order of the Templars and offered a new mission in the fabled city of Constantinople. There Talon makes new friendships, but winning the Emperor's favor obligates him to follow Manuel to war in a willful expedition to free Byzantine lands from the Seljuk Turks. And beneath the pageantry of the great city, seditious plans are being fomented by disaffected aristocrats who have made a reckless deal to sell the one weapon the Byzantine Empire has to defend itself, *Greek fire*, to an implacable enemy bent upon the Empire's destruction.

Talon and Max find themselves sailing into perilous battles, and in the labyrinthine back streets of Constantinople Talon must outwit his own kind - assassins - in the pay of a treacherous alliance.

PENMORE PRESS
www.penmorepress.com

Historical fiction and nonfiction
Paperback available for order on line
and as Ebook with all major distributers

When the Jungle Is Silent

by

James Boschert

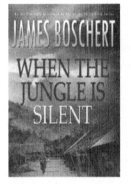

Set in Borneo during a little known war known as "the Confrontation," this story tells of the British soldiers who fought in one of the densest jungles in the world.

Jason, a young soldier of the Light Infantry who is good with guns, is stationed in Penang, an idyllic island off the coast of Malaysia. He is living aimlessly in paradise until he meets Megan, a bright and intelligent young American from the Peace Corps. Megan challenges his complacent existence and a romance develops, but then the regiment is sent off to Borneo.

After a dismal shipping upriver, the regiment arrives in Kuching, the capital of Sarawak. Jason is moved up to Padawan, close to local populations of Ibans and Dyak headhunters, and right in the path of the Indonesian offensive. Fighting erupts along the border of Sarawak and a small fort is turned into a muddy hell from which Jason is an unlikely survivor.

An SAS Sergeant and his trackers have been drawn to the vicinity by the battle, but who will find Jason first: rescuers or hostiles? Jason is forced to wake up to the cruel harshness of real soldiering while he endeavors stay one step ahead of the Indonesians who are combing the Jungle. And the jungle itself, although neutral, is deadly enough.

James Boschert served in Borneo with the British Army and is the author of *Assassins of Alamut*, a story of Persia in the time of the Crusades.

PENMORE PRESS
www.penmorepress.com

Historical fiction and nonfiction
Paperback available for order on line
and as Ebook with all major distributers

Penmore Press

Challenging, Intriguing, Adventurous , Historical and Imaginative

www.penmorepress.com

CPSIA information can be obtained
at www.ICGtesting.com
Printed in the USA
FSOW03n0401020415
6076FS